Y0-AJZ-275

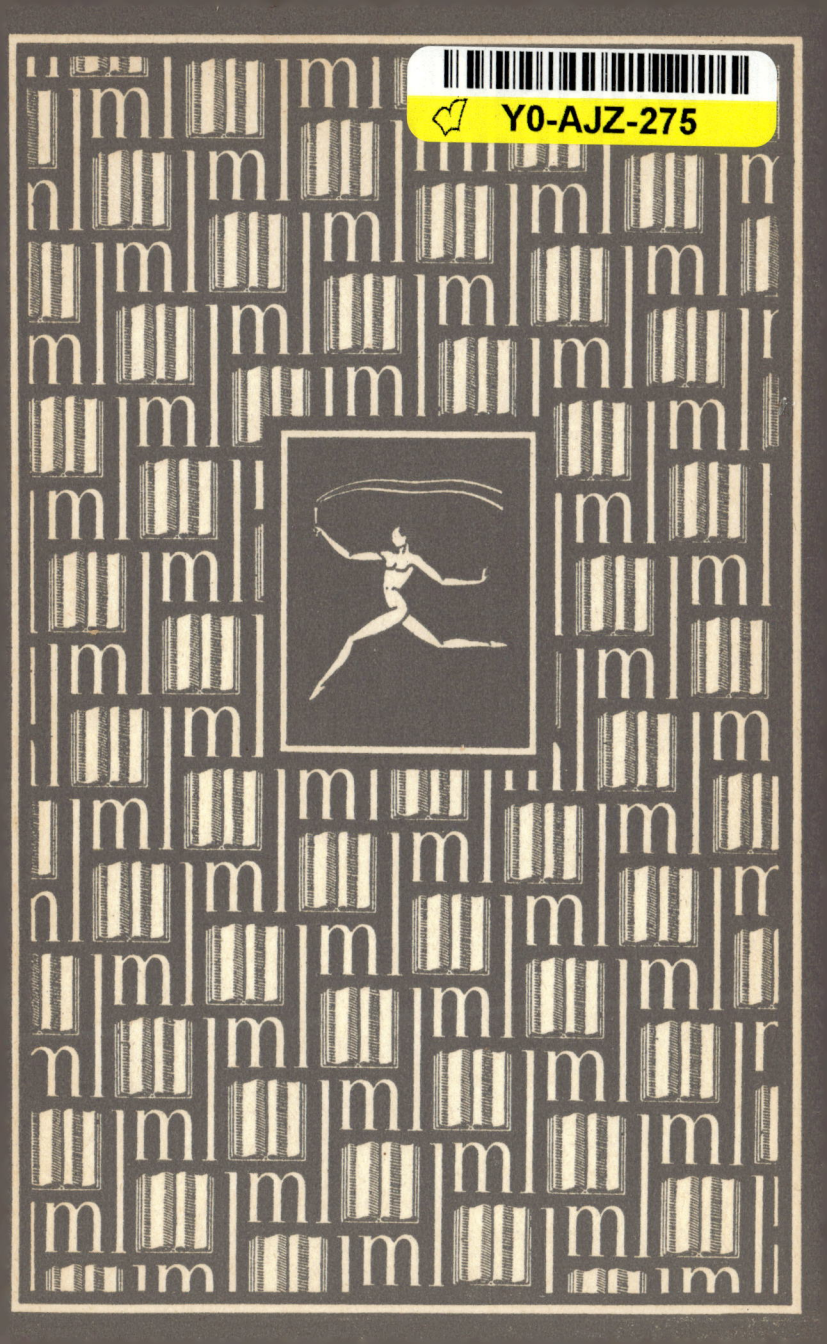

THE MODERN LIBRARY
of the World's Best Books

FAMOUS GHOST STORIES

The publishers will be pleased to send, upon request, an illustrated folder setting forth the purpose and scope of THE MODERN LIBRARY, *and listing each volume in the series. Every reader of books will find titles he has been looking for, handsomely printed, in unabridged editions, and at an unusually low price.*

FAMOUS GHOST STORIES

Compiled and with an Introductory Note

BY BENNETT A. CERF

THE MODERN LIBRARY · NEW YORK

COPYRIGHT, 1944, BY RANDOM HOUSE, INC.

Random House IS THE PUBLISHER OF

THE MODERN LIBRARY

BENNETT A. CERF · DONALD S. KLOPFER · ROBERT K. HAAS

Manufactured in the United States of America

By H. Wolff

ACKNOWLEDGMENTS

For permission to reprint copyrighted material in this volume the editor is indebted to the following:

Dodd, Mead and Co. for "The Monkey's Paw"
E. P. Dutton and Co. for "The Willows"
The Modern Library for "The Rival Ghosts" and "The Man Who Went Too Far"
Edward Arnold and Co. for "The Mezzotint"
The Viking Press for "The Open Window"
Secker and Warburg for "The Beckoning Fair One"
Ernest Benn, Ltd. for "On the Brighton Road"
Matson and Duggan for "The Considerate Hosts"
J. M. Dent and Sons, Ltd. for "August Heat"
Derleth and Schorer for "The Return of Andrew Bentley"
Random House for "The Supper at Elsinore" and "The Current Crop of Ghost Stories"

The other stories in this volume are in the public domain.

B. C.

CONTENTS

Introductory Note by Bennett Cerf	ix
1. The Haunted and the Haunters, by Edward Bulwer-Lytton	3
2. The Damned Thing, by Ambrose Bierce	32
3. The Monkey's Paw, by W. W. Jacobs	42
4. The Phantom 'Rickshaw, by Rudyard Kipling	54
5. The Willows, by Algernon Blackwood	78
6. The Rival Ghosts, by Brander Matthews	131
7. The Man Who Went Too Far, by E. F. Benson	150
8. The Mezzotint, by Montague Rhodes James	173
9. The Open Window, by "Saki"	186
10. The Beckoning Fair One, by Oliver Onions	190
11. On the Brighton Road, by Richard Middleton	260
12. The Considerate Hosts, by Thorp McClusky	264
13. August Heat, by W. F. Harvey	276
14. The Return of Andrew Bentley, by August W. Derleth and Mark Schorer	282
15. The Supper at Elsinore, by Isak Dinesen	300
16. The Current Crop of Ghost Stories, by Bennett Cerf	351

INTRODUCTORY NOTE

I NEVER HAVE enjoyed a literary task more genuinely than the compilation of this volume of famous ghost stories. On my bedside table were piled volume upon volume of tales of terror and the other world. What unalloyed pleasure it was to escape from omniscient strategists bent upon planning new world orders and self-appointed critics of the government and military, and lose myself in a world of fantasy and macabre goings-on!

Do I believe in ghost stories? Of course I do. So do you. Deep in the souls of the most sophisticated of us is a lurking fear of the supernatural which all the discoveries of scientists cannot eradicate. The greatest skeptic I ever met was asked point-blank if he would sleep alone in a house that had been haunted, according to common belief, for a hundred years or more. "No, sirree, not on your life!" said the skeptic. *"Why should I take the chance?"*

You may recall the story of the lady who asked Coleridge if he believed in ghosts. "No, Madame," was the reply. "I have seen far too many of them to believe in them!"

The fundamental difference between the mystery story and the ghost story is the fact that a mystery story demands a solution for its effectiveness; a ghost story is necessarily insoluble; the reader must be willing to accept the fact that nothing can be proved, and that its very thesis is, by all sensible standards, utterly impossible.

I have tried to include examples of every kind of ghost story in this volume. "The Haunted and the Haunters" has long been considered a typical and unsurpassable model of the standard, spine-tickling tale of "things that walk in the night." "The Supper at Elsinore" (never before included in an anthology) is a perfect example of the purely literary ghost story.

INTRODUCTORY NOTE

Note how Miss Dinesen takes her ghost as a matter of course, and how easy it is for the reader to accept his appearance in the same manner! "The Rival Ghosts" strikes me as a worthy example of the humorous ghost story, although I found the telling old-fashioned and cumbersome. (I have omitted anything remotely resembling those loathsome dialect stories of Negro and Irish visitations that enjoyed a certain vogue some years ago.) "The Willows" is only one of a number of superb ghost stories by Algernon Blackwood; a collected volume of his best work was published by Heinemann, in London, under the title of *Strange Stories*. "The Mezzotint," another of the traditional ghost-story classics included here, comes from *Ghost Stories of an Antiquary*. Probably the most familiar story of all is W. W. Jacobs' "The Monkey's Paw," but what anthology of stories of this character would be complete without it? Side by side with old stand-bys that simply could not be omitted, I think you will find a handful that you have not heard of before.

The two best ghost stories I have ever read, or ever expect to read, are "The Turn of the Screw" by Henry James, and "The Beckoning Fair One" by Oliver Onions. "The Turn of the Screw" is one hundred and thirty-odd pages in length; I omitted it because it is obtainable in another Modern Library volume (Number 169); "The Beckoning Fair One," however, is here to thrill and delight you. William Lyon Phelps called it "one of the most terrifying, nerve-shattering tales of horror I ever read. . . . If you have weak nerves, I advise you to skip it!" Its author, Oliver Onions, now seventy years old, is a Yorkshireman who became so understandably provoked by witticisms about his name that he changed it legally to George Oliver. "The Beckoning Fair One" appeared originally in 1911 in a volume of short tales called *Widdershins*.

I have also set down a few of the current ghost stories that are guaranteed to rivet the attention of any dinner party. The late Alexander Woollcott delighted in collecting tales of this sort, and added trimmings of his own that not always heightened their effectiveness.

INTRODUCTORY NOTE

I must ruefully admit that I myself have not yet encountered anything that even remotely resembled a ghost. Since I have been poring over the varied examples of literature on the subject, however, I can report some very promising creakings in distant corners of my own house, and a couple of peculiar shadows that may develop into something extraordinary at any moment. Probably you have heard the story of the timid soul who was hurrying down a dark, dark corridor, when he suddenly collided with a stout and shadowy personage whom he certainly had not seen approaching him. "My, my!" said the timid one. "You gave me a start! For a moment I could have sworn you were a ghost!" "What, my friend," answered the other, "makes you believe I'm not?"—and promptly disappeared!

BENNETT CERF

New York, 1943

FAMOUS GHOST STORIES

THE HAUNTED AND THE HAUNTERS

or, The House and the Brain

BY EDWARD BULWER-LYTTON

A FRIEND of mine, who is a man of letters and a philosopher, said to me one day, as if between jest and earnest, "Fancy! since we last met, I have discovered a haunted house in the midst of London."

"Really haunted?—and by what? ghosts?"

"Well, I can't answer that question: all I know is this—six weeks ago my wife and I were in search of a furnished apartment. Passing a quiet street, we saw on the window of one of the houses a bill, 'Apartments Furnished.' The situation suited us; we entered the house—liked the rooms—engaged them by the week—and left them the third day. No power on earth could have reconciled my wife to stay longer; and I don't wonder at it."

"What did you see?"

"Excuse me—I have no desire to be ridiculed as a superstitious dreamer—nor, on the other hand, could I ask you to accept on my affirmation what you would hold to be incredible without the evidence of your own senses. Let me only say this, it was not so much what we saw or heard (in which you might fairly suppose that we were the dupes of our own excited fancy, or the victims of imposture in others) that drove us away, as it was an undefinable terror which seized both of us whenever we passed by the door of a certain unfurnished room, in which we neither saw nor heard anything. And the strangest marvel of all was, that for once in my life I agreed with my wife, silly woman though she be—and allowed, after the third night, that it was impossible to stay a fourth in that house. Accordingly, on the fourth morning I summoned the woman who kept the house and attended on us, and told her that the rooms did not quite suit us, and we would not stay out our week. She said, dryly, 'I know why: you have stayed longer than any other lodger. Few ever stayed a second night; none before you a third. But I take it they have been very kind to you.'

" 'They—who?' I asked, affecting to smile.

" 'Why, they who haunt the house, whoever they are. I don't mind them; I remember them many years ago, when I lived in this house, not as a servant; but I know they will be the death of me some day. I don't care—I'm old, and must die soon anyhow; and then I shall be with them, and in this house still.' The woman spoke with so dreary a calmness, that really it was a sort of awe that prevented my conversing with her further. I paid for my week, and too happy were my wife and I to get off so cheaply."

"You excite my curiosity," said I; "nothing I should like better than to sleep in a haunted house. Pray give me the address of the one which you left so ignominiously."

My friend gave me the address; and when we parted, I walked straight towards the house thus indicated.

It is situated on the north side of Oxford Street (in a dull but respectable thoroughfare). I found the house shut up —no bill at the window, and no response to my knock. As I was turning away, a beer-boy, collecting pewter pots at the neighboring areas, said to me, "Do you want any one at that house, sir?"

"Yes, I heard it was to be let."

"Let!—why, the woman who kept it is dead—has been dead these three weeks, and no one can be found to stay there, though Mr. J—— offered ever so much. He offered Mother, who chars for him, £1 a week just to open and shut the windows, and she would not."

"Would not!—and why?"

"The house is haunted: and the old woman who kept it was found dead in her bed, with her eyes wide open. They say the devil strangled her."

"Pooh!—you speak of Mr. J——. Is he the owner of the house?"

"Yes."

"Where does he live?"

"In G—— Street, No. —."

"What is he—in any business?"

"No, sir—nothing particular; a single gentleman."

I gave the pot-boy the gratuity earned by his liberal information, and proceeded to Mr. J——, in G—— Street, which was close by the street that boasted the haunted house. I was lucky enough to find Mr. J—— at home, an elderly man, with intelligent countenance and prepossessing manners.

I communicated my name and my business frankly. I said I heard the house was considered to be haunted—that I had a strong desire to examine a house with so equivocal a reputation—that I should be greatly obliged if he would allow me to hire it, though only for a night. I was willing to pay for that privilege whatever he might be inclined to ask. "Sir," said Mr. J——, with great courtesy, "the house is at your service, for as short or as long a time as you please. Rent is out of the question—the obligation will be on my side should you be able to discover the cause of the strange phenomena which at present deprive it of all value. I cannot let it, for I cannot even get a servant to keep it in order or answer the door. Unluckily the house is haunted, if I may use that expression, not only by night, but by day; though at night the disturbances are of a more unpleasant and sometimes of a more alarming character. The poor old woman who died in it three weeks ago was a pauper whom I took out of a workhouse, for in her childhood she had been known to some of my family, and had once been in such good circumstances that she had rented that house of my uncle. She was a woman of superior education and strong mind, and was the only person I could ever induce to remain in the house. Indeed, since her death, which was sudden, and the coroner's inquest, which gave it a notoriety in the neighborhood, I have so despaired of finding any person to take charge of the house, much more a tenant, that I would willingly let it rent-free for a year to any one who would pay its rates and taxes."

"How long is it since the house acquired this sinister character?"

"That I can scarcely tell you, but very many years since. The old woman I spoke of said it was haunted when she rented it between thirty and forty years ago. The fact is, that my life has been spent in the East Indies, and in the civil service of the Company. I returned to England last year, on inheriting the fortune of an uncle, among whose possessions was the house in question. I found it shut up and uninhabited. I was told that it was haunted, that no one would inhabit it. I smiled at what seemed to me so idle a story. I spent some money in repairing it—added to its old-fashioned furniture a few modern articles—advertised it, and obtained a lodger for a year. He was a colonel retired on half-pay. He came in with his family, a son and a daughter, and four or five servants: they all left the house the next day; and, although each of them declared that he had seen something different from that which had scared the others, a something still was equally terrible to all. I really could not in conscience sue, nor even blame, the colonel for breach of agreement. Then I put in the old woman I have spoken of, and she was empowered to let the house in apartments. I never had one lodger who stayed more than three days. I do not tell you their stories—to no two lodgers have there been exactly the same phenomena repeated. It is better that you should judge for yourself, than enter the house with an imagination influenced by previous narratives; only be prepared to see and to hear something or other, and take whatever precautions you yourself please."

"Have you never had a curiosity yourself to pass a night in that house?"

"Yes. I passed not a night, but three hours in broad daylight alone in that house. My curiosity is not satisfied but it is quenched. I have no desire to renew the experiment. You cannot complain, you see, sir, that I am not sufficiently candid; and unless your interest be exceedingly eager and your nerves unusually strong, I honestly add, that I advise you not to pass a night in that house."

"My interest *is* exceedingly keen," said I, "and though only a coward will boast of his nerves in situations wholly unfamiliar to him, yet my nerves have been seasoned in such variety of danger that I have the right to rely on them—even in a haunted house."

Mr. J—— said very little more; he took the keys of the house out of his bureau, gave them to me—and, thanking him cordially for his frankness, and his urbane concession to my wish, I carried off my prize.

Impatient for the experiment, as soon as I reached home, I summoned my confidential servant—a young man of gay spirits, fearless temper, and as free from superstitious prejudices as any one I could think of.

"F——," said I, "you remember in Germany how disappointed we were at not finding a ghost in that old castle, which was said to be haunted by a headless apparition? Well, I have heard of a house in London which, I have reason to hope, is decidedly haunted. I mean to sleep there to-night. From what I hear, there is no doubt that something will allow itself to be seen or to be heard—something, perhaps, excessively horrible. Do you think if I take you with me, I may rely on your presence of mind, whatever may happen?"

"Oh, sir! pray trust me," answered F——, grinning with delight.

"Very well; then here are the keys of the house—this is the address. Go now—select for me any bedroom you please; and since the house has not been inhabited for weeks, make up a good fire—air the bed well—see, of course, that there are candles as well as fuel. Take with you my revolver and my dagger—so much for my weapons—arm yourself equally well; and if we are not a match for a dozen ghosts, we shall be but a sorry couple of Englishmen."

I was engaged for the rest of the day on business so urgent that I had not leisure to think much on the nocturnal adventure to which I had plighted my honor. I dined alone, and very late, and while dining, read, as is my habit. I selected one of the volumes of Macaulay's *Essays*. I thought to myself that I would take the book with me; there was so much of the healthfulness in the style, and practical life in the subjects, that it would serve as an antidote against the influence of superstitious fancy.

Accordingly, about half-past nine, I put the book into my pocket, and strolled leisurely towards the haunted house. I took with me a favorite dog—an exceedingly sharp, bold and vigilant bull-terrier—a dog fond of prowling about strange ghostly corners and passages at night in search of rats—a dog of dogs for a ghost.

It was a summer night, but chilly, the sky somewhat gloomy and overcast. Still there was a moon—faint and sickly, but still a moon—and if the clouds permitted, after midnight it would be brighter.

I reached the house, knocked, and my servant opened with a cheerful smile.

"All right, sir, and very comfortable."

"Oh!" said I, rather disappointed; "have you not seen nor heard anything remarkable?"

"Well, sir, I must own I have heard something queer."

"What—what?"

"The sound of feet pattering behind me; and once or twice small noises like whispers close at my ear—nothing more."

"You are not at all frightened?"

"I! not a bit of it, sir," and the man's bold look reassured me on one point—viz., that happen what might, he would not desert me.

We were in the hall, the street-door closed, and my attention was now drawn to my dog. He had at first run in eagerly enough, but had sneaked back to the door, and was scratching and whining to get out. After patting him on the head, and encouraging him gently, the dog seemed to reconcile himself to the situation, and followed me and F—— through the house, but keeping close at my heels instead of hurrying inquisitively in advance, which was his usual and normal habit in all strange places. We first visited the subterranean apartments, the kitchen and other offices, and especially the cellars, in which last there were two or three bottles of wine still left in a bin, covered with cobwebs, and evidently, by their appearance, undisturbed for many years. It was clear that the ghosts were not wine-bibbers. For the rest we discovered nothing of interest. There was a gloomy little back-yard with very high walls. The stones of this yard were very damp; and what with the damp, and what with the dust and smoke-grime on the pavement, our feet left a slight impression where we passed.

And now appeared the first strange phenomenon witnessed by myself in this strange abode. I saw, just before me, the print of a foot suddenly form itself, as it were. I stopped, caught hold of my servant, and pointed to it. In advance of that footprint as suddenly dropped another. We both saw it. I advanced quickly to the place; the footprint kept advancing before me, a small footprint—the foot of a child; the impression was too faint thoroughly to distinguish the shape, but it seemed to us both that it was the print of a naked foot. This phenomenon ceased when we arrived at the opposite wall, nor did it repeat itself on returning. We remounted the stairs, and entered the rooms on the ground floor, a dining-parlor, a small back parlor, and a still smaller third room that had been probably appropriated to a footman—all still as death. We then visited the drawing-rooms, which seemed fresh and new. In the front room I seated myself in an armchair. F—— placed on the table the candlestick with which he had lighted us. I told him to shut the door. As he turned to do so, a chair opposite to me moved from the wall quickly and noiselessly, and dropped itself about a yard from my own chair, immediately fronting it.

"Why, this is better than the turning tables," said I, with a half-laugh; and as I laughed, my dog put back his head and howled.

F——, coming back, had not observed the movement of the chair. He employed himself now in stilling the dog. I continued to gaze on the chair, and fancied I saw on it a pale blue misty outline of a human figure, but an outline so indistinct that I could only distrust my own vision. The dog now was quiet.

"Put back that chair opposite me," said I to F——; "put it back to the wall."

F—— obeyed. "Was that you, sir?" said he, turning abruptly.

"I!—what?"

"Why, something struck me. I felt it sharply on the shoulder —just here."

"No," said I. "But we have jugglers present, and though we may not discover their tricks, we shall catch *them* before they frighten *us*."

We did not stay long in the drawing-rooms—in fact, they felt so damp and so chilly that I was glad to get to the fire upstairs. We locked the doors of the drawing-rooms—a precaution which, I should observe, we had taken with all the rooms we had searched below. The bedroom my servant had selected for me was the best on the floor—a large one, with two windows fronting the street. The four-posted bed, which took up no inconsiderable space, was opposite to the fire, which burnt clear and bright; a door in the wall to the left, between the bed and the window, communicated with the room which my servant appropriated to himself. This last was a small room with a sofa-bed, and had no communication with the landing-place—no other door but that which conducted to the bedroom I was to occupy. On either side of my fireplace was a cupboard, without locks, flush with the wall and covered with the same dull-brown paper. We examined these cupboards— only hooks to suspend female dresses—nothing else; we sounded the walls—evidently solid—the outer walls of the building. Having finished the survey of these apartments, warmed myself a few moments, and lighted my cigar, I then, still accompanied by F——, went forth to complete my reconnoiter. In the landing-place there was another door; it was closed firmly. "Sir," said my servant, in surprise, "I unlocked this door with all the others when I first came; it cannot have got locked from the inside, for——"

Before he had finished his sentence, the door, which neither of us then was touching, opened quietly of itself. We looked at each other a single instant. The same thought seized both —some human agency might be detected here. I rushed in first, my servant followed. A small blank dreary room without furniture—few empty boxes and hampers in a corner—a small window—the shutters closed—not even a fireplace—no other door than that by which we had entered—no carpet on the floor, and the floor seemed very old, uneven, worm-eaten, mended here and there, as was shown by the whiter patches on the wood; but no living being, and no visible place in which a living being could have hidden. As we stood gazing round, the door by which we had entered closed as quietly as it had before opened: we were imprisoned.

For the first time I felt a creep of undefinable horror. Not so my servant. "Why, they don't think to trap us, sir; I could break the trumpery door with a kick of my foot."

"Try first if it will open to your hand," said I, shaking off the vague apprehension that had seized me, "while I unclose the shutters and see what is without."

I unbarred the shutters—the window looked on the little backyard I have before described; there was no ledge without —nothing to break the sheer descent of the wall. No man getting out of that window would have found any footing till he had fallen on the stones below.

F——, meanwhile, was vainly attempting to open the door. He now turned round to me and asked my permission to use force. And I should here state, in justice to the servant, that, far from evincing any superstitious terrors, his nerve, composure, and even gayety amidst circumstances so extraordinary, compelled my admiration, and made me congratulate myself on having secured a companion in every way fitted to the occasion. I willingly gave him the permission he required. But though he was a remarkably strong man, his force was as idle as his milder efforts; the door did not even shake to his stoutest kick. Breathless and panting, he desisted. I then tried the door myself, equally in vain. As I ceased from the effort, again that creep of horror came over me; but this time it was more cold and stubborn. I felt as if some strange and ghastly exhalation were rising up from the chinks of that rugged floor, and filling the atmosphere with a venomous influence hostile to human life. The door now very slowly and quietly opened as of its own accord. We precipitated ourselves into the landing-place. We both saw a large pale light—as large as the human figure but shapeless and unsubstantial—move before us, and ascend the stairs that led from the landing into the attics. I followed the light, and my servant followed me. It entered, to the right of the landing, a small garret, of which the door stood open. I entered in the same instant. The light then collapsed into a small globule, exceedingly brilliant and vivid; rested a moment on a bed in the corner, quivered, and vanished.

We approached the bed and examined it—a half-tester, such as is commonly found in attics devoted to servants. On the drawers that stood near it we perceived an old faded silk kerchief, with the needle still left in a rent half repaired. The kerchief was covered with dust; probably it had belonged to the old woman who had last died in that house, and this might have been her sleeping room. I had sufficient curiosity to open the drawers: there were a few odds and ends of female dress, and two letters tied round with a narrow ribbon of faded yellow. I took the liberty to possess myself of the letters. We found nothing else in the room worth noticing—nor did the light reappear; but we distinctly heard, as we turned to go, a pattering footfall on the floor—just before us. We went through the other attics (in all four), the footfall still preceding us. Nothing to be seen—nothing but the footfall heard. I had the letters in my hand: just as I was descending the stairs I distinctly felt my wrist seized, and a faint soft effort made to draw the letters from my clasp. I only held them the more tightly, and the effort ceased.

We regained the bedchamber appropriated to myself, and I then remarked that my dog had not followed us when we had left it. He was thrusting himself close to the fire, and trembling. I was impatient to examine the letters; and while I read them, my servant opened a little box in which he had deposited the weapons I had ordered him to bring; took them out, placed them on a table close at my bed-head, and then occupied himself in soothing the dog, who, however, seemed to heed him very little.

The letters were short—they were dated; the dates exactly thirty-five years ago. They were evidently from a lover to his mistress, or a husband to some young wife. Not only the terms of expression, but a distinct reference to a former voyage, indicated the writer to have been a seafarer. The spelling and handwriting were those of a man imperfectly educated, but still the language itself was forcible. In the expressions of endearment there was a kind of rough wild love; but here and there were dark and unintelligible hints at some secret not of love—some secret that seemed of crime. "We ought to love each other," was one of the sentences I remember, "for how every one else would execrate us if all was known." Again: "Don't let any one be in the same room with you at night— you talk in your sleep." And again: "What's done can't be undone; and I tell you there's nothing against us unless the dead could come to life." Here there was underlined in a better handwriting (a female's), "They do!" At the end of the letter latest in date the same female hand had written these words: "Lost at sea the 4th of June, the same day as ———."

I put down the letters, and began to muse over their contents.

Fearing, however, that the train of thought into which I fell might unsteady my nerves, I fully determined to keep my mind in a fit state to cope with whatever of marvelous the advancing night might bring forth. I roused myself—laid the letters on the table—stirred up the fire, which was still bright and cheering—and opened my volume of Macaulay. I read quietly enough till about half-past eleven. I then threw myself dressed upon the bed, and told my servant he might retire to his own room, but must keep himself awake. I bade him leave open the door between the two rooms. Thus alone, I kept two candles burning on the table by my bed-head. I placed my watch beside the weapons, and calmly resumed my Macaulay. Opposite to me the fire burned clear; and on the hearthrug, seemingly asleep, lay the dog. In about twenty minutes I felt an exceedingly cold air pass by my cheek, like a sudden draught. I fancied the door to my right, communicating with the landing-place, must have got open; but no—it was closed. I then turned my glance to my left, and saw the flame of the candles violently swayed as by a wind. At the same moment the watch beside the revolver softly slid from the table—softly, softly—no visible hand—it was gone. I sprang up, seizing the revolver with the one hand, the dagger with the other: I was not willing that my weapons should share the fate of the watch. Thus armed, I looked round the floor—no sign of the watch. Three slow, loud, distinct knocks were now heard at the bed-head; my servant called out, "Is that you, sir?"

"No; be on your guard."

The dog now roused himself and sat on his haunches, his ears moving quickly backwards and forwards. He kept his eyes fixed on me with a look so strange that he concentered all my attention on himself. Slowly he rose up, all his hair bristling, and stood perfectly rigid, and with the same wild stare. I had no time, however, to examine the dog. Presently my servant emerged from his room; and if ever I saw horror in the human face, it was then. I should not have recognized him had we met in the street, so altered was every lineament. He passed by me quickly, saying in a whisper that seemed scarcely to come from his lips, "Run—run! it is after me!" He gained the door to the landing, pulled it open, and rushed forth. I followed him into the landing involuntarily, calling him to stop; but, without heeding me, he bounded down the stairs, clinging to the balusters, and taking several steps at a time. I heard, where I stood, the street-door open—heard it again clap to. I was left alone in the haunted house.

It was but for a moment that I remained undecided whether or not to follow my servant; pride and curiosity alike forbade so dastardly a flight. I re-entered my room, closing the door after me, and proceeded cautiously into the interior chamber. I encountered nothing to justify my servant's terror. I again carefully examined the walls, to see if there were any concealed door. I could find no trace of one—not even a seam in the dull-brown paper with which the room was hung. How, then, had the THING, whatever it was, which had so scared him, obtained ingress except through my own chamber?

I returned to my room, shut and locked the door that opened upon the interior one, and stood on the hearth, expectant and prepared. I now perceived that the dog had slunk into an angle of the wall, and was pressing himself close against it, as if literally striving to force his way into it. I approached the animal and spoke to it; the poor brute was evidently beside itself with terror. It showed all its teeth, the slaver dropping from its jaws, and would certainly have bitten me if I had touched it. It did not seem to recognize me. Whoever has seen at the Zoological Gardens a rabbit fascinated by a serpent, cowering in a corner, may form some idea of the anguish which the dog exhibited. Finding all efforts to soothe the animal in vain, and fearing that his bite might be as venomous in that state as in the madness of hydrophobia, I left him alone, placed my weapons on the table beside the fire, seated myself, and recommenced my Macaulay.

Perhaps, in order not to appear seeking credit for a courage, or rather a coolness, which the reader may conceive I exaggerate, I may be pardoned if I pause to indulge in one or two egotistical remarks.

As I hold presence of mind, or what is called courage, to be precisely proportioned to familiarity with the circumstances that lead to it, so I should say that I had been long sufficiently familiar with all experiments that appertain to the Marvelous.

I had witnessed many very extraordinary phenomena in various parts of the world—phenomena that would be either totally disbelieved if I stated them, or ascribed to supernatural agencies. Now, my theory is that the Supernatural is the Impossible, and that what is called supernatural is only a something in the laws of nature of which we have been hitherto ignorant. Therefore, if a ghost rise before me, I have not the right to say, "So, then, the supernatural is possible," but rather, "So, then, the apparition of a ghost is, contrary to received opinion, within the laws of nature—*i.e.*, not supernatural."

Now, in all that I had hitherto witnessed, and indeed in all the wonders which the amateurs of mystery in our age record as facts, a material living agency is always required. On the continent you will find still magicians who assert that they can raise spirits. Assume for the moment that they assert truly, still the living material form of the magician is present; and he is the material agency by which, from some constitutional peculiarities, certain strange phenomena are represented to your natural senses.

Accept, again, as truthful, the tales of spirit Manifestation in America—musical or other sounds—writings on paper, produced by no discernible hand—articles of furniture moved without apparent human agency—or the actual sight and touch of hands, to which no bodies seem to belong—still there must be found the MEDIUM or living being, with constitutional peculiarities capable of obtaining these signs. In fine, in all such marvels, supposing even that there is no imposture, there must be a human being like ourselves by whom, or through whom, the effects presented to human beings are produced. It is so with the now familiar phenomena of mesmerism or electro-biology; the mind of the person operated on is affected through a material living agent. Nor, supposing it true that a mesmerized patient can respond to the will or passes of a mesmerizer a hundred miles distant, is the response less occasioned by a material fluid—call it Electric, call it Odic, call it what you will—which has the power of traversing space and passing obstacles, that the material effect is communicated from one to the other.

Hence all that I had hitherto witnessed, or expected to witness, in this strange house, I believed to be occasioned through some agency or medium as mortal as myself: and this idea necessarily prevented the awe with which those who regard as supernatural things that are not within the ordinary operations of nature might have been impressed by the adventures of that memorable night.

As, then, it was my conjecture that all that was presented, or would be presented to my senses, must originate in some human being gifted by constitution with the power so to present them, and having some motive so to do, I felt an interest in my theory which, in its way, was rather philosophical than superstitious. And I can sincerely say that I was in as tranquil a temper for observation as any practical experimentalist could be in awaiting the effect of some rare, though perhaps perilous, chemical combination. Of course, the more I kept my mind detached from fancy, the more the temper fitted for observation would be obtained; and I therefore riveted eye and thought on the strong daylight sense in the page of my Macaulay.

I now became aware that something interposed between the page and the light—the page was over-shadowed: I looked up, and I saw what I shall find it very difficult, perhaps impossible, to describe.

It was a Darkness shaping itself forth from the air in very undefined outline. I cannot say it was of a human form, and yet it had more resemblance to a human form, or rather shadow, than to anything else. As it stood, wholly apart and distinct from the air and the light around it, its dimensions seemed gigantic, the summit nearly touching the ceiling. While I gazed, a feeling of intense cold seized me. An iceberg before me could not more have chilled me; nor could the cold of an iceberg have been more purely physical. I feel convinced that it was not the cold caused by fear. As I continued to gaze, I thought—but this I cannot say with precision—that I distinguished two eyes looking down on me from the height. One moment I fancied that I distinguished them clearly, the next they seemed gone; but still two rays of a pale-blue light frequently shot through the darkness, as from the height on which I half believed, half doubted, that I had encountered the eyes.

I strove to speak—my voice utterly failed me; I could only think to myself, "Is this fear? it is *not* fear!" I strove to rise—in vain; I felt as if weighed down by an irresistible force. Indeed, my impression was that of an immense and overwhelming Power opposed to any volition—that sense of utter inadequacy to cope with a force beyond man's, which one may feel *physically* in a storm at sea, in a conflagration, or when confronting some terrible wild beast, or rather, perhaps, the shark of the ocean, I felt *morally*. Opposed to my will was another will, as far superior to its strength as storm, fire, and shark are superior in material force to the force of man.

And now, as this impression grew on me—now came, at last, horror—horror to a degree that no words can convey. Still I retained pride, if not courage; and in my own mind I said, "This is horror, but it is not fear; unless I fear I cannot be harmed; my reason rejects this thing, it is an illusion—I do not fear." With a violent effort I succeeded at last in stretching out my hand towards the weapon on the table; as I did so, on the arm and shoulder I received a strange shock, and my arm fell to my side powerless. And now, to add to my horror, the light began slowly to wane from the candles; they were not, as it were, extinguished, but their flame seemed very gradually withdrawn; it was the same with the fire—the light was extracted from the fuel; in a few minutes the room was in utter darkness.

The dread that came over me, to be thus in the dark with that dark Thing, whose power was so intensely felt, brought a reaction of nerve. In fact, terror had reached that climax, that either my senses must have deserted me, or I must have burst through the spell. I did burst through it. I found voice, though the voice was a shiek. I remember that I broke forth with words like these—"I do not fear, my soul does not fear"; and at the same time I found the strength to rise. Still in that profound gloom I rushed to one of the windows—tore aside the curtain—flung open the shutters; my first thought was—LIGHT. And when I saw the moon high, clear, and calm, I felt a joy that almost compensated for the previous terror. There was the moon, there was also the light from the gas-lamps in the deserted slumberous street. I turned to look back into the room; the moon penetrated its shadow very palely and partially—but still there was light. The dark Thing, whatever it might be, was gone—except that I could yet see a dim shadow, which seemed the shadow of that shade, against the opposite wall.

My eye now rested on the table, and from under the table (which was without cloth or cover—an old mahogany round table) there rose a hand, visible as far as the wrist. It was a hand, seemingly, as much of flesh and blood as my own, but the hand of an aged person—lean, wrinkled, small, too—a woman's hand. That hand very softly closed on the two letters that lay on the table: hand and letters both vanished. There then came the same three loud measured knocks I heard at the bed-head before this extraordinary drama had commenced.

As those sounds slowly ceased, I felt the whole room vibrate sensibly; and at the far end there rose, as from the floor, sparks or globules like bubbles of light, many-colored—green, yellow, fire-red, azure. Up and down, to and fro, hither, thither, as tiny Will-o'-the-Wisps the sparks moved slow or swift, each at his own caprice. A chair (as in the drawing-room below) was now advanced from the wall without apparent agency, and placed at the opposite side of the table. Suddenly as forth from the chair, there grew a shape—a woman's shape. It was distinct as a shape of life—ghastly as a shape of death. The face was that of youth, with a strange mournful beauty: the throat and shoulders were bare, the rest of the form in a loose robe of cloudy white. It began sleeking its long yellow hair, which fell over its shoulders; its eyes were not turned towards me, but to the door; it seemed listening, watching, waiting. The shadow of the shade in the background grew darker; and again I thought I beheld the eyes gleaming out from the summit of the shadow—eyes fixed upon that shape.

As if from the door, though it did not open, there grew out another shape, equally distinct, equally ghastly—a man's shape

—a young man's. It was in the dress of the last century, or rather in a likeness of such dress (for both the male shape and the female, though defined, were evidently unsubstantial, impalpable—simulacra—phantasms); and there was something incongruous, grotesque, yet fearful, in the contrast between the elaborate finery, the courtly precision of that old-fashioned garb, with its ruffles and lace and buckles, and the corpse-like aspect and ghost-like stillness of the flitting wearer. Just as the male shape approached the female, the dark shadow started from the wall, all three for a moment wrapped in darkness. When the pale light returned, the two phantoms were as in the grasp of the shadow that towered between them; and there was a bloodstain on the breast of the female; and the phantom male was leaning on its phantom sword, and blood seemed trickling fast from the ruffles, from the lace; and the darkness of the intermediate Shadow swallowed them up—they were gone. And again the bubbles of light shot, and sailed, and undulated, growing thicker and thicker and more wildly confused in their movements.

The closet door to the right of the fireplace now opened, and from the aperture there came the form of an aged woman. In her hand she held letters—the very letters over which I had seen *the* Hand close; and behind her I heard a footstep. She turned round as if to listen, and then she opened the letters and seemed to read; and over her shoulder I saw a livid face, the face as of a man long drowned—bloated, bleached, seaweed tangled in its dripping hair; and at her feet lay a form as of a corpse, and beside the corpse there cowered a child, a miserable squalid child, with famine in its cheeks and fear in its eyes. And as I looked in the old woman's face, the wrinkles and lines vanished and it became a face of youth—hard-eyed, stony, but still youth; and the Shadow darted forth, and darkened over these phantoms as it had darkened over the last.

Nothing now was left but the Shadow, and on that my eyes were intently fixed, till again eyes grew out of the Shadow—malignant, serpent eyes. And the bubbles of light again rose and fell, and in their disorder, irregular, turbulent maze, mingled with the wan moonlight. And now from these globules themselves, as from the shell of an egg, monstrous things burst out; the air grew filled with them; larvæ so bloodless and so hideous that I can in no way describe them except to remind the reader of the swarming life which the solar microscope brings before his eyes in a drop of water—things transparent, supple, agile, chasing each other, devouring each other—forms like nought ever beheld by the naked eye. As the shapes were without symmetry, so their movements were without order. In their very vagrancies there was no sport; they came round me and round, thicker and faster and swifter, swarming over my head, crawling over my right arm, which was outstretched in involuntary command against all evil beings. Sometimes I felt myself touched, but not by them; invisible hands touched me. Once I felt the clutch as of cold soft fingers at my throat. I was still equally conscious that if I gave way to fear I should be in bodily peril; and I concentrated all my faculties in the single focus of resisting, stubborn will. And I turned my sight from the Shadow—above all, from those strange serpent eyes—eyes that had now become distinctly visible. For there, though in nought else round me, I was aware that there was a WILL, and a will of intense, creative, working evil, which might crush down my own.

The pale atmosphere in the room began now to redden as if in the air of some near conflagration. The larvæ grew lurid as things that live in fire. Again the room vibrated; again were heard the three measured knocks; and again all things were swallowed up in the darkness of the dark Shadow, as if out of that darkness all had come, into that darkness all returned.

As the gloom receded, the Shadow was wholly gone. Slowly as it had been withdrawn, the flame grew again into the candles on the table, again into the fuel in the grate. The whole room came once more calmly, healthfully into sight.

The two doors were still closed, the door communicating with the servant's room still locked. In the corner of the wall into which he had so convulsively niched himself, lay the dog. I called to him—no movement; I approached—the animal was dead; his eyes protruded; his tongue out of his mouth; the froth gathered round his jaws. I took him in my arms; I brought him to the fire, I felt acute grief for the loss of my poor favorite—acute self-reproach; I accused myself of his death; I imagined he had died of fright. But what was my surprise on finding that his neck was actually broken. Had this been done in the dark?—must it not have been by a hand human as mine?—must there not have been a human agency all the while in that room? Good cause to suspect it. I cannot tell. I cannot do more than state the fact fairly; the reader may draw his own inference.

Another surprising circumstance—my watch was restored to the table from which it had been so mysteriously withdrawn; but it had stopped at the very moment it was so withdrawn; nor, despite all the skill of the watchmaker, has it ever gone since—that is, it will go in a strange erratic way for a few hours, and then come to a dead stop—it is worthless.

Nothing more chanced for the rest of the night. Nor, indeed, had I long to wait before the dawn broke. Nor till it was broad daylight did I quit the haunted house. Before I did so, I revisited the little blind room in which my servant and myself had been for a time imprisoned. I had a strong impression—for which I could not account—that from that room had originated the mechanism of the phenomena—if I may use the term—which had been experienced in my chamber. And though I entered it now in the clear day, with the sun peering through the filmy window, I still felt, as I stood on its floor, the creep of the horror which I had first there experienced the night before, and which had been so aggravated by what had passed in my own chamber. I could not, indeed, bear to stay more than half a minute within those walls. I descended the stairs, and again I heard the footfall before me; and when I opened the street door, I thought I could distinguish a very low laugh. I gained my own home, expecting to find my runaway servant there. But he had not presented himself; nor did I hear more of him for three days, when I received a letter from him, dated from Liverpool to this effect:

"HONORED SIR—I humbly entreat your pardon, though I can scarcely hope that you will think I deserve it, unless—which Heaven forbid—

you saw what I did. I feel that it will be years before I can recover myself: and as to being fit for service, it is out of the question. I am therefore going to my brother-in-law at Melbourne. The ship sails to-morrow. Perhaps the long voyage may set me up. I do nothing now but start and tremble, and fancy IT is behind me. I humbly beg you, honored sir, to order my clothes, and whatever wages are due to me, to be sent to my mother's, at Walworth. John knows her address."

The letter ended with additional apologies, somewhat incoherent, and explanatory details as to effects that had been under the writer's charge.

This flight may perhaps warrant a suspicion that the man wished to go to Australia, and had been somehow or other fraudulently mixed up with the events of the night. I say nothing in refutation of that conjecture; rather, I suggest it as one that would seem to many persons the most probable solution of improbable occurrences. My belief in my own theory remained unshaken. I returned in the evening to the house, to bring away in a hack cab the things I had left there, with my poor dog's body. In this task I was not disturbed, nor did any incident worth note befall me, except that still, on ascending and descending the stairs, I heard the same footfall in advance. On leaving the house, I went to Mr. J——'s. He was at home. I returned him the keys, told him that my curiosity was sufficiently gratified, and was about to relate quickly what had passed, when he stopped me, and said, though with much politeness, that he had no longer any interest in a mystery which none had ever solved.

I determined at least to tell him of the two letters I had read, as well as of the extraordinary manner in which they had disappeared, and I then inquired if he thought they had been addressed to the woman who had died in the house, and if there were anything in her early history which could possibly confirm the dark suspicions to which the letters gave rise. Mr. J—— seemed startled, and, after musing a few moments, answered, "I am but little acquainted with the woman's earlier history, except, as I before told you, that her family were known to mine. But you revive some vague reminiscences to her prejudice. I will make inquiries, and inform you of their result. Still, even if we could admit the popular superstition that a person who had been either the perpetrator or the victim of dark crimes in life could revisit, as a restless spirit, the scene in which those crimes had been committed, I should observe that the house was infested by strange sights and sounds before the old woman died—you smile—what would you say?"

"I would say this, that I am convinced, if we could get to the bottom of these mysteries, we should find a living human agency."

"What! you believe it is all an imposture? for what object?"

"Not an imposture in the ordinary sense of the word. If suddenly I were to sink into a deep sleep, from which you could not awake me, but in that sleep could answer questions with an accuracy which I could not pretend to when awake—tell you what money you had in your pocket—nay, describe your very thoughts—it is not necessarily an imposture, any more than it is necessarily supernatural. I should be, unconsciously to myself, under a mesmeric influence, conveyed to me from a distance by a human being who had acquired power over me by previous *rapport*."

"But if a mesmerizer could so affect another living being, can you suppose that a mesmerizer could also affect inanimate objects: move chairs—open and shut doors?"

"Or impress our senses with the belief in such effects—we never having been *en rapport* with the person acting on us? No. What is commonly called mesmerism could not do this; but there may be a power akin to mesmerism, and superior to it—the power that in the old days was called Magic. That such a power may extend to all inanimate objects of matter I do not say; but if so, it would not be against nature—it would be only a rare power in nature which might be given to constitutions with certain peculiarities, and cultivated by practice to an extraordinary degree. That such a power might extend over the dead—that is, over certain thoughts and memories that the dead may still retain—and compel, not that which ought properly to be called the Soul, and which is far beyond human reach, but rather a phantom of what has been most earth-stained on earth, to make itself apparent to our senses—is a very ancient though obsolete theory, upon which I will hazard no opinion. But I do not conceive the power would be supernatural. Let me illustrate what I mean from an experiment which Paracelsus describes as not difficult, and which the author of the *Curiosities of Literature* cites as credible: A flower perishes; you burn it. Whatever were the elements of that flower while it lived are gone, dispersed, you know not wither; you can never discover nor recollect them. But you can, by chemistry, out of the burnt dust of that flower, raise a spectrum of the flower, just as it seemed in life. It may be the same with the human being. The soul has as much escaped you as the essence or elements of the flower. Still you may make a spectrum of it.

"And this phantom, though in the popular superstition it is held to be the soul of the departed, must not be confounded with the true soul; it is but eidolon of the dead form. Hence, like the best attested stories of ghosts or spirits, the thing that most strikes us is the absence of what we hold to be soul; that is, of superior emancipated intelligence. These apparitions come for little or no object—they seldom speak when they do come; if they speak, they utter no ideas above those of an ordinary person on earth. American spirit-seers have published volumes of communications in prose and verse, which they assert to be given in the names of the most illustrious dead—Shakespeare, Bacon—heaven knows whom. Those communications, taking the best, are certainly not a whit of higher order than would be communications from living persons of fair talent and education; they are wondrously inferior to what Bacon, Shakespeare, and Plato said and wrote when on earth. Nor, what is more noticeable, do they ever contain an idea that was not on the earth before. Wonderful, therefore, as such phenomena may be (granting them to be truthful), I see much that philosophy may question, nothing that it is incumbent on philosophy to deny, viz., nothing supernatural. They are but ideas conveyed somehow or other (we have not yet discovered the means) from one mortal brain to another. Whether, in so doing, tables walk of their own accord, or fiend-like shapes appear in a magic circle, or bodyless hands rise and remove material objects, or a Thing of Darkness, such as presented itself to me, freeze our blood—still am I persuaded that these are but agencies conveyed, as if by electric wires, to my own brain from the brain of another. In some constitutions there is a natural chemistry, and these constitutions may produce chemic wonders—in others a natural fluid, call it electricity, and these may produce electric wonders.

"But the wonders differ from Normal Science in this—they are alike objectless, purposeless, puerile, frivolous. They lead on to no grand results; and therefore the world does not heed, and true sages have not cultivated them. But sure I am, that of all I saw or heard, a man, human as myself, was the remote originator; and I believe unconsciously to himself as to the exact effects produced, for this reason: no two persons, you say, have ever told you that they experienced exactly the same thing. Well, observe, no two persons ever experience exactly the same dream. If this were an ordinary imposture, the machinery would be arranged for results that would but little vary; if it were a supernatural agency permitted by the Almighty, it would surely be for some definite end. These phenomena belong to neither class; my persuasion is, that they originate in some brain now far distant; that that brain had no distinct volition in anything that occurred; that what does occur reflects but its devious, motley, ever-shifting, half-formed thoughts; in short, that it has been but the dreams of such a brain put into action and invested with a semi-substance. That this brain is of immense power, that it can set matter into movement, that it is malignant and destructive, I believe; some material force must have killed my dog; the same force might, for aught I know, have sufficed to kill myself, had I been as subjugated by terror as the dog—had my intellect or my spirit given me no countervailing resistance in my will."

"It killed your dog! that is fearful! indeed it is strange that no animal can be induced to stay in that house; not even a cat. Rats and mice are never found in it."

"The instincts of the brute creation detect influences deadly to their existence. Man's reason has a sense less subtle, because it has a resisting power more supreme. But enough; do you comprehend my theory?"

"Yes, though imperfectly—and I accept any crotchet (pardon the word), however odd, rather than embrace at once the notion of ghosts and hobgoblins we imbibed in our nurseries. Still, to my unfortunate house the evil is the same. What on earth can I do with the house?"

"I will tell you what I would do. I am convinced from my own internal feelings that the small unfurnished room at right angles to the door of the bedroom which I occupied, forms a starting point or receptacle for the influences which haunt the house; and I strongly advise you to have the walls opened, the floor removed—nay, the whole room pulled down. I observe that it is detached from the body of the house, built over the small backyard, and could be removed without injury to the rest of the building."

"And you think, if I did that——"

"You would cut off the telegraph wires. Try it. I am so persuaded that I am right, that I will pay half the expense if you will allow me to direct the operations."

"Nay, I am well able to afford the cost; for the rest, allow me to write to you."

About ten days afterwards I received a letter from Mr. J——, telling me that he had visited the house since I had seen him; that he had found the two letters I had described replaced in the drawer from which I had taken them; that he had read them with misgivings like my own; that he had instituted a cautious inquiry about the woman to whom I rightly conjectured they had been written. It seemed that thirty-six years ago (a year before the date of the letters) she had married, against the wish of her relations, an American of very suspicious character, in fact, he was generally believed to have been a pirate. She herself was the daughter of very respectable tradespeople, and had served in the capacity of nursery governess before her marriage. She had a brother, a widower, who was considered wealthy, and who had one child of about six years old. A month after the marriage, the body of this brother was found in the Thames, near

London Bridge; there seemed some marks of violence about his throat, but they were not deemed sufficient to warrant the inquest in any other verdict than that of "found drowned."

The American and his wife took charge of the little boy, the deceased brother having by his will left his sister the guardian of his only child—and in the event of the child's death, the sister inherited. The child died about six months afterwards—it was supposed to have been neglected and ill-treated. The neighbors deposed to have heard it shriek at night. The surgeon who had examined it after death said that it was emaciated as if from want of nourishment, and the body was covered with livid bruises. It seemed that one winter night the child had sought to escape—crept out into the backyard—tried to scale the wall—fallen back exhausted, and been found at morning on the stones in a dying state. But though there was some evidence of cruelty, there was none of murder; and the aunt and her husband had sought to palliate cruelty by alleging the exceeding stubbornness and perversity of the child, who was declared to be half-witted. Be that as it may, at the orphan's death the aunt inherited her brother's fortune. Before the first wedded year was out the American quitted England abruptly, and never returned to it. He obtained a cruising vessel, which was lost in the Atlantic two years afterwards. The widow was left in affluence; but reverses of various kinds had befallen her; a bank broke—an investment failed—she went into a small business and became insolvent—then she entered into service, sinking lower and lower, from housekeeper down to maid-of-all work—never long retaining a place, though nothing decided against her character was ever alleged. She was considered sober, honest, and peculiarly quiet in her ways; still nothing prospered with her. And so she had dropped into the workhouse, from which Mr. J—— had taken her, to be placed in charge of the very house which she had rented as mistress in the first year of her wedded life.

Mr. J—— added that he had passed an hour alone in the unfurnished room which I had urged him to destroy, and that his impressions of dread while there were so great, though he had neither heard nor seen anything, that he was eager to have the walls bared and the floors removed as I had suggested. He had engaged persons for the work, and would commence any day I would name.

The day was accordingly fixed. I repaired to the haunted house—he went into the blind dreary room, took up the skirting, and then the floors. Under the rafters, covered with rubbish, was found a trap-door, quite large enough to admit a man. It was closely nailed down, with clamps and rivets of iron. On removing these we descended into a room below, the existence of which had never been suspected. In this room there had been a window and a flue, but they had been bricked over, evidently for many years. By the help of candles we examined this place; it still retained some mouldering furniture—three chairs, an oak settle, a table—all of the fashion of about eighty years ago. There was a chest of drawers against the wall, in which we found, half-rotted away, old-fashioned articles of a man's dress, such as might have been worn eighty or a hundred years ago by a gentleman of some rank—costly steel buckles and buttons, like those yet worn in court-dresses, a handsome court sword—in a waistcoat which had once been rich with gold-lace, but which was now blackened and foul with damp, we found five guineas, a few silver coins, and an ivory ticket, probably for some place of entertainment long since passed away. But our main discovery was in a kind of iron safe fixed to the wall, the lock of which it cost us much trouble to get picked.

In this safe were three shelves, and two small drawers. Ranged on the shelves were several small bottles of crystal, hermetically stopped. They contained colorless volatile essences, of the nature of which I shall only say that they were not poisons—phosphor and ammonia entered into some of them. There were also some very curious glass tubes, and a small pointed rod of iron, with a large lump of rock-crystal, and another of amber—also a loadstone of great power.

In one of the drawers we found a miniature portrait set in gold, and retaining the freshness of its colors most remarkably, considering the length of time it had probably been there. The portrait was that of a man who might be somewhat advanced in middle life, perhaps forty-seven or forty-eight.

It was a remarkable face—a most impressive face. If you could fancy some mighty serpent transformed into a man, preserving in the human lineaments the old serpent type, you would have a better idea of that countenance than long descriptions can convey: the width and flatness of frontal—the tapering elegance of contour disguising the strength of the deadly jaw—the long, large, terrible eye, glittering and green as the emerald—and withal a certain ruthless calm, as if from the consciousness of an immense power.

Mechanically I turned round the miniature to examine the back of it, and on the back was engraved a pentacle; in the middle of the pentacle a ladder, and the third step of the ladder was formed by the date 1765. Examining still more minutely, I detected a spring; this, on being pressed, opened the back of the miniature as a lid. Withinside the lid were engraved, "Marianna to thee—be faithful in life and in death to ——." Here follows a name that I will not mention, but it was not unfamiliar to me. I had heard it spoken of by old men in my childhood as the name borne by a dazzling charlatan who had made a great sensation in London for a year or so, and had fled the country on the charge of a double murder within his own house—that of his mistress and his rival. I said nothing of this to Mr. J——, to whom reluctantly I resigned the miniature.

We had found no difficulty in opening the first drawer within the iron safe; we found great difficulty in opening the second: it was not locked, but it resisted all efforts, till we inserted in the clinks the edge of a chisel. When we had thus drawn it forth we found a very singular apparatus in the nicest order. Upon a small thin book, or rather tablet, was placed a saucer of crystal: this saucer was filled with a clear liquid—on that liquid floated a kind of compass, with a needle shifting rapidly round; but instead of the usual points of a compass were seven strange characters, not very unlike those used by astrologers to denote the planets.

A peculiar, but not strong nor displeasing odor came from this drawer, which was lined with a wood that we afterwards discovered to be hazel. Whatever the cause of this odor, it produced a material effect on the nerves. We all felt it, even the two workmen who were in the room—a creeping tingling sensation from the tips of the fingers to the roots of the hair. Impatient to examine the tablet, I removed the saucer. As I did so the needle of the compass went round and round with exceeding swiftness, and I felt a shock that ran through my whole frame, so that I dropped the saucer on the floor. The liquid was spilt—the saucer was broken—the compass rolled to the end of the room—and at that instant the walls shook to and fro, as if a giant had swayed and rocked them.

The two workmen were so frightened that they ran up the ladder by which we had descended from the trap-door; but seeing that nothing more happened, they were easily induced to return.

Meanwhile I had opened the tablet: it was bound in plain red leather, with a silver clasp; it contained but one sheet of thick vellum, and on that sheet were inscribed within a double pentacle, words in old monkish Latin, which are literally to be translated thus: "On all that it can reach within these walls—sentient or inanimate, living or dead—as moves the needle, so work my will! Accursed be the house, and restless be the dwellers therein."

We found no more. Mr. J—— burnt the tablet and its anathema. He razed to the foundations the part of the building containing the secret room with the chamber over it. He had then the courage to inhabit the house himself for a month, and a quieter, better-conditioned house could not be found in all London. Subsequently he let it to advantage, and his tenant has made no complaints.

THE DAMNED THING

BY AMBROSE BIERCE

I

ONE DOES NOT ALWAYS EAT WHAT IS ON THE TABLE

BY THE LIGHT of a tallow candle which had been placed on one end of a rough table a man was reading something written in a book. It was an old account book, greatly worn; and the writing was not, apparently, very legible, for the man sometimes held the page close to the flame of the candle to get a stronger light on it. The shadow of the book would then throw into obscurity a half of the room, darkening a number of faces and figures; for besides the reader, eight other men were present. Seven of them sat against the rough log walls, silent, motionless, and the room being small, not very far from the table. By extending an arm any one of them could have touched the eighth man, who lay on the table, face upward, partly covered by a sheet, his arms at his sides. He was dead.

The man with the book was not reading aloud, and no one spoke; all seemed to be waiting for something to occur; the dead man only was without expectation. From the blank darkness outside came in, through the aperture that served for a window, all the ever unfamiliar noises of night in the wilderness—the long nameless note of a distant coyote; the stilly pulsing trill of tireless insects in trees; strange cries of night birds, so different from those of the birds of day; the drone of great blundering beetles, and all that mysterious chorus of small sounds that seem always to have been but half heard when they have suddenly ceased, as if conscious of an indiscretion. But nothing of all this was noted in that company; its members were not overmuch addicted to idle interest in matters of no practical importance; that was obvious in every line of their rugged faces—obvious even in the dim light of the single candle. They were evidently men of the vicinity—farmers and woodsmen.

The person reading was a trifle different; one would have said of him that he was of the world, worldly, albeit there was that in his attire which attested a certain fellowship with the organisms of his environment. His coat would hardly have passed muster in San Francisco; his foot-gear was not of urban origin, and the hat that lay by him on the floor (he was the only one uncovered) was such that if one had considered it as an article of mere personal adornment he would have missed its meaning. In countenance the man was rather prepossessing, with just a hint of sternness; though that he may have assumed or cultivated, as appropriate to one in authority. For he was a coroner. It was by virtue of his office that he had possession of the book in which he was reading; it had been found among the dead man's effects—in his cabin, where the inquest was now taking place.

When the coroner had finished reading he put the book into his breast pocket. At that moment the door was pushed open and a young man entered. He, clearly, was not of mountain birth and breeding: he was clad as those who dwell in cities. His clothing was dusty, however, as from travel. He had, in fact, been riding hard to attend the inquest.

The coroner nodded; no one else greeted him.

"We have waited for you," said the coroner. "It is necessary to have done with this business to-night."

The young man smiled. "I am sorry to have kept you," he said. "I went away, not to evade your summons, but to post to my newspaper an account of what I suppose I am called back to relate."

The coroner smiled.

"The account that you posted to your newspaper," he said,

"differs, probably, from that which you will give here under oath."

"That," replied the other, rather hotly and with a visible flush, "is as you please. I used manifold paper and have a copy of what I sent. It was not written as news, for it is incredible, but as fiction. It may go as a part of my testimony under oath."

"But you say it is incredible."

"That is nothing to you, sir, if I also swear that it is true."

The coroner was silent for a time, his eyes upon the floor. The men about the sides of the cabin talked in whispers, but seldom withdrew their gaze from the face of the corpse. Presently the coroner lifted his eyes and said: "We will resume the inquest."

The men removed their hats. The witness was sworn.

"What is your name?" the coroner asked.

"William Harker."

"Age?"

"Twenty-seven."

"You knew the deceased, Hugh Morgan?"

"Yes."

"You were with him when he died?"

"Near him."

"How did that happen—your presence, I mean?"

"I was visiting him at this place to shoot and fish. A part of my purpose, however, was to study him and his odd, solitary way of life. He seemed a good model for a character in fiction. I sometimes write stories."

"I sometimes read them."

"Thank you."

"Stories in general—not yours."

Some of the jurors laughed. Against a somber background humor shows high lights. Soldiers in the intervals of battle laugh easily, and a jest in the death chamber conquers by surprise.

"Relate the circumstances of this man's death," said the coroner. "You may use any notes or memoranda that you please."

The witness understood. Pulling a manuscript from his breast pocket he held it near the candle and turning the leaves until he found the passage that he wanted began to read.

II

WHAT MAY HAPPEN IN A FIELD OF WILD OATS

". . . The sun had hardly risen when we left the house. We were looking for quail, each with a shotgun, but we had only one dog. Morgan said that our best ground was beyond a certain ridge that he pointed out, and we crossed it by a trail through the *chaparral*. On the other side was comparatively level ground, thickly covered with wild oats. As we emerged from the *chaparral* Morgan was but a few yards in advance. Suddenly we heard, at a little distance to our right and partly in front, a noise as of some animal thrashing about in the bushes, which we could see were violently agitated.

" 'We've started a deer,' I said. 'I wish we had brought a rifle.'

"Morgan, who had stopped and was intently watching the agitated *chaparral*, said nothing, but had cocked both barrels of his gun and was holding it in readiness to aim. I thought him a trifle excited, which surprised me, for he had a reputation for exceptional coolness, even in moments of sudden and imminent peril.

" 'Oh, come,' I said. 'You are not going to fill up a deer with quail-shot, are you?'

"Still he did not reply; but catching a sight of his face as he turned it slightly toward me I was struck by the intensity of his look. Then I understood that we had serious business in hand and my first conjecture was that we had 'jumped' a grizzly. I advanced to Morgan's side, cocking my piece as I moved.

"The bushes were now quiet and the sounds had ceased, but Morgan was as attentive to the place as before.

" 'What is it? What the devil is it?' I asked.

" 'That Damned Thing!' he replied, without turning his head. His voice was husky and unnatural. He trembled visibly.

"I was about to speak further, when I observed the wild oats near the place of the disturbance moving in the most inexplicable way. I can hardly describe it. It seemed as if stirred by a streak of wind, which not only bent it, but pressed it down—crushed it so that it did not rise; and this movement was slowly prolonging itself directly toward us.

"Nothing that I had ever seen had affected me so strangely as this unfamiliar and unaccountable phenomenon, yet I am unable to recall any sense of fear. I remember—and tell it here because, singularly enough, I recollected it then—that once in looking carelessly out of an open window I momentarily mistook a small tree close at hand for one of a group of larger trees at a little distance away. It looked the same size as the others, but being more distinctly and sharply defined in mass and detail seemed out of harmony with them. It was a mere falsification of the law of aërial perspective, but it startled, almost terrified me. We so rely upon the orderly operation of familiar natural laws that any seeming suspension of them is noted as a menace to our safety, a warning of unthinkable calamity. So now the apparently causeless movement of the herbage and the slow, undeviating approach of the line of disturbances were distinctly disquieting. My companion appeared actually frightened, and I could hardly credit my senses when I saw him suddenly throw his gun to his shoulder and fire both barrels at the agitated grain! Before the smoke of the discharge had cleared away I heard a loud savage cry—a scream like that of a wild animal—and flinging his gun upon the ground Morgan sprang away and ran swiftly from the spot. At the same instant I was thrown violently to the ground by the impact of something unseen in the smoke—some soft, heavy substance that seemed thrown against me with great force.

"Before I could get upon my feet and recover my gun, which seemed to have been struck from my hands, I heard Morgan crying out as if in mortal agony, and mingling with his cries were such hoarse, savage sounds as one hears from fighting dogs. Inexpressibly terrified, I struggled to my feet and looked in the direction of Morgan's retreat; and may Heaven in mercy spare me from another sight like that! At a distance of less than thirty yards was my friend, down upon one knee, his head thrown back at a frightful angle, hatless, his long hair in disorder and his whole body in violent movement from side to side, backward and forward. His right arm was lifted and seemed to lack the hand—at least, I could see none. The other arm was invisible. At times, as my memory now reports this extraordinary scene, I could discern but a part of his body; it was as if he had been partly blotted out—I cannot otherwise express it—then a shifting of his position would bring it all into view again.

"All this must have occurred within a few seconds, yet in that time Morgan assumed all the postures of a determined wrestler vanquished by superior weight and strength. I saw nothing but him, and him not always distinctly. During the entire incident his shouts and curses were heard, as if through an enveloping uproar of such sounds of rage and fury as I had never heard from the throat of man or brute!

"For a moment only I stood irresolute, then throwing down my gun I ran forward to my friend's assistance. I had a vague belief that he was suffering from a fit, or some form of convulsion. Before I could reach his side he was down and quiet. All sounds had ceased, but with a feeling of such terror as even these awful events had not inspired I now saw again the mysterious movement of the wild oats, prolonging itself from the trampled area about the prostrate man toward the edge of a wood. It was only when it had reached the wood that I was able to withdraw my eyes and look at my companion. He was dead."

III

A MAN THOUGH NAKED MAY BE IN RAGS

The coroner rose from his seat and stood beside the dead man. Lifting an edge of the sheet he pulled it away, exposing the entire body, altogether naked and showing in the candle-light a claylike yellow. It had, however, broad maculations of bluish black, obviously caused by extravasated blood from contusions. The chest and sides looked as if they had been beaten with a bludgeon. There were dreadful lacerations; the skin was torn in strips and shreds.

The coroner moved round to the end of the table and undid a silk handkerchief which had been passed under the chin and knotted on the top of the head. When the handkerchief was drawn away it exposed what had been the throat. Some of the jurors who had risen to get a better view repented their curiosity and turned away their faces. Witness Harker went to the open window and leaned out across the sill, faint and sick. Dropping the handkerchief upon the dead man's neck the coroner stepped to an angle of the room and from a pile of clothing produced one garment after another, each of which he held up a moment for inspection All were torn, and stiff with blood. The jurors did not make a closer inspection. They seemed rather uninterested. They had, in truth, seen all this before; the only thing that was new to them being Harker's testimony.

"Gentlemen," the coroner said, "we have no more evidence, I think. Your duty has been already explained to you; if there is nothing you wish to ask you may go outside and consider your verdict."

The foreman rose—a tall, bearded man of sixty, coarsely clad.

"I should like to ask one question, Mr. Coroner," he said. "What asylum did this yer last witness escape from?"

"Mr. Harker," said the coroner, gravely and tranquilly, "from what asylum did you last escape?"

Harker flushed crimson again, but said nothing, and the seven jurors rose and solemnly filed out of the cabin.

"If you have done insulting me, sir," said Harker, as soon as he and the officer were left alone with the dead man, "I suppose I am at liberty to go?"

"Yes."

Harker started to leave, but paused, with his hand on the door latch. The habit of his profession was strong in him—stronger than his sense of personal dignity. He turned about and said:

"The book that you have there—I recognize it as Morgan's diary. You seemed greatly interested in it; you read in it while I was testifying. May I see it? The public would like——"

"The book will cut no figure in this matter," replied the

official, slipping it into his coat pocket; "all the entries in it were made before the writer's death."

As Harker passed out of the house the jury reëntered and stood about the table, on which the now covered corpse showed under the sheet with sharp definition. The foreman seated himself near the candle, produced from his breast pocket a pencil and scrap of paper and wrote rather laboriously the following verdict, which with various degrees of effort all signed:

"We, the jury, do find that the remains come to their death at the hands of a mountain lion, but some of us thinks, all the same, they had fits."

IV

AN EXPLANATION FROM THE TOMB

In the diary of the late Hugh Morgan are certain interesting entries having, possibly, a scientific value as suggestions. At the inquest upon his body the book was not put in evidence; possibly the coroner thought it not worth while to confuse the jury. The date of the first of the entries mentioned cannot be ascertained; the upper part of the leaf is torn away; the part of the entry remaining follows:

". . . would run in a half-circle, keeping his head turned always toward the center, and again he would stand still, barking furiously. At last he ran away into the brush as fast as he could go. I thought at first that he had gone mad, but on returning to the house found no other alteration in his manner than what was obviously due to fear of punishment.

"Can a dog see with his nose? Do odors impress some cerebral center with images of the thing that emitted them? . . .

"Sept. 2.—Looking at the stars last night as they rose above the crest of the ridge east of the house, I observed them successively disappear—from left to right. Each was eclipsed but an instant, and only a few at the same time, but along the entire length of the ridge all that were within a degree or two of the crest were blotted out. It was as if something had passed along between me and them; but I could not see it, and the stars were not thick enough to define its outline. Ugh! I don't like this."

Several weeks' entries are missing, three leaves being torn from the book.

"Sept. 27.—It has been about here again—I find evidences of its presence every day. I watched again all last night in the same cover, gun in hand, double-charged with buckshot. In the morning the fresh footprints were there, as before. Yet I would have sworn that I did not sleep—indeed, I hardly sleep at all. It is terrible, insupportable! If these amazing experiences are real I shall go mad; if they are fanciful I am mad already.

"Oct. 3.—I shall not go—it shall not drive me away. No, this is *my* house, *my* land. God hates a coward. . . .

"Oct. 5.—I can stand it no longer; I have invited Harker to pass a few weeks with me—he has a level head. I can judge from his manner if he thinks me mad.

"Oct. 7.—I have the solution of the mystery; it came to me last night—suddenly, as by revelation. How simple—how terribly simple!

"There are sounds that we cannot hear. At either end of the scale are notes that stir no chord of that imperfect instrument, the human ear. They are too high or too grave. I have observed a flock of blackbirds occupying an entire tree-top—the tops of several trees—and all in full song. Suddenly—in a moment—at absolutely the same instant—all spring into the air and fly away. How? They could not all see one another—whole tree-tops intervened. At no point could a leader have been visible to all. There must have been a signal of warning or command, high and shrill above the din, but by me unheard. I have observed, too, the same simultaneous flight when all were silent, among not only blackbirds, but other birds—quail, for example, widely separated by bushes—even on opposite sides of a hill.

"It is known to seamen that a school of whales basking or sporting on the surface of the ocean, miles apart, with the convexity of the earth between, will sometimes dive at the same instant—all gone out of sight in a moment. The signal has been sounded—too grave for the ear of the sailor at the masthead and his comrades on the deck—who nevertheless feel its vibrations in the ship as the stones of a cathedral are stirred by the bass of the organ.

"As with sounds, so with colors. At each end of the solar spectrum the chemist can detect the presence of what are known as 'actinic' rays. They represent colors—integral colors in the composition of light—which we are unable to discern. The human eye is an imperfect instrument; its range is but a few octaves of the real 'chromatic scale.' I am not mad; there are colors that we cannot see.

"And, God help me! the Damned Thing is of such a color!"

THE MONKEY'S PAW

BY W. W. JACOBS

I

WITHOUT, the night was cold and wet, but in the small parlor of Laburnam Villa the blinds were drawn and the fire burned brightly. Father and son were at chess, the former, who possessed ideas about the game involving radical changes, putting his king into such sharp and unnecessary perils that it even provoked comment from the white-haired old lady knitting placidly by the fire.

"Hark at the wind," said Mr. White, who, having seen a fatal mistake after it was too late, was amiably desirous of preventing his son from seeing it.

"I'm listening," said the latter, grimly surveying the board as he stretched out his hand. "Check."

"I should hardly think that he'd come to-night," said his father, with his hand poised over the board.

"Mate," replied the son.

"That's the worst of living so far out," bawled Mr. White, with sudden and unlooked-for violence; "of all the beastly, slushy, out-of-the-way places to live in, this is the worst. Pathway's a bog, and the road's a torrent. I don't know what people are thinking about. I suppose because only two houses in the road are let, they think it doesn't matter."

"Never mind, dear," said his wife, soothingly; "perhaps you'll win the next one."

Mr. White looked up sharply, just in time to intercept a knowing glance between mother and son. The words died away on his lips, and he hid a guilty grin in his thin gray beard.

"There he is," said Herbert White, as the gate banged to loudly and heavy footsteps came toward the door.

The old man rose with hospitable haste, and opening the door, was heard condoling with the new arrival. The new arrival also condoled with himself, so that Mrs. White said, "Tut, tut!" and coughed gently as her husband entered the room, followed by a tall, burly man, beady of eye and rubicund of visage.

"Sergeant-Major Morris," he said, introducing him.

The sergeant-major shook hands, and taking the proffered seat by the fire, watched contentedly while his host got out whisky and tumblers and stood a small copper kettle on the fire.

At the third glass his eyes got brighter, and he began to talk, the little family circle regarding with eager interest this visitor from distant parts, as he squared his broad shoulders in the chair and spoke of wild scenes and doughty deeds; of wars and plagues and strange peoples.

"Twenty-one years of it," said Mr. White, nodding at his wife and son. "When he went away he was a slip of a youth in the warehouse. Now look at him."

"He don't look to have taken much harm," said Mrs. White, politely.

"I'd like to go to India myself," said the old man, "just to look round a bit, you know."

"Better where you are," said the sergeant-major, shaking his head. He put down the empty glass, and sighing softly, shook it again.

"I should like to see those old temples and fakirs and jugglers," said the old man. "What was that you started telling me the other day about a monkey's paw or something, Morris?"

"Nothing," said the soldier hastily. "Leastways nothing worth hearing."

"Monkey's paw?" said Mrs. White, curiously.

"Well, it's just a bit of what you might call magic, perhaps," said the sergeant-major off-handedly.

His three listeners leaned forward eagerly. The visitor absentmindedly put his empty glass to his lips and then set it down again. His host filled it for him.

"To look at," said the sergeant-major, fumbling in his pocket, "it's just an ordinary little paw, dried to a mummy."

He took something out of his pocket and proffered it. Mrs. White drew back with a grimace, but her son, taking it, examined it curiously.

"And what is there special about it?" inquired Mr. White as he took it from his son, and having examined it, placed it upon the table.

"It had a spell put on it by an old fakir," said the sergeant-major, "a very holy man. He wanted to show that fate ruled people's lives, and that those who interfered with it did so to their sorrow. He put a spell on it so that three separate men could each have three wishes from it."

His manner was so impressive that his hearers were conscious that their light laughter jarred somewhat.

"Well, why don't you have three, sir?" said Herbert White cleverly.

The soldier regarded him in the way that middle age is wont to regard presumptuous youth. "I have," he said quietly, and his blotchy face whitened.

"And did you really have the three wishes granted?" asked Mrs. White.

"I did," said the sergeant-major, and his glass tapped against his strong teeth.

"And has anybody else wished?" persisted the old lady.

"The first man had his three wishes. Yes," was the reply; "I don't know what the first two were, but the third was for death. That's how I got the paw."

His tones were so grave that a hush fell upon the group.

"If you've had your three wishes, it's no good to you now, then, Morris," said the old man at last. "What do you keep it for?"

The soldier shook his head. "Fancy, I suppose," he said slowly. "I did have some idea of selling it, but I don't think I will. It has caused enough mischief already. Besides, people won't buy. They think it's a fairy tale; some of them, and those who do think anything of it want to try it first and pay me afterward."

"If you could have another three wishes," said the old man, eyeing him keenly, "would you have them?"

"I don't know," said the other. "I don't know."

He took the paw, and dangling it between his forefinger and thumb, suddenly threw it upon the fire. White, with a slight cry, stooped down and snatched it off.

"Better let it burn," said the soldier solemnly.

"If you don't want it, Morris," said the other, "give it to me."

"I won't," said his friend doggedly. "I threw it on the fire. If you keep it, don't blame me for what happens. Pitch it on the fire again like a sensible man."

The other shook his head and examined his new possession closely. "How do you do it?" he inquired.

"Hold it up in your right hand and wish aloud," said the sergeant-major, "but I warn you of the consequences."

"Sounds like the *Arabian Nights*," said Mrs. White, as she rose and began to set the supper. "Don't you think you might wish for four pairs of hands for me?"

Her husband drew the talisman from his pocket, and then all three burst into laughter as the sergeant-major, with a look of alarm on his face, caught him by the arm.

"If you must wish," he said gruffly, "wish for something sensible."

Mr. White dropped it back in his pocket, and placing chairs, motioned his friend to the table. In the business of supper the talisman was partly forgotten, and afterward the three sat listening in an enthralled fashion to a second instalment of the soldier's adventures in India.

"If the tale about the monkey's paw is not more truthful than those he has been telling us," said Herbert, as the door closed behind their guest, just in time for him to catch the last train, "we shan't make much out of it."

"Did you give him anything for it, father?" inquired Mrs. White, regarding her husband closely.

"A trifle," said he, coloring slightly. "He didn't want it, but I made him take it. And he pressed me again to throw it away."

"Likely," said Herbert, with pretended horror. "Why, we're going to be rich, and famous and happy. Wish to be an emperor, father, to begin with; then you can't be henpecked."

He darted round the table, pursued by the maligned Mrs. White armed with an antimacassar.

Mr. White took the paw from his pocket and eyed it dubiously. "I don't know what to wish for, and that's a fact," he said slowly. "It seems to me I've got all I want."

"If you only cleared the house, you'd be quite happy wouldn't you?" said Herbert, with his hand on his shoulder. "Well, wish for two hundred pounds, then; that'll just do it."

His father, smiling shamefacedly at his own credulity, held up the talisman, as his son, with a solemn face, somewhat marred by a wink at his mother, sat down at the piano and struck a few impressive chords.

"I wish for two hundred pounds," said the old man distinctly.

A fine crash from the piano greeted the words, interrupted by a shuddering cry from the old man. His wife and son ran toward him.

"It moved," he cried, with a glance of disgust at the object as it lay on the floor. "As I wished, it twisted in my hand like a snake."

"Well, I don't see the money," said his son as he picked it up and placed it on the table, "and I bet I never shall."

"It must have been your fancy, father," said his wife, regarding him anxiously.

He shook his head. "Never mind, though; there's no harm done, but it gave me a shock all the same."

They sat down by the fire again while the two men finished their pipes. Outside, the wind was higher than ever, and the old man started nervously at the sound of a door banging upstairs. A silence unusual and depressing settled upon all three, which lasted until the old couple rose to retire for the night.

"I expect you'll find the cash tied up in a big bag in the middle of your bed," said Herbert, as he bade them good night, "and something horrible squatting up on top of the wardrobe watching you as you pocket your ill-gotten gains."

He sat alone in the darkness, gazing at the dying fire, and seeing faces in it. The last face was so horrible and so simian that he gazed at it in amazement. It got so vivid that, with a little uneasy laugh, he felt on the table for a glass containing a little water to throw over it. His hand grasped the monkey's paw, and with a little shiver he wiped his hand on his coat and went up to bed.

II

In the brightness of the wintry sun next morning as it streamed over the breakfast table he laughed at his fears. There was an air of prosaic wholesomeness about the room which it had lacked on the previous night, and the dirty, shriveled little paw was pitched on the sideboard with a carelessness which betokened no great belief in its virtues.

"I suppose all old soldiers are the same," said Mrs. White. "The idea of our listening to such nonsense! How could wishes be granted in these days? And if they could, how could two hundred pounds hurt you, father?"

"Might drop on his head from the sky," said the frivolous Herbert.

"Morris said the things happened so naturally," said his father, "that you might if you so wished attribute it to coincidence."

"Well, don't break into the money before I come back," said Herbert as he rose from the table. "I'm afraid it'll turn you into a mean, avaricious man, and we shall have to disown you."

His mother laughed, and following him to the door, watched him down the road; and returning to the breakfast table, was very happy at the expense of her husband's credulity. All of which did not prevent her from scurrying to the door at the postman's knock, nor prevent her from referring somewhat shortly to retired sergeant-majors of bibulous habits when she found that the post brought a tailor's bill.

"Herbert will have some more of his funny remarks, I expect, when he comes home," she said, as they sat at dinner.

"I dare say," said Mr. White, pouring himself out some beer; "but for all that, the thing moved in my hand; that I'll swear to."

"You thought it did," said the old lady soothingly.

"I say it did," replied the other. "There was no thought about it; I had just—— What's the matter?"

His wife made no reply. She was watching the mysterious movements of a man outside, who, peering in an undecided fashion at the house, appeared to be trying to make up his mind to enter. In mental connection with the two hundred pounds, she noticed that the stranger was well dressed, and wore a silk hat of glossy newness. Three times he paused at the gate, and then walked on again. The fourth time he stood with his hand upon it, and then with sudden resolution flung it open and walked up the path. Mrs. White at the same moment placed her hands behind her, and hurriedly unfastening the strings of her apron, put that useful article of apparel beneath the cushion of her chair.

She brought the stranger, who seemed ill at ease, into the room. He gazed at her furtively, and listened in a preoccupied fashion as the old lady apologized for the appearance of the room, and her husband's coat, a garment which he usually reserved for the garden. She then waited as patiently as her sex would permit, for him to broach his business, but he was at first strangely silent.

"I—was asked to call," he said at last, and stooped and picked a piece of cotton from his trousers. "I come from Maw and Meggins."

The old lady started. "Is anything the matter?" she asked breathlessly. "Has anything happened to Herbert? What is it? What is it?"

Her husband interposed. "There, there, mother," he said hastily. "Sit down, and don't jump to conclusions. You've not brought bad news, I'm sure, sir;" and he eyed the other wistfully.

"I'm sorry——" began the visitor.

"Is he hurt?" demanded the mother wildly.

The visitor bowed in assent. "Badly hurt," he said quietly, "but he is not in any pain."

"Oh, thank God!" said the old woman, clasping her hands. "Thank God for that! Thank——"

She broke off suddenly as the sinister meaning of the assurance dawned upon her and she saw the awful confirmation of her fears in the other's averted face. She caught her breath, and turning to her slower-witted husband, laid her trembling old hand upon his. There was a long silence.

"He was caught in the machinery," said the visitor at length in a low voice.

"Caught in the machinery," repeated Mr. White, in a dazed fashion, "yes."

He sat staring blankly out at the window, and taking his wife's hand between his own, pressed it as he had been wont to do in their old courting-days nearly forty years before.

"He was the only one left to us," he said, turning gently to the visitor. "It is hard."

The other coughed, and rising, walked slowly to the window. "The firm wished me to convey their sincere sympathy with you in your great loss," he said, without looking round. "I beg that you will understand I am only their servant and merely obeying orders."

There was no reply; the old woman's face was white, her eyes staring, and her breath inaudible; on the husband's face was a look such as his friend the sergeant-major might have carried into his first action.

"I was to say that Maw and Meggins disclaim all responsibility," continued the other. "They admit no liability at all, but in consideration of your son's services, they wish to present you with a certain sum as compensation."

Mr. White dropped his wife's hand, and rising to his feet,

gazed with a look of horror at his visitor. His dry lips shaped the words, "How much?"

"Two hundred pounds," was the answer.

Unconscious of his wife's shriek, the old man smiled faintly, put out his hands like a sightless man, and dropped, a senseless heap, to the floor.

III

In the huge new cemetery, some two miles distant, the old people buried their dead, and came back to a house steeped in shadow and silence. It was all over so quickly that at first they could hardly realize it, and remained in a state of expectation as though of something else to happen—something else which was to lighten this load, too heavy for old hearts to bear.

But the days passed, and expectation gave place to resignation—the hopeless resignation of the old, sometimes miscalled apathy. Sometimes they hardly exchanged a word, for now they had nothing to talk about, and their days were long to weariness.

It was about a week after that the old man, waking suddenly in the night, stretched out his hand and found himself alone. The room was in darkness, and the sound of subdued weeping came from the window. He raised himself in bed and listened.

"Come back," he said tenderly. "You will be cold."

"It is colder for my son," said the old woman, and wept afresh.

The sound of her sobs died away on his ears. The bed was warm, and his eyes heavy with sleep. He dozed fitfully, and then slept until a sudden wild cry from his wife awoke him with a start.

"*The paw!*" she cried wildly. "The monkey's paw!"

He started up in alarm. "Where? Where is it? What's the matter?"

She came stumbling across the room toward him. "I want it," she said quietly. "You've not destroyed it?"

"It's in the parlor, on the bracket," he replied, marvelling. "Why?"

She cried and laughed together, and bending over, kissed his cheek.

"I only just thought of it," she said hysterically. "Why didn't I think of it before? Why didn't *you* think of it?"

"Think of what?" he questioned.

"The other two wishes," she replied rapidly. "We've only had one."

"Was not that enough?" he demanded fiercely.

"No," she cried triumphantly; "we'll have one more. Go down and get it quickly, and wish our boy alive again."

The man sat up in bed and flung the bedclothes from his quaking limbs. "Good God, you are mad!" he cried, aghast.

"Get it," she panted; "get it quickly, and wish—— Oh, my boy, my boy!"

Her husband struck a match and lit the candle. "Get back to bed," he said unsteadily. "You don't know what you are saying."

"We had the first wish granted," said the old woman feverishly; "why not the second?"

"A coincidence," stammered the old man.

"Go and get it and wish," cried his wife, quivering with excitement.

The old man turned and regarded her, and his voice shook. "He has been dead ten days, and besides he—I would not tell you else, but—I could only recognize him by his clothing. If he was too terrible for you to see then, how now?"

"Bring him back," cried the old woman, and dragged him toward the door. "Do you think I fear the child I have nursed?"

He went down in the darkness, and felt his way to the parlor, and then to the mantelpiece. The talisman was in its place, and a horrible fear that the unspoken wish might bring his mutilated son before him ere he could escape from the room seized upon him, and he caught his breath as he found that he had lost the direction of the door. His brow cold with sweat, he felt his way round the table, and groped along the wall until he found himself in the small passage with the unwholesome thing in his hand.

Even his wife's face seemed changed as he entered the room. It was white and expectant, and to his fears seemed to have an unnatural look upon it. He was afraid of her.

"*Wish!*" she cried, in a strong voice.

"It is foolish and wicked," he faltered.

"*Wish!*" repeated his wife.

He raised his hand. "I wish my son alive again."

The talisman fell to the floor, and he regarded it fearfully. Then he sank trembling into a chair as the old woman, with burning eyes, walked to the window and raised the blind.

He sat until he was chilled with the cold, glancing occasionally at the figure of the old woman peering through the window. The candle-end, which had burned below the rim of the china candestick, was throwing pulsating shadows on the ceiling and walls, until, with a flicker larger than the rest, it expired. The old man, with an unspeakable sense of relief at the failure of the talisman, crept back to his bed, and a minute or two afterward the old woman came silently and apathetically beside him.

Neither spoke, but lay silently listening to the ticking of the clock. A stair creaked, and a squeaky mouse scurried noisily through the wall. The darkness was oppressive, and after lying for some time screwing up his courage, he took the box of matches, and striking one, went downstairs for a candle.

At the foot of the stairs the match went out, and he paused to strike another; and at the same moment a knock, so quiet and stealthy as to be scarcely audible, sounded on the front door.

The matches fell from his hand and spilled in the passage. He stood motionless, his breath suspended until the knock was repeated. Then he turned and fled swiftly back to his room, and closed the door behind him. A third knock sounded through the house.

"*What's that?*" cried the old woman, starting up.

"A rat," said the old man in shaking tones, "a rat. It passed me on the stairs."

His wife sat up in bed listening. A loud knock resounded through the house.

"It's Herbert!" she screamed. "It's Herbert!"

She ran to the door, but her husband was before her, and catching her by the arm, held her tightly.

"What are you going to do?" he whispered hoarsely.

"It's my boy; it's Herbert!" she cried, struggling mechanically. "I forgot it was two miles away. What are you holding me for? Let go. I must open the door."

"For God's sake don't let it in," cried the old man, trembling.

"You're afraid of your own son," she cried, struggling. "Let me go. I'm coming, Herbert; I'm coming."

There was another knock, and another. The old woman with a sudden wrench broke free and ran from the room. Her husband followed to the landing, and called after her appealingly as she hurried downstairs. He heard the chain rattle back and the bottom bolt drawn slowly and stiffly from the socket. Then the old woman's voice, strained and panting.

"The bolt," she cried loudly. "Come down. I can't reach it."

But her husband was on his hands and knees groping wildly on the floor in search of the paw. If he could only find it before the thing outside got in. A perfect fusillade of knocks reverberated through the house, and he heard the scraping of a chair as his wife put it down in the passage against the door. He heard the creaking of the bolt as it came slowly back, and at the same moment he found the monkey's paw, and frantically breathed his third and last wish.

The knocking ceased suddenly, although the echoes of it were still in the house. He heard the chair drawn back, and the door opened. A cold wind rushed up the staircase, and a long loud wail of disappointment and misery from his wife gave him courage to run down to her side, and then to the gate beyond. The street lamp flickering opposite shone on a quiet and deserted road.

THE PHANTOM 'RICKSHAW

BY RUDYARD KIPLING

> "May no ill dreams disturb my rest,
> Nor Powers of Darkness me molest."
> —*Evening Hymn*

ONE OF THE few advantages that India has over England is a certain great Knowability. After five years' service a man is directly or indirectly acquainted with the two or three hundred Civilians in his Province, all the Messes of ten or twelve Regiments and Batteries, and some fifteen hundred other people of the non-official castes. In ten years his knowledge should be doubled, and at the end of twenty he knows, or knows something about, almost every Englishman in the Empire, and may travel anywhere and everywhere without paying hotel bills.

Globe-trotters who expect entertainment as a right, have, even within my memory, blunted this open-heartedness, but, none the less, to-day if you belong to the Inner Circle and are neither a bear nor a black sheep all houses are open to you and our small world is very kind and helpful.

Rickett of Kamartha stayed with Polder of Kumaon, some fifteen years ago. He meant to stay two nights only, but was knocked down by rheumatic fever, and for six weeks disorganized Polder's establishment, stopped Polder's work, and nearly died in Polder's bedroom. Polder behaves as though he had been placed under eternal obligation by Rickett, and yearly sends the little Ricketts a box of presents and toys. It is the same everywhere. The men who do not take the trouble to conceal from you their opinion that you are an incompetent ass, and the women who blacken your character and misunderstand your wife's amusements, will work themselves to the bone in your behalf if you fall sick or into serious trouble.

Heatherlegh, the doctor, kept, in addition to his regular practice, a hospital on his private account—an arrangement of loose-boxes for Incurables, his friends called it—but it was really a sort of fitting-up shed for craft that had been damaged by stress of weather. The weather in India is often sultry, and since the tale of bricks is a fixed quantity, and the only liberty allowed is permission to work overtime and get no thanks, men occasionally break down and become as mixed as the metaphors in this sentence.

Heatherlegh is the nicest doctor that ever was, and his invariable prescription to all his patients is "lie low, go slow, and keep cool." He says that more men are killed by overwork than the importance of this world justifies. He maintains that overwork slew Pansay who died under his hands about three years ago. He has, of course, the right to speak authoritatively, and he laughs at my theory that there was a crack in Pansay's head and a little bit of the Dark World came through and pressed him to death. "Pansay went off the handle," says Heatherlegh, "after the stimulus of long leave at Home. He may or he may not have behaved like a blackguard to Mrs. Keith-Wessington. My notion is that the work of the Katabundi Settlement ran him off his legs, and that he took to brooding and making much of an ordinary P. & O. flirtation. He certainly was engaged to Miss Mannering, and she certainly broke off the engagement. Then he took a feverish chill and all that nonsense about ghosts developed itself. Overwork started his illness, kept it alight, and killed him, poor devil. Write him off to the System—one man to do the work of two-and-a-half men."

I do not believe this. I used to sit up with Pansay sometimes when Heatherlegh was called out to visit patients and I happened to be within claim. The man would make me most unhappy by describing in a low, even voice the procession of men, women, children, and devils that was always passing at the bottom of his bed. He had a sick man's command of language. When he recovered I suggested that he should write out the whole affair from beginning to end, knowing that ink might assist him to ease his mind. When little boys have learned a new bad word they are never happy till they have chalked it up on a door. And this also is Literature.

He was in high fever while he was writing, and the blood-and-thunder Magazine style he adopted did not calm him. Two months afterwards he was reported fit for duty, but, in spite of the fact that he was urgently needed to help an undermanned Commission stagger through a deficit, he preferred to die; vowing at the last that he was hag-ridden. I secured his manuscript before he died, and this is his version of the affair, dated 1885:

My doctor tells me that I need rest and change of air. It is not improbable that I shall get both ere long—rest that neither the red-coated orderly nor the mid-day gun can break, and change of air far beyond that which any homeward-bound steamer can give me. In the meantime I am resolved to stay where I am; and, in flat defiance of my doctor's orders, to take all the world into my confidence. You shall learn for yourselves the precise nature of my malady; and shall, too, judge for yourselves whether any man born of woman on this weary earth was ever so tormented as I.

Speaking now as a condemned criminal might speak ere the drop-bolts are drawn, my story, wild and hideously improbable as it may appear, demands at least attention. That it will ever receive credence I utterly disbelieve. Two months ago I should have scouted as mad or drunk the man who had dared tell me the like. Two months ago I was the happiest man in India. To-day, from Peshawar to the sea, there is no one more wretched. My doctor and I are the only two who know this. His explanation is that my brain, digestion and eyesight are all slightly affected; giving rise to my frequent and persistent "delusions." Delusions, indeed! I call him a fool; but he attends me still with the same unwearied smile, the same bland professional manner, the same neatly-trimmed red whiskers, till I begin to suspect that I am an ungrateful, evil-tempered invalid. But you shall judge for yourselves.

Three years ago it was my fortune—my great misfortune—to sail from Gravesend to Bombay, on return from long leave, with one Agnes Keith-Wessington, wife of an officer on the Bombay side. It does not in the least concern you to know what manner of woman she was. Be content with the knowledge that, ere the voyage had ended, both she and I were desperately and unreasoningly in love with one another. Heaven knows that I can make the admission now without one particle of vanity. In matters of this sort there is always one who gives and another who accepts. From the first day of our ill-omened attachment, I was conscious that Agnes's passion was a stronger, a more dominant, and—if I may use the expression—a purer sentiment than mine. Whether she recognized the fact then, I do not know. Afterwards it was bitterly plain to both of us.

Arrived at Bombay in the spring of the year, we went our respective ways, to meet no more for the next three or four months, when my leave and her love took us both to Simla. There we spent the season together; and there my fire of straw burnt itself out to a pitiful end with the closing year. I attempt no excuse. I make no apology. Mrs. Wessington had given up much for my sake, and was prepared to give up all. From my own lips, in August, 1882, she learnt that I was sick of her presence, tired of her company, and weary of the sound of her voice. Ninety-nine women out of a hundred would have wearied of me as I wearied of them; seventy-five of that number would have promptly avenged themselves by active and obtrusive flirtation with other men. Mrs. Wessington was the hundredth. On her neither my openly-expressed aversion, nor the cutting brutalities with which I garnished our interviews had the least effect.

"Jack, darling!" was her one eternal cuckoo-cry, "I'm sure it's all a mistake—a hideous mistake; and we'll be good friends again some day. *Please* forgive me, Jack, dear."

I was the offender, and I knew it. That knowledge transformed my pity into passive endurance, and, eventually, into blind hate—the same instinct, I suppose, which prompts a man to savagely stamp on the spider he has but half killed. And with this hate in my bosom the season of 1882 came to an end.

Next year we met again at Simla—she with her monotonous face and timid attempts at reconciliation, and I with loathing of her in every fiber of my frame. Several times I could not avoid meeting her alone; and on each occasion her words were identically the same. Still the unreasoning wail that it was all a "mistake"; and still the hope of eventually "making friends." I might have seen, had I cared to look, that that hope only was keeping her alive. She grew more wan and thin month by month. You will agree with me, at least, that such conduct would have driven any one to despair. It was uncalled for, childish, unwomanly. I maintain that she was much to blame. And again, sometimes, in the black, fever-stricken night watches, I have begun to think that I might have been a little kinder to her. But that really *is* a "delusion." I could not have continued pretending to love her when I didn't; could I? It would have been unfair to us both.

Last year we met again—on the same terms as before. The same weary appeals, and the same curt answers from my lips. At least I would make her see how wholly wrong and hopeless were her attempts at resuming the old relationship. As the season wore on, we fell apart—that is to say, she found it difficult to meet me, for I had other and more absorbing interests to attend to. When I think it over quietly in my sick-room, the season of 1884 seems a confused nightmare wherein light and shade were fantastically intermingled—my courtship of little Kitty Mannering; my hopes, doubts and fears; our long rides together; my trembling avowal of attachment; her reply; and now and again a vision of a white face flitting by in the 'rickshaw with the black and white liveries I once watched for so earnestly; the wave of Mrs. Wessington's gloved hand; and, when she met me alone, which was but seldom, the irksome monotony of her appeal. I loved Kitty Mannering, honestly, heartily loved her, and with my love for her grew my hatred for Agnes. In August Kitty and I were engaged. The next day I met those accursed "magpie" *jhampanies* at the back of Jakko, and, moved by some passing sentiment of pity, stopped to tell Mrs. Wessington everything. She knew it already.

"So I hear you're engaged, Jack, dear." Then, without a moment's pause: "I'm sure it's all a mistake—a hideous mistake. We shall be as good friends some day, Jack, as we ever were."

My answer might have made even a man wince. It cut the dying woman before me like the blow of a whip. "Please forgive me, Jack; I didn't mean to make you angry; but it's true, it's true!"

And Mrs. Wessington broke down completely. I turned away and left her to finish her journey in peace, feeling, but only for a moment or two, that I had been an unutterably mean hound. I looked back, and saw that she had turned her 'rickshaw with the idea, I suppose, of overtaking me.

The scene and its surroundings were photographed on my memory. The rain-swept sky (we were at the end of the wet weather), the sodden, dingy pines, the muddy road, and the black powder-driven cliffs formed a gloomy background against which the black and white liveries of the *jhampanies*, the yellow-paneled 'rickshaw and Mrs. Wessington's down-bowed golden head stood out clearly. She was holding her handkerchief in her left hand and was leaning back exhausted against the 'rickshaw cushions. I turned my horse up a bypath near the Sanjowlie Reservoir and literally ran away. Once I fancied I heard a faint call of "Jack!" This may have been imagination. I never stopped to verify it. Ten minutes later I came across Kitty on horseback; and, in the delight of a long ride with her, forgot all about the interview.

A week later Mrs. Wessington died, and the inexpressible burden of her existence was removed from my life. I went Plainsward perfectly happy. Before three months were over I had forgotten all about her, except that at times the discovery of some of her old letters reminded me unpleasantly of our bygone relationship. By January I had disinterred what was left of our correspondence from among my scattered belongings and had burnt it. At the beginning of April of this year, 1885, I was at Simla—semi-deserted Simla—once more, and was deep in lover's talks and walks with Kitty. It was decided that we should be married at the end of June. You will understand, therefore, that, loving Kitty as I did, I am not saying too much when I pronounce myself to have been, at the time, the happiest man in India.

Fourteen delightful days passed almost before I noticed their flight. Then, aroused to the sense of what was proper among mortals circumstanced as we were, I pointed out to Kitty that an engagement-ring was the outward and visible sign of her dignity as an engaged girl; and that she must forthwith come to Hamilton's to be measured for one. Up to that moment, I give you my word, we had completely forgotten so trivial a matter. To Hamilton's we accordingly went on the 15th of April, 1885. Remember that—whatever my doctor may say to the contrary—I was then in perfect health, enjoying a well-balanced mind and an absolutely tranquil spirit. Kitty and I entered Hamilton's shop together, and there, regardless of the order of affairs, I measured Kitty's finger for the ring in the presence of the amused assistant. The ring was a sapphire with two diamonds. We then rode out down the slope that leads to the Combermere Bridge and Peliti's shop.

While my Waler was cautiously feeling his way over the loose shale, and Kitty was laughing and chattering at my side —while all Simla, that is to say as much of it as had then come from the Plains, was grouped round the Reading-room and Peliti's veranda—I was aware that some one, apparently at a vast distance, was calling me by my Christian name. It struck me that I had heard the voice before, but when and where I could not at once determine. In the short space it took to cover the road between the path from Hamilton's shop and the first plank of the Combermere Bridge I had thought over half-a-dozen people who might have committed such a solecism, and had eventually decided that it must have been some singing in my ears. Immediately opposite Peliti's shop my eye was arrested by the sight of four *jhampanies* in black and white livery, pulling a yellow-paneled, cheap, bazar 'rickshaw. In a moment my mind flew back to the previous season and Mrs. Wessington with a sense of irritation and disgust. Was it not enough that the woman was dead and done with, without her black and white servitors re-appearing to spoil the day's happiness? Whoever employed them now I thought I would call upon, and ask as a personal favor to change her *jhampanies'* livery. I would hire the men myself, and, if necessary, buy their coats from off their backs. It is impossible to say here what a flood of undesirable memories their presence evoked.

"Kitty," I cried, "there are poor Mrs. Wessington's *jhampanies* turned up again! I wonder who has them now?"

Kitty had known Mrs. Wessington slightly last season, and had always been interested in the sickly woman.

"What? Where?" she asked. "I can't see them anywhere."

Even as she spoke, her horse, swerving from a laden mule, threw himself directly in front of the advancing 'rickshaw. I had scarcely time to utter a word of warning when, to my unutterable horror, horse and rider passed *through* men and carriage as if they had been thin air.

"What's the matter?" cried Kitty; "what made you call out so foolishly, Jack? If I *am* engaged I don't want all creation to know about it. There was lots of space between the mule and the veranda; and, if you think I can't ride—— There!"

Whereupon willful Kitty set off, her dainty little head in the air, at a hand-gallop in the direction of the Band-stand; fully expecting, as she herself afterwards told me, that I should follow her. What was the matter? Nothing, indeed. Either that I was mad or drunk, or that Simla was haunted with devils. I reined in my impatient cob, and turned round. The 'rickshaw had turned too, and now stood immediately facing me, near the left railing of the Combermere Bridge.

"Jack! Jack, darling." (There was no mistake about the words this time: they rang through my brain as if they had been shouted in my ear.) "It's some hideous mistake, I'm sure. *Please* forgive me, Jack, and let's be friends again."

The 'rickshaw-hood had fallen back, and inside, as I hope and daily pray for the death I dread by night, sat Mrs. Keith-Wessington, handkerchief in hand, and golden head bowed on her breast.

How long I stared motionless I do not know. Finally, I was aroused by my groom taking the Waler's bridle and asking whether I was ill. I tumbled off my horse and dashed, half fainting, into Peliti's for a glass of cherry-brandy. There two or three couples were gathered round the coffee-tables discussing the gossip of the day. Their trivialities were more comforting to me just then than the consolations of religion could have been. I plunged into the midst of the conversation at once; chatted, laughed and jested with a face (when I caught a glimpse of it in a mirror) as white and drawn as that of a corpse. Three or four men noticed my condition; and, evidently setting it down to the results of over many pegs, charitably endeavored to draw me apart from the rest of the loungers. But I refused to be led away. I wanted the company of my kind—as a child rushes into the midst of the dinner-party after a fright in the dark. I must have talked for about ten minutes or so, though it seemed an eternity to me, when I heard Kitty's clear voice outside inquiring for me. In another minute she had entered the shop, prepared to upbraid me roundly for failing so signally in my duties. Something in my face stopped her.

"Why, Jack," she cried, "what *have* you been doing? What *has* happened? Are you ill?" Thus driven into a direct lie, I said that the sun had been a little too much for me. It was close upon five o'clock of a cloudy April afternoon, and the sun had been hidden all day. I saw my mistake as soon as the words were out of my mouth; attempted to recover it; blundered hopelessly and followed Kitty, in a regal rage, out of doors, amid the smiles of my acquaintances. I made some excuse (I have forgotten what) on the score of my feeling faint; and cantered away to my hotel, leaving Kitty to finish the ride by herself.

In my room I sat down and tried calmly to reason out the matter. Here was I, Theobald Jack Pansay, a well-educated Bengal Civilian in the year of grace 1885, presumably sane, certainly healthy, driven in terror from my sweetheart's side by the apparition of a woman who had been dead and buried eight months ago. These were facts that I could not blink. Nothing was further from my thought than any memory of Mrs. Wessington when Kitty and I left Hamilton's shop. Nothing was more utterly commonplace than the stretch of wall opposite Peliti's. It was broad daylight. The road was full of people; and yet here, look you, in defiance of every law of probability, in direct outrage of Nature's ordinance, there had appeared to me a face from the grave.

Kitty's Arab had gone *through* the 'rickshaw: so that my first hope that some woman marvelously like Mrs. Wessington had hired the carriage and the coolies with their old livery was lost. Again and again I went round this treadmill of thought; and again and again gave up baffled and in despair. The voice was as inexplicable as the apparition. I had originally some wild notion of confiding it all to Kitty; of begging her to marry me at once; and in her arms defying the ghostly occupant of the 'rickshaw. "After all," I argued, "the presence of the 'rickshaw is in itself enough to prove the existence of a spectral illusion. One may see ghosts of men and women, but surely never of coolies and carriages. The whole thing is absurd. Fancy the ghost of a hill-man!"

Next morning I sent a penitent note to Kitty, imploring her to overlook my strange conduct of the previous afternoon. My Divinity was still very wroth, and a personal apology was necessary. I explained, with a fluency born of night-long pondering over a falsehood, that I had been attacked with a sudden palpitation of the heart—the result of indigestion. This eminently practical solution had its effect; and Kitty and I rode out that afternoon with the shadow of my first lie dividing us.

Nothing would please her save a canter round Jakko. With my nerves still unstrung from the previous night I feebly protested against the notion, suggesting Observatory Hill, Jutogh, the Boileaugunge road—anything rather than the Jakko round. Kitty was angry and a little hurt, so I yielded from fear of provoking further misunderstanding, and we set out together towards Chota Simla. We walked a greater part of the way, and, according to our custom, cantered from a mile or so below the Convent to the stretch of level road by the Sanjowlie Reservoir. The wretched horses appeared to fly, and my heart beat quicker and quicker as we neared the crest of the ascent. My mind had been full of Mrs. Wessington all the afternoon; and every inch of the Jakko road bore witness to our old-time walks and talks. The boulders were full of it; the pines sang it aloud overhead; the rain-fed torrents giggled and chuckled unseen over the shameful story; and the wind in my ears chanted the iniquity aloud.

As a fitting climax, in the middle of the level men call the Ladies' Mile, the Horror was awaiting me. No other 'rickshaw was in sight—only the four black and white *jhampanies,* the yellow-paneled carriage, and the golden head of the woman within—all apparently just as I had left them eight months and one fortnight ago! For an instant I fancied that Kitty must see what I saw—we were so marvelously sympathetic in all things. Her next words undeceived me—"Not a soul in sight! Come along, Jack, and I'll race you to the Reservoir buildings!" Her wiry little Arab was off like a bird, my Waler following close behind, and in this order we dashed under the cliffs. Half a minute brought us within fifty yards of the 'rickshaw. I pulled my Waler and fell back a little. The 'rickshaw was directly in the middle of the road: and once more the Arab passed through it, my horse following. "Jack, Jack, dear! *Please* forgive me," rang with a wail in my ears, and, after an interval: "It's all a mistake, a hideous mistake!"

I spurred my horse like a man possessed. When I turned my head at the Reservoir works the black and white liveries were still waiting—patiently waiting—under the gray hillside, and the wind brought me a mocking echo of the words I had just heard. Kitty bantered me a good deal on my silence throughout the remainder of the ride. I had been talking up till then wildly and at random. To save my life I could not speak afterwards naturally, and from Sanjowlie to the Church wisely held my tongue.

I was to dine with the Mannerings that night and had barely time to canter home to dress. On the road to Elysium Hill I overheard two men talking together in the dusk—"It's a curious thing," said one, "how completely all trace of it disappeared. You know my wife was insanely fond of the woman (never could see anything in her myself) and wanted me to pick up her old 'rickshaw and coolies if they were to be got for love or money. Morbid sort of fancy I call it, but I've got to do what the *Memsahib* tells me. Would you believe that the man she hired it from tells me that all four of the men, they were brothers, died of cholera, on the way to Hardwár, poor devils; and the 'rickshaw has been broken up by the man himself. Told me he never used a dead *Memsahib's* 'rickshaw. Spoilt his luck. Queer notion, wasn't it? Fancy poor little Mrs. Wessington spoiling any one's luck except her own!" I laughed aloud at this point; and my laugh jarred on me as I uttered it. So there *were* ghosts of 'rickshaws after all, and ghostly employments in the other world! How much did Mrs. Wessington give her men? What were their hours? Where did they go?

And for visible answer to my last question I saw the infernal thing blocking my path in the twilight. The dead travel fast and by short-cuts unknown to ordinary coolies. I laughed aloud a second time and checked my laughter suddenly, for I was afraid I was going mad. Mad to a certain extent I must have been, for I recollect that I reined in my horse at the head of the 'rickshaw, and politely wished Mrs. Wessington "good evening." Her answer was one I knew only too well. I listened to the end; and replied that I had heard it all before, but should be delighted if she had anything further to say. Some malignant devil stronger than I must have entered into me that evening, for I have a dim recollection of talking the commonplaces of the day for five minutes to the thing in front of me.

"Mad as a hatter, poor devil—or drunk. Max, try and get him to come home."

Surely *that* was not Mrs. Wessington's voice! The two men had overheard me speaking to the empty air, and had returned to look after me. They were very kind and considerate, and from their words evidently gathered that I was extremely drunk. I thanked them confusedly and cantered away to my hotel, there changed, and arrived at the Mannerings' ten minutes late. I pleaded the darkness of the night as an excuse; was rebuked by Kitty for my unlover-like tardiness; and sat down.

The conversation had already become general; and, under cover of it, I was addressing some tender small talk to my sweetheart when I was aware that at the further end of the table a short red-whiskered man was describing with much broidery his encounter with a mad unknown that evening. A few sentences convinced me that he was repeating the incident of half an hour ago. In the middle of the story he looked round for applause, as professional story-tellers do, caught my eye, and straightway collapsed. There was a moment's awkward silence, and the red-whiskered man muttered something to the effect that he had "forgotten the rest"; thereby sacrificing a reputation as a good story-teller which he had built up for six seasons past. I blessed him from the bottom of my heart and—went on with my fish.

In the fullness of time that dinner came to an end; and with genuine regret I tore myself away from Kitty—as certain as I was of my own existence that It would be waiting for me outside the door. The red-whiskered man, who had been introduced to me as Dr. Heatherlegh of Simla, volunteered to bear me company as far as our roads lay together. I accepted his offer with gratitude.

My instinct had not deceived me. It lay in readiness in the Mall, and, in what seemed devilish mockery of our ways, with a lighted head-lamp. The red-whiskered man went to the point at once, in a manner that showed he had been thinking over it all dinner time.

"I say, Pansay, what the deuce was the matter with you this evening on the Elysium road?" The suddenness of the question wrenched an answer from me before I was aware.

"That!" said I, pointing to It.

"*That* may be either *D. T.* or eyes for aught I know. Now you don't liquor. I saw as much at dinner, so it can't be *D. T.* There's nothing whatever where you're pointing, though you're sweating and trembling with fright like a scared pony. Therefore, I conclude that it's eyes. And I ought to understand all about them. Come along home with me. I'm on the Blessington lower road."

To my intense delight the 'rickshaw instead of waiting for us kept about twenty yards ahead—and this, too, whether we walked, trotted, or cantered. In the course of that long night ride I had told my companion almost as much as I have told you here.

"Well, you've spoilt one of the best tales I've ever laid tongue to," said he, "but I'll forgive you for the sake of what you've gone through. Now come home and do what I tell you; and when I've cured you, young man, let this be a lesson to you to steer clear of women and indigestible food till the day of your death."

The 'rickshaw kept steadily in front; and my red-whiskered friend seemed to derive great pleasure from my account of its exact whereabouts.

"Eyes, Pansay—all eyes, brain and stomach; and the greatest of these three is stomach. You've too much conceited brain, too little stomach, and thoroughly unhealthy eyes. Get your stomach straight and the rest follows. And all that's French for a liver pill. I'll take sole medical charge of you from this hour; for you're too interesting a phenomenon to be passed over."

By this time we were deep in the shadow of the Blessington lower road and the 'rickshaw came to a dead stop under a pine-clad, overhanging shale cliff. Instinctively I halted too, giving my reason. Heatherlegh rapped out an oath.

"Now, if you think I'm going to spend a cold night on the hillside for the sake of a stomach-*cum*-brain-*cum*-eye illusion . . . Lord ha' mercy! What's that?"

There was a muffled report, a blinding smother of dust just in front of us, a crack, the noise of rent boughs, and about ten yards of the cliffside—pines, undergrowth, and all—slid down into the road below, completely blocking it up. The uprooted trees swayed and tottered for a moment like drunken giants in the gloom, and then fell prone among their fellows with a thunderous crash. Our two horses stood motionless and sweating with fear. As soon as the rattle of falling earth and stone had subsided, my companion muttered: "Man, if we'd gone forward we should have been ten feet deep in our graves by now! 'There are more things in heaven and earth' . . . Come home, Pansay, and thank God. I want a drink badly."

We retraced our way over the Church Ridge, and I arrived at Dr. Heatherlegh's house shortly after midnight.

His attempts towards my cure commenced almost immediately, and for a week I never left his sight. Many a time in the course of that week did I bless the good fortune which had thrown me in contact with Simla's best and kindest doctor. Day by day my spirits grew lighter and more equable. Day by day, too, I became more and more inclined to fall in with Heatherlegh's "spectral illusion" theory, implicating eyes, brain, and stomach. I wrote to Kitty, telling her that a slight sprain caused by a fall from my horse kept me indoors for a few days; and that I should be recovered before she had time to regret my absence.

Heatherlegh's treatment was simple to a degree. It consisted of liver-pills, cold-water baths and strong exercise, taken in the dusk or at early dawn—for, as he sagely observed: "A man with a sprained ankle doesn't walk a dozen miles a day, and your young woman might be wondering if she saw you."

At the end of the week, after much examination of pupil and pulse and strict injunctions as to diet and pedestrianism, Heatherlegh dismissed me as brusquely as he had taken charge of me. Here is his parting benediction: "Man, I certify to your mental cure, and that's as much as to say I've cured most of your bodily ailments. Now, get your traps out of this as soon as you can; and be off to make love to Miss Kitty."

I was endeavoring to express my thanks for his kindness. He cut me short:

"Don't think I did this because I like you. I gather that

you've behaved like a blackguard all through. But, all the same you're a phenomenon, and as queer a phenomenon as you are a blackguard. Now, go out and see if you can find the eyes-brain-and-stomach business again. I'll give you a lakh for each time you see it."

Half an hour later I was in the Mannerings' drawing-room with Kitty—drunk with the intoxication of present happiness and the foreknowledge that I should never more be troubled with Its hideous presence. Strong in the sense of my new-found security, I proposed a ride at once; and, by preference, a canter round Jakko.

Never have I felt so well, so overladen with vitality and mere animal spirits as I did on the afternoon of the 30th of April. Kitty was delighted at the change in my appearance, and complimented me on it in her delightfully frank and outspoken manner. We left the Mannerings' house together, laughing and talking, and cantered along the Chota Simla road as of old.

I was in haste to reach the Sanjowlie Reservoir and there make my assurance doubly sure. The horses did their best, but seemed all too slow to my impatient mind. Kitty was astonished at my boisterousness. "Why, Jack!" she cried at last, "you are behaving like a child! What are you doing?"

We were just below the Convent, and from sheer wantonness I was making my Waler plunge and curvet across the road as I tickled it with the loop of my riding-whip.

"Doing," I answered, "nothing, dear. That's just it. If you'd been doing nothing for a week except lie up, you'd be as riotous as I.

> *'Singing and murmuring in your feastful mirth,*
> *Joying to feel yourself alive;*
> *Lord over nature, Lord of the visible Earth,*
> *Lord of the senses five.'"*

My quotation was hardly out of my lips before we had rounded the corner above the Convent; and a few yards further on could see across to Sanjowlie. In the center of the level road stood the black and white liveries, the yellow-paneled 'rickshaw and Mrs. Keith-Wessington. I pulled up, looked, rubbed my eyes, and, I believe, must have said something. The next thing I knew was that I was lying face downward on the road, with Kitty kneeling above me in tears.

"Has it gone, child?" I gasped. Kitty only wept more bitterly.

"Has what gone? Jack dear: what does it all mean? There must be a mistake somewhere, Jack. A hideous mistake." Her last words brought me to my feet—mad—raving for the time being.

"Yes, there *is* a mistake somewhere," I repeated, "a hideous mistake. Come and look at It!"

I have an indistinct idea that I dragged Kitty by the wrist along the road up to where It stood, and implored her for pity's sake to speak to It; to tell It that we were betrothed! that neither Death nor Hell could break the tie between us; and Kitty only knows how much more to the same effect. Now and again I appealed passionately to the Terror in the 'rickshaw to bear witness to all I had said, and to release me from a torture that was killing me. As I talked I suppose I must have told Kitty of my old relations with Mrs. Wessington, for I saw her listen intently with white face and blazing eyes.

"Thank you, Mr. Pansay," she said, "that's *quite* enough. Bring my horse."

The grooms, impassive as Orientals always are, had come up with the recaptured horses; and as Kitty sprang into her saddle I caught hold of the bridle entreating her to hear me out and forgive. My answer was the cut of her riding-whip across my face from mouth to eye, and a word or two of farewell that even now I cannot write down. So I judged, and judged rightly, that Kitty knew all; and I staggered back to the side of the 'rickshaw. My face was cut and bleeding, and the blow of the riding-whip had raised a livid blue weal on it. I had no self-respect. Just then, Heatherlegh, who must have been following Kitty and me at a distance, cantered up.

"Doctor," I said, pointing to my face, "here's Miss Mannering's signature to my order of dismissal and . . . I'll thank you for that lakh as soon as convenient."

Heatherlegh's face, even in my abject misery, moved me to laugh.

"I'll stake my professional reputation," he began. "Don't be a fool," I whispered. "I've lost my life's happiness and you'd better take me home."

As I spoke the 'rickshaw was gone. Then I lost all knowledge of what was passing. The crest of Jakko seemed to heave and roll like the crest of a cloud and fall in upon me.

Seven days later (on the 7th of May, that is to say) I was aware that I was lying in Heatherlegh's room as weak as a little child. Heatherlegh was watching me intently from behind the papers on his writing table. His first words were not very encouraging; but I was too far spent to be much moved by them.

"Here's Miss Kitty has sent back your letters. You corresponded a good deal, you young people. Here's a packet that looks like a ring, and a cheeful sort of a note from Mannering Papa, which I've taken the liberty of reading and burning. The old gentleman's not pleased with you."

"And Kitty?" I asked dully.

"Rather more drawn than her father from what she says. By the same token you must have been letting out any number of queer reminiscences just before I met you. Says that a man who would have behaved to a woman as you did to Mrs. Wessington ought to kill himself out of sheer pity for his kind. She's a hot-headed little virago, your mash. Will have it too that you were suffering from *D. T.* when that row on the Jakko road turned up. Says she'll die before she ever speaks to you again."

I groaned and turned over on the other side.

"Now you've got your choice, my friend. This engagement has to be broken off; and the Mannerings don't want to be too hard on you. Was it broken through *D. T.* or epileptic fits? Sorry I can't offer you a better exchange unless you'd prefer hereditary insanity. Say the word and I'll tell 'em it's fits. All Simla knows about that scene on the Ladies' Mile. Come! I'll give you five minutes to think over it."

During those five minutes I believe that I explored thoroughly the lowest circles of the Inferno which it is permitted man to tread on earth. And at the same time I myself was watching myself faltering through the dark labyrinths of doubt, misery, and utter despair. I wondered, as Heatherlegh in his chair might have wondered, which dreadful alternative I should adopt. Presently I heard myself answering in a voice that I hardly recognized:

"They're confoundedly particular about morality in these parts. Give 'em fits, Heatherlegh, and my love. Now let me sleep a bit longer."

Then my two selves joined, and it was only I (half crazed, devil-driven I) that tossed in my bed, tracing step by step the history of the past month.

"But I am in Simla," I kept repeating to myself. "I, Jack Pansay, am in Simla, and there are no ghosts here. It's unreasonable of that woman to pretend there are. Why couldn't Agnes have left me alone? I never did her any harm. It might just as well have been me as Agnes. Only I'd never have come back on purpose to kill *her*. Why can't I be left alone—left alone and happy?"

It was high noon when I first awoke: and the sun was low in the sky before I slept—slept as the tortured criminal sleeps on his rack, too worn to feel further pain.

Next day I could not leave my bed. Heatherlegh told me in the morning that he had received an answer from Mr. Mannering, and that, thanks to his (Heatherlegh's) friendly offices, the story of my affliction had traveled through the length and breadth of Simla, where I was on all sides much pitied.

"And that's rather more than you deserve," he concluded pleasantly, "though the Lord knows you've been going through a pretty severe mill. Never mind; we'll cure you yet, you perverse phenomenon."

I declined firmly to be cured. "You've been much too good to me already, old man," said I; "but I don't think I need trouble you further."

In my heart I knew that nothing Heatherlegh could do would lighten the burden that had been laid upon me.

With that knowledge came also a sense of hopeless, impotent rebellion against the unreasonableness of it all. There were scores of men no better than I whose punishments had at least been reserved for another world and I felt that it was bitterly, cruelly unfair that I alone should have been singled out for so hideous a fate. This mood would in time give place to another where it seemed that the 'rickshaw and I were the only realities in a world of shadows; that Kitty was a ghost; that Mannering, Heatherlegh, and all the other men and women I knew were all ghosts and the great, gray hills themselves but vain shadows devised to torture me. From mood to mood I tossed backwards and forwards for seven weary days, my body growing daily stronger and stronger, until the bedroom looking-glass told me that I had returned to everyday life, and was as other men once more. Curiously enough, my face showed no signs of the struggle I had gone through. It was pale indeed, but as expressionless and commonplace as ever. I had expected some permanent alteration—visible evidence of the disease that was eating me away. I found nothing.

On the 15th of May I left Heatherlegh's house at eleven o'clock in the morning; and the instinct of the bachelor drove me to the Club. There I found that every man knew my story as told by Heatherlegh, and was, in clumsy fashion, abnormally kind and attentive. Nevertheless I recognized that for the rest of my natural life I should be among, but not of, my fellows; and I envied very bitterly indeed the laughing coolies on the Mall below. I lunched at the Club, and at four o'clock wandered aimlessly down the Mall in the vague hope of meeting Kitty. Close to the Band-stand the black and white liveries joined me; and I heard Mrs. Wessington's old appeal at my side. I had been expecting this ever since I came out; and was only surprised at her delay. The phantom 'rickshaw and I went side by side along the Chota Simla road in silence. Close to the bazaar, Kitty and a man on horseback overtook and passed us. For any sign she gave I might have been a dog in the road. She did not even pay me the compliment of quickening her pace; though the rainy afternoon had served for an excuse.

So Kitty and her companion, and I and my ghostly Light-o'-Love, crept round Jakko in couples. The road was streaming with water; the pines dripped like roof-pipes on the rocks below, and the air was full of fine, driving rain. Two or three times I found myself saying to myself almost aloud: "I'm Jack Pansay on leave at Simla—*at Simla!* Everyday, ordinary Simla. I mustn't forget that—I mustn't forget that." Then I would try to recollect some of the gossip I had heard at the Club; the prices of So-and-So's horses—anything, in fact, that related to the work-a-day Anglo-Indian world I knew so well. I even repeated the multiplication-table rapidly to myself, to make quite sure that I was not taking leave of my senses. It gave me much comfort; and must have prevented my hearing Mrs. Wessington for a time.

Once more I wearily climbed the Convent slope and entered the level road. Here Kitty and the man started off at a canter, and I was left alone with Mrs. Wessington. "Agnes," said I, "will you put back your hood and tell me what it all means?" The hood dropped noiselessly and I was face to face with my dead and buried mistress. She was wearing the dress in which I had last seen her alive: carried the same tiny handkerchief in her right hand; and the same card-case in her left. (A woman eight months dead with a card-case!) I had to pin myself down to the multiplication-table, and to set both hands on the stone parapet of the road to assure myself that that at least was real.

"Agnes," I repeated, "for pity's sake tell me what it all means." Mrs. Wessington leant forward, with that odd, quick turn of the head I used to know so well, and spoke.

If my story had not already so madly overleaped the bounds of all human belief I should apologize to you now. As I know that no one—no, not even Kitty, for whom it is written as some sort of justification of my conduct—will believe me, I will go on. Mrs. Wessington spoke and I walked with her from the Sanjowlie road to the turning below the Commander-in-Chief's house as I might walk by the side of any living woman's 'rickshaw, deep in conversation. The second and most tormenting of my moods of sickness had suddenly laid hold upon me, and like the prince in Tennyson's poem, "I seemed to move amid a world of ghosts." There had been a garden-party at the Commander-in-Chief's, and we two joined the crowd of homeward-bound folk. As I saw them then it seemed that *they* were the shadows—impalpable fantastic shadows—that divided for Mrs. Wessington's 'rickshaw to pass through. What we said during the course of that weird interview I cannot—indeed, I dare not—tell. Heatherlegh's comment would have been a short laugh and a remark that I had been "mashing a brain-eye-and-stomach chimera." It was a ghastly and yet in some indefinable way a marvelously dear experience. Could it be possible, I wondered, that I was in this life to woo a second time the woman I had killed by my own neglect and cruelty?

I met Kitty on the homeward road—a shadow among shadows.

If I were to describe all the incidents of the next fortnight in their order, my story would never come to an end; and your patience would be exhausted. Morning after morning and evening after evening the ghostly 'rickshaw and I used to wander through Simla together. Wherever I went, there the four black and white liveries followed me and bore me company to and from my hotel. At the theater I found them amid the crowd of yelling *jhampanies;* outside the Club veranda, after a long evening of whist; at the birthday ball, waiting patiently for my reappearance; and in broad daylight when I went calling. Save that it cast no shadow, the 'rickshaw was in every respect as real to look upon as one of wood and iron. More than once, indeed, I have had to check myself from warning some hard-riding friend against cantering over it. More than once I have walked down the Mall deep in conversation with Mrs. Wessington to the unspeakable amazement of the passers-by.

Before I had been out and about a week I learnt that the "fit" theory had been discarded in favor of insanity. However, I made no change in my mode of life. I called, rode, and dined out as freely as ever. I had a passion for the society of my kind which I had never felt before; I hungered to be among the realities of life; and at the same time I felt vaguely unhappy when I had been separated too long from my ghostly companion. It would be almost impossible to describe my varying moods from the 15th of May up to to-day.

The presence of the 'rickshaw filled me by turns with horror, blind fear, a dim sort of pleasure, and utter despair. I dared not leave Simla; and I knew that my stay there was killing me. I knew, moreover, that it was my destiny to die slowly and a little every day. My only anxiety was to get the penance over as quietly as might be. Alternately I hungered for a sight of Kitty and watched her outrageous flirtations with my successor—to speak more accurately, my successors—with amused interest. She was as much out of my life as I was out of hers. By day I wandered with Mrs. Wessington almost content. By night I implored Heaven to let me return to the world as I used to know it. Above all these varying moods lay the sensation of dull, numbing wonder that the seen and the unseen should mingle so strangely on this earth to hound one poor soul to its grave.

 .   .   .   .   .   .

August 27th.—Heatherlegh has been indefatigable in his attendance on me; and only yesterday told me that I ought to send in an application for sick-leave. An application to escape the company of a phantom! A request that the Government would graciously permit me to get rid of five ghosts and an airy 'rickshaw by going to England! Heatherlegh's proposition moved me to almost hysterical laughter. I told him that I should await the end quietly at Simla; and I am sure that the end is not far off. Believe me that I dread its advent more than any word can say; and I torture myself nightly with a thousand speculations as to the manner of my death.

Shall I die in my bed decently and as an English gentlemen should die; or, in one last walk on the Mall, will my soul be wrenched from me to take its place for ever and ever by the side of that ghastly phantasm? Shall I return to my old lost allegiance in the next world, or shall I meet Agnes loathing her and bound to her side through all eternity? Shall we two hover over the scene of our lives till the end of time? As the day of my death draws nearer, the intense horror that all living flesh feels towards escaped spirits from beyond the grave grows more and more powerful. It is an awful thing to go down quick among the dead with scarcely one half of your life completed. It is a thousand times more awful to wait as I do in your midst, for I know not what unimaginable terror. Pity me, at least on the score of my "delusion," for I know you will never believe what I have written here. Yet as surely as ever a man was done to death by the Powers of Darkness I am that man.

In justice, too, pity her. For as surely as ever woman was killed by man, I killed Mrs. Wessington. And the last portion of my punishment is even now upon me.

THE WILLOWS

BY ALGERNON BLACKWOOD

I

AFTER LEAVING Vienna, and long before you come to Buda-Pesth, the Danube enters a region of singular loneliness and desolation, where its waters spread away on all sides regardless of a main channel, and the country becomes a swamp for miles upon miles, covered by a vast sea of low willow-bushes. On the big maps this deserted area is painted in a fluffy blue, growing fainter in color as it leaves the banks, and across it may be seen in large straggling letters the word *Sümpfe,* meaning marshes.

In high flood this great acreage of sand, shingle-beds, and willow-grown islands is almost topped by the water, but in normal seasons the bushes bend and rustle in the free winds, showing their silver leaves to the sunshine in an ever-moving plain of bewildering beauty. These willows never attain to the dignity of trees; they have no rigid trunks; they remain humble bushes, with rounded tops and soft outline, swaying on slender stems that answer to the least pressure of the wind; supple as grasses, and so continually shifting that they somehow give the impression that the entire plain is moving and *alive.* For the wind sends waves rising and falling over the whole surface, waves of leaves instead of waves of water, green swells like the sea, too, until the branches turn and lift, and then silvery white as their under-side turns to the sun.

Happy to slip beyond the control of stern banks, the Danube

here wanders about at will among the intricate network of channels intersecting the islands everywhere with broad avenues down which the waters pour with a shouting sound; making whirlpools, eddies, and foaming rapids; tearing at the sandy banks; carrying away masses of shore and willow-clumps; and forming new islands innumerable which shift daily in size and shape and possess at best an impermanent life, since the flood-time obliterates their very existence.

Properly speaking, this fascinating part of the river's life begins soon after leaving Pressburg, and we, in our Canadian canoe, with gipsy tent and frying-pan on board, reached it on the crest of a rising flood about mid-July. That very same morning, when the sky was reddening before sunrise, we had slipped swiftly through still-sleeping Vienna, leaving it a couple of hours later a mere patch of smoke against the blue hills of the Wienerwald on the horizon; we had breakfasted below Fischamend under a grove of birch trees roaring in the wind; and had then swept on the tearing current past Orth, Hainburg, Petronell (the old Roman Carnuntum of Marcus Aurelius), and so under the frowning heights of Theben on a spur of the Carpathians, where the March steals in quietly from the left and the frontier is crossed between Austria and Hungary.

Racing along at twelve kilometers an hour soon took us well into Hungary, and the muddy waters—sure sign of flood— sent us aground on many a shingle-bed, and twisted us like a cork in many a sudden belching whirlpool before the towers of Pressburg (Hungarian, Poszóny) showed against the sky; and then the canoe, leaping like a spirited horse, flew at top speed under the gray walls, negotiated safely the sunken chain of the Fliegende Brücke ferry, turned the corner sharply to the left, and plunged on yellow foam into the wilderness of islands, sand-banks, and swamp-land beyond—the land of the willows.

The change came suddenly, as when a series of bioscope pictures snaps down on the streets of a town and shifts without warning into the scenery of lake and forest. We entered the land of desolation on wings, and in less than half an hour there was neither boat nor fishing-hut nor red roof, nor any single sign of human habitation and civilization within sight. The sense of remoteness from the world of human kind, the utter isolation, the fascination of this singular world of willows, winds, and waters, instantly laid its spell upon us both, so that we allowed laughingly to one another that we ought by rights to have held some special kind of passport to admit us, and that we had, somewhat audaciously, come without asking leave into a separate little kingdom of wonder and magic—a kingdom that was reserved for the use of others who had a right to it, with everywhere unwritten warnings to trespassers for those who had the imagination to discover them.

Though still early in the afternoon, the ceaseless buffetings of a most tempestuous wind made us feel weary, and we at once began casting about for a suitable camping-ground for the night. But the bewildering character of the islands made landing difficult; the swirling flood carried us in-shore and then swept us out again; the willow branches tore our hands as we seized them to stop the canoe, and we pulled many a yard of sandy bank into the water before at length we shot with a great sideways blow from the wind into a backwater and managed to beach the bows in a cloud of spray. Then we lay panting and laughing after our exertions on hot yellow sand, sheltered from the wind, and in the full blaze of a scorching sun, a cloudless blue sky above, and an immense army of dancing, shouting willow bushes, closing in from all sides, shining with spray and clapping their thousand little hands as though to applaud the success of our efforts.

"What a river!" I said to my companion, thinking of all the way we had traveled from the source in the Black Forest, and how we had often been obliged to wade and push in the upper shallows at the beginning of June.

"Won't stand much nonsense now, will it?" he said, pulling the canoe a little farther into safety up the sand, and then composing himself for a nap.

I lay by his side, happy and peaceful in the bath of the elements—water, wind, sand, and the great fire of the sun—

thinking of the long journey that lay behind us, and of the great stretch before us to the Black Sea, and how lucky I was to have such a delightful and charming traveling companion as my friend, the Swede.

We had made many similar journeys together, but the Danube, more than any other river I knew, impressed us from the very beginning with its *aliveness*. From its tiny bubbling entry into the world among the pinewood gardens of Donaueschingen, until this moment when it began to play the great river-game of losing itself among the deserted swamps, unobserved, unrestrained, it had seemed to us like following the growth of some living creature. Sleepy at first, but later developing violent desires as it became conscious of its deep soul, it rolled, like some huge fluid being, through all the countries we had passed, holding our little craft on its mighty shoulders, playing roughly with us sometimes, yet always friendly and well-meaning, till at length we had come inevitably to regard it as a Great Personage.

How, indeed, could it be otherwise, since it told us so much of its secret life? At night we heard it singing to the moon as we lay in our tent, uttering that odd sibilant note peculiar to itself and said to be caused by the rapid tearing of the pebbles along its bed, so great is its hurrying speed. We knew, too, the voice of its gurgling whirlpools, suddenly bubbling up on a surface previously quite calm; the roar of its shallows and swift rapids; its constant steady thundering below all mere surface sounds; and that ceaseless tearing of its icy waters at the banks. How it stood up and shouted when the rains fell flat upon its face! And how its laughter roared out when the wind blew upstream and tried to stop its growing speed! We knew all its sounds and voices, its tumblings and foamings, its unnecessary splashing against the bridges; that self-conscious chatter when there were hills to look on; the affected dignity of its speech when it passed through the little towns, far too important to laugh; and all these faint, sweet whisperings when the sun caught it fairly in some slow curve and poured down upon it till the steam rose.

It was full of tricks, too, in its early life before the great world knew it. There were places in the upper reaches among the Swabian forests, when yet the first whispers of its destiny had not reached it, where it elected to disappear through holes in the ground, to appear again on the other side of the porous limestone hills and start a new river with another name; leaving, too, so little water in its own bed that we had to climb out and wade and push the canoe through miles of shallows!

And a chief pleasure, in those early days of its irresponsible youth, was to lie low, like Brer Fox, just before the little turbulent tributaries came to join it from the Alps, and to refuse to acknowledge them when in, but to run for miles side by side, the dividing line well marked, the very levels different, the Danube utterly declining to recognize the newcomer. Below Passau, however, it gave up this particular trick, for there the Inn comes in with a thundering power impossible to ignore, and so pushes and incommodes the parent river that there is hardly room for them in the long twisting gorge that follows, and the Danube is shoved this way and that against the cliffs, and forced to hurry itself with great waves and much dashing to and fro in order to get through in time. And during the fight our canoe slipped down from its shoulder to its breast, and had the time of its life among the struggling waves. But the Inn taught the old river a lesson, and after Passau it no longer pretended to ignore new arrivals.

This was many days back, of course, and since then we had come to know other aspects of the great creature, and across the Bavarian wheat plain of Straubing she wandered so slowly under the blazing June sun that we could well imagine only the surface inches were water, while below there moved, concealed as by a silken mantle, a whole army of Undines, passing silently and unseen down to the sea, and very leisurely too, lest they be discovered.

Much, too, we forgave her because of her friendliness to the birds and animals that haunted the shores. Cormorants lined the banks in lonely places in rows like short black palings; gray crows crowded the shingle-beds; storks stood fishing in the vistas of shallower water that opened up between the islands, and hawks, swans, and marsh birds of all sorts filled the air with glinting wings and singing, petulant cries. It was impossible to feel annoyed with the river's vagaries after seeing a deer leap with a splash into the water at sunrise and swim past the bows of the canoe; and often we saw fawns peering at us from the underbrush, or looked straight into the brown eyes of a stag as we charged full tilt round a corner and entered another reach of the river. Foxes, too, everywhere haunted the banks, tripping daintily among the driftwood and disappearing so suddenly that it was impossible to see how they managed it.

But now, after leaving Pressburg, everything changed a little, and the Danube became more serious. It ceased trifling. It was half-way to the Black Sea, within scenting distance almost of other, stranger countries where no tricks would be permitted or understood. It became suddenly grown-up, and claimed our respect and even our awe. It broke out into three arms, for one thing, that only met again a hundred kilometers farther down, and for a canoe there were no indications which one was intended to be followed.

"If you take a side channel," said the Hungarian officer we met in the Pressburg shop while buying provisions, "you may find yourselves, when the flood subsides, forty miles from anywhere, high and dry, and you may easily starve. There are no people, no farms, no fishermen. I warn you not to continue. The river, too, is still rising, and this wind will increase."

The rising river did not alarm us in the least, but the matter of being left high and dry by a sudden subsidence of the waters might be serious, and we had consequently laid in an extra stock of provisions. For the rest, the officer's prophecy held true, and the wind, blowing down a perfectly clear sky, increased steadily till it reached the dignity of a westerly gale.

It was earlier than usual when we camped, for the sun was a good hour or two from the horizon, and leaving my friend still asleep on the hot sand, I wandered about in desultory examination of our hotel. The island, I found, was less than an acre in extent, a mere sandy bank standing some two or three feet above the level of the river. The far end, pointing into the sunset, was covered with flying spray which the tremendous wind drove off the crests of the broken waves. It was triangular in shape, with the apex upstream.

I stood there for several minutes, watching the impetuous crimson flood bearing down with a shouting roar, dashing in waves against the bank as though to sweep it bodily away, and then swirling by in two foaming streams on either side. The ground seemed to shake with the shock and rush, while the furious movement of the willow bushes as the wind poured over them increased the curious illusion that the island itself actually moved. Above, for a mile or two, I could see the great river descending upon me: it was like looking up the slope of a sliding hill, white with foam, and leaping up everywhere to show itself to the sun.

The rest of the island was too thickly grown with willows to make walking pleasant, but I made the tour, nevertheless. From the lower end the light, of course, changed, and the river looked dark and angry. Only the backs of the flying waves were visible, streaked with foam, and pushed forcibly by the great puffs of wind that fell upon them from behind. For a short mile it was visible, pouring in and out among the islands, and then disappearing with a huge sweep into the willows, which closed about it like a herd of monstrous antediluvian creatures crowding down to drink. They made me think of gigantic sponge-like growths that sucked the river up into themselves. They caused it to vanish from sight. They herded there together in such overpowering numbers.

Altogether it was an impressive scene, with its utter loneliness, its bizarre suggestion; and as I gazed, long and curiously, a singular emotion began to stir somewhere in the depths of me. Midway in my delight of the wild beauty, there crept, unbidden and unexplained, a curious feeling of disquietude, almost of alarm.

A rising river, perhaps, always suggests something of the ominous: many of the little islands I saw before me would probably have been swept away by the morning; this resistless, thundering flood of water touched the sense of awe. Yet I was aware that my uneasiness lay deeper far than the emotions of awe and wonder. It was not that I felt. Nor had it directly to do with the power of the driving wind—this shouting hurricane that might almost carry up a few acres of willows into the air and scatter them like so much chaff over the landscape. The wind was simply enjoying itself, for nothing rose out of the flat landscape to stop it, and I was conscious of sharing its great game with a kind of pleasurable excitement. Yet this novel emotion had nothing to do with the wind. Indeed, so vague was the sense of distress I experienced, that it was impossible to trace it to its source and deal with it accordingly, though I was aware somehow that it had to do with my realization of our utter insignificance before this unrestrained power of the elements about me. The huge-grown river had something to do with it too—a vague, unpleasant idea that we had somehow trifled with these great elemental forces in whose power we lay helpless every hour of the day and night. For here, indeed, they were gigantically at play together, and the sight appealed to the imagination.

But my emotion, so far as I could understand it, seemed to attach itself more particularly to the willow bushes, to these acres and acres of willows, crowding, so thickly growing there, swarming everywhere the eye could reach, pressing upon the river as though to suffocate it, standing in dense array mile after mile beneath the sky, watching, waiting, listening. And, apart quite from the elements, the willows connected themselves subtly with my malaise, attacking the mind insidiously somehow by reason of their vast numbers, and contriving in some way or other to represent to the imagination a new and mighty power, a power, moreover, not altogether friendly to us.

Great revelations of nature, of course, never fail to impress in one way or another, and I was no stranger to moods of the kind. Mountains overawe and oceans terrify, while the mystery of great forests exercises a spell peculiarly its own. But all these, at one point or another, somewhere link on intimately with human life and human experience. They stir comprehensible, even if alarming, emotions. They tend on the whole to exalt.

With this multitude of willows, however, it was something far different, I felt. Some essence emanated from them that besieged the heart. A sense of awe awakened, true, but of awe touched somewhere by a vague terror. Their serried ranks, growing everywhere darker about me as the shadows deepened, moving furiously yet softly in the wind, woke in me the curious and unwelcome suggestion that we had trespassed here upon the borders of an alien world, a world where we were intruders, a world where we were not wanted or invited to remain—where we ran grave risks perhaps!

The feeling, however, though it refused to yield its meaning entirely to analysis, did not at the time trouble me by passing into menace. Yet it never left me quite, even during the very practical business of putting up the tent in a hurricane of wind and building a fire for the stew-pot. It remained, just enough to bother and perplex, and to rob a most delightful camping-ground of a good portion of its charm. To my companion, however, I said nothing, for he was a man I considered devoid of imagination. In the first place, I could never have explained to him what I meant, and in the second, he would have laughed stupidly at me if I had.

There was a slight depression in the center of the island, and here we pitched the tent. The surrounding willows broke the wind a bit.

"A poor camp," observed the imperturbable Swede when at last the tent stood upright; "no stones and precious little firewood. I'm for moving on early tomorrow—eh? This sand won't hold anything."

But the experience of a collapsing tent at midnight had taught us many devices, and we made the cozy gipsy house as safe as possible, and then set about collecting a store of wood to last till bedtime. Willow bushes drop no branches, and driftwood was our only source of supply. We hunted the shores pretty thoroughly. Everywhere the banks were crumbling as

THE WILLOWS

the rising tide flood tore at them and carried away great portions with a splash and a gurgle.

"The island's much smaller than when we landed," said the accurate Swede. "It won't last long at this rate. We'd better drag the canoe close to the tent, and be ready to start at a moment's notice. *I* shall sleep in my clothes."

He was a little distance off, climbing along the bank, and I heard his rather jolly laugh as he spoke.

"By Jove!" I heard him call, a moment later, and turned to see what had caused his exclamation. But for the moment he was hidden by the willows, and I could not find him.

"What in the world's this?" I heard him cry again, and this time his voice had become serious.

I ran up quickly and joined him on the bank. He was looking over the river, pointing at something in the water.

"Good Heavens, it's a man's body!" he cried excitedly. "Look!"

A black thing, turning over and over in the foaming waves, swept rapidly past. It kept disappearing and coming up to the surface again. It was about twenty feet from the shore, and just as it was opposite to where we stood it lurched round and looked straight at us. We saw its eyes reflecting the sunset, and gleaming an odd yellow as the body turned over. Then it gave a swift, gulping plunge, and dived out of sight in a flash.

"An otter, by gad!" we exclaimed in the same breath, laughing.

It *was* an otter, alive, and out on the hunt; yet it had looked exactly like the body of a drowned man turning helplessly in the current. Far below it came to the surface once again, and we saw its black skin, wet and shining in the sunlight.

Then, too, just as we turned back, our arms full of driftwood, another thing happened to recall us to the river bank. This time it really was a man, and what was more, a man in a boat. Now a small boat on the Danube was an unusual sight at any time, but here in this deserted region, and at flood time, it was so unexpected as to constitute a real event. We stood and stared.

Whether it was due to the slanting sunlight, or the refraction from the wonderfully illumined water, I cannot say, but, whatever the cause, I found it difficult to focus my sight properly upon the flying apparition. It seemed, however, to be a man standing upright in a sort of flat-bottomed boat, steering with a long oar, and being carried down the opposite shore at a tremendous pace. He apparently was looking across in our direction, but the distance was too great and the light too uncertain for us to make out very plainly what he was about. It seemed to me that he was gesticulating and making signs at us. His voice came across the water to us shouting something furiously, but the wind drowned it so that no single word was audible. There was something curious about the whole appearance—man, boat, signs, voice—that made an impression on me out of all proportion to its cause.

"He's crossing himself!" I cried. "Look, he's making the sign of the Cross!"

"I believe you're right," the Swede said, shading his eyes with his hand and watching the man out of sight. He seemed to be gone in a moment, melting away down there into the sea of willows where the sun caught them in the bend of the river and turned them into a great crimson wall of beauty. Mist, too, had begun to rise, so that the air was hazy.

"But what in the world is he doing at night-fall on this flooded river?" I said, half to myself. "Where is he going at such a time, and what did he mean by his signs and shouting? D'you think he wished to warn us about something?"

"He saw our smoke, and thought we were spirits probably," laughed my companion. "These Hungarians believe in all sorts of rubbish: you remember the shopwoman at Pressburg warning us that no one ever landed here because it belonged to some sort of beings outside man's world! I suppose they believe in fairies and elementals, possibly demons too. That peasant in the boat saw people on the islands for the first time in his life," he added, after a slight pause, "and it scared him, that's all."

The Swede's tone of voice was not convincing, and his manner lacked something that was usually there. I noted the change instantly while he talked, though without being able to label it precisely.

"If they had enough imagination," I laughed loudly— I remember trying to make as much *noise* as I could—"they might well people a place like this with the old gods of antiquity. The Romans must have haunted all this region more or less with their shrines and sacred groves and elemental deities."

The subject dropped and we returned to our stew-pot, for my friend was not given to imaginative conversation as a rule. Moreover, just then I remember feeling distinctly glad that he was not imaginative; his stolid, practical nature suddenly seemed to me welcome and comforting. It was an admirable temperament, I felt: he could steer down rapids like a red Indian, shoot dangerous bridges and whirlpools better than any white man I ever saw in a canoe. He was a grand fellow for an adventurous trip, a tower of strength when untoward things happened. I looked at his strong face and light curly hair as he staggered along under his pile of driftwood (twice the size of mine!), and I experienced a feeling of relief. Yes, I was distinctly glad just then that the Swede was—what he was, and that he never made remarks that suggested more than they said.

"The river's still rising," he added, as if following out some thoughts of his own, and dropping his load with a gasp. "This island will be under water in two days if it goes on."

"I wish the *wind* would go down," I said. "I don't care a fig for the river."

The flood, indeed, had no terrors for us; we could get off at ten minutes' notice, and the more water the better we liked it. It meant an increasing current and the obliteration of the treacherous shingle-beds that so often threatened to tear the bottom out of our canoe.

Contrary to our expectations, the wind did not go down with the sun. It seemed to increase with the darkness, howling overhead and shaking the willows round us like straws. Curious sounds accompanied it sometimes, like the explosion of heavy guns, and it fell upon the water and the island in great flat blows of immense power. It made me think of the sounds a planet must make, could we only hear it, driving along through space.

But the sky kept wholly clear of clouds, and soon after supper the full moon rose up in the east and covered the river and the plain of shouting willows with a light like the day.

We lay on the sandy patch beside the fire, smoking, listening to the noises of the night round us, and talking happily of the journey we had already made, and of our plans ahead. The map lay spread in the door of the tent, but the high wind made it hard to study, and presently we lowered the curtain and extinguished the lantern. The firelight was enough to smoke and see each other's faces by, and the sparks flew about overhead like fireworks. A few yards beyond, the river gurgled and hissed, and from time to time a heavy splash announced the falling away of further portions of the bank.

Our talk, I noticed, had to do with the far-away scenes and incidents of our first camps in the Black Forest, or of other subjects altogether remote from the present setting, for neither of us spoke of the actual moment more than was necessary—almost as though we had agreed tacitly to avoid discussion of the camp and its incidents. Neither the otter nor the boatman, for instance, received the honor of a single mention, though ordinarily these would have furnished discussion for the greater part of the evening. They were, of course, distinct events in such a place.

The scarcity of wood made it a business to keep the fire going, for the wind, that drove the smoke in our faces wherever we sat, helped at the same time to make a forced draught. We took it in turn to make foraging expeditions into the darkness, and the quantity the Swede brought back always made me feel that he took an absurdly long time finding it; for the fact was I did not care much about being left alone, and yet it always seemed to be my turn to grub about among the bushes or scramble along the slippery banks in the moonlight. The long day's battle with wind and water—such wind and such water!—had tired us both, and an early bed was the obvious program.

Yet neither of us made the move for the tent. We lay there, tending the fire, talking in desultory fashion, peering about us into the dense willow bushes, and listening to the thunder of wind and river. The loneliness of the place had entered our very bones, and silence seemed natural, for after a bit the sound of our voices became a trifle unreal and forced; whispering would have been the fitting mode of communication, I felt, and the human voice, always rather absurd amid the roar of the elements, now carried with it something almost illegitimate. It was like talking out loud in church, or in some place where it was not lawful, perhaps not quite *safe,* to be overheard.

The eeriness of this lonely island, set among a million willows, swept by a hurricane, and surrounded by hurrying deep waters, touched us both, I fancy. Untrodden by man, almost unknown to man, it lay there beneath the moon, remote from human influence, on the frontier of another world, an alien world, a world tenanted by willows only and the souls of willows. And we, in our rashness, had dared to invade it, even to make use of it! Something more than the power of its mystery stirred in me as I lay on the sand, feet to fire, and peered up through the leaves at the stars. For the last time I rose to get firewood.

"When this has burnt up," I said firmly, "I shall turn in," and my companion watched me lazily as I moved off into the surrounding shadows.

For an unimaginative man I thought he seemed unusually receptive that night, unusually open to suggestion of things other than sensory. He too was touched by the beauty and loneliness of the place. I was not altogether pleased, I remember, to recognize this slight change in him, and instead of immediately collecting sticks, I made my way to the far point of the island where the moonlight on plain and river could be seen to better advantage. The desire to be alone had come suddenly upon me; my former dread returned in force; there was a vague feeling in me I wished to face and probe to the bottom.

When I reached the point of sand jutting out among the waves, the spell of the place descended upon me with a positive shock. No mere "scenery" could have produced such an effect. There was something more here, something to alarm.

I gazed across the waste of wild waters; I watched the whispering willows; I heard the ceaseless beating of the tireless wind; and, one and all, each in its own way, stirred in me this sensation of a strange distress. But the *willows* especially: for ever they went on chattering and talking among themselves, laughing a little, shrilly crying out, sometimes sighing—but what it was they made so much to-do about belonged to the secret life of the great plain they inhabited. And it was utterly alien to the world I knew, or to that of the wild yet kindly elements. They made me think of a host of beings from another plane of life, another evolution altogether, perhaps, all discussing a mystery known only to themselves. I watched them moving busily together, oddly shaking their big bushy heads, twirling their myriad leaves even when there was no wind. They moved of their own will as though alive, and they touched, by some incalculable method, my own keen sense of the *horrible*.

There they stood in the moonlight, like a vast army surrounding our camp, shaking their innumerable silver spears defiantly, formed all ready for an attack.

The psychology of places, for some imaginations at least, is very vivid; for the wanderer, especially, camps have their "note" either of welcome or rejection. At first it may not always be apparent, because the busy preparations of tent and cooking prevent, but with the first pause—after supper usually—it comes and announces itself. And the note of this willow-camp now became unmistakably plain to me: we were interlopers, trespassers; we were not welcomed. The sense of unfamiliarity grew upon me as I stood there watching. We touched the frontier of a region where our presence was resented. For a night's lodging we might perhaps be tolerated; but for a prolonged and inquisitive stay—No! by all the gods of the trees and the wilderness, no! We were the first human influences upon this island, and we were not wanted. *The willows were against us.*

Strange thoughts like these, bizarre fancies, borne I know not whence, found lodgment in my mind as I stood listening.

What, I thought, if, after all, these crouching willows proved to be alive; if suddenly they should rise up, like a swarm of living creatures, marshaled by the gods whose territory we had invaded, sweep toward us off the vast swamps, booming overhead in the night—and then *settle* down! As I looked it was so easy to imagine they actually moved, crept nearer, retreated a little, huddled together in masses, hostile, waiting for the great wind that should finally start them a-running. I could have sworn their aspect changed a little, and their ranks deepened and pressed more closely together.

The melancholy shrill cry of a night-bird sounded overhead, and suddenly I nearly lost my balance as the piece of bank I stood upon fell with a great splash into the river, undermined by the flood. I stepped back just in time, and went on hunting for firewood again, half laughing at the odd fancies that crowded so thickly into my mind and cast their spell upon me. I recalled the Swede's remark about moving on next day, and I was just thinking that I fully agreed with him, when I turned with a start and saw the subject of my thoughts standing immediately in front of me. He was quite close. The roar of the elements had covered his approach.

"You've been gone so long," he shouted above the wind, "I thought something must have happened to you."

But there was that in his tone, and a certain look in his face as well, that conveyed to me more than his actual words, and in a flash I understood the real reason for his coming. It was because the spell of the place had entered his soul too, and he did not like being alone.

"River still rising," he cried, pointing to the flood in the moonlight, "and the wind's simply awful."

He always said the same things, but it was the cry for companionship that gave the real importance to his words.

"Lucky," I cried back, "our tent's in the hollow. I think it'll hold all right." I added something about the difficulty of finding wood, in order to explain my absence, but the wind caught my words and flung them across the river, so that he did not hear, but just looked at me through the branches, nodding his head.

"Lucky if we get away without disaster!" he shouted, or words to that effect; and I remember feeling half angry with him for putting the thought into words, for it was exactly what I felt myself. There was disaster impending somewhere, and the sense of presentiment lay unpleasantly upon me.

We went back to the fire and made a final blaze, poking it up with our feet. We took a last look round. But for the wind the heat would have been unpleasant. I put this thought into words, and I remember my friend's reply struck me oddly: that he would rather have the heat, the ordinary July weather than this "diabolical wind."

Everything was snug for the night; the canoe lying turned over beside the tent, with both yellow paddles beneath her; the provision sack hanging from a willow-stem, and the washed-up dishes removed to a safe distance from the fire, all ready for the morning meal.

We smothered the embers of the fire with sand, and then turned in. The flap of the tent door was up, and I saw the branches and the stars and the white moonlight. The shaking willows and the heavy buffetings of the wind against our taut little house were the last things I remembered as sleep came down and covered all with its soft and delicious forgetfulness.

II

Suddenly I found myself lying awake, peering from my sandy mattress through the door of the tent. I looked at my watch pinned against the canvas, and saw by the bright moonlight that it was past twelve o'clock—the threshold of a new day—and I had therefore slept a couple of hours. The Swede was asleep still beside me; the wind howled as before; something plucked at my heart and made me feel afraid. There was a sense of disturbance in my immediate neighborhood.

I sat up quickly and looked out. The trees were swaying violently to and fro as the gusts smote them, but our little bit of green canvas lay snugly safe in the hollow, for the wind passed over it without meeting enough resistance to make it vicious. The feeling of disquietude did not pass, however, and I crawled quietly out of the tent to see if our belongings were safe. I moved carefully so as not to waken my companion. A curious excitement was on me.

I was halfway out, kneeling on all fours, when my eye first took in that the tops of the bushes opposite, with their moving tracery of leaves, made shapes against the sky. I sat back on my haunches and stared. It was incredible, surely, but there, opposite and slightly above me, were shapes of some indeterminate sort among the willows, and as the branches swayed in the wind they seemed to group themselves about these shapes, forming a series of monstrous outlines that shifted rapidly beneath the moon. Close, about fifty feet in front of me, I saw these things.

My first instinct was to waken my companion, that he too might see them, but something made me hesitate—the sudden realization, probably, that I should not welcome corroboration; and meanwhile I crouched there staring in amazement with smarting eyes. I was wide awake. I remember saying to myself that I was *not* dreaming.

They first became properly visible, these huge figures, just within the tops of the bushes—immense, bronze-colored, moving, and wholly independent of the swaying of the branches. I saw them plainly and noted, now I came to examine them more calmly, that they were very much larger than human, and indeed that something in their appearance proclaimed them to be *not human* at all. Certainly they were not merely the moving tracery of the branches against the moonlight. They shifted independently. They rose upward in a continuous stream from earth to sky, vanishing utterly as soon as they reached the dark of the sky. They were interlaced one with another, making a great column, and I saw their limbs and huge bodies melting in and out of each other, forming this serpentine line that bent and swayed and twisted spirally with the contortions of the wind-tossed trees. They were nude, fluid shapes, passing up the bushes, *within* the leaves almost—rising up in a living column into the heavens. Their faces I never could see. Unceasingly they poured upward, swaying in great bending curves, with a hue of dull bronze upon their skins.

I stared, trying to force every atom of vision from my eyes. For a long time I thought they *must* every moment disappear and resolve themselves into the movements of the branches and prove to be an optical illusion. I searched everywhere for a proof of reality, when all the while I understood quite well that the standard of reality had changed. For the longer I looked the more certain I became that these figures were real and living, though perhaps not according to the standards that the camera and the biologist would insist upon.

Far from feeling fear, I was possessed with a sense of awe and wonder such as I have never known. I seemed to be gazing at the personified elemental forces of this haunted and primeval region. Our intrusion had stirred the powers of the place into activity. It was we who were the cause of the disturbance, and my brain filled to bursting with stories and legends of the spirits and deities of places that have been acknowledged and worshipped by men in all ages of the world's history. But, before I could arrive at any possible explanation, something impelled me to go farther out, and I crept forward on to the sand and stood upright. I felt the ground still warm under my bare feet; the wind tore at my hair and face; and the sound of the river burst upon my ears with a sudden roar. These things, I knew, were real, and proved that my senses were acting normally. Yet the figures still rose from earth to heaven, silent, majestically, in a great spiral of grace and strength that overwhelmed me at length with a genuine deep emotion of worship. I felt that I must fall down and worship—absolutely worship.

Perhaps in another minute I might have done so, when a gust of wind swept against me with such force that it blew me sideways, and I nearly stumbled and fell. It seemed to shake the dream violently out of me. At least it gave me another point of view somehow. The figures still remained, still ascended into heaven from the heart of the night, but my reason at last began to assert itself. It must be a subjective experience, I argued—none the less real for that, but still subjective. The moonlight and the branches combined to work out these pictures upon the mirror of my imagination, and for some reason I projected them outward and made them appear objective. I knew this must be the case, of course. I was the subject of a vivid and interesting hallucination. I took courage, and began to move forward across the open patches of sand. By Jove, though, was it all hallucination? Was it merely subjective? Did not my reason argue in the old futile way from the little standard of the known?

I only know that great column of figures ascended darkly into the sky for what seemed a very long period of time, and with a very complete measure of reality as most men are accustomed to gauge reality. Then suddenly they were gone!

And, once they were gone and the immediate wonder of their great presence had passed, fear came down upon me with a cold rush. The esoteric meaning of this lonely and haunted region suddenly flamed up within me, and I began to tremble dreadfully. I took a quick look round—a look of horror that came near to panic—calculating vainly ways of escape; and then, realizing how helpless I was to achieve anything really effective, I crept back silently into the tent and lay down again upon my sandy mattress, first lowering the door-curtain to shut out the sight of the willows in the moonlight, and then burying my head as deeply as possible beneath the blankets to deaden the sound of the terrifying wind.

III

As though further to convince me that I had not been dreaming, I remember that it was a long time before I fell again into a troubled and restless sleep; and even then only the upper crust of me slept, and underneath there was something that never quite lost consciousness, but lay alert and on the watch.

But this second time I jumped up with a genuine start of terror. It was neither the wind nor the river that woke me, but the slow approach of something that caused the sleeping portion of me to grow smaller and smaller till at last it vanished altogether, and I found myself sitting bolt upright—listening.

Outside there was a sound of multitudinous little patterings. They had been coming, I was aware, for a long time, and in my sleep they had first become audible. I sat there nervously wide awake as though I had not slept at all. It seemed to me that my breathing came with difficulty, and that there was a great weight upon the surface of my body. In spite of the hot night, I felt clammy with cold and shivered. Something surely was pressing steadily against the sides of the tent and weighing down upon it from above. Was it the body of the wind? Was this the pattering rain, the dripping of the leaves? The spray blown from the river by the wind and gathering in big drops? I thought quickly of a dozen things.

Then suddenly the explanation leaped into my mind: a bough from the poplar, the only large tree on the island, had fallen with the wind. Still half caught by the other branches, it would fall with the next gust and crush us, and meanwhile its leaves brushed and tapped upon the tight canvas surface of the tent. I raised the loose flap and rushed out, calling to the Swede to follow.

But when I got out and stood upright I saw that the tent was free. There was no hanging bough; there was no rain or spray; nothing approached.

A cold, gray light filtered down through the bushes and lay on the faintly gleaming sand. Stars still crowded the sky directly overhead, and the wind howled magnificently, but the fire no longer gave out any glow, and I saw the east reddening in streaks through the trees. Several hours must have passed since I stood there before watching the ascending figures, and the memory of it now came back to me horribly, like an evil dream. Oh, how tired it made me feel, that ceaseless raging wind! Yet, though the deep lassitude of a sleepless night was on me, my nerves were tingling with the activity of an equally tireless apprehension, and all idea of repose was out of the question. The river I saw had risen further. Its thunder filled the air, and a fine spray made itself felt through my thin sleeping shirt.

Yet nowhere did I discover the slightest evidences of anything to cause alarm. This deep, prolonged disturbance in my heart remained wholly unaccounted for.

My companion had not stirred when I called him, and there was no need to waken him now. I looked about me carefully, noting everything: the turned-over canoe; the yellow paddles —two of them, I'm certain; the provision sack and the extra lantern hanging together from the tree; and, crowding everywhere about me, enveloping all, the willows, those endless, shaking willows. A bird uttered its morning cry, and a string of ducks passed with whirring flight overhead in the twilight. The sand whirled, dry and stinging, about my bare feet in the wind.

I walked round the tent and then went out a little way into the bush, so that I could see across the river to the farther landscape, and the same profound yet indefinable emotion of distress seized upon me again as I saw the interminable sea of bushes stretching to the horizon, looking ghostly and unreal in the wan light of dawn. I walked softly here and there, still puzzling over that odd sound of infinite pattering, and of that pressure upon the tent that had wakened me. It *must* have been the wind, I reflected—the wind beating upon the loose, hot sand, driving the dry particles smartly against the taut canvas—the wind dropping heavily upon our fragile roof.

Yet all the time my nervousness and malaise increased appreciably.

I crossed over to the farther shore and noted how the coastline had altered in the night, and what masses of sand the river had torn away. I dipped my hands and feet into the cool current, and bathed my forehead. Already there was a glow of sunrise in the sky and the exquisite freshness of coming day. On my way back I passed purposely beneath the very bushes where I had seen the column of figures rising into the air, and midway among the clumps I suddenly found myself overtaken by a sense of vast terror. From the shadows a large figure went swiftly by. Someone passed me, as sure as ever man did. . . .

It was a great staggering blow from the wind that helped me forward again, and once out in the more open space, the sense of terror diminished strangely. The winds were about and walking, I remember saying to myself; for the winds often move like great presences under the trees. And altogether the fear that hovered about me was such an unknown and immense kind of fear, so unlike anything I had ever felt before, that it woke a sense of awe and wonder in me that did much to counteract its worst effects; and when I reached a high point in the middle of the island from which I could see the wide stretch of river, crimson in the sunrise, the whole magical beauty of it all was so overpowering that a sort of wild yearning woke in me and almost brought a cry up into the throat.

But this cry found no expression, for as my eyes wandered from the plain beyond to the island round me and noted our little tent half hidden among the willows, a dreadful discovery leaped out at me, compared to which my terror of the walking winds seemed as nothing at all.

For a change, I thought, had somehow come about in the arrangement of the landscape. It was not that my point of vantage gave me a different view, but that an alteration had apparently been effected in the relation of the tent to the willows, and of the willows to the tent. Surely the bushes now crowded much closer—unnecessarily, unpleasantly close. *They had moved nearer.*

Creeping with silent feet over the shifting sands, drawing imperceptibly nearer by soft, unhurried movements, the willows had come closer during the night. But had the wind moved them, or had they moved of themselves? I recalled the sound of infinite small patterings and the pressure upon the tent and upon my own heart that caused me to wake in terror. I swayed for a moment in the wind like a tree, finding it hard to keep my upright position on the sandy hillock. There was a suggestion here of personal agency, of deliberate intention, of aggressive hostility, and it terrified me into a sort of rigidity.

Then the reaction followed quickly. The idea was so bizarre, so absurd, that I felt inclined to laugh. But the laughter came no more readily than the cry, for the knowledge that my mind was so receptive to such dangerous imaginings brought the additional terror that it was through our minds and not through our physical bodies that the attack would come, and was coming.

The wind buffeted me about, and, very quickly it seemed, the sun came up over the horizon, for it was after four o'clock, and I must have stood on that little pinnacle of sand longer than I knew, afraid to come down at close quarters with the willows. I returned quietly, creepily, to the tent, first taking another exhaustive look round and—yes, I confess it—making a few measurements. I paced out on the warm sand the distances between the willows and the tent, making a note of the shortest distance particularly.

I crawled stealthily into my blankets. My companion, to all appearances, still slept soundly, and I was glad that this was so. Provided my experiences were not corroborated, I could find strength somehow to deny them, perhaps. With the daylight I could persuade myself that it was all a subjective hallucination, a fantasy of the night, a projection of the excited imagination.

Nothing further came to disturb me, and I fell asleep almost at once, utterly exhausted, yet still in dread of hearing again that weird sound of multitudinous pattering, or of feeling the pressure upon my heart that had made it difficult to breathe.

IV

The sun was high in the heavens when my companion woke me from a heavy sleep and announced that the porridge was cooked and there was just time to bathe. The grateful smell of frizzling bacon entered the tent door.

"River still rising," he said, "and several islands out in midstream have disappeared altogether. Our own island's much smaller."

"Any wood left?" I asked sleepily.

"The wood and the island will finish tomorrow in a dead heat," he laughed, "but there's enough to last us till then."

I plunged in from the point of the island, which had indeed altered a lot in size and shape during the night, and was swept down in a moment to the landing place opposite the tent. The water was icy, and the banks flew by like the country from an express train. Bathing under such conditions was an exhilarating operation, and the terror of the night seemed cleansed out of me by a process of evaporation in the brain. The sun was blazing hot; not a cloud showed itself anywhere; the wind, however, had not abated one little jot.

Quite suddenly then the implied meaning of the Swede's words flashed across me, showing that he no longer wished to leave post-haste, and had changed his mind. "Enough to last till tomorrow"—he assumed we should stay on the island another night. It struck me as odd. The night before he was so positive the other way. How had the change come about?

Great crumblings of the banks occurred at breakfast, with heavy splashings and clouds of spray which the wind brought into our frying-pan, and my fellow-traveler talked incessantly about the difficulty the Vienna-Pesth steamers must have to find the channel in flood. But the state of his mind interested and impressed me far more than the state of the river or the difficulties of the steamers. He had changed somehow since the evening before. His manner was different—a trifle excited, a trifle shy, with a sort of suspicion about his voice and gestures. I hardly know how to describe it now in cold blood, but at the time I remember being quite certain of one thing, viz., that he had become frightened!

He ate very little breakfast, and for once omitted to smoke his pipe. He had the map spread open beside him, and kept studying its markings.

"We'd better get off sharp in an hour," I said presently, feeling for an opening that must bring him indirectly to a partial confession at any rate. And his answer puzzled me uncomfortably: "Rather! If they'll let us."

"Who'll let us? The elements?" I asked quickly, with affected indifference.

"The powers of this awful place, whoever they are," he replied, keeping his eyes on the map. "The gods are here, if they are anywhere at all in the world."

"The elements are always the true immortals," I replied, laughing as naturally as I could manage, yet knowing quite well that my face reflected my true feelings when he looked up gravely at me and spoke across the smoke:

"We shall be fortunate if we get away without further disaster."

This was exactly what I had dreaded, and I screwed myself up to the point of the direct question. It was like agreeing to allow the dentist to extract the tooth; it *had* to come anyhow in the long run, and the rest was all pretense.

"Further disaster! Why, what's happened?"

"For one thing—the steering paddle's gone," he said quietly

"The steering paddle gone!" I repeated, greatly excited, for this was our rudder, and the Danube in flood without a rudder was suicide. "But what——"

"And there's a tear in the bottom of the canoe," he added, with a genuine little tremor in his voice.

I continued staring at him, able only to repeat the words in his face somewhat foolishly. There, in the heat of the sun, and on this burning sand, I was aware of a freezing atmosphere descending round us. I got up to follow him, for he merely nodded his head gravely and led the way toward the tent a few yards on the other side of the fireplace. The canoe still lay there as I had last seen her in the night, ribs uppermost, the paddles, or rather, *the* paddle, on the sand beside her.

"There's only one," he said, stooping to pick it up. "And here's the rent in the base-board."

It was on the tip of my tongue to tell him that I had clearly noticed *two* paddles a few hours before, but a second impulse made me think better of it, and I said nothing. I approached to see.

There was a long, finely made tear in the bottom of the canoe where a little slither of wood had been neatly taken clean out; it looked as if the tooth of a sharp rock or snag had eaten down her length, and investigation showed that the hole went through. Had we launched out in her without observing it we must inevitably have foundered. At first the water would have made the wood swell so as to close the hole, but once out in midstream the water must have poured in, and the canoe, never more than two inches above the surface, would have filled and sunk very rapidly.

"There, you see, an attempt to prepare a victim for the sacrifice," I heard him saying, more to himself than to me, "two victims rather," he added as he bent over and ran his fingers along the slit.

I began to whistle—a thing I always do unconsciously when utterly nonplussed—and purposely paid no attention to his words. I was determined to consider them foolish.

"It wasn't there last night," he said presently, straightening up from his examination and looking anywhere but at me.

"We must have scratched her in landing, of course," I stopped whistling to say. "The stones are very sharp———"

I stopped abruptly, for at that moment he turned round and met my eye squarely. I knew just as well as he did how impossible my explanation was. There were no stones, to begin with.

"And then there's this to explain too," he added quietly, handing me the paddle and pointing to the blade.

A new and curious emotion spread freezingly over me as I took and examined it. The blade was scraped down all over, beautifully scraped, as though someone had sand-papered it with care, making it so thin that the first vigorous stroke must have snapped it off at the elbow.

"One of us walked in his sleep and did this thing," I said feebly, "or—or it has been filed by the constant stream of sand particles blown against it by the wind, perhaps."

"Ah," said the Swede, turning away, laughing a little, "you can explain everything!"

"The same wind that caught the steering paddle and flung it

so near the bank that it fell in with the next lump that crumbled," I called out after him, absolutely determined to find an explanation for everything he showed me.

"I see," he shouted back, turning his head to look at me before disappearing among the willow bushes.

Once alone with these perplexing evidences of personal agency, I think my first thought took the form of "One of us must have done this thing, and it certainly was not I." But my second thought decided how impossible it was to suppose, under all the circumstances, that either of us had done it. That my companion, the trusted friend of a dozen similar expeditions, could have knowingly had a hand in it, was a suggestion not to be entertained for a moment. Equally absurd seemed the explanation that this imperturbable and densely practical nature had suddenly become insane and was busied with insane purposes.

Yet the fact remained that what disturbed me most, and kept my fear actively alive even in this blaze of sunshine and wild beauty, was the clear certainty that some curious alteration had come about in his *mind*—that he was nervous, timid, suspicious, aware of goings on he did not speak about, watching a series of secret and hitherto unmentionable events—waiting, in a word, for a climax that he expected, and, I thought, expected very soon. This grew up in my mind intuitively—I hardly knew how.

I made a hurried examination of the tent and its surroundings, but the measurements of the night remained the same. There were deep hollows formed in the sand, I now noticed for the first time, basin-shaped and of various depths and sizes, varying from that of a tea-cup to a large bowl. The wind, no doubt, was responsible for these miniature craters, just as it was for lifting the paddle and tossing it toward the water. The rent in the canoe was the only thing that seemed quite inexplicable; and, after all, it *was* conceivable that a sharp point had caught it when we landed. The examination I made of the shore did not assist this theory, but all the same I clung to it with that diminishing portion of my intelligence which I called my "reason." An explanation of some kind was an absolute necessity, just as some working explanation of the universe is necessary—however absurd—to the happiness of every individual who seeks to do his duty in the world and face the problems of life. The simile seemed to me at the time an exact parallel.

I at once set the pitch melting, and presently the Swede joined me at the work, though under the best conditions in the world the canoe could not be safe for traveling till the following day. I drew his attention casually to the hollows in the sand.

"Yes," he said, "I know. They're all over the island. But *you* can explain them, no doubt!"

"Wind, of course," I answered without hesitation. "Have you never watched those little whirlwinds in the street that twist and twirl everything into a circle? This sand's loose enough to yield, that's all."

He made no reply, and we worked on in silence for a bit. I watched him surreptitiously all the time, and I had an idea he was watching me. He seemed, too, to be always listening attentively to something I could not hear, or perhaps for something that he expected to hear, for he kept turning about and staring into the bushes, and up into the sky, and out across the water where it was visible through the openings among the willows. Sometimes he even put his hand to his ear and held it there for several minutes. He said nothing to me, however, about it, and I asked no questions. And meanwhile, as he mended that torn canoe with the skill and address of a red Indian, I was glad to notice his absorption in the work, for there was a vague dread in my heart that he would speak of the changed aspect of the willows. And, if he had noticed *that*, my imagination could no longer be held a sufficient explanation of it.

At length, after a long pause, he began to talk.

"Queer thing," he added in a hurried sort of voice, as though he wanted to say something and get it over. "Queer thing, I mean, about that otter last night."

I had expected something so totally different that he caught me with surprise, and I looked up sharply.

"Shows how lonely this place is. Otters are awfully shy things——"

"I don't mean that, of course," he interrupted. "I mean—do you think—did you think it really *was* an otter?"

"What else, in the name of Heaven, what else?"

"You know, I saw it before you did, and at first it seemed—so *much* bigger than an otter."

"The sunset as you looked upstream magnified it, or something," I replied.

He looked at me absently a moment, as though his mind were busy with other thoughts.

"It had such extraordinary yellow eyes," he went on half to himself.

"That was the sun too," I laughed, a trifle boisterously. "I suppose you'll wonder next if that fellow in the boat——"

I suddenly decided not to finish the sentence. He was in the act again of listening, turning his head to the wind, and something in the expression of his face made me halt. The subject dropped, and we went on with our calking. Apparently he had not noticed my unfinished sentence. Five minutes later, however, he looked at me across the canoe, the smoking pitch in his hand, his face exceedingly grave.

"I *did* rather wonder, if you want to know," he said slowly, "what that thing in the boat was. I remember thinking at the time it was not a man. The whole business seemed to rise quite suddenly out of the water."

I laughed again boisterously in his face, but this time there was impatience, and a strain of anger too, in my feeling.

"Look here now," I cried, "this place is quite queer enough without going out of our way to imagine things! That boat was an ordinary boat, and the man in it was an ordinary man, and they were both going downstream as fast as they could lick. And that otter *was* an otter, so don't let's play the fool about it!"

He looked steadily at me with the same grave expression. He was not in the least annoyed. I took courage from his silence.

"And, for Heaven's sake," I went on, "don't keep pretending

you hear things, because it only gives me the jumps, and there's nothing to hear but the river and this cursed old thundering wind."

"You *fool*!" he answered in a low, shocked voice, "you utter fool. That's just the way all victims talk. As if you didn't understand just as well as I do!" He sneered with scorn in his voice, and a sort of resignation. "The best thing you can do is to keep quiet and try to hold your mind as firm as possible. This feeble attempt at self-deception only makes the truth harder when you're forced to meet it."

My little effort was over, and I found nothing more to say, for I knew quite well his words were true, and that *I* was the fool, not *he*. Up to a certain stage in the adventure he kept ahead of me easily, and I think I felt annoyed to be out of it, to be thus proved less psychic, less sensitive than himself to these extraordinary happenings, and half ignorant all the time of what was going on under my very nose. He *knew* from the beginning, apparently. But at the moment I wholly missed the point of his words about the necessity of there being a victim, and that we ourselves were destined to satisfy the want. I dropped all pretense thenceforward, but thenceforward likewise my fear increased steadily to the climax.

"But you're quite right about one thing," he added, before the subject passed, "and that is that we're wiser not to talk about it, or even to think about it, because what one *thinks* finds expression in words, and what one *says*, happens."

That afternoon, while the canoe dried and hardened, we spent trying to fish, testing the leak, collecting wood, and watching the enormous flood of rising water. Masses of driftwood swept near our shores sometimes, and we fished for them with long willow branches. The island grew perceptibly smaller as the banks were torn away with great gulps and splashes. The weather kept brilliantly fine till about four o'clock, and then for the first time for three days the wind showed signs of abating. Clouds began to gather in the south-west, spreading thence slowly over the sky.

This lessening of the wind came as a great relief, for the

incessant roaring, banging, and thundering had irritated our nerves. Yet the silence that came about five o'clock with its sudden cessation was in a manner quite as oppressive. The booming of the river had everything its own way then: filled the air with deep murmurs, more musical than the wind noises, but infinitely more monotonous. The wind held many notes, rising, falling, always beating out some sort of great elemental tune; whereas the river's song lay between three notes at most —dull pedal notes, that held a lugubrious quality foreign to the wind, and somehow seemed to me, in my then nervous state, to sound wonderfully well the music of doom.

It was extraordinary, too, how the withdrawal suddenly of bright sunlight took everything out of the landscape that made for cheerfulness; and since this particular landscape had already managed to convey the suggestion of something sinister, the change of course was all the more unwelcome and noticeable. For me, I know, the darkening outlook became distinctly more alarming, and I found myself more than once calculating how soon after sunset the full moon would get up in the east, and whether the gathering clouds would greatly interfere with her lighting of the little island.

With this general hush of the wind—though it still indulged in occasional brief gusts—the river seemed to me to grow blacker, the willows to stand more densely together. The latter, too, kept up a sort of independent movement of their own, rustling among themselves when no wind stirred, and shaking oddly from the roots upward. When common objects in this way become charged with the suggestion of horror, they stimulate the imagination far more than things of unusual appearance; and these bushes, crowding huddled about us, assumed for me in the darkness a bizarre *grotesquerie* of appearance that lent to them somehow the aspect of purposeful and living creatures. Their very ordinariness, I felt, masked what was malignant and hostile to us. The forces of the region drew nearer with the coming of night. They were focusing upon our island, and more particularly upon ourselves. For thus, somehow, in the terms of the imagination, did my really indescribable sensations in this extraordinary place present themselves.

I had slept a good deal in the early afternoon, and had thus recovered somewhat from the exhaustion of a disturbed night, but this only served apparently to render me more susceptible than before to the obsessing spell of the haunting. I fought against it, laughing at my feelings as absurd and childish, with very obvious physiological explanations, yet, in spite of every effort, they gained in strength upon me so that I dreaded the night as a child lost in a forest must dread the approach of darkness.

The canoe we had carefully covered with a waterproof sheet during the day, and the one remaining paddle had been securely tied by the Swede to the base of a tree, lest the wind should rob us of that too. From five o'clock onward I busied myself with the stew-pot and preparations for dinner, it being my turn to cook that night. We had potatoes, onions, bits of bacon fat to add flavor, and a general thick residue from former stews at the bottom of the pot; with black bread broken up into it the result was most excellent, and it was followed by a stew of plums with sugar and a brew of strong tea with dried milk. A good pile of wood lay close at hand, and the absence of wind made my duties easy. My companion sat lazily watching me, dividing his attentions between cleaning his pipe and giving useless advice—an admitted privilege of the off-duty man. He had been very quiet all the afternoon, engaged in re-calking the canoe, strenthening the tent ropes, and fishing for driftwood while I slept. No more talk about undesirable things had passed between us, and I think his only remarks had to do with the gradual destruction of the island, which he declared was now fully a third smaller than when we first landed.

The pot had just begun to bubble when I heard his voice calling to me from the bank, where he had wandered away without my noticing. I ran up.

"Come and listen," he said, "and see what you make of it." He held his hand cupwise to his ear, as so often before.

"*Now* do you hear anything?" he asked, watching me curiously.

We stood there, listening attentively together. At first I heard only the deep note of the water and the hissings rising from its turbulent surface. The willows, for once, were motionless and silent. Then a sound began to reach my ears faintly, a peculiar sound—something like the humming of a distant gong. It seemed to come across to us in the darkness from the waste of swamps and willows opposite. It was repeated at regular intervals, but it was certainly neither the sound of a bell nor the hooting of a distant steamer. I can liken it to nothing so much as to the sound of an immense gong, suspended far up in the sky, repeating incessantly its muffled metallic note, soft and musical, as it was repeatedly struck. My heart quickened as I listened.

"I heard it all day," said my companion. "While you slept this afternoon it came all round the island. I hunted it down, but could never get near enough to see—to localize it correctly. Sometimes it was overhead, and sometimes it seemed under the water. Once or twice, too, I could have sworn it was not outside at all, but *within myself*—you know—the way a sound in the fourth dimension is supposed to come."

I was too much puzzled to pay much attention to his words. I listened carefully, striving to associate it with any known familiar sound I could think of, but without success. It changed in direction, too, coming nearer, and then sinking utterly away into remote distance. I cannot say that it was ominous in quality, because to me it seemed distinctly musical, yet I must admit it set going a distressing feeling that made me wish I had never heard it.

"The wind blowing in those sand-funnels," I said, determined to find an explanation, "or the bushes rubbing together after the storm perhaps."

"It comes off the whole swamp," my friend answered. "It comes from everywhere at once." He ignored my explanations. "It comes from the willow bushes somehow——"

"But now the wind has dropped," I objected. "The willows can hardly make a noise by themselves, can they?"

His answer frightened me, first because I had dreaded it, and secondly, because I knew intuitively it was true.

"It is *because* the wind has dropped we now hear it. It was drowned before. It is the cry, I believe, of the——"

I dashed back to my fire, warned by a sound of bubbling that the stew was in danger, but determined at the same time to escape from further conversation. I was resolute, if possible, to avoid the exchanging of views. I dreaded, too, that he would begin again about the gods, or the elemental forces, or something else disquieting, and I wanted to keep myself well in hand for what might happen later. There was another night to be faced before we escaped from this distressing place, and there was no knowing yet what it might bring forth.

"Come and cut up bread for the pot," I called to him, vigorously stirring the appetizing mixture. That stew-pot held sanity for us both, and the thought made me laugh.

He came over slowly and took the provision sack from the tree, fumbling in its mysterious depths, and then emptying the entire contents upon the ground-sheet at his feet.

"Hurry up!" I cried; "it's boiling."

The Swede burst out into a roar of laughter that startled me. It was forced laughter, not artificial exactly, but mirthless.

"There's nothing here!" he shouted, holding his sides.

"Bread, I mean."

"It's gone. There is no bread. They've taken it!"

I dropped the long spoon and ran up. Everything the sack had contained lay upon the ground-sheet, but there was no loaf.

The whole dead weight of my growing fear fell upon me and shook me. Then I burst out laughing too. It was the only thing to do: and the sound of my own laughter also made me understand his. The strain of physical pressure caused it—this explosion of unnatural laughter in both of us; it was an effort of repressed forces to seek relief; it was a temporary safety valve. And with both of us it ceased quite suddenly.

"How criminally stupid of me!" I cried, still determined to be consistent and find an explanation. "I clean forgot to buy a loaf at Pressburg. That chattering woman put everything out of my head, and I must have left it lying on the counter or——"

"The oatmeal, too, is much less than it was this morning," the Swede interrupted.

Why in the world need he draw attention to it? I thought angrily.

"There's enough for tomorrow," I said, stirring vigorously, "and we can get lots more at Komorn or Gran. In twenty-four hours we shall be miles from here."

"I hope so—to God," he muttered, putting the things back into the sack, "unless we're claimed first as victims for the sacrifice," he added with a foolish laugh. He dragged the sack into the tent, for safety's sake, I suppose, and I heard him mumbling on to himself, but so indistinctly that it seemed quite natural for me to ignore his words.

Our meal was beyond question a gloomy one, and we ate it almost in silence, avoiding one another's eyes, and keeping the fire bright. Then we washed up and prepared for the night, and, once smoking, our minds unoccupied with any definite duties, the apprehension I had felt all day long became more and more acute. It was not then active fear, I think, but the very vagueness of its origin distressed me far more than if I had been able to ticket and face it squarely. The curious sound I have likened to the note of a gong became now almost incessant, and filled the stillness of the night with a faint, continuous ringing rather than a series of distinct notes. At one time it was behind and at another time in front of us. Sometimes I fancied it came from the bushes on our left, and then again from the clumps on our right. More often it hovered directly overhead like the whirring of wings. It was really everywhere at once, behind, in front, at our sides and over our heads, completely surrounding us. The sound really defies description. But nothing within my knowledge is like that ceaseless muffled humming rising off the deserted world of swamps and willows.

We sat smoking in comparative silence, the strain growing every minute greater. The worst feature of the situation seemed to me that we did not know what to expect, and could therefore make no sort of preparation by way of defense. We could anticipate nothing. My explanations made in the sunshine, moreover, now came to haunt me with their foolish and wholly unsatisfactory nature, and it was more and more clear to us that some kind of plain talk with my companion was inevitable, whether I liked it or not. After all, we had to spend the night together, and to sleep in the same tent side by side. I saw that I could not get along much longer without the support of his mind, and for that, of course, plain talk was imperative. As long as possible, however, I postponed this little climax, and tried to ignore or laugh at the occasional sentences he flung into the emptiness.

Some of these sentences, moreover, were confoundedly disquieting to me, coming as they did to corroborate much that I felt myself: corroboration, too—which made it so much more convincing—from a totally different point of view. He composed such curious sentences, and hurled them at me in such an inconsequential sort of way, as though his main line of thought was secret to himself, and these fragments were the bits he found it impossible to digest. He got rid of them by uttering them. Speech relieved him. It was like being sick.

"There are things about us, I'm sure, that make for disorder, disintegration, destruction, our destruction," he said once, while the fire blazed between us. "We've strayed out of a safe line somewhere."

And another time, when the gong sounds had come nearer, ringing much louder than before, and directly over our heads, he said, as though talking to himself:

"I don't think a phonograph would show any record of that. The sound doesn't come to me by the ears at all. The vibrations reach me in another manner altogether, and seem to be within me, which is precisely how a fourth dimensional sound might be supposed to make itself heard."

I purposely made no reply to this, but I sat up a little closer to the fire and peered about me into the darkness. The clouds were massed all over the sky and no trace of moonlight came through. Very still, too, everything was, so that the river and the frogs had things all their own way.

"It has that about it," he went on, "which is utterly out of common experience. It is *unknown*. Only one thing describes it really: it is a non-human sound; I mean a sound outside humanity."

Having rid himself of this indigestible morsel, he lay quiet for a time; but he had so admirably expressed my own feeling that it was a relief to have the thought out, and to have confined it by the limitation of words from dangerous wandering to and fro in the mind.

The solitude of that Danube camping place, can I ever forget it? The feeling of being utterly alone on an empty planet! My thoughts ran incessantly upon cities and the haunts of men. I would have given my soul, as the saying is, for the "feel" of those Bavarian villages we had passed through by the score; for the normal, human commonplaces: peasants drinking beer, tables beneath the trees, hot sunshine, and a ruined castle on the rocks behind the red-roofed church. Even the tourists would have been welcome.

Yet what I felt of dread was no ordinary ghostly fear. It was infinitely greater, stranger, and seemed to arise from some dim ancestral sense of terror more profoundly disturbing than anything I had known or dreamed of. We had "strayed," as the Swede put it, into some region or some set of conditions where the risks were great, yet unintelligible to us; where the frontiers of some unknown world lay close about us. It was a spot held by the dwellers in some outer space, a sort of peephole whence they could spy upon the earth, themselves unseen, a point where the veil between had worn a little thin. As the final result of too long a sojourn here, we should be carried over the border and deprived of what we called "our lives," yet by mental, not physical, processes. In that sense, as he said, we should be the victims of our adventure—a sacrifice.

It took us in different fashion, each according to the measure of his sensitiveness and powers of resistance. I translated it vaguely into a personification of the mightily disturbed elements, investing them with the horror of a deliberate and malefic purpose, resentful of our audacious intrusion into their breeding place; whereas my friend threw it into the unoriginal form at first of a trespass on some ancient shrine, some place where the old gods still held sway, where the emotional forces of former worshippers still clung, and the ancestral portion of him yielded to the old pagan spell.

At any rate, here was a place unpolluted by men, kept clean by the winds from coarsening human influences, a place where spiritual agencies were within reach and aggressive. Never, before or since, have I been so attacked by indescribable suggestions of a "beyond region," of another scheme of life, another evolution not parallel to the human. And in the end our minds would succumb under the weight of the awful spell, and we should be drawn across the frontier into *their* world.

Small things testified to this amazing influence of the place, and now in the silence round the fire they allowed themselves to be noted by the mind. The very atmosphere had proved itself a magnifying medium to distort every indication: the otter rolling in the current, the hurrying boatman making signs, the shifting willows, one and all had been robbed of its natural character, and revealed in something of its other aspect—as it existed across the border in that other region. And this changed aspect I felt was new not merely to me, but to the race. The whole experience whose verge we touched was unknown to humanity at all. It was a new order of experience, and in the true sense of the word *unearthly*.

"It's the deliberate, calculating purpose that reduces one's courage to zero," the Swede said suddenly, as if he had been actually following my thoughts. "Otherwise imagination might count for much. But the paddle, the canoe, the lessening food——"

"Haven't I explained all that once?" I interrupted viciously.

"You have," he answered dryly; "you have indeed."

He made other remarks too, as usual, about what he called the "plain determination to provide a victim"; but, having arranged my thoughts better, I recognized that this was simply the cry of his frightened soul against the knowledge that he was being attacked in a vital part, and that he would be somehow taken or destroyed. The situation called for a courage and calmness of reasoning that neither of us could compass, and I have never before been so clearly conscious of two persons in me—the one that explained everything, and the other that laughed at such foolish explanations, yet was horribly afraid.

Meanwhile, in the pitchy night the fire died down and the wood pile grew small. Neither of us moved to replenish the stock, and the darkness consequently came up very close to our faces. A few feet beyond the circle of firelight it was inky black. Occasionally a stray puff of wind set the willows shivering about us, but apart from this not very welcome sound a deep and depressing silence reigned, broken only by the gurgling of the river and the humming in the air overhead.

We both missed, I think, the shouting company of the winds.

At length, at a moment when a stray puff prolonged itself as though the wind were about to rise again, I reached the point for me of saturation, the point where it was absolutely necessary to find relief in plain speech, or else to betray myself by some hysterical extravagance that must have been far worse in its effect upon both of us. I kicked the fire into a blaze, and turned to my companion abruptly. He looked up with a start.

"I can't disguise it any longer," I said; "I don't like this place, and the darkness, and the noises, and the awful feelings I get. There's something here that beats me utterly. I'm in a blue funk, and that's the plain truth. If the other shore was—different, I swear I'd be inclined to swim for it!"

The Swede's face turned very white beneath the deep tan of sun and wind. He stared straight at me and answered quietly, but his voice betrayed his huge excitement by its unnatural calmness. For the moment, at any rate, he was the strong man of the two. He was the more phlegmatic, for one thing.

"It's not a physical condition we can escape from by running away," he replied, in the tone of a doctor diagnosing some grave disease; "we must sit tight and wait. There are forces close here that could kill a herd of elephants in a second as easily as you or I could squash a fly. Our only chance is to keep perfectly still. Our insignificance perhaps may save us."

I put a dozen questions into my expression of face, but found no words. It was precisely like listening to an accurate description of a disease whose symptoms had puzzled me.

"I mean that so far, although aware of our disturbing presence, they have not *found* us—not 'located' us, as the Americans say," he went on. "They're blundering about like men hunting for a leak of gas. The paddle and canoe and provisions prove that. I think they *feel* us, but cannot actually see us. We must keep our minds quiet—it's our minds they feel. We must control our thoughts, or it's all up with us."

"Death you mean?" I stammered, icy with the horror of his suggestion.

"Worse—by far," he said. "Death, according to one's belief, means either annihilation or release from the limitations of the senses, but it involves no change of character. *You* don't suddenly alter just because the body's gone. But this means a radical alteration, a complete change, a horrible loss of oneself by substitution—far worse than death, and not even annihilation. We happen to have camped in a spot where their region touches ours, where the veil between has worn thin"—horrors! he was using my very own phrase, my actual words—"so that they are aware of our being in their neighborhood."

"But *who* are aware?" I asked.

I forgot the shaking of the willows in the windless calm, the humming overhead, everything except that I was waiting for an answer that I dreaded more than I can possibly explain.

He lowered his voice at once to reply, leaning forward a little over the fire, an indefinable change in his face that made me avoid his eyes and look down upon the ground.

"All my life," he said, "I have been strangely, vividly conscious of another region—not far removed from our own world in one sense, yet wholly different in kind—where great things go on unceasingly, where immense and terrible personalities hurry by, intent on vast purposes compared to which earthly affairs, the rise and fall of nations, the destinies of empires, the fate of armies and continents, are all as dust in the balance; vast purposes, I mean, that deal directly with the soul, and not indirectly with mere expressions of the soul——"

"I suggest just now——" I began, seeking to stop him, feeling as though I was face to face with a madman. But he instantly overbore me with his torrent that *had* to come.

"You think," he said, "it is the spirits of the elements, and I thought perhaps it was the old gods. But I tell you now it is—*neither*. These would be comprehensible entities, for they have relations with men, depending upon them for worship or sacrifice, whereas these beings who are now about us have absolutely nothing to do with mankind, and it is mere chance that their space happens just at this spot to touch our own."

The mere conception, which his words somehow made so convincing, as I listened to them there in the dark stillness of that lonely island, set me shaking a little all over. I found it impossible to control my movements.

"And what do you propose?" I began again.

"A sacrifice, a victim, might save us by distracting them until we could get away," he went on, "just as the wolves stop to devour the dogs and give the sleigh another start. But—I see no chance of any other victim now."

I stared blankly at him. The gleam in his eyes was dreadful. Presently he continued.

"It's the willows, of course. The willows *mask* the others, but the others are feeling about for us. If we let our minds betray our fear, we're lost, lost utterly." He looked at me with an expression so calm, so determined, so sincere, that I no longer had any doubts as to his sanity. He was as sane as any man ever was. "If we can hold out through the night," he added, "we may get off in the daylight unnoticed, or rather, *undiscovered*."

"But you really think a sacrifice would——"

That gong-like humming came down very close over our heads as I spoke, but it was my friend's scared face that really stopped my mouth.

"Hush!" he whispered, holding up his hand. "Do not mention them more than you can help. Do not refer to them by *name*. To name is to reveal: it is the inevitable clue, and our only hope lies in ignoring them, in order that they may ignore us."

"Even in thought?"

He was extraordinarily agitated. "Especially in thought. Our thoughts make spirals in their world. We must keep them *out of our minds* at all costs if possible."

I raked the fire together to prevent the darkness having everything its own way. I never longed for the sun as I longed for it then in the awful blackness of that summer night.

"Were you awake all last night?" he went on suddenly.

"I slept badly a little after dawn," I replied evasively, trying to follow his instructions, which I knew instinctively were true, "but the wind, of course——"

"I know. But the wind won't account for all the noises."

"Then you heard it too?"

"The multiplying countless little footsteps I heard," he said, adding, after a moment's hesitation, "and that other sound——"

"You mean above the tent, and the pressing down upon us of something tremendous, gigantic?"

He nodded significantly.

"It was like the beginning of a sort of inner suffocation?" I said.

"Partly, yes. It seemed to me that the weight of the atmosphere had been altered—had increased enormously, so that we should be crushed."

"And *that*," I went on, determined to have it all out, pointing upward where the gong-like note hummed ceaselessly, rising and falling like wind. "What do you make of that?"

"It's *their* sound," he whispered gravely. "It's the sound of their world, the humming in their region. The division here is so thin that it leaks through somehow. But, if you listen carefully, you'll find it's not above so much as around us. It's in the willows. It's the willows themselves humming, because here the willows have been made symbols of the forces that are against us."

I could not follow exactly what he meant by this, yet the thought and idea in my mind were beyond question the thought and idea in his. I realized what he realized, only with less power of analysis than his. It was on the tip of my tongue to tell him at last about my hallucination of the ascending figures and the moving bushes, when he suddenly thrust his face again close into mine across the firelight and began to speak in a very earnest whisper. He amazed me by his calmness and pluck, his apparent control of the situation. This man I had for years deemed unimaginative, stolid!

"Now listen," he said. "The only thing for us to do is to go on as though nothing had happened, follow our usual habits, go to bed, and so forth; pretend we feel nothing and notice nothing. It is a question wholly of the mind, and the less we think about them the better our chance of escape. Above all, don't *think*, for what you think happens!"

"All right," I managed to reply, simply breathless with his words and the strangeness of it all; "all right, I'll try, but tell me one thing more first. Tell me what you make of those hollows in the ground all about us, those sand-funnels?"

"No!" he cried, forgetting to whisper in his excitement. "I dare not, simply dare not, put the thought into words. If you have not guessed I am glad. Don't try to. *They* have put it into my mind; try your hardest to prevent their putting it into yours."

He sank his voice again to a whisper before he finished, and I did not press him to explain. There was already just about as much horror in me as I could hold. The conversation came to an end, and we smoked our pipes busily in silence.

Then something happened, something unimportant apparently, as the way is when the nerves are in a very great state of tension, and this small thing for a brief space gave me an entirely different point of view. I chanced to look down at my sand-shoe—the sort we used for the canoe—and something to do with the hole at the toe suddenly recalled to me the London shop where I had bought them, the difficulty the man had in fitting me, and other details of the uninteresting but practical operation. At once, in its train, followed a wholesome view of the modern skeptical world I was accustomed to move in at home. I thought of roast beef and ale, motor cars, policemen, brass bands, and a dozen other things that proclaimed the soul of ordinariness or utility. The effect was immediate and astonishing even to myself. Psychologically, I suppose, it was simply a sudden and violent reaction after the strain of living in an atmosphere of things that to the normal consciousness must seem impossible and incredible. But, whatever the cause, it momentarily lifted the spell from my heart, and left me for the short space of a minute feeling free and utterly unafraid. I looked up at my friend opposite.

"You damned old pagan!" I cried, laughing aloud in his face. "You imaginative idiot! You superstitious idolator! You——"

I stopped in the middle, seized anew by the old horror. I tried to smother the sound of my voice as something sacrilegious. The Swede, of course, heard it too—that strange cry overhead in the darkness—and that sudden drop in the air as though something had come nearer.

He had turned ashen white under the tan. He stood bolt upright in front of the fire, stiff as a rod, staring at me.

"After that," he said in a sort of helpless, frantic way, "we must go! We can't stay now; we must strike camp this very instant and go on—down the river."

He was talking, I saw, quite wildly, his words dictated by abject terror—the terror he had resisted so long, but which had caught him at last.

"In the dark?" I exclaimed, shaking with fear after my hysterical outburst, but still realizing our position better than he did. "Sheer madness! The river's in flood, and we've only got a single paddle. Besides, we only go deeper into their country! There's nothing ahead for fifty miles but willows, willows, willows!"

He sat down again in a state of semi-collapse. The positions, by one of those kaleidoscopic changes nature loves, were suddenly reversed, and the control of our forces passed over into my hands. His mind at last had reached the point where it was beginning to weaken.

"What on earth possessed you to do such a thing?" he whispered, with the awe of genuine terror in his voice and face.

I crossed round to his side of the fire. I took both his hands

THE WILLOWS

in mine, kneeling down beside him and looking straight into his frightened eyes.

"We'll make one more blaze," I said firmly, "and then turn in for the night. At sunrise we'll be off full speed for Komorn. Now, pull yourself together a bit, and remember your own advice about *not thinking fear!*"

He said no more, and I saw that he would agree and obey. In some measure, too, it was a sort of relief to get up and make an excursion into the darkness for more wood. We kept close together, almost touching, groping among the bushes and along the bank. The humming overhead never ceased, but seemed to me to grow louder as we increased our distance from the fire. It was shivery work!

We were grubbing away in the middle of a thickish clump of willows where some driftwood from a former flood had caught high among the branches, when my body was seized in a grip that made me half drop upon the sand. It was the Swede. He had fallen against me, and was clutching me for support. I heard his breath coming and going in short gasps.

"Look! By my soul!" he whispered, and for the first time in my experience I knew what it was to hear tears of terror in a human voice. He was pointing to the fire, some fifty feet away. I followed the direction of his finger, and I swear my heart missed a beat.

There, in front of the dim glow, *something was moving*.

I saw it through a veil that hung before my eyes like the gauze drop-curtain used at the back of a theater—hazily a little. It was neither a human figure nor an animal. To me it gave the strange impression of being as large as several animals grouped together, like horses, two or three, moving slowly. The Swede, too, got a similar result, though expressing it differently, for he thought it was shaped and sized like a clump of willow bushes, rounded at the top, and moving all over upon its surface—"coiling upon itself like smoke," he said afterward.

"I watched it settle downward through the bushes," he sobbed at me. "Look, by God! It's coming this way! Oh, oh!" He gave a kind of whistling cry. *"They've found us."*

I gave one terrified glance, which just enabled me to see that the shadowy form was swinging toward us through the bushes, and then I collapsed backward with a crash into the branches. These failed, of course, to support my weight, so that with the Swede on the top of me we fell in a struggling heap upon the sand. I really hardly knew what was happening. I was conscious only of a sort of enveloping sensation of icy fear that plucked the nerves out of their fleshly covering, twisted them this way and that, and replaced them quivering. My eyes were tightly shut; something in my throat choked me; a feeling that my consciousness was expanding, extending out into space, swiftly gave way to another feeling that I was losing it altogether, and about to die.

An acute spasm of pain passed through me, and I was aware that the Swede had hold of me in such a way that he hurt me abominably. It was the way he caught at me in falling.

But it was this pain, he declared afterward, that saved me: it caused me to *forget them* and think of something else at the very instant when they were about to find me. It concealed my mind from them at the moment of discovery, yet just in time to evade their terrible seizing of me. He himself, he says, actually swooned at the same moment, and that was what saved him.

I only know that at a later time, how long or short is impossible to say, I found myself scrambling up out of the slippery network of willow branches, and saw my companion standing in front of me holding out a hand to assist me. I stared at him in a dazed way, rubbing the arm he had twisted for me. Nothing came to me to say, somehow.

"I lost consciousness for a moment or two," I heard him say. "That's what saved me. It made me stop thinking about them."

"You nearly broke my arm in two," I said, uttering my only connected thought at the moment. A numbness came over me.

"That's what saved *you!*" he replied. "Between us, we've managed to set them off on a false tack somewhere. The humming has ceased. It's gone—for the moment at any rate!"

A wave of hysterical laughter seized me again, and this time spread to my friend too—great healing gusts of shaking laughter that brought a tremendous sense of relief in their train. We made our way back to the fire and put the wood on so that it blazed at once. Then we saw that the tent had fallen over and lay in a tangled heap upon the ground.

We picked it up, and during the process tripped more than once and caught our feet in sand.

"It's those sand-funnels," exclaimed the Swede, when the tent was up again and the firelight lit up the ground for several yards about us. "And look at the size of them!"

All round the tent and about the fireplace where we had seen the moving shadows there were deep funnel-shaped hollows in the sand, exactly similar to the ones we had already found over the island, only far bigger and deeper, beautifully formed, and wide enough in some instances to admit the whole of my foot and leg.

Neither of us said a word. We both knew that sleep was the safest thing we could do, and to bed we went accordingly without further delay, having first thrown sand on the fire and taken the provision sack and the paddle inside the tent with us. The canoe, too, we propped in such a way at the end of the tent that our feet touched it, and the least motion would disturb and wake us.

In case of emergency, too, we again went to bed in our clothes, ready for a sudden start.

V

It was my firm intention to lie awake all night and watch, but the exhaustion of nerves and body decreed otherwise, and sleep after a while came over me with a welcome blanket of oblivion. The fact that my companion also slept quickened its approach. At first he fidgeted and constantly sat up, asking me if I "heard this" or "heard that." He tossed about on his cork mattress, and said the tent was moving and the river had risen over the point of the island; but each time I went out to look I returned with the report that all was well, and finally he grew calmer and lay still. Then at length his breathing became regular and I heard unmistakable sounds of snoring—the first and only time in my life when snoring has been a welcome and calming influence.

This, I remember, was the last thought in my mind before dozing off.

A difficulty in breathing woke me, and I found the blanket over my face. But something else besides the blanket was pressing upon me, and my first thought was that my companion had rolled off his mattress on to my own in his sleep. I called to him and sat up, and at the same moment it came to me that the tent was *surrounded*. That sound of multitudinous soft pattering was again audible outside, filling the night with horror.

I called again to him, louder than before. He did not answer, but I missed the sound of his snoring, and also noticed that the flap of the tent door was down. This was the unpardonable sin. I crawled out in the darkness to hook it back securely, and it was then for the first time I realized positively that the Swede was not there. He had gone.

I dashed out in a mad run, seized by a dreadful agitation, and the moment I was out I plunged into a sort of torrent of humming that surrounded me completely and came out of every quarter of the heavens at once. It was that same familiar humming—gone mad! A swarm of great invisible bees might have been about me in the air. The sound seemed to thicken the very atmosphere, and I felt that my lungs worked with difficulty.

But my friend was in danger, and I could not hesitate.

The dawn was just about to break, and a faint whitish light spread upward over the clouds from a thin strip of clear horizon. No wind stirred. I could just make out the bushes and river beyond, and the pale sandy patches. In my excitement I ran frantically to and fro about the island, calling him by name, shouting at the top of my voice the first words that came into my head. But the willows smothered my voice, and the humming muffled it, so that the sound only traveled a few feet round me. I plunged among the bushes, tripping headlong, tumbling over roots, and scraping my face as I tore this way and that among the preventing branches.

Then, quite unexpectedly, I came out upon the island's point and saw a dark figure outlined between the water and the sky. It was the Swede. And already he had one foot in the river! A moment more and he would have taken the plunge.

I threw myself upon him, flinging my arms about his waist and dragging him shoreward with all my strength. Of course he struggled furiously, making a noise all the time just like that cursed humming, and using the most outlandish phrases in his anger about "going *inside* to Them," and "taking the way of the water and the wind," and God only knows what more besides, that I tried in vain to recall afterward, but which turned me sick with horror and amazement as I listened. But in the end I managed to get him into the comparative safety of the tent, and flung him breathless and cursing upon the mattress, where I held him until the fit had passed.

I think the suddenness with which it all went and he grew calm, coinciding as it did with the equally abrupt cessation of the humming and pattering outside—I think this was almost the strangest part of the whole business perhaps. For he just opened his eyes and turned his tired face up to me so that the dawn threw a pale light upon it through the doorway, and said, for all the world just like a frightened child:

"My life, old man—it's my life I owe you. But it's all over now anyhow. They've found a victim in our place!"

Then he dropped back upon his blankets and went to sleep literally under my eyes. He simply collapsed, and began to snore again as healthily as though nothing had happened and he had never tried to offer his own life as a sacrifice by drowning. And when the sunlight woke him three hours later—hours of ceaseless vigil for me—it became so clear to me that he remembered absolutely nothing of what he had attempted to do, that I deemed it wise to hold my peace and ask no dangerous questions.

He woke naturally and easily, as I have said, when the sun was already high in a windless hot sky, and he at once got up and set about the preparation of the fire for breakfast. I followed him anxiously at bathing, but he did not attempt to plunge in, merely dipping his head and making some remark about the extra coldness of the water.

"River's falling at last," he said, "and I'm glad of it."

"The humming has stopped too," I said.

He looked up at me quietly with his normal expression. Evidently he remembered everything except his own attempt at suicide.

"Everything has stopped," he said, "because——"

He hesitated. But I knew some reference to that remark he had made just before he fainted was in his mind, and I was determined to know it.

"Because 'They've found another victim'?" I said, forcing a little laugh.

"Exactly," he answered, "exactly! I feel as positive of it as though—as though—I feel quite safe again, I mean," he finished.

He began to look curiously about him. The sunlight lay in hot patches on the sand. There was no wind. The willows were motionless. He slowly rose to his feet.

"Come," he said; "I think if we look, we shall find it."

He started off on a run, and I followed him. He kept to the banks, poking with a stick among the sandy bays and caves and little back-waters, myself always close on his heels.

"Ah!" he exclaimed presently, "ah!"

The tone of his voice somehow brought back to me a vivid sense of the horror of the last twenty-four hours, and I hurried up to join him. He was pointing with his stick at a large black object that lay half in the water and half on the sand. It appeared to be caught by some twisted willow roots so that the river could not sweep it away. A few hours before the spot must have been under water.

"See," he said quietly, "the victim that made our escape possible!"

And when I peered across his shoulder I saw that his stick rested on the body of a man. He turned it over. It was the corpse of a peasant, and the face was hidden in the sand. Clearly the man had been drowned but a few hours before, and his body must have been swept down upon our island somewhere about the hour of the dawn—*at the very time the fit had passed.*

"We must give it a decent burial, you know."

"I suppose so," I replied. I shuddered a little in spite of myself, for there was something about the appearance of that poor drowned man that turned me cold.

The Swede glanced up sharply at me, an undecipherable expression on his face, and began clambering down the bank. I followed him more leisurely. The current, I noticed, had torn away much of the clothing from the body, so that the neck and part of the chest lay bare.

Halfway down the bank my companion suddenly stopped and held up his hand in warning; but either my foot slipped, or I had gained too much momentum to bring myself quickly to a halt, for I bumped into him and sent him forward with a sort of leap to save himself. We tumbled together on to the hard sand so that our feet splashed into the water. And, before anything could be done, we had collided a little heavily against the corpse.

The Swede uttered a sharp cry. And I sprang back as if I had been shot.

At the moment we touched the body there rose from its surface the loud sound of humming—the sound of several hummings—which passed with a vast commotion as of winged things in the air about us and disappeared upward into the sky, growing fainter and fainter till they finally ceased in the distance. It was exactly as though we had disturbed some living yet invisible creatures at work.

My companion clutched me, and I think I clutched him, but before either of us had time properly to recover from the unexpected shock, we saw that a movement of the current was turning the corpse round so that it became released from the grip of the willow roots. A moment later it had turned completely over, the dead face uppermost, staring at the sky. It lay on the edge of the main stream. In another moment it would be swept away.

The Swede started to save it, shouting again something I did not catch about a "proper burial"—and then abruptly dropped upon his knees on the sand and covered his eyes with his hands. I was beside him in an instant.

I saw what he had seen.

For just as the body swung round to the current the face and the exposed chest turned full toward us, and showed plainly how the skin and flesh were indented with small hollows, beautifully formed, and exactly similar in shape and kind to the sand-funnels that we had found all over the island.

"Their mark!" I heard my companion mutter under his breath. "Their awful mark!"

And when I turned my eyes again from his ghastly face to the river, the current had done its work, and the body had been swept away into midstream and was already beyond our reach and almost out of sight, turning over and over on the waves like an otter.

THE RIVAL GHOSTS

BY BRANDER MATTHEWS

THE GOOD SHIP sped on her way across the calm Atlantic. It was an outward passage, according to the little charts which the company had charily distributed, but most of the passengers were homeward bound, after a summer of rest and recreation, and they were counting the days before they might hope to see Fire Island Light. On the lee side of the boat, comfortably sheltered from the wind, and just by the door of the captain's room (which was theirs during the day), sat a little group of returning Americans. The Duchess (she was down on the purser's list as Mrs. Martin, but her friends and familiars called her the Duchess of Washington Square) and Baby Van Rensselaer (she was quite old enough to vote, had her sex been entitled to that duty, but as the younger of two sisters she was still the baby of the family)—the Duchess and Baby Van Rensselaer were discussing the pleasant English voice and the not unpleasant English accent of a manly young lordling who was going to America for sport. Uncle Larry and Dear Jones were enticing each other into a bet on the ship's run of the morrow.

"I'll give you two to one she don't make 420," said Dear Jones.

"I'll take it," answered Uncle Larry. "We made 427 the fifth day last year." It was Uncle Larry's seventeenth visit to Europe, and this was therefore his thirty-fourth voyage.

"And when did you get in?" asked Baby Van Rensselaer. "I don't care a bit about the run, so long as we get in soon."

"We crossed the bar Sunday night, just seven days after we

left Queenstown, and we dropped anchor off Quarantine at three o'clock on Monday morning."

"I hope we shan't do that this time. I can't seem to sleep any when the boat stops."

"I can; but I didn't," continued Uncle Larry; "because my state-room was the most for'ard in the boat, and the donkey-engine that let down the anchor was right over my head."

"So you got up and saw the sunrise over the bay," said Dear Jones, "with the electric lights of the city twinkling in the distance, and the first faint flush of the dawn in the east just over Fort Lafayette, and the rosy tinge which spread softly upward, and——"

"Did you both come back together?" asked the Duchess.

"Because he has crossed thirty-four times you must not suppose that he has a monopoly in sunrises," retorted Dear Jones. "No, this was my own sunrise; and a mighty pretty one it was, too."

"I'm not matching sunrises with you," remarked Uncle Larry, calmly; "but I'm willing to back a merry jest called forth by my sunrise against any two merry jests called forth by yours."

"I confess reluctantly that my sunrise evoked no merry jest at all." Dear Jones was an honest man, and would scorn to invent a merry jest on the spur of the moment.

"That's where my sunrise has the call," said Uncle Larry, complacently.

"What was the merry jest?" was Baby Van Rensselaer's inquiry, the natural result of a feminine curiosity thus artistically excited.

"Well, here it is. I was standing aft, near a patriotic American and a wandering Irishman, and the patriotic American rashly declared that you couldn't see a sunrise like that anywhere in Europe, and this gave the Irishman his chance, and he said, 'Sure ye don't have 'em here till we're through with 'em over there.'"

"It is true," said Dear Jones, thoughtfully, "that they do have some things over there better than we do; for instance, umbrellas."

"And gowns," added the Duchess.

"And antiquities,"—this was Uncle Larry's contribution.

"And we do have some things so much better in America!" protested Baby Van Rensselaer, as yet uncorrupted by any worship of the effete monarchies of despotic Europe. "We make lots of things a great deal nicer than you can get them in Europe—especially ice-cream."

"And pretty girls," added Dear Jones; but he did not look at her.

"And spooks," remarked Uncle Larry casually.

"Spooks?" queried the Duchess.

"Spooks. I maintain the word. Ghosts, if you like that better, or specters. We turn out the best quality of spook——"

"You forget the lovely ghost stories about the Rhine, and the Black Forest," interrupted Miss Van Rensselaer, with feminine inconsistency.

"I remember the Rhine and the Black Forest and all the other haunts of elves and fairies and hobgoblins; but for good honest spooks there is no place like home. And what differentiates our spook—*Spiritus Americanus*—from the ordinary ghost of literature is that it responds to the American sense of humor. Take Irving's stories for example. *The Headless Horseman,* that's a comic ghost story. And Rip Van Winkle—consider what humor, and what good-humor, there is in the telling of his meeting with the goblin crew of Hendrik Hudson's men! A still better example of this American way of dealing with legend and mystery is the marvelous tale of the rival ghosts."

"The rival ghosts?" queried the Duchess and Baby Van Rensselaer together. "Who were they?"

"Didn't I ever tell you about them?" answered Uncle Larry, a gleam of approaching joy flashing from his eye.

"Since he is bound to tell us sooner or later, we'd better be resigned and hear it now," said Dear Jones.

"If you are not more eager, I won't tell it at all."

"Oh, do, Uncle Larry; you know I just dote on ghost stories," pleaded Baby Van Rensselaer.

"Once upon a time," began Uncle Larry—"in fact, a very

few years ago—there lived in the thriving town of New York a young American called Duncan—Eliphalet Duncan. Like his name, he was half Yankee and half Scotch, and naturally he was a lawyer, and had come to New York to make his way. His father was a Scotchman, who had come over and settled in Boston, and married a Salem girl. When Eliphalet Duncan was about twenty he lost both of his parents. His father left him with enough money to give him a start, and a strong feeling of pride in his Scotch birth; you see there was a title in the family in Scotland, and although Eliphalet's father was the younger son of a younger son, yet he always remembered, and always bade his only son to remember, that his ancestry was noble. His mother left him her full share of Yankee grit, and a little house in Salem which has belonged to her family for more than two hundred years. She was a Hitchcock, and the Hitchcocks had been settled in Salem since the year 1. It was a great-great-grandfather of Mr. Eliphalet Hitchcock who was foremost in the time of the Salem witchcraft craze. And this little old house which she left to my friend Eliphalet Duncan was haunted."

"By the ghost of one of the witches, of course," interrupted Dear Jones.

"Now how could it be the ghost of a witch, since the witches were all burned at the stake? You never heard of anybody who was burned having a ghost, did you?"

"That's an argument in favor of cremation, at any rate," replied Jones, evading the direct question.

"It is, if you don't like ghosts; I do," said Baby Van Rensselaer.

"And so do I," added Uncle Larry. "I love a ghost as dearly as an Englishman loves a lord."

"Go on with your story," said the Duchess, majestically overruling all extraneous discussion.

"This little old house at Salem was haunted," resumed Uncle Larry. "And by a very distinguished ghost—or at least by a ghost with very remarkable attributes."

"What was he like?" asked Baby Van Rensselaer, with a premonitory shiver of anticipatory delight.

"It had a lot of peculiarities. In the first place, it never appeared to the master of the house. Mostly it confined its visitations to unwelcome guests. In the course of the last hundred years it had frightened away four successive mothers-in-law, while never intruding on the head of the household."

"I guess that ghost had been one of the boys when he was alive and in the flesh." This was Dear Jones's contribution to the telling of the tale.

"In the second place," continued Uncle Larry, "it never frightened anybody the first time it appeared. Only on the second visit were the ghost-seers scared; but then they were scared enough for twice, and they rarely mustered up courage enough to risk a third interview. One of the most curious characteristics of this well-meaning spook was that it had no face —or at least that nobody ever saw its face."

"Perhaps he kept his countenance veiled?" queried the Duchess, who was beginning to remember that she never did like ghost stories.

"That was what I was never able to find out. I have asked several people who saw the ghost, and none of them could tell me anything about its face, and yet while in its presence they never noticed its features, and never remarked on their absence or concealment. It was only afterward when they tried to recall calmly all the circumstances of meeting with the mysterious stranger, that they became aware that they had not seen its face. And they could not say whether the features were covered, or whether they were wanting, or what the trouble was. They knew only that the face was never seen. And no matter how often they might see it, they never fathomed this mystery. To this day nobody knows whether the ghost which used to haunt the little old house in Salem had a face, or what manner of face it had."

"How awfully weird!" said Baby Van Rensselaer. "And why did the ghost go away?"

"I haven't said it went away," answered Uncle Larry, with much dignity.

"But you said it *used* to haunt the little house at Salem, so I supposed it had moved. Didn't it?"

"You shall be told in due time. Eliphalet Duncan used to spend most of his summer vacations at Salem, and the ghost never bothered him at all, for he was the master of the house—much to his disgust, too, because he wanted to see for himself the mysterious tenant at will of his property. But he never saw it, never. He arranged with friends to call him whenever it might appear, and he slept in the next room with the door open; and yet when their frightened cries waked him the ghost was gone, and his only reward was to hear reproachful sighs as soon as he went back to bed. You see, the ghost thought it was not fair of Eliphalet to seek an introduction which was plainly unwelcome."

Dear Jones interrupted the story-teller by getting up and tucking a heavy rug snugly around Baby Van Rensselaer's feet, for the sky was now overcast and gray, and the air was damp and penetrating.

"One fine spring morning," pursued Uncle Larry, "Eliphalet Duncan received great news. I told you that there was a title in the family in Scotland, and that Eliphalet's father was the younger son of a younger son. Well, it happened that all Eliphalet's father's brothers and uncles had died off without male issue except the eldest son of the eldest, and he, of course, bore the title, and was Baron Duncan of Duncan. Now the great news that Eliphalet Duncan received in New York one fine spring morning was that Baron Duncan and his only son had been yachting in the Hebrides, and they had been caught in a black squall, and they were both dead. So my friend Eliphalet Duncan inherited the title and the estates."

"How romantic!" said the Duchess. "So he was a baron!"

"Well," answered Uncle Larry, "he was a baron if he chose. But he didn't choose."

"More fool he," said Dear Jones sententiously.

"Well," answered Uncle Larry, "I'm not so sure of that. You

see, Eliphalet Duncan was half Scotch and half Yankee, and he had two eyes to the main chance. He held his tongue about his windfall of luck until he could find out whether the Scotch estates were enough to keep up the Scotch title. He soon discovered that they were not, and that the late Lord Duncan, having married money, kept up such state as he could out of the revenues of the dowry of Lady Duncan. And Eliphalet, he decided that he would rather be a well-fed lawyer in New York, living comfortably on his practice, than a starving lord in Scotland, living scantily on his title."

"But he kept his title?" asked the Duchess.

"Well," answered Uncle Larry, "he kept it quiet. I knew it, and a friend or two more. But Eliphalet was a sight too smart to put Baron Duncan of Duncan, Attorney and Counselor at Law, on his shingle."

"What has all this got to do with your ghost?" asked Dear Jones pertinently.

"Nothing with that ghost, but a good deal with another ghost. Eliphalet was very learned in spirit lore—perhaps because he owned the haunted house at Salem, perhaps because he was a Scotchman by descent. At all events, he had made a special study of the wraiths and white ladies and banshees and bogies of all kinds whose sayings and doings and warnings are recorded in the annals of the Scottish nobility. In fact, he was acquainted with the habits of every reputable spook in the Scotch peerage. And he knew that there was a Duncan ghost attached to the person of the holder of the title of Baron Duncan of Duncan."

"So, besides being the owner of a haunted house in Salem, he was also a haunted man in Scotland?" asked Baby Van Rensselaer.

"Just so. But the Scotch ghost was not unpleasant, like the Salem ghost, although it had one peculiarity in common with its trans-Atlantic fellow-spook. It never appeared to the holder of the title, just as the other never was visible to the owner of the house. In fact, the Duncan ghost was never seen at all. It was a guardian angel only. Its sole duty was to be in personal attendance on Baron Duncan of Duncan, and to warn him of impending evil. The traditions of the house told that the Barons of Duncan had again and again felt a premonition of ill fortune. Some of them had yielded and withdrawn from the venture they had undertaken, and it had failed dismally. Some had been obstinate, and had hardened their hearts, and had gone on reckless of defeat and to death. In no case had a Lord Duncan been exposed to peril without fair warning."

"Then how came it that the father and son were lost in the yacht off the Hebrides?" asked Dear Jones.

"Because they were too enlightened to yield to superstition. There is extant now a letter of Lord Duncan, written to his wife a few minutes before he and his son set sail, in which he tells her how hard he has had to struggle with an almost overmastering desire to give up the trip. Had he obeyed the friendly warning of the family ghost, the latter would have been spared a journey across the Atlantic."

"Did the ghost leave Scotland for America as soon as the old baron died?" asked Baby Van Rensselaer, with much interest.

"How did he come over," queried Dear Jones, "in the steerage, or as a cabin passenger?"

"I don't know," answered Uncle Larry calmly, "and Eliphalet, he didn't know. For as he was in no danger, and stood in no need of warning, he couldn't tell whether the ghost was on duty or not. Of course he was on the watch for it all the time. But he never got any proof of its presence until he went down to the little old house of Salem, just before the Fourth of July. He took a friend down with him—a young fellow who had been in the regular army since the day Fort Sumter was fired on, and who thought that after four years of the little unpleasantness down South, including six months in Libby, and after ten years of fighting the bad Indians on the plains, he wasn't likely to be much frightened by a ghost. Well, Eliphalet and the officer sat out on the porch all the evening smoking and talking over points in military law. A little after twelve o'clock, just as they began to think it was about time to turn in, they heard the most ghastly noise in the house. It wasn't a shriek, or a howl, or a yell, or anything they could put a name to. It was an undeterminate, inexplicable shiver and shudder of sound, which went wailing out of the window. The officer had been at Cold Harbor, but he felt himself getting colder this time. Eliphalet knew it was the ghost who haunted the house. As this weird sound died away, it was followed by another, sharp, short, blood-curdling in its intensity. Something in this cry seemed familiar to Eliphalet, and he felt sure that it proceeded from the family ghost, the warning wraith of the Duncans."

"Do I understand you to intimate that both ghosts were there together?" inquired the Duchess anxiously.

"Both of them were there," answered Uncle Larry. "You see, one of them belonged to the house, and had to be there all the time, and the other was attached to the person of Baron Duncan, and had to follow him there; wherever he was there was the ghost also. But Eliphalet, he had scarcely time to think this out when he heard both sounds again, not one after another, but both together, and something told him—some sort of an instinct he had—that those two ghosts didn't agree, didn't get on together, didn't exactly hit it off; in fact, that they were quarreling."

"Quarreling ghosts! Well, I never!" was Baby Van Rensselaer's remark.

"It is a blessed thing to see ghosts dwell together in unity," said Dear Jones.

And the Duchess added, "It would certainly be setting a better example."

"You know," resumed Uncle Larry, "that two waves of light or of sound may interfere and produce darkness or silence. So it was with these rival spooks. They interfered, but they did not produce silence or darkness. On the contrary, as soon as Eliphalet and the officer went into the house, there began at once a series of spiritualistic manifestations, a regular dark séance. A tambourine was played upon, a bell was rung, and a flaming banjo went singing around the room."

"Where did they get the banjo?" asked Dear Jones skeptically.

"I don't know. Materialized it, maybe, just as they did the tambourine. You don't suppose a quiet New York lawyer kept a stock of musical instruments large enough to fit out a strolling minstrel troupe just on the chance of a pair of ghosts coming to give him a surprise party, do you? Every spook has its own instrument of torture. Angels play on harps, I'm informed, and spirits delight in banjos and tambourines. These spooks of Eliphalet Duncan's were ghosts with all the modern improvements, and I guess they were capable of providing their own musical weapons. At all events, they had them there in the little old house at Salem the night Eliphalet and his friend came down. And they played on them, and they rang the bell, and they rapped here, there, and everywhere. And they kept it up all night."

"All night?" asked the awe-stricken Duchess.

"All night long," said Uncle Larry solemnly; "and the next night, too. Eliphalet did not get a wink of sleep, neither did his friend. On the second night the house ghost was seen by the officer; on the third night it showed itself again; and the next morning the officer packed his grip-sack and took the first train to Boston. He was a New Yorker, but he said he'd sooner go to Boston than see that ghost again. Eliphalet, he wasn't scared at all, partly because he never saw either the domiciliary or the titular spook, and partly because he felt himself on friendly terms with the spirit world, and didn't scare easily. But after losing three nights' sleep and the society of his friend, he began to be a little impatient, and to think that the thing had gone far enough. You see, while in a way he was fond of ghosts, yet he liked them best one at a time. Two ghosts were one too many. He wasn't bent on making a collection of spooks. He and one ghost were company, but he and two ghosts were a crowd."

"What did he do?" asked Baby Van Rensselaer.

"Well, he couldn't do anything. He waited awhile, hoping they would get tired; but he got tired out first. You see, it comes natural to a spook to sleep in the daytime, but a man wants to sleep nights, and they wouldn't let him sleep nights. They kept on wrangling and quarreling incessantly; they manifested and they dark-séanced as regularly as the old clock on the stairs struck twelve; they rapped and they rang bells and they banged the tambourine and they threw the flaming banjo about the house, and worse than all, they swore."

"I did not know that spirits were addicted to bad language," said the Duchess.

"How did he know they were swearing? Could he hear them?" asked Dear Jones.

"That was just it," responded Uncle Larry; "he could not hear them—at least not distinctly. There were inarticulate murmurs and stifled rumblings. But the impression produced on him was that they were swearing. If they had only sworn right out, he would not have minded it so much, because he would have known the worst. But the feeling that the air was full of suppressed profanity was very wearing and after standing it for a week, he gave up in disgust and went to the White Mountains."

"Leaving them to fight it out, I suppose," interjected Baby Van Rensselaer.

"Not at all," explained Uncle Larry. "They could not quarrel unless he was present. You see, he could not leave the titular ghost behind him, and the domiciliary ghost could not leave the house. When he went away he took the family ghost with him, leaving the house ghost behind. Now spooks can't quarrel when they are a hundred miles apart any more than men can."

"And what happened afterward?" asked Baby Van Rensselaer, with a pretty impatience.

"A most marvelous thing happened. Eliphalet Duncan went to the White Mountains, and in the car of the railroad that runs to the top of Mount Washington he met a classmate whom he had not seen for years, and this classmate introduced Duncan to his sister, and this sister was a remarkably pretty girl, and Duncan fell in love with her at first sight, and by the time he got to the top of Mount Washington he was so deep in love that he began to consider his own unworthiness, and to wonder whether she might ever be induced to care for him a little—ever so little."

"I don't think that is so marvelous a thing," said Dear Jones glancing at Baby Van Rensselaer.

"Who was she?" asked the Duchess, who had once lived in Philadelphia.

"She was Miss Kitty Sutton, of San Francisco, and she was a daughter of old Judge Sutton, of the firm of Pixley and Sutton."

"A very respectable family," assented the Duchess.

"I hope she wasn't a daughter of that loud and vulgar old Mrs. Sutton whom I met at Saratoga, one summer, four or five years ago?" said Dear Jones.

"Probably she was."

"She was a horrid old woman. The boys used to call her Mother Gorgon."

"The pretty Kitty Sutton with whom Eliphalet Duncan had fallen in love was the daughter of Mother Gorgon. But he never saw the mother, who was in 'Frisco, or Los Angeles, or Santa Fe, or somewhere out West, and he saw a great deal of the daughter, who was up in the White Mountains. She was traveling with her brother and his wife, and as they journeyed from hotel to hotel, Duncan went with them, and filled out the quartette. Before the end of the summer he began to think about proposing. Of course he had lots of chances, going on excursions as they were every day. He made up his mind to seize the first opportunity, and that very evening he took her out for a moonlight row on Lake Winnipiseogee. As he handed her into the boat he resolved to do it, and he had a glimmer of a suspicion that she knew he was going to do it, too."

"Girls," said Dear Jones, "never go out in a rowboat at night with a young man unless you mean to accept him."

"Sometimes it's best to refuse him, and get it over once for all," said Baby Van Rensselaer.

"As Eliphalet took the oars he felt a sudden chill. He tried to shake it off, but in vain. He began to have a growing consciousness of impending evil. Before he had taken ten strokes—and he was a swift oarsman—he was aware of a mysterious presence between him and Miss Sutton."

"Was it the guardian-angel ghost warning him off the match?" interrupted Dear Jones.

"That's just what it was," said Uncle Larry. "And he yielded to it, and kept his peace, and rowed Miss Sutton back to the hotel with his proposal unspoken."

"More fool he," said Dear Jones. "It will take more than one ghost to keep me from proposing when my mind is made up." And he looked at Baby Van Rensselaer.

"The next morning," continued Uncle Larry, "Eliphalet overslept himself, and when he went down to a late breakfast he found that the Suttons had gone to New York by the morning train. He wanted to follow them at once, and again he felt the mysterious presence overpowering his will. He struggled two days, and at last he roused himself to do what he wanted in spite of the spook. When he arrived in New York it was late in the evening. He dressed himself hastily and went to the hotel where the Suttons put up, in the hope of seeing at least her brother. The guardian angel fought every inch of the walk with him, until he began to wonder whether, if Miss Sutton were to take him, the spook would forbid the banns. At the hotel he saw no one that night, and he went home determined to call as early as he could the next afternoon, and make an end of it. When he left his office about two o'clock the next day to learn his fate, he had not walked five blocks before he discovered that the wraith of the Duncans had withdrawn his opposition to the suit. There was no feeling of impending evil, no resistance, no struggle, no consciousness of an opposing presence. Eliphalet was greatly encouraged. He walked briskly to the hotel; he found Miss Sutton alone. He asked her the question, and got his answer."

"She accepted him, of course," said Baby Van Rensselaer.

"Of course," said Uncle Larry. "And while they were in the first flush of joy, swapping confidences and confessions, her brother came into the parlor with an expression of pain on his face and a telegram in his hand. The former was caused by the latter, which was from 'Frisco, and which announced the sudden death of Mrs. Sutton, their mother."

"And that was why the ghost no longer opposed the match?" questioned Dear Jones.

"Exactly. You see, the family ghost knew that Mother Gorgon was an awful obstacle to Duncan's happiness, so it warned him. But the moment the obstacle was removed, it gave its consent at once."

The fog was lowering its thick damp curtain, and it was beginning to be difficult to see from one end of the boat to the other. Dear Jones tightened the rug which enwrapped Baby Van Rensselaer, and then withdrew again into his own substantial coverings.

Uncle Larry paused in his story long enough to light another of the tiny cigars he always smoked.

"I infer that Lord Duncan"—the Duchess was scrupulous in the bestowal of titles—"saw no more of the ghosts after he was married."

"He never saw them at all, at any time, either before or since. But they came very near breaking off the match, and thus breaking two young hearts."

"You don't mean to say that they knew any just cause or impediment why they should not forever after hold their peace?" asked Dear Jones.

"How could a ghost, or even two ghosts, keep a girl from marrying the man she loved?" This was Baby Van Rensselaer's question.

"It seems curious, doesn't it?" and Uncle Larry tried to warm himself by two or three sharp pulls at his fiery little cigar. "And the circumstances are quite as curious as the fact itself. You see, Miss Sutton wouldn't be married for a year after her mother's death, so she and Duncan had lots of time to tell each other all they knew. Eliphalet, he got to know a good deal about the girls she went to school with, and Kitty, she learned all about his family. He didn't tell her about the title for a long time, as he wasn't one to brag. But he described to her the little old house at Salem. And one evening toward the end of the summer, the wedding-day having been appointed for early in September, she told him that she didn't want to bridal tour at all; she just wanted to go down to the little old house at Salem to spend her honeymoon in peace and quiet, with nothing to do and nobody to bother them. Well, Eliphalet jumped at the suggestion. It suited him down to the ground. All of a sudden he remembered the spooks, and it knocked him all of a heap. He had told her about the Duncan Banshee, and the idea of having an ancestral ghost in personal attendance on her husband tickled her immensely. But he had never said anything about the ghost which haunted the little old house at Salem. He knew she would be frightened out of her wits if the house ghost revealed itself to her, and he saw at once that it would be impossible to go to Salem on their wedding trip. So he told her all about it, and how whenever he went to Salem the two ghosts interfered, and gave dark séances and manifested and materialized and made the place absolutely impossible. Kitty, she listened in silence, and Eliphalet, he thought she had changed her mind. But she hadn't done anything of the kind."

"Just like a man—to think she was going to," remarked Baby Van Rensselaer.

"She just told him she could not bear ghosts herself, but she would not marry a man who was afraid of them."

"Just like a girl—to be so inconsistent," remarked Dear Jones.

Uncle Larry's tiny cigar had long been extinct. He lighted a new one, and continued: "Eliphalet protested in vain. Kitty said her mind was made up. She was determined to pass her honeymoon in the little old house at Salem, and she was equally determined not to go there as long as there were any ghosts there. Until he could assure her that the spectral tenants had received notice to quit, and that there was no danger of manifestations and materializing, she refused to be married at all. She did not intend to have her honeymoon interrupted by two wrangling ghosts, and the wedding could be postponed until he had made ready the house for her."

"She was an unreasonable young woman," said the Duchess.

"Well, that's what Eliphalet thought, much as he was in love with her. And he believed he could talk her out of her determination. But he couldn't. She was set. And when a girl is set, there's nothing to do but yield to the inevitable. And that's just what Eliphalet did. He saw he would either have to give her up or to get the ghosts out; and as he loved her and did not care for the ghosts, he resolved to tackle the ghosts. He had clear grit, Eliphalet had—he was half Scotch and half Yankee, and neither breed turns tail in a hurry. So he made his plans and he went down to Salem. As he said good-bye to Kitty he had an impression that she was sorry she had made him go, but she kept up bravely, and put a bold face on it, and saw him off, and went home and cried for an hour, and was perfectly miserable until he came back the next day."

"Did he succeed in driving the ghosts away?" asked Baby Van Rensselaer, with great interest.

"That's just what I'm coming to," said Uncle Larry, pausing at the critical moment, in the manner of the trained story teller. "You see, Eliphalet had got a rather tough job, and he would gladly have had an extension of time on the contract, but he had to choose between the girl and the ghosts, and he wanted the girl. He tried to invent or remember some short and easy way with ghosts, but he couldn't. He wished that somebody had invented a specific for spooks—something that would make the ghosts come out of the house and die in the yard. He wondered if he could not tempt the ghosts to run in debt, so that he might get the sheriff to help him. He wondered also whether the ghosts could not be overcome with strong drink —a dissipated spook, a spook with delirium tremens, might be committed to the inebriate asylum. But none of these things seemed feasible."

"What did he do?" interrupted Dear Jones. "The learned counsel will please speak to the point."

THE RIVAL GHOSTS 147

"You will regret this unseemly haste," said Uncle Larry, gravely, "when you know what really happened."

"What was it, Uncle Larry?" asked Baby Van Rensselaer. "I'm all impatience."

And Uncle Larry proceeded:

"Eliphalet went down to the little old house at Salem, and as soon as the clock struck twelve the rival ghosts began wrangling as before. Raps here, there, and everywhere, ringing bells, banging tambourines, strumming banjos sailing about the room, and all the other manifestations and materializations followed one another just as they had the summer before. The only difference Eliphalet could detect was a stronger flavor in the spectral profanity; and this, of course, was only a vague impression, for he did not actually hear a single word. He waited awhile in patience, listening and watching. Of course he never saw either of the ghosts, because neither of them could appear to him. At last he got his dander up, and he thought it was about time to interfere, so he rapped on the table, and asked for silence. As soon as he felt that the spooks were listening to him he explained the situation to them. He told them he was in love, and that he could not marry unless they vacated the house. He appealed to them as old friends, and he laid claim to their gratitude. The titular ghost had been sheltered by the Duncan family for hundreds of years, and the domiciliary ghost had had free lodging in the little old house at Salem for nearly two centuries. He implored them to settle their differences, and to get him out of his difficulty at once. He suggested they'd better fight it out then and there, and see who was master. He had brought down with him all needful weapons. And he pulled out his valise, and spread on the table a pair of navy revolvers, a pair of shot-guns, a pair of dueling swords, and a couple of bowie-knives. He offered to serve as second for both parties, and to give the word when to begin. He also took out of his valise a pack of cards and a bottle of poison, telling them that if they wished to avoid carnage they might cut the cards to see which one should take the poison. Then he waited anxiously for their reply. For a little space there was silence. Then he became conscious of a tremulous shivering in one corner of the room, and he remembered that he had heard from that direction what sounded like a frightened sigh when he made the first suggestion of the duel. Something told him that this was the domiciliary ghost, and that it was badly scared. Then he was impressed by a certain movement in the opposite corner of the room, as though the titular ghost were drawing himself up with offended dignity. Eliphalet couldn't exactly see these things, because he never saw the ghosts, but he felt them. After a silence of nearly a minute a voice came from the corner where the family ghost stood—a voice strong and full, but trembling slightly with suppressed passion. And this voice told Eliphalet it was plain enough that he had not long been the head of the Duncans, and that he had never properly considered the characteristics of his race if now he supposed that one of his blood could draw his sword against a woman. Eliphalet said he had never suggested that the Duncan ghost should raise his hand against a woman and all he wanted was that the Duncan ghost should fight the other ghost. And then the voice told Eliphalet that the other ghost was a woman."

"What?" said Dear Jones, sitting up suddenly. "You don't mean to tell me that the ghost which haunted the house was a woman?"

"Those were the very words Eliphalet Duncan used," said Uncle Larry; "but he did not need to wait for the answer. All at once he recalled the traditions about the domiciliary ghost, and he knew that what the titular ghost said was the fact. He had never thought of the sex of a spook, but there was no doubt whatever that the house ghost was a woman. No sooner was this firmly fixed in Eliphalet's mind than he saw his way out of the difficulty. The ghosts must be married!—for then there would be no more interference, no more quarreling, no more manifestations and materializations, no more dark séances, with their raps and bells and tambourines and banjos. At first the ghosts would not hear of it. The voice in the corner declared that the Duncan wraith had never thought of matrimony. But

Eliphalet argued with them, and pleaded and persuaded and coaxed, and dwelt on the advantages of matrimony. He had to confess, of course, that he did not know how to get a clergyman to marry them; but the voice from the corner gravely told him that there need be no difficulty in regard to that, as there was no lack of spiritual chaplains. Then, for the first time, the house ghost spoke, in a low, clear, gentle voice, and with a quaint, old-fashioned New England accent, which contrasted sharply with the broad Scotch speech of the family ghost. She said that Eliphalet Duncan seemed to have forgotten that she was married. But this did not upset Eliphalet at all; he remembered the whole case clearly, and he told her she was not a married ghost, but a widow, since her husband had been hung for murdering her. Then the Duncan ghost drew attention to the great disparity of their ages, saying that he was nearly four hundred and fifty years old, while she was barely two hundred. But Eliphalet had not talked to juries for nothing; he just buckled to, and coaxed those ghosts into matrimony. Afterward he came to the conclusion that they were willing to be coaxed, but at the time he thought he had pretty hard work to convince them of the advantages of the plan."

"Did he succeed?" asked Baby Van Rensselaer, with a young lady's interest in matrimony.

"He did," said Uncle Larry. "He talked the wraith of the Duncans and the specter of the little old house at Salem into a matrimonial engagement. And from the time they were engaged he had no more trouble with them. They were rival ghosts no longer. They were married by their spiritual chaplain the very same day that Eliphalet Duncan met Kitty Sutton in front of the railing of Grace Church. The ghostly bride and bridegroom went away at once on their bridal tour, and Lord and Lady Duncan went down to the little old house at Salem to pass their honeymoon."

Uncle Larry stopped. His tiny cigar was out again. The tale of the rival ghosts was told. A solemn silence fell on the little party on the deck of the ocean steamer, broken harshly by the hoarse roar of the fog-horn.

THE MAN WHO WENT TOO FAR

BY E. F. BENSON

THE LITTLE VILLAGE of St. Faith's nestles in a hollow of wooded hill up on the north bank of the river Fawn in the county of Hampshire, huddling close round its gray Norman church as if for spiritual protection against the fays and fairies, the trolls and "little people," who might be supposed still to linger in the vast empty spaces of the New Forest, and to come after dusk and do their doubtful businesses. Once outside the hamlet you may walk in any direction (so long as you avoid the high road which leads to Brockenhurst) for the length of a summer afternoon without seeing sign of human habitation, or possibly even catching sight of another human being. Shaggy wild ponies may stop their feeding for a moment as you pass, the white scuts of rabbits will vanish into their burrows, a brown viper perhaps will glide from your path into a clump of heather, and unseen birds will chuckle in the bushes, but it may easily happen that for a long day you will see nothing human. But you will not feel in the least lonely; in summer, at any rate, the sunlight will be gay with butterflies, and the air thick with all those woodland sounds which like instruments in an orchestra combine to play the great symphony of the yearly festival of June. Winds whisper in the birches, and sigh among the firs; bees are busy with their redolent labor among the heather, a myriad birds chirp in the green temples of the forest trees, and the voice of the river prattling over stony places, bubbling into pools, chuckling and gulping round corners, gives you the sense that many presences and companions are near at hand.

Yet, oddly enough, though one would have thought that these benign and cheerful influences of wholesome air and spaciousness of forest were very healthful comrades for a man, in so far as nature can really influence this wonderful human genus which has in these centuries learned to defy her most violent storms in its well-established houses, to bridle her torrents and make them light its streets, to tunnel her mountains and plow her seas, the inhabitants of St. Faith's will not willingly venture into the forest after dark. For in spite of the silence and loneliness of the hooded night it seems that a man is not sure in what company he may suddenly find himself, and though it is difficult to get from these villagers any very clear story of occult appearances, the feeling is widespread. One story indeed I have heard with some definiteness, the tale of a monstrous goat that has been seen to skip with hellish glee about the woods and shady places, and this perhaps is connected with the story which I have here attempted to piece together. It too is well-known to them; for all remember the young artist who died here not long ago, a young man, or so he struck the beholder, of great personal beauty, with something about him that made men's faces to smile and brighten when they looked on him. His ghost they will tell you "walks" constantly by the stream and through the woods which he loved so, and in especial it haunts a certain house, the last of the village, where he lived, and its garden in which he was done to death. For my part I am inclined to think that the terror of the Forest dates chiefly from that day. So, such as the story is, I have set it forth in connected form. It is based partly on the accounts of the villagers, but mainly on that of Darcy, a friend of mine and a friend of the man with whom these events were chiefly concerned.

The day had been one of untarnished midsummer splendor, and as the sun drew near to its setting, the glory of the evening grew every moment more crystalline, more miraculous. Westward from St. Faith's the beechwood which stretched for some miles toward the heathery upland beyond already cast its veil of clear shadow over the red roofs of the village, but the spire of the gray church, overtopping all, still pointed a flaming orange finger into the sky. The river Fawn, which runs below, lay in sheets of sky-reflected blue, and wound its dreamy devious course round the edge of this wood, where a rough two-planked bridge crossed from the bottom of the garden of the last house in the village, and communicated by means of a little wicker gate with the wood itself. Then once out of the shadow of the wood the stream lay in flaming pools of the molten crimson of the sunset, and lost itself in the haze of woodland distances.

This house at the end of the village stood outside the shadow, and the lawn which sloped down to the river was still flecked with sunlight. Garden-beds of dazzling color lined its gravel walks, and down the middle of it ran a brick pergola, half-hidden in clusters of rambler-rose and purple with starry clematis. At the bottom end of it, between two of its pillars, was slung a hammock containing a shirt-sleeved figure.

The house itself lay somewhat remote from the rest of the village, and a footpath leading across two fields, now tall and fragrant with hay, was its only communication with the high road. It was low-built, only two stories in height, and like the garden, its walls were a mass of flowering roses. A narrow stone terrace ran along the garden front, over which was stretched an awning, and on the terrace a young silent-footed man-servant was busied with the laying of the table for dinner. He was neat-handed and quick with his job, and having finished it he went back into the house, and reappeared again with a large rough bath-towel on his arm. With this he went to the hammock in the pergola.

"Nearly eight, sir," he said.

"Has Mr. Darcy come yet?" asked a voice from the hammock.

"No, sir."

THE MAN WHO WENT TOO FAR 153

"If I'm not back when he comes, tell him that I'm just having a bathe before dinner."

The servant went back to the house, and after a moment or two Frank Halton struggled to a sitting posture, and slipped out on to the grass. He was of medium height and rather slender in build, but the supple ease and grace of his movements gave the impression of great physical strength: even his descent from the hammock was not an awkward performance. His face and hands were of very dark complexion, either from constant exposure to wind and sun, or, as his black hair and dark eyes tended to show, from some strain of southern blood. His head was small, his face of an exquisite beauty of modeling, while the smoothness of its contour would have led you to believe that he was a beardless lad still in his teens. But something, some look which living and experience alone can give, seemed to contradict that, and finding yourself completely puzzled as to his age, you would next moment probably cease to think about that, and only look at this glorious specimen of young manhood with wondering satisfaction.

He was dressed as became the season and the heat, and wore only a shirt open at the neck, and a pair of flannel trousers. His head, covered very thickly with a somewhat rebellious crop of short curly hair, was bare as he strolled across the lawn to the bathing-place that lay below. Then for a moment there was silence, then the sound of splashed and divided waters, and presently after, a great shout of ecstatic joy, as he swam upstream with the foamed water standing in a frill round his neck. Then after some five minutes of limb-stretching struggle with the flood, he turned over on his back, and with arms thrown wide, floated downstream, ripple-cradled and inert. His eyes were shut, and between half-parted lips he talked gently to himself.

"I am one with it," he said to himself, "the river and I, I and the river. The coolness and splash of it is I, and the water-herbs that wave in it are I also. And my strength and my limbs are not mine but the river's. It is all one, all one, dear Fawn."

A quarter of an hour later he appeared again at the bottom of the lawn, dressed as before, his wet hair already drying into its crisp short curls again. There he paused a moment, looking back at the stream with the smile with which men look on the face of a friend, then turned towards the house. Simultaneously his servant came to the door leading on to the terrace, followed by a man who appeared to be some half-way through the fourth decade of his years. Frank and he saw each other across the bushes and garden-beds, and each quickening his step, they met suddenly face to face round an angle of the garden walk, in the fragrance of syringa.

"My dear Darcy," cried Frank, "I am charmed to see you."

But the other stared at him in amazement.

"Frank!" he exclaimed.

"Yes, that is my name," he said laughing, "what is the matter?"

Darcy took his hand.

"What have you done to yourself?" he asked. "You are a boy again."

"Ah, I have a lot to tell you," said Frank. "Lots that you will hardly believe, but I shall convince you——"

He broke off suddenly, and held up his hand.

"Hush, there is my nightingale," he said.

The smile of recognition and welcome with which he had greeted his friend faded from his face, and a look of rapt wonder took its place, as of a lover listening to the voice of his beloved. His mouth parted slightly, showing the white line of teeth, and his eyes looked out and out till they seemed to Darcy to be focused on things beyond the vision of man. Then something perhaps startled the bird, for the song ceased.

"Yes, lots to tell you," he said. "Really I am delighted to see you. But you look rather white and pulled down; no wonder after that fever. And there is to be no nonsense about this visit. It is June now, you stop here till you are fit to begin work again. Two months at least."

"Ah, I can't trespass quite to that extent."

Frank took his arm and walked him down the grass.

"Trespass? Who talks of trespass? I shall tell you quite openly when I am tired of you, but you know when we had the studio together, we used not to bore each other. However, it is ill talking of going away on the moment of your arrival. Just a stroll to the river, and then it will be dinner-time."

Darcy took out his cigarette case, and offered it to the other. Frank laughed.

"No, not for me. Dear me, I suppose I used to smoke once. How very odd!"

"Given it up?"

"I don't know. I suppose I must have. Anyhow I don't do it now. I would as soon think of eating meat."

"Another victim on the smoking altar of vegetarianism?"

"Victim?" asked Frank. "Do I strike you as such?"

He paused on the margin of the stream and whistled softly. Next moment a moor-hen made its splashing flight across the river, and ran up the bank. Frank took it very gently in his hands and stroked its head, as the creature lay against his shirt.

"And is the house among the reeds still secure?" he half-crooned to it. "And is the missus quite well, and are the neighbors flourishing? There, dear, home with you," and he flung it into the air.

"That bird's very tame," said Darcy, slightly bewildered.

"It is rather," said Frank, following its flight.

During dinner Frank chiefly occupied himself in bringing himself up-to-date in the movements and achievements of this old friend whom he had not seen for six years. Those six years, it now appeared, had been full of incident and success for Darcy; he had made a name for himself as a portrait painter which bade fair to outlast the vogue of a couple of seasons, and his leisure time had been brief. Then some four months previously he had been through a severe attack of typhoid, the result of which as concerns this story was that he had come down to this sequestered place to recruit.

"Yes, you've got on," said Frank at the end. "I always knew you would. A.R.A. with more in prospect. Money? You roll in it, I suppose, and, O Darcy, how much happiness have you had all these years? That is the only imperishable possession. And how much have you learned? Oh, I don't mean in Art. Even I could have done well in that."

Darcy laughed.

"Done well? My dear fellow, all I have learned in these six years you knew, so to speak, in your cradle. Your old pictures fetch huge prices. Do you never paint now?"

Frank shook his head.

"No, I'm too busy," he said.

"Doing what? Please tell me. That is what every one is for ever asking me."

"Doing? I suppose you would say I do nothing."

Darcy glanced up at the brilliant young face opposite him.

"It seems to suit you, that way of being busy," he said. "Now, it's your turn. Do you read? Do you study? I remember you saying that it would do us all—all us artists, I mean—a great deal of good if we would study any one human face carefully for a year, without recording a line. Have you been doing that?"

Frank shook his head again.

"I mean exactly what I say," he said, "I have been *doing* nothing. And I have never been so occupied. Look at me; have I not done something to myself to begin with?"

"You are two years younger than I," said Darcy, "at least you used to be. You therefore are thirty-five. But had I never seen you before I should say you were just twenty. But was it worth while to spend six years of greatly occupied life in order to look twenty? Seems rather like a woman of fashion."

Frank laughed boisterously.

"First time I've ever been compared to that particular bird of prey," he said. "No, that has not been my occupation—in fact I am only very rarely conscious that one effect of my occupation has been that. Of course, it must have been if one comes to think of it. It is not very important. Quite true my body has become young. But that is very little; I have become young."

Darcy pushed back his chair and sat sideways to the table looking at the other.

"Has that been your occupation then?" he asked.

"Yes, that anyhow is one aspect of it. Think what youth means! It is the capacity for growth, mind, body, spirit, all grow, all get stronger, all have a fuller, firmer life every day. That is something, considering that every day that passes after the ordinary man reaches the full-blown flower of his strength, weakens his hold on life. A man reaches his prime, and remains, we say, in his prime, for ten years, or perhaps twenty. But after his primest prime is reached, he slowly, insensibly weakens. These are the signs of age in you, in your body, in your art probably, in your mind. You are less electric than you were. But I, when I reach my prime—I am nearing it—ah, you shall see."

The stars had begun to appear in the blue velvet of the sky, and to the east the horizon seen above the black silhouette of the village was growing dove-colored with the approach of moonrise. White moths hovered dimly over the garden-beds, and the footsteps of night tip-toed through the bushes. Suddenly Frank rose.

"Ah, it is the supreme moment," he said softly. "Now more than at any other time the current of life, the eternal imperishable current runs so close to me that I am almost enveloped in it. Be silent a minute."

He advanced to the edge of the terrace and looked out standing stretched with arms outspread. Darcy heard him draw a long breath into his lungs, and after many seconds expel it again. Six or eight times he did this, then turned back into the lamplight.

"It will sound to you quite mad, I expect," he said, "but if you want to hear the soberest truth I have ever spoken and shall ever speak, I will tell you about myself. But come into the garden if it is not too damp for you. I have never told any one yet, but I shall like to tell you. It is long, in fact, since I have even tried to classify what I have learned."

They wandered into the fragrant dimness of the pergola, and sat down. Then Frank began:

"Years ago, do you remember," he said, "we used often to talk about the decay of joy in the world. Many impulses, we settled, had contributed to this decay, some of which were good in themselves, others that were quite completely bad. Among the good things, I put what we may call certain Christian virtues, renunciation, resignation, sympathy with suffering, and the desire to relieve sufferers. But out of those things spring very bad ones, useless renunciations, asceticism for its own sake, mortification of the flesh with nothing to follow, no corresponding gain that is, and that awful and terrible disease which devastated England some centuries ago, and from which by heredity of spirit we suffer now, Puritanism. That was a dreadful plague, the brutes held and taught that joy and laughter and merriment were evil: it was a doctrine the most profane and wicked. Why, what is the commonest crime one sees? A sullen face. That is the truth of the matter.

"Now all my life I have believed that we are intended to be happy, that joy is of all gifts the most divine. And when I left London, abandoned my career, such as it was, I did so because I intended to devote my life to the cultivation of joy, and, by continuous and unsparing effort, to be happy. Among people, and in constant intercourse with others, I did not find it possible; there were too many distractions in towns and work-rooms, and also too much suffering. So I took one step backwards or forwards, as you may choose to put it, and went straight to Nature, to trees, birds, animals, to all those things which quite clearly pursue one aim only, which blindly follow the great native instinct to be happy without any care at all for morality, or human law or divine law. I wanted, you understand, to get all joy first-hand and unadulterated, and I think it scarcely exists among men; it is obsolete."

Darcy turned in his chair.

"Ah, but what makes birds and animals happy?" he asked. "Food, food and mating."

Frank laughed gently in the stillness.

"Do not think I became a sensualist," he said. "I did not make that mistake. For the sensualist carries his miseries pick-a-back, and round his feet is wound the shroud that shall soon enwrap him. I may be mad, it is true, but I am not so stupid anyhow as to have tried that. No, what is it that makes puppies play with their own tails, that sends cats on their prowling ecstatic errands at night?"

He paused a moment.

"So I went to Nature," he said. "I sat down here in this New Forest, sat down fair and square, and looked. That was my first difficulty, to sit here quiet without being bored, to wait without being impatient, to be receptive and very alert, though for a long time nothing particular happened. The change in fact was slow in those early stages."

"Nothing happened?" asked Darcy rather impatiently, with the sturdy revolt against any new idea which to the English mind is synonymous with nonsense. "Why, what in the world *should* happen?"

Now Frank as he had known him was the most generous but most quick-tempered of mortal men; in other words his anger would flare to a prodigious beacon, under almost no provocation, only to be quenched again under a gust of no less impulsive kindliness. Thus the moment Darcy had spoken, an apology for his hasty question was half-way up his tongue. But there was no need for it to have traveled even so far, for Frank laughed again with kindly, genuine mirth.

"Oh, how I should have resented that a few years ago," he said. "Thank goodness that resentment is one of the things I have got rid of. I certainly wish that you should believe my story—in fact, you are going to—but that you at this moment should imply that you do not, does not concern me."

"Ah, your solitary sojournings have made you inhuman," said Darcy, still very English.

"No, human," said Frank. "Rather more human, at least rather less of an ape."

"Well, that was my first quest," he continued, after a moment, "the deliberate and unswerving pursuit of joy, and my method, the eager contemplation of Nature. As far as motive went, I daresay it was purely selfish, but as far as effect goes, it seems to me about the best thing one can do for one's fellow-creatures, for happiness is more infectious than small-pox. So, as I said, I sat down and waited; I looked at happy things, zealously avoided the sight of anything unhappy, and by degrees a little trickle of the happiness of this blissful world began to filter into me. The trickle grew more abundant, and now, my dear fellow, if I could for a moment divert from me into you one half of the torrent of joy that pours through me day and night, you would throw the world, art, everything aside, and just live, exist. When a man's body dies, it passes into trees and flowers. Well, that is what I have been trying to do with my soul before death."

The servant had brought into the pergola a table with syphons and spirits, and had set a lamp upon it. As Frank spoke he leaned forward towards the other, and Darcy for all his matter-of-fact common-sense could have sworn that his companion's face shone, was luminous in itself. His dark brown eyes glowed from within, the unconscious smile of a child irradiated and transformed his face. Darcy felt suddenly excited, exhilarated.

"Go on," he said. "Go on. I can feel you are somehow telling me sober truth. I daresay you are mad; but I don't see that matters."

Frank laughed again.

"Mad?" he said. "Yes, certainly, if you wish. But I prefer to call it sane. However, nothing matters less than what anybody chooses to call things. God never labels his gifts; He just puts them into our hands; just as He put animals in the garden of Eden, for Adam to name if he felt disposed.

"So by the continual observance and study of things that were happy," continued he, "I got happiness, I got joy. But seeking it, as I did, from Nature, I got much more which I did not seek, but stumbled upon originally by accident. It is difficult to explain, but I will try.

"About three years ago I was sitting one morning in a place I will show you to-morrow. It is down by the river brink, very green, dappled with shade and sun, and the river passes there through some little clumps of reeds. Well, as I sat there, doing nothing, but just looking and listening, I heard the sound quite distinctly of some flute-like instrument playing a strange unending melody. I thought at first it was some musical yokel on the highway and did not pay much attention. But before long the strangeness and indescribable beauty of the tune struck me. It never repeated itself, but it never came to an end, phrase after phrase ran its sweet course, it worked gradually and inevitably up to a climax, and having attained it, it went on; another climax was reached and another and another. Then with a sudden gasp of wonder I localized where it came from. It came from the reeds and from the sky and from the trees. It was everywhere, it was the sound of life. It was, my dear Darcy, as the Greeks would have said, it was Pan playing on his pipes, the voice of Nature. It was the life-melody, the world-melody."

Darcy was far too interested to interrupt, though there was a question he would have liked to ask, and Frank went on:

"Well, for the moment I was terrified, terrified with the impotent horror of nightmare, and I stopped my ears and just ran from the place and got back to the house panting, trembling, literally in a panic. Unknowingly, for at that time I only pursued joy, I had begun, since I drew my joy from Nature, to get in touch with Nature. Nature, force, God, call it what you will, had drawn across my face a little gossamer web of essential life. I saw that when I emerged from my terror, and I went very humbly back to where I had heard the Pan-pipes. But it was nearly six months before I heard them again."

"Why was that?" asked Darcy.

"Surely because I had revolted, rebelled, and worst of all been frightened. For I believe that just as there is nothing in the world which so injures one's body as fear, so there is nothing that so much shuts up the soul. I was afraid, you see, of the one thing in the world which has real existence. No wonder its manifestation was withdrawn."

"And after six months?"

"After six months one blessed morning I heard the piping again. I wasn't afraid that time. And since then it has grown louder, it has become more constant. I now hear it often, and I can put myself into such an attitude towards Nature that the pipes will almost certainly sound. And never yet have they played the same tune, it is always something new, something fuller, richer, more complete than before."

"What do you mean by 'such an attitude towards Nature'?" asked Darcy.

"I can't explain that; but by translating it into a bodily attitude it is this."

Frank sat up for a moment quite straight in his chair, then slowly sunk back with arms outspread and head drooped.

"That," he said, "an effortless attitude, but open, resting, receptive. It is just that which you must do with your soul."

Then he sat up again.

"One word more," he said, "and I will bore you no further. Nor unless you ask me questions shall I talk about it again. You will find me, in fact, quite sane in my mode of life. Birds and beasts you will see behaving somewhat intimately to me, like that moor-hen, but that is all. I will walk with you, ride with you, play golf with you, and talk with you on any subject you like. But I wanted you on the threshold to know what has happened to me. And one thing more will happen."

He paused again, and a slight look of fear crossed his eyes.

"There will be a final revelation," he said, "a complete and blinding stroke which will throw open to me, once and for all, the full knowledge, the full realization and comprehension that I am one, just as you are, with life. In reality there is no 'me,' no 'you,' no 'it.' Everything is part of the one and only thing which is life. I know that that is so, but the realization of it is not yet mine. But it will be, and on that day, so I take it, I shall see Pan. It may mean death, the death of my body, that is, but I don't care. It may mean immortal, eternal life lived here and now and for ever. Then having gained that, ah, my dear Darcy, I shall preach such a gospel of joy, showing myself as the living proof of the truth, that Puritanism, the dismal religion of sour faces, shall vanish like a breath of smoke, and be dispersed and disappear in the sunlit air. But first the full knowledge must be mine."

Darcy watched his face narrowly.

"You are afraid of that moment," he said.

Frank smiled at him.

"Quite true; you are quick to have seen that. But when it comes I hope I shall not be afraid."

For some little time there was silence; then Darcy rose.

"You have bewitched me, you extraordinary boy," he said. "You have been telling me a fairy-story, and I find myself saying, 'Promise me it is true.'"

"I promise you that," said the other.

"And I know I shan't sleep," added Darcy.

Frank looked at him with a sort of mild wonder as if he scarcely understood.

"Well, what does that matter?" he said.

"I assure you it does. I am wretched unless I sleep."

"Of course I can make you sleep if I want," said Frank in a rather bored voice.

"Well, do."

"Very good: go to bed. I'll come upstairs in ten minutes."

Frank busied himself for a little after the other had gone, moving the table back under the awning of the veranda and quenching the lamp. Then he went with his quick silent tread upstairs and into Darcy's room. The latter was already in bed, but very wide-eyed and wakeful, and Frank with an amused smile of indulgence, as for a fretful child, sat down on the edge of the bed.

"Look at me," he said, and Darcy looked.

"The birds are sleeping in the brake," said Frank softly, "and the winds are asleep. The sea sleeps, and the tides are but the heaving of its breast. The stars swing slow, rocked in the great cradle of the Heavens, and——"

He stopped suddenly, gently blew out Darcy's candle, and left him sleeping.

Morning brought to Darcy a flood of hard commonsense, as clear and crisp as the sunshine that filled his room. Slowly as he woke he gathered together the broken threads of the memories of the evening which had ended, so he told himself, in a trick of common hypnotism. That accounted for it all; the whole strange talk he had had was under a spell of suggestion from the extraordinary vivid boy who had once been a man; all his own excitement, his acceptance of the incredible had been merely the effect of a stronger, more potent will imposed on his own. How strong that will was, he guessed from his own instantaneous obedience to Frank's suggestion of sleep. And armed with impenetrable commonsense he came down to breakfast. Frank had already begun, and was consuming a large plateful of porridge and milk with the most prosaic and healthy appetite.

"Slept well?" he asked.

"Yes, of course. Where did you learn hypnotism?"

"By the side of the river."

"You talked an amazing quantity of nonsense last night," remarked Darcy, in a voice prickly with reason.

"Rather. I felt quite giddy. Look, I remembered to order a dreadful daily paper for you. You can read about money markets or politics or cricket matches."

Darcy looked at him closely. In the morning light Frank looked even fresher, younger, more vital than he had done the night before, and the sight of him somehow dinted Darcy's armor of commonsense.

"You are the most extraordinary fellow I ever saw," he said. "I want to ask you some more questions."

"Ask away," said Frank.

For the next day or two Darcy plied his friend with many questions, objections and criticisms on the theory of life and gradually got out of him a coherent and complete account of his experience. In brief then, Frank believed that "by lying naked," as he put it, to the force which controls the passage of the stars, the breaking of a wave, the budding of a tree, the love of a youth and maiden, he had succeeded in a way hitherto undreamed of in possessing himself of the essential principle of life. Day by day, so he thought, he was getting nearer to, and in closer union with the great power itself which caused all life to be, the spirit of nature, of force, or the spirit of God. For himself, he confessed to what others would call paganism; it was sufficient for him that there existed a principle of life. He did not worship it, he did not pray to it, he did not praise it. Some of it existed in all human beings, just as it existed in trees and animals; to realize and make living to himself the fact that it was all one, was his sole aim and object.

Here perhaps Darcy would put in a word of warning.

"Take care," he said. "To see Pan meant death, did it not?"

Frank's eyebrows would rise at this.

"What does that matter?" he said. "True, the Greeks were always right, and they said so, but there is another possibility. For the nearer I get to it, the more living, the more vital and young I become."

"What then do you expect the final revelation will do for you?"

"I have told you," said he. "It will make me immortal."

But it was not so much from speech and argument that Darcy grew to grasp his friend's conception, as from the ordinary conduct of his life. They were passing, for instance, one morning down the village street, when an old woman, very bent and decrepit, but with an extraordinary cheerfulness of face, hobbled out from her cottage. Frank instantly stopped when he saw her.

"You old darling! How goes it all?" he said.

But she did not answer, her dim old eyes were riveted on his face; she seemed to drink in like a thirsty creature the beautiful radiance which shone there. Suddenly she put her two withered old hands on his shoulders.

"You're just the sunshine itself," she said, and he kissed her and passed on.

But scarcely a hundred yards further a strange contradiction of such tenderness occurred. A child running along the path towards them fell on its face, and set up a dismal cry of fright and pain. A look of horror came into Frank's eyes, and, putting his fingers in his ears, he fled at full speed down the street, and did not pause till he was out of hearing. Darcy, having ascertained that the child was not really hurt, followed him in bewilderment.

"Are you without pity then?" he asked.

Frank shook his head impatiently.

"Can't you see?" he asked. "Can't you understand that that sort of thing, pain, anger, anything unlovely throws me back, retards the coming of the great hour! Perhaps when it comes I shall be able to piece that side of life on to the other, on to the true religion of joy. At present I can't."

"But the old woman. Was she not ugly?"

Frank's radiance gradually returned.

"Ah, no. She was like me. She longed for joy, and knew it when she saw it, the old darling."

Another question suggested itself.

"Then what about Christianity?" asked Darcy.

"I can't accept it. I can't believe in any creed of which the central doctrine is that God who is Joy should have had to suffer. Perhaps it was so; in some inscrutable way I believe it may have been so, but I don't understand how it was possible. So I leave it alone; my affair is joy."

They had come to the weir above the village, and the thunder of riotous cool water was heavy in the air. Trees dipped into the translucent stream with slender trailing branches, and the meadow where they stood was starred with midsummer blossomings. Larks shot up caroling into the crystal dome of blue, and a thousand voices of June sang round them. Frank, bare-headed as was his wont, with his coat slung over his arm and his shirt sleeves rolled up above the elbow, stood there like some beautiful wild animal with eyes half-shut and mouth half-open, drinking in the scented warmth of the air. Then suddenly he flung himself face downwards on the grass at the edge of the stream, burying his face in the daisies and cowslips, and lay stretched there in wide-armed ecstasy, with his long fingers pressing and stroking the dewy herbs of the field. Never before had Darcy seen him thus fully possessed by his idea; his caressing fingers, his half-buried face pressed close to the grass, even the clothed lines of his figure were instinct with a vitality that somehow was different from that of other men. And some faint glow from it reached Darcy, some thrill, some vibration from that charged recumbent body passed to him, and for a moment he understood as he had not understood before, despite his persistent questions and the candid answers they received, how real, and how realized by Frank, his idea was.

Then suddenly the muscles in Frank's neck became stiff and alert, and he half-raised his head, whispering, "The Pan-pipes, the Pan-pipes. Close, oh, so close."

Very slowly, as if a sudden movement might interrupt the melody, he raised himself and leaned on the elbow of his bent arm. His eyes opened wider, the lower lids drooped as if he focused his eyes on something very far away, and the smile on his face broadened and quivered like sunlight on still water, till the exultance of its happiness was scarcely human. So he remained motionless and rapt for some minutes, then the look of listening died from his face, and he bowed his head satisfied.

"Ah, that was good," he said. "How is it possible you did not hear? Oh, you poor fellow! Did you really hear nothing?"

A week of this outdoor and stimulating life did wonders in restoring to Darcy the vigor and health which his weeks of fever had filched from him, and as his normal activity and higher pressure of vitality returned, he seemed to himself to fall even more under the spell which the miracle of Frank's youth cast over him. Twenty times a day he found himself saying to himself suddenly at the end of some ten minutes' silent resistance to the absurdity of Frank's idea: "But it isn't possible; it can't be possible," and from the fact of his having to assure himself so frequently of this, he knew that he was struggling and arguing with a conclusion which already had taken root in his mind. For in any case a visible living miracle confronted him, since it was equally impossible that this youth, this boy, trembling on the verge of manhood, was thirty-five. Yet such was the fact.

July was ushered in by a couple of days of blustering and fretful rain, and Darcy, unwilling to risk a chill, kept to the house. But to Frank this weeping change of weather seemed to have no bearing on the behavior of man, and he spent his days exactly as he did under the suns of June, lying in his hammock, stretched on the dripping grass, or making huge rambling excursions into the forest, the birds hopping from tree to tree after him, to return in the evening, drenched and soaked, but with the same unquenchable flame of joy burning within him.

"Catch cold?" he would ask, "I've forgotten how to do it, I think. I suppose it makes one's body more sensible always to sleep out-of-doors. People who live indoors always remind me of something peeled and skinless."

"Do you mean to say you slept out-of-doors last night in that deluge?" asked Darcy. "And where, may I ask?"

Frank thought a moment.

"I slept in the hammock till nearly dawn," he said. "For I remember the light blinked in the east when I awoke. Then I went—where did I go?—oh, yes, to the meadow where the Pan-pipes sounded so close a week ago. You were with me, do you remember? But I always have a rug if it is wet."

And he went whistling upstairs.

Somehow that little touch, his obvious effort to recall where he had slept, brought strangely home to Darcy the wonderful romance of which he was the still half-incredulous beholder. Sleep till close on dawn in a hammock, then the tramp—or probably scamper—underneath the windy and weeping heavens to the remote and lonely meadow by the weir! The picture of other such nights rose before him; Frank sleeping perhaps by the bathing-place under the filtered twilight of the stars, or the white blaze of moonshine, a stir and awakening at some dead hour, perhaps a space of silent wide-eyed thought, and then a wandering through the hushed woods to some other dormitory, alone with his hapiness, alone with the joy and the life that suffused and enveloped him, without other thought or desire or aim except the hourly and never-ceasing communion with the joy of nature.

They were in the middle of dinner that night, talking on indifferent subjects, when Darcy suddenly broke off in the middle of a sentence.

"I've got it," he said. "At last I've got it."

"Congratulate you," said Frank. "But what?"

"The radical unsoundness of your idea. It is this: All nature from highest to lowest is full, crammed full of suffering; every

THE MAN WHO WENT TOO FAR 169

living organism in nature preys on another, yet in your aim to get close to, to be one with nature, you leave suffering altogether out; you run away from it, you refuse to recognize it. And you are waiting, you say, for the final revelation."

Frank's brow clouded slightly.

"Well?" he asked, rather wearily.

"Cannot you guess then when the final revelation will be? In joy you are supreme, I grant you that; I did not know a man could be so master of it. You have learned perhaps practically all that nature can teach. And if, as you think, the final revelation is coming to you, it will be the revelation of horror, suffering, death, pain in all its hideous forms. Suffering does exist: you hate it and fear it."

Frank held up his hand.

"Stop; let me think," he said.

There was silence for a long minute.

"That never struck me," he said at length. "It is possible that what you suggest is true. Does the sight of Pan mean that, do you think? Is it that nature, take it altogether, suffers horribly, suffers to a hideous inconceivable extent? Shall I be shown all the suffering?"

He got up and came round to where Darcy sat.

"If it is so, so be it," he said. "Because, my dear fellow, I am near, so splendidly near to the final revelation. To-day the pipes have sounded almost without pause. I have even heard the rustle in the bushes, I believe, of Pan's coming. I have seen, yes, I saw to-day, the bushes pushed aside as if by a hand, and piece of a face, not human, peered through. But I was not frightened, at least I did not run away this time."

He took a turn up to the window and back again.

"Yes, there is suffering all through," he said, "and I have left it all out of my search. Perhaps, as you say, the revelation will be that. And in that case, it will be good-bye. I have gone on one line. I shall have gone too far along one road, without having explored the other. But I can't go back now. I wouldn't if I could; not a step would I retrace! In any case, whatever the revelation is, it will be God. I'm sure of that."

The rainy weather soon passed, and with the return of the sun Darcy again joined Frank in long rambling days. It grew extraordinarily hotter, and with the fresh bursting of life, after the rain, Frank's vitality seemed to blaze higher and higher. Then, as is the habit of the English weather, one evening clouds began to bank themselves up in the west, the sun went down in a glare of coppery thunder-rack, and the whole earth broiling under an unspeakable oppression and sultriness paused and panted for the storm. After sunset the remote fires of lightning began to wink and flicker on the horizon, but when bed-time came the storm seemed to have moved no nearer, though a very low unceasing noise of thunder was audible. Weary and oppressed by the stress of the day, Darcy fell at once into a heavy uncomforting sleep.

He woke suddenly into full consciousness, with the din of some appalling explosion of thunder in his ears, and sat up in bed with racing heart. Then for a moment, as he recovered himself from the panic-land which lies between sleeping and waking, there was silence, except for the steady hissing of rain on the shrubs outside his window. But suddenly that silence was shattered and shredded into fragments by a scream from somewhere close at hand outside in the black garden, a scream of supreme and despairing terror. Again and once again it shrilled up, and then a babble of awful words was interjected. A quivering sobbing voice that he knew, said:

"My God, oh, my God; oh, Christ!"

And then followed a little mocking, bleating laugh. Then was silence again; only the rain hissed on the shrubs.

All this was but the affair of a moment, and without pause either to put on clothes or light a candle, Darcy was already fumbling at his door-handle. Even as he opened it he met a terror-stricken face outside, that of the man-servant who carried a light.

"Did you hear?" he asked.

The man's face was bleached to a dull shining whiteness.

"Yes, sir," he said. "It was the master's voice."

Together they hurried down the stairs, and through the dining-room where an orderly table for breakfast had already been laid, and out on to the terrace. The rain for the moment had been utterly stayed, as if the tap of the heavens had been turned off, and under the lowering black sky, not quite dark, since the moon rode somewhere serene behind the conglomerated thunder-clouds, Darcy stumbled into the garden, followed by the servant with the candle. The monstrous leaping shadow of himself was cast before him on the lawn; lost and wandering odors of rose and lily and damp earth were thick about him, but more pungent was some sharp and acrid smell that suddenly reminded him of a certain châlet in which he had once taken refuge in the Alps. In the blackness of the hazy light from the sky, and the vague tossing of the candle behind him, he saw that the hammock in which Frank so often lay was tenanted. A gleam of white shirt was there, as if a man sitting up in it, but across that there was an obscure dark shadow, and as he approached the acrid odor grew more intense.

He was now only some few yards away, when suddenly the black shadow seemed to jump into the air, then came down with tappings of hard hoofs on the brick path that ran down the pergola, and with frolicsome skippings galloped off into the bushes. When that was gone Darcy could see quite clearly that a shirted figure sat up in the hammock. For one moment, from sheer terror of the unseen, he hung on his step, and the servant joining him they walked together to the hammock.

It was Frank. He was in shirt and trousers only, and he sat up with braced arms. For one half-second he stared at them, his face a mask of horrible contorted terror. His upper lip was drawn back so that the gums of the teeth appeared, and his eyes were focused not on the two who approached him but on something quite close to him; his nostrils were widely expanded, as if he panted for breath, and terror incarnate and repulsion and deathly anguish ruled dreadful lines on his smooth cheeks and forehead. Then even as they looked the body sank backwards, and the ropes of the hammock wheezed and strained.

Darcy lifted him out and carried him indoors. Once he

thought there was a faint convulsive stir of the limbs that lay with so dead a weight in his arms, but when they got inside, there was no trace of life. But the look of supreme terror and agony of fear had gone from his face, a boy tired with play but still smiling in his sleep was the burden he laid on the floor. His eyes had closed, and the beautiful mouth lay in smiling curves, even as when a few mornings ago, in the meadow by the weir, it had quivered to the music of the unheard melody of Pan's pipes. Then they looked further.

Frank had come back from his bath before dinner that night in his usual costume of shirt and trousers only. He had not dressed, and during dinner, so Darcy remembered, he had rolled up the sleeves of his shirt to above the elbow. Later, as they sat and talked after dinner on the close sultriness of the evening, he had unbuttoned the front of his shirt to let what little breath of wind there was play on his skin. The sleeves were rolled up now, the front of the shirt was unbuttoned, and on his arms and on the brown skin of his chest were strange discolorations which grew momently more clear and defined, till they saw that the marks were pointed prints, as if caused by the hoofs of some monstrous goat that had leaped and stamped upon him.

THE MEZZOTINT

BY MONTAGUE RHODES JAMES

SOME TIME ago I believe I had the pleasure of telling you the story of an adventure which happened to a friend of mine by the name of Dennistoun, during his pursuit of objects of art for the museum at Cambridge.

He did not publish his experiences very widely upon his return to England; but they could not fail to become known to a good many of his friends, and among others to the gentleman who at that time presided over an art museum at another University. It was to be expected that the story should make a considerable impression on the mind of a man whose vocation lay in lines similar to Dennistoun's, and that he should be eager to catch at any explanation of the matter which tended to make it seem improbable that he should ever be called upon to deal with so agitating an emergency. It was, indeed, somewhat consoling to him to reflect that he was not expected to acquire ancient MSS. for his institution; that was the business of the Shelburnian Library. The authorities of that institution might, if they pleased, ransack obscure corners of the Continent for such matters. He was glad to be obliged at the moment to confine his attention to enlarging the already unsurpassed collection of English topographical drawings and engravings possessed by his museum. Yet, as it turned out, even a department so homely and familiar as this may have its dark corners, and to one of these Mr. Williams was unexpectedly introduced.

Those who have taken even the most limited interest in the acquisition of topographical pictures are aware that there is one

London dealer whose aid is indispensable to their researches. Mr. J. W. Britnell publishes at short intervals very admirable catalogues of a large and constantly changing stock of engravings, plans, and the old sketches of mansions, churches, and towns in England and Wales. These catalogues were, of course, the ABC of his subject to Mr. Williams: but as his museum already contained an enormous accumulation of topographical pictures, he was a regular, rather than a copious, buyer; and he rather looked to Mr. Britnell to fill up gaps in the rank and file of his collection than to supply him with rarities.

Now, in February of last year there appeared upon Mr. Williams's desk at the museum a catalogue from Mr. Britnell's emporium, and accompanying it was a typewritten communication from the dealer himself. This latter ran as follows:

Dear Sir,
We beg to call your attention to No. 978 in our accompanying catalogue, which we shall be glad to send on approval

Yours faithfully,
J. W. BRITNELL.

To turn to No. 978 in the accompanying catalogue was with Mr. Williams (as he observed to himself) the work of a moment, and in the place indicated he found the following entry:

978—Unknown. Interesting mezzotint: View of a manor-house, early part of the century. 15 by 10 inches; black frame. £2 2s.

It was not specially exciting, and the price seemed high. However, as Mr. Britnell, who knew his business and his customer, seemed to set store by it, Mr. Williams wrote a postcard asking for the article to be sent on approval, along with some other engravings and sketches which appeared in the same catalogue. And so he passed without much excitement of anticipation to the ordinary labors of the day.

A parcel of any kind always arrives a day later than you expect it, and that of Mr. Britnell proved, as I believe the right phrase goes, no exception to the rule. It was delivered at the museum by the afternoon post of Saturday, after Mr. Williams had left his work, and it was accordingly brought round to his rooms in college by the attendant, in order that he might not have to wait over Sunday before looking through it and returning such of the contents as he did not propose to keep. And here he found it when he came in to tea, with a friend.

The only item with which I am concerned was the rather large, black-framed mezzotint of which I have already quoted the short description given in Mr. Britnell's catalogue. Some more details of it will have to be given, though I cannot hope to put before you the look of the picture as clearly as it is present to my own eye. Very nearly the exact duplicate of it may be seen in a good many old inn parlors, or in the passages of undisturbed country mansions at the present moment. It was a rather indifferent mezzotint, and an indifferent mezzotint is perhaps, the worst form of engraving known. It presented a full-face view of a not very large manor-house of the last century, with three rows of plain sashed windows with rusticated masonry about them, a parapet with balls or vases at the angles, and a small portico in the center. On either side were trees, and in front a considerable expanse of lawn. The legend "A. W. F. sculpsit" was engraved on the narrow margin; and there was no further inscription. The whole thing gave the impression that it was the work of an amateur. What in the world Mr. Britnell could mean by affixing the price of £2 2s. to such an object was more than Mr. Williams could imagine. He turned it over with a good deal of contempt; upon the back was a paper label, the left-hand half of which had been torn off. All that remained were the ends of two lines of writing: the first had the letters—*ngley Hall;* the second—*ssex.*

It would, perhaps, be just worth while to identify the place represented, which he could easily do with the help of a gazetteer, and then he would send it back to Mr. Britnell, with some remarks reflecting upon the judgment of that gentleman.

He lighted the candles, for it was now dark, made the tea, and supplied the friend with whom he had been playing golf (for I believe the authorities of the University I write of indulge in that pursuit by way of relaxation); and tea was taken to the accompaniment of a discussion which golfing persons can imagine for themselves, but which the conscientious writer has no right to inflict upon any non-golfing persons.

The conclusion arrived at was that certain strokes might have been better, and that in certain emergencies neither player had experienced the amount of luck which a human being has a right to expect. It was now that the friend—let us call him Professor Binks—took up the framed engraving, and said:

"What's this place, Williams?"

"Just what I am going to try to find out," said Williams, going to the shelf for a gazetteer. "Look at the back. Somethingley Hall, either in Sussex or Essex. Half the name's gone, you see. You don't happen to know it, I suppose?"

"It's from that man Britnell, I suppose, isn't it?" said Binks. "Is it for the museum?"

"Well, I think I should buy it if the price was five shillings," said Williams; "but for some unearthly reason he wants two guineas for it. I can't conceive why. It's a wretched engraving, and there aren't even any figures to give it life."

"It's not worth two guineas, I should think," said Binks; "but I don't think it's so badly done. The moonlight seems rather good to me; and I should have thought there *were* figures, or at least a figure, just on the edge in front."

"Let's look," said Williams. "Well, it's true that light is rather cleverly given. Where's your figure? Oh, yes! Just the head, in the very front of the picture."

And indeed there was—hardly more than a black blot on the extreme edge of the engraving—the head of a man or woman, a good deal muffled up, the back turned to the spectator, and looking towards the house.

Williams had not noticed it before.

"Still," he said, "though it's a cleverer thing than I thought, I can't spend two guineas of museum money on a picture of a place I don't know."

Professor Binks had his work to do, and soon went; and very nearly up to Hall time Williams was engaged in a vain attempt to identify the subject of his picture. "If the vowel before the *ng* had only been left, it would have been easy enough," he thought;

"but as it is, the name may be anything from Guestingley to Langley, and there are many more names ending like this than I thought; and this rotten book has no index of terminations."

Hall in Mr. Williams's college was at seven. It need not be dwelt upon; the less so as he met there colleagues who had been playing golf during the afternoon, and words with which we have no concern were freely bandied across the table—merely golfing words, I would hasten to explain.

I suppose an hour or more to have been spent in what is called common-room after dinner. Later in the evening some few retired to Williams's rooms, and I have little doubt that whist was played and tobacco smoked. During a lull in these operations Williams picked up the mezzotint from the table without looking at it, and handed it to a person mildly interested in art, telling him where it had come from, and the other particulars which we already know.

The gentleman took it carelessly, looked at it, then said, in a tone of some interest:

"It's really a very good piece of work, Williams; it has quite a feeling of the romantic period. The light is admirably managed, it seems to me, and the figure, though it's rather too grotesque, is somehow very impressive."

"Yes, isn't it?" said Williams, who was just then busy giving whisky-and-soda to the others of the company, and was unable to come across the room to look at the view again.

It was by this time rather late in the evening, and the visitors were on the move. After they went Williams was obliged to write a letter or two and clear up some odd bits of work. At last, some time past midnight, he was disposed to turn in, and he put out his lamp after lighting his bedroom candle. The picture lay face upward on the table where the last man who looked at it had put it, and it caught his eye as he turned the lamp down. What he saw made him very nearly drop the candle on the floor, and he declares now that if he had been left in the dark at that moment he would have had a fit. But, as that did not happen, he was able to put down the light on the table and take a good look at the picture. It was indubitable—rankly impossible, no doubt, but absolutely certain. In the middle of the lawn in front of the unknown house there was a figure where no figure had been at five o'clock that afternoon. It was crawling on all fours toward the house, and it was muffled in a strange black garment with a white cross on the back.

I do not know what is the ideal course to pursue in a situation of this kind. I can only tell you what Mr. Williams did. He took the picture by one corner and carried it across the passage to a second set of rooms which he possessed. There he locked it up in a drawer, sported the doors of both sets of rooms, and retired to bed; but first he wrote out and signed an account of the extraordinary change which the picture had undergone since it had come into his possession.

Sleep visited him rather late; but it was consoling to reflect that the behavior of the picture did not depend upon his own unsupported testimony. Evidently the man who had looked at it the night before had seen something of the same kind as he had, otherwise he might have been tempted to think that something gravely wrong was happening either to his eyes or his mind. This possibility being fortunately precluded two matters awaited him on the morrow. He must take stock of the picture very carefully, and call in a witness for the purpose, and he must make a determined effort to ascertain what house it was that was represented. He would therefore ask his neighbor Nisbet to breakfast with him, and he would subsequently spend a morning over the gazetteer.

Nisbet was disengaged, and arrived about 9:30. His host was not quite dressed, I am sorry to say, even at this late hour. During breakfast nothing was said about the mezzotint by Williams, save that he had a picture on which he wished for Nisbet's opinion. But those who are familiar with University life can picture for themselves the wide and delightful range of subjects over which the conversation of two Fellows of Canterbury College is likely to extend during a Sunday morning breakfast. Hardly a topic was left unchallenged, from golf to lawn-tennis. Yet I am bound to say that Williams was rather distraught; for his interest naturally centered in that very strange picture which was now reposing, face downward, in the drawer in the room opposite.

The morning pipe was at last lighted, and the moment had arrived for which he looked. With very considerable—almost tremulous—excitement, he ran across, unlocked the drawer, and, extracting the picture—still face downward—ran back, and put it into Nisbet's hands.

"Now," he said, "Nisbet, I want you to tell me exactly what you see in that picture. Describe it, if you don't mind, rather minutely. I'll tell you why afterward."

"Well," said Nisbet, "I have here a view of a country-house— English, I presume—by moonlight."

"Moonlight? You're sure of that?"

"Certainly. The moon appears to be on the wane, if you wish for details, and there are clouds in the sky."

"All right. Go on. I'll swear," added Williams in an aside, "there was no moon when I saw it first."

"Well, there's not much more to be said," Nisbet continued. "The house has one—two—three rows of windows, five in each row, except at the bottom, where there's a porch instead of the middle one, and——"

"But what about figures?" said Williams, with marked interest.

"There aren't any," said Nisbet; "but——"

"What! No figure on the grass in front?"

"Not a thing."

"You'll swear to that?"

"Certainly I will. But there's just one other thing."

"What?"

"Why, one of the windows on the ground-floor—left of the door—is open."

"Is it really so? My goodness! he must have got in," said Williams, with great excitement; and he hurried to the back of the sofa on which Nisbet was sitting, and, catching the picture from him, verified the matter for himself.

It was quite true. There was no figure, and there was the open window. Williams, after a moment of speechless surprise, went to the writing-table and scribbled for a short time. Then he brought two papers to Nisbet, and asked him first to sign one—it was his own description of the picture, which you have just heard—and then to read the other which was Williams's statement written the night before.

"What can it all mean?" said Nisbet.

"Exactly," said Williams. "Well, one thing I must do—or three things, now I think of it. I must find out from Garwood"—this was his last night's visitor—"what he saw, and then I must get the thing photographed before it goes further, and then I must find out what the place is."

"I can do the photographing myself," said Nisbet, "and I will. But, you know, it looks very much as if we were assisting at the working out of a tragedy somewhere. The question is, Has it happened already, or is it going to come off? You must find out what the place is. Yes," he said, looking at the picture again, "I expect you're right: he has got in. And if I don't mistake there'll be the devil to pay in one of the rooms upstairs."

"I'll tell you what," said Williams: "I'll take the picture across to old Green." (This was the senior Fellow of the College, who had been Bursar for many years.) "It's quite likely he'll know it. We have property in Essex and Sussex, and he must have been over the two counties a lot in his time."

"Quite likely he will," said Nisbet; "but just let me take my photograph first. But look here, I rather think Green isn't up today. He wasn't in Hall last night, and I think I heard him say he was going down for the Sunday."

"That's true, too," said Williams; "I know he's gone to Brighton. Well, if you'll photograph it now, I'll go across to Garwood and get his statement, and you keep an eye on it while I'm gone. I'm beginning to think two guineas is not a very exorbitant price for it now."

In a short time he had returned, and brought Mr. Garwood with him. Garwood's statement was to the effect that the figure, when he had seen it, was clear of the edge of the picture, but had not got far across the lawn. He remembered a white mark on the back of its drapery, but could not have been sure it was a cross. A document to this effect was then drawn up and signed, and Nisbet proceeded to photograph the picture.

"Now what do you mean to do?" he said. "Are you going to sit and watch it all day?"

"Well, no, I think not," said Williams. "I rather imagine we're meant to see the whole thing. You see, between the time I saw it last night and this morning there was time for lots of things to happen, but the creature only got into the house. It could easily have got through its business in the time and gone to its own place again; but the fact of the window being open, I think, must mean that it's in there now. So I feel quite easy about leaving it. And besides, I have a kind of idea that it wouldn't change much, if at all, in the daytime. We might go out for a walk this afternoon, and come in to tea, or whenever it gets dark. I shall leave it out on the table here, and sport the door. My skip can get in, but no one else."

The three agreed that this would be a good plan; and, further, that if they spent the afternoon together they would be less likely to talk about the business to other people; for any rumor of such a transaction as was going on would bring the whole of the Phasmatological Society about their ears.

We may give them a respite until five o'clock.

At or near that hour the three were entering Williams's staircase. They were at first slightly annoyed to see that the door of his rooms was unsported; but in a moment it was remembered that on Sunday the skips came for orders an hour or so earlier than on week-days. However, a surprise was awaiting them. The first thing they saw was the picture leaning up against a pile of books on the table, as it had been left, and the next thing was Williams's skip, seated on a chair opposite, gazing at it with undisguised horror. How was this? Mr. Filcher (the name is not my own invention) was a servant of considerable standing, and set the standard of etiquette to all his own college and to several neighboring ones, and nothing could be more alien to his practice than to be found sitting on his master's chair, or appearing to take any particular notice of his master's furniture or pictures. Indeed, he seemed to feel this himself. He started violently when the three men were in the room, and got up with a marked effort. Then he said:

"I ask your pardon, sir, for taking such a freedom as to set down."

"Not at all, Robert," interposed Mr. Williams. "I was meaning to ask you some time what you thought of that picture."

"Well, sir, of course I don't set up my opinion again yours, but it ain't the picture I should 'ang where my little girl could see it, sir."

"Wouldn't you, Robert? Why not?"

"No, sir. Why, the pore child, I recollect once she see a Door Bible, with pictures not 'alf what that is, and we 'ad to set up with her three or four nights afterward, if you'll believe me; and if she was to ketch a sight of this skelinton here, or whatever it is, carrying off the pore baby, she would be in a taking. You know 'ow it is with children; 'ow nervish they git with a little thing and all. But what I should say, it don't seem a right picture to be laying about, sir, not where anyone that's liable to be startled could come on it. Should you be wanting anything this evening, sir? Thank you, sir."

With these words the excellent man went to continue the round of his masters, and you may be sure the gentlemen whom he left lost no time in gathering round the engraving. There was the house, as before, under the waning moon and the drifting clouds. The window that had been open was shut, and the figure was once more on the lawn: but not this time crawling cautiously on hands and knees. Now it was erect and stepping swiftly, with long strides, toward the front of the picture. The moon was behind it, and the black drapery hung down over its face so that only hints of that could be seen, and what was visible made the spectators profoundly thankful that they could see no more than a white dome-like forehead and a few straggling hairs. The head was bent down, and the arms were tightly clasped over an object which could be dimly seen and identified as a child, whether dead or living it was not possible to say. The legs of the appearance alone could be plainly discerned, and they were horribly thin.

From five to seven the three companions sat and watched the picture by turns. But it never changed. They agreed at last that it would be safe to leave it, and that they would return after Hall and await further developments.

When they assembled again, at the earliest possible moment, the engraving was there, but the figure was gone, and the house was quiet under the moonbeams. There was nothing for it but to spend the evening over gazetteers and guide-books. Williams was the lucky one at last, and perhaps he deserved it. At 11.30 p.m. he read from Murray's *Guide to Essex* the following lines:

> 16½ miles, Anningley. The church has been an interesting building of Norman date, but was extensively classicized in the last century. It contains the tomb of the family of Francis, whose mansion, Anningley Hall, a solid Queen Anne house, stands immediately beyond the churchyard in a park of about 80 acres. The family is now extinct, the last heir having disappeared mysteriously in infancy in the year 1802. The father, Mr. Arthur Francis, was locally known as a talented amateur engraver in mezzotint. After his son's disappearance he lived in complete retirement at the Hall, and was found dead in his studio on the third anniversary of the disaster, having just completed an engraving of the house, impressions of which are of considerable rarity.

This looked like business, and, indeed, Mr. Green on his return at once identified the house as Anningley Hall.

"Is there any kind of explanation of the figure, Green?" was the question which Williams naturally asked.

"I don't know, I'm sure, Williams. What used to be said in the place when I first knew it, which was before I came up here, was just this: old Francis was always very much down on these poaching fellows, and whenever he got a chance he used to get a man whom he suspected of it turned off the estate, and by degrees he got rid of them all but one. Squires could do a lot of things then that they daren't think of now. Well, this man that was left was what you find pretty often in that country—

the last remains of a very old family. I believe they were Lords of the Manor at one time. I recollect just the same thing in my own parish."

"What, like the man in *Tess of the d'Urbervilles*," Williams put in.

"Yes, I dare say; it's not a book I could ever read myself. But this fellow could show a row of tombs in the church there that belonged to his ancestors, and all that went to sour him a bit; but Francis, they said, could never get at him—he always kept just on the right side of the law—until one night the keepers found him at it in a wood right at the end of the estate. I could show you the place now; it marches with some land that used to belong to an uncle of mine. And you can imagine there was a row; and this man Gawdy (that was the name, to be sure—Gawdy; I thought I should get it—Gawdy), he was unlucky enough, poor chap! to shoot a keeper. Well, that was what Francis wanted, and grand juries—you know what they would have been then—and poor Gawdy was strung up in double-quick time; and I've been shown the place he was buried in, on the north side of the church—you know the way in that part of the world: anyone that's been hanged or made away with themselves, they bury them that side. And the idea was that some friend of Gawdy's—not a relation, because he had none, poor devil! he was the last of his line: kind of *spes ultima gentis*—must have planned to get hold of Francis's boy and put an end to *his* line, too. I don't know—it's rather an out-of-the-way thing for an Essex poacher to think of—but, you know, I should say now it looks more as if ole Gawdy had managed the job himself. Booh! I hate to think of it! have some whisky, Williams!"

The facts were communicated by Williams to Dennistoun, and by him to a mixed company, of which I was one, and the Sadducean Professor of Ophiology another. I am sorry to say that the latter when asked what he thought of it, only remarked: "Oh, those Bridgeford people will say anything"—a sentiment which met with the reception it deserved.

I have only to add that the picture is now in the Ashleian

Museum; that it has been treated with a view to discovering whether sympathetic ink has been used in it, but without effect; that Mr. Britnell knew nothing of it save that he was sure it was uncommon; and that, though carefully watched, it has never been known to change again.

THE OPEN WINDOW *

BY "SAKI" (H. H. MUNRO)

"MY AUNT will be down presently, Mr. Nuttel," said a very self-possessed young lady of fifteen; "in the meantime you must try and put up with me."

Framton Nuttel endeavoured to say the correct something which should duly flatter the niece of the moment without unduly discounting the aunt that was to come. Privately he doubted more than ever whether these formal visits on a succession of total strangers would do much towards helping the nerve cure which he was supposed to be undergoing.

"I know how it will be," his sister had said when he was preparing to migrate to this rural retreat; "you will bury yourself down there and not speak to a living soul, and your nerves will be worse than ever from moping. I shall just give you letters of introduction to all the people I know there. Some of them, as far as I can remember, were quite nice."

Framton wondered whether Mrs. Sappleton, the lady to whom he was presenting one of the letters of introduction, came into the nice division.

"Do you know many of the people round here?" asked the niece, when she judged that they had had sufficient silent communion.

"Hardly a soul," said Framton. "My sister was staying here, at the rectory, you know, some four years ago, and she gave me letters of introduction to some of the people here."

* From *The Short Stories of Saki (H. H. Munro)*, copyright 1930. By permission of The Viking Press, Inc., New York.

THE OPEN WINDOW

He made the last statement in a tone of distinct regret.

"Then you know practically nothing about my aunt?" pursued the self-possessed young lady.

"Only her name and address," admitted the caller. He was wondering whether Mrs. Sappleton was in the married or widowed state. An indefinable something about the room seemed to suggest masculine habitation.

"Her great tragedy happened just three years ago," said the child; "that would be since your sister's time."

"Her tragedy?" asked Framton; somehow in this restful country spot tragedies seemed out of place.

"You may wonder why we keep that window wide open on an October afternoon," said the niece, indicating a large French window that opened on to a lawn.

"It is quite warm for the time of the year," said Framton; "but has that window got anything to do with the tragedy?"

"Out through that window, three years ago to a day, her husband and her two young brothers went off for their day's shooting. They never came back. In crossing the moor to their favorite snipe-shooting ground they were all three engulfed in a treacherous piece of bog. It had been that dreadful wet summer, you know, and places that were safe in other years gave way suddenly without warning. Their bodies were never recovered. That was the dreadful part of it." Here the child's voice lost its self-possessed note and became falteringly human. "Poor aunt always thinks that they will come back some day, they and the little brown spaniel that was lost with them, and walk in at that window just as they used to do. That is why the window is kept open every evening till it is quite dusk. Poor dear aunt, she has often told me how they went out, her husband with his white waterproof coat over his arm, and Ronnie, her youngest brother, singing 'Bertie, why do you bound?' as he always did to tease her, because she said it got on her nerves. Do you know, sometimes on still, quiet evenings like this, I almost get a creepy feeling that they will all walk in through that window——"

She broke off with a little shudder. It was a relief to Framton when the aunt bustled into the room with a whirl of apologies for being late in making her appearance.

"I hope Vera has been amusing you?" she said.

"She has been very interesting," said Framton.

"I hope you don't mind the open window," said Mrs. Sappleton briskly; "my husband and brothers will be home directly from shooting, and they always come in this way. They've been out for snipe in the marshes to-day, so they'll make a fine mess over my poor carpets. So like you menfolks, isn't it?"

She rattled on cheerfully about the shooting and the scarcity of birds, and the prospects for duck in the winter. To Framton it was all purely horrible. He made a desperate but only partially successful effort to turn the talk on to a less ghastly topic; he was conscious that his hostess was giving him only a fragment of her attention, and her eyes were constantly straying past him to the open window and the lawn beyond. It was certainly an unfortunate coincidence that he should have paid his visit on this tragic anniversary.

"The doctors agree in ordering me complete rest, an absence of mental excitement, and avoidance of anything in the nature of violent physical exercise," announced Framton, who labored under the tolerably wide-spread delusion that total strangers and chance acquaintances are hungry for the least detail of one's ailments and infirmities, their cause and cure. "On the matter of diet they are not so much in agreement," he continued.

"No?" said Mrs. Sappleton, in a voice which only replaced a yawn at the last moment. Then she suddenly brightened into alert attention—but not to what Framton was saying.

"Here they are at last!" she cried. "Just in time for tea, and don't they look as if they were muddy up to the eyes!"

Framton shivered slightly and turned toward the niece with a look intended to convey sympathetic comprehension. The child was staring out through the open window with dazed horror in her eyes. In a chill shock of nameless fear Framton swung round in his seat and looked in the same direction.

In the deepening twilight three figures were walking across

the lawn towards the window; they all carried guns under their arms, and one of them was additionally burdened with a white coat hung over his shoulders. A tired brown spaniel kept close at their heels. Noiselessly they neared the house, and then a hoarse young voice chanted out of the dusk: "I said, Bertie, why do you bound?"

Framton grabbed wildly at his stick and hat; the hall-door, the gravel-drive, and the front gate were dimly noted stages in his headlong retreat. A cyclist coming along the road had to run into the hedge to avoid imminent collision.

"Here we are, my dear," said the bearer of the white mackintosh, coming in through the window; "fairly muddy, but most of it's dry. Who was that who bolted out as we came up?"

"A most extraordinary man, a Mr. Nuttel," said Mrs. Sappleton; "could only talk about his illness, and dashed off without a word of good-bye or apology when you arrived. One would think he had seen a ghost."

"I expect it was the spaniel," said the niece calmly; "he told me he had a horror of dogs. He was once hunted into a cemetery somewhere on the banks of the Ganges by a pack of pariah dogs, and had to spend the night in a newly dug grave with the creatures snarling and grinning and foaming just above him. Enough to make anyone lose their nerve."

Romance at short notice was her specialty.

THE BECKONING FAIR ONE

BY OLIVER ONIONS

I

THE THREE OR FOUR "To Let" boards had stood within the low paling as long as the inhabitants of the little triangular "Square" could remember, and if they had ever been vertical it was a very long time ago. They now overhung the palings each at its own angle, and resembled nothing so much as a row of wooden choppers, ever in the act of falling upon some passer-by, yet never cutting off a tenant for the old house from the stream of his fellows. Not that there was ever any great "stream" through the square; the stream passed a furlong and more away, beyond the intricacy of tenements and alleys and byways that had sprung up since the old house had been built, hemming it in completely; and probably the house itself was only suffered to stand pending the falling-in of a lease or two, when doubtless a clearance would be made of the whole neighborhood.

It was of bloomy old red brick, and built into its walls were the crowns and clasped hands and other insignia of insurance companies long since defunct. The children of the secluded square had swung upon the low gate at the end of the entrance alley until little more than the solid top bar of it remained, and the alley itself ran past boarded basement windows on which tramps had chalked their cryptic marks. The path was washed and worn uneven by the spilling of water from the eaves of the encroaching next house, and cats and dogs had made the approach their own. The chances of a tenant did not seem such as to warrant the keeping of the "To Let" boards in a state of legibility and repair, and as a matter of fact they were not so kept.

For six months Oleron had passed the old place twice a day or oftener, on his way from his lodgings to the room, ten minutes' walk away, he had taken to work in; and for six months no hatchet-like notice-board had fallen across his path. This might have been due to the fact that he usually took the other side of the square. But he chanced one morning to take the side that ran past the broken gate and the rain-worn entrance alley, and to pause before one of the inclined boards. The board bore, beside the agent's name, the announcement, written apparently about the time of Oleron's own early youth, that the key was to be had at Number Six.

Now Oleron was already paying, for his separate bedroom and workroom, more than an author who, without private means, habitually disregards his public, can afford; and he was paying in addition a small rent for the storage of the greater part of his grandmother's furniture. Moreover, it invariably happened that the book he wished to read in bed was at his working-quarters half a mile or more away, while the note or letter he had sudden need of during the day was as likely as not to be in the pocket of another coat hanging behind his bedroom door. And there were other inconveniences in having a divided domicile. Therefore Oleron, brought suddenly up by the hatchet-like notice-board, looked first down through some scanty privet-bushes at the boarded basement windows, then up at the blank and grimy windows of the first floor, and so up to the second floor and the flat stone coping of the leads. He stood for a minute thumbing his lean and shaven jaw; then, with another glance at the board, he walked slowly across the square to Number Six.

He knocked, and waited for two or three minutes, but, although the door stood open, received no answer. He was knocking again when a long-nosed man in shirt-sleeves appeared.

"I was arsking a blessing on our food," he said in a severe explanation.

Oleron asked if he might have the key of the old house; and the long-nosed man withdrew again.

Oleron waited for another five minutes on the step; then the man, appearing again and masticating some of the food of which he had spoken, announced that the key was lost.

"But you won't want it," he said. "The entrance door isn't closed, and a push'll open any of the others. I'm a agent for it, if you're thinking of taking it——"

Oleron recrossed the square, descended the two steps at the broken gate, passed along the alley, and turned in at the old wide doorway. To the right, immediately within the door, steps descended to the roomy cellars, and the staircase before him had a carved rail, and was broad and handsome and filthy. Oleron ascended it, avoiding contact with the rail and wall, and stopped at the first landing. A door facing him had been boarded up, but he pushed at that on his right hand, and an insecure bolt or staple yielded. He entered the empty first floor.

He spent a quarter of an hour in the place, and then came out again. Without mounting higher, he descended and recrossed the square to the house of the man who had lost the key.

"Can you tell me how much the rent is?" he asked.

The man mentioned a figure, the comparative lowness of which seemed accounted for by the character of the neighborhood and the abominable state of unrepair of the place.

"Would it be possible to rent a single floor?"

The long-nosed man did not know; they might. . . .

"Who are they?"

The man gave Oleron the name of a firm of lawyers in Lincoln's Inn.

"You might mention my name—Barrett," he added.

Pressure of work prevented Oleron from going down to Lincoln's Inn that afternoon, but he went on the morrow, and was instantly offered the whole house as a purchase for fifty pounds down, the remainder of the purchase-money to remain on mortgage. It took him half an hour to disabuse the lawyer's mind of the idea that he wished anything more of the place than to rent a single floor of it. This made certain hums and haws of a difference, and the lawyer was by no means certain that it lay within his power to do as Oleron suggested; but it was finally extracted from him that, provided the notice-boards were allowed to remain up, and that, provided it was agreed that in the event of the whole house letting, the arrangement should terminate automatically without further notice, something might be done. That the old place should suddenly let over his head seemed to Oleron the slightest of risks to take, and he promised a decision within a week. On the morrow he visited the house again, went through it from top to bottom, and then went home to his lodgings to take a bath.

He was immensely taken with that portion of the house he had already determined should be his own. Scraped clean and repainted, and with that old furniture of Oleron's grandmother's, it ought to be entirely charming. He went to the storage warehouse to refresh his memory of his half-forgotten belongings, and to take the measurements; and thence he went to a decorator's. He was very busy with his regular work, and could have wished that the notice-board had caught his attention either a few months earlier or else later in the year; but the quickest way would be to suspend work entirely until after his removal. . . .

A fortnight later his first floor was painted throughout in a tender, elder-flower white, the paint was dry, and Oleron was in the middle of his installation. He was animated, delighted; and he rubbed his hands as he polished and made disposals of his grandmother's effects—the tall lattice-paned china cupboard with its Derby and Mason and Spode, the large folding Sheraton table, the long, low bookshelves (he had had two of them "copied"), the chairs, the Sheffield candlesticks, the riveted rose-bowls. These things he set against his newly painted elder-white walls—walls of wood paneled in the happiest proportions, and molded and coffered to the low-seated window-recesses in a mood of gaiety and rest that the builders of rooms no longer know. The ceilings were lofty, and faintly painted with an old pattern of stars; even the tapering moldings of his iron fireplace were as delicately designed as jewelry; and Oleron walked about rubbing his hands, frequently stopping for the mere pleasure of the glimpses from white room to white room. . . .

"Charming, charming!" he said to himself. "I wonder what Elsie Bengough will think of this!"

He bought a bolt and a Yale lock for his door, and shut off his quarters from the rest of the house. If he now wanted to read in bed, his book could be had for stepping into the next room. All the time, he thought how exceedingly lucky he was to get the place. He put up a hat-rack in the little square hall, and hung up his hats and caps and coats; and passers through the small triangular square late at night, looking up over the little serried row of wooden "To Let" hatchets, could see the light within Oleron's red blinds, or else the sudden darkening of one blind and the illumination of another, as Oleron, candlestick in hand, passed from room to room, making final settlings of his furniture, or preparing to resume the work that his removal had interrupted.

II

As far as the chief business of his life—his writing—was concerned, Paul Oleron treated the world a good deal better than he was treated by it; but he seldom took the trouble to strike a balance, or to compute how far, at forty-four years of age, he was behind his points on the handicap. To have done so wouldn't have altered matters, and it might have depressed Oleron. He had chosen his path, and was committed to it beyond possibility of withdrawal. Perhaps he had chosen it in the days when he had been easily swayed by something a little disinterested, a little generous, a little noble; and had he ever thought of questioning himself he would still have held to it that a life without nobility and generosity and disinterestedness was no life for him. Only quite recently, and rarely, had he even vaguely suspected that there was more in it than this; but it was no good anticipating the day when, he supposed, he would reach that maximum point of his powers beyond which he must inevitably decline, and be left face to face with the question whether it would not have profited him better to have ruled his life by less exigent ideals.

In the meantime, his removal into the old house with the insurance marks built into its brick merely interrupted *Romilly Bishop* at the fifteenth chapter.

As this tall man with the lean, ascetic face moved about his new abode, arranging, changing, altering, hardly yet into his working stride again, he gave the impression of almost spinsterlike precision and nicety. For twenty years past, in a score of lodgings, garrets, flats, and rooms furnished and unfurnished, he had been accustomed to do many things for himself, and he had discovered that it saves time and temper to be methodical. He had arranged with the wife of the long-nosed Barrett, a stout Welsh woman with a falsetto voice, the Merionethshire accent of which long residence in London had not perceptibly modified, to come across the square each morning to prepare his breakfast and also to "turn the place out" on Saturday mornings; and for the rest, he even welcomed a little housework as a relaxation from the strain of writing.

His kitchen, together with the adjoining strip of an apartment into which a modern bath had been fitted, overlooked the alley at the side of the house; and at one end of it was a large closet with a door, and a square sliding hatch in the upper part of the door. This had been a powder-closet, and through the hatch the elaborately dressed head had been thrust to receive the click and puff of the powder-pistol. Oleron puzzled a little over this closet; then, as its use occurred to him, he smiled faintly, a little moved, he knew not by what. . . . He would have to put it to a very different purpose from its original one; it would probably have to serve as a larder. . . . It was in this closet that he made a discovery. The back of it was shelved, and, rummaging on an upper shelf that ran deeply into the wall, Oleron found a couple of mushroom-shaped old wooden wig-stands. He did not know how they had come to be there. Doubtless the painters had turned them up somewhere or other, and had put them there. But his five rooms, as a whole, were short of cupboard and closetroom; and it was only by the exercise of some ingenuity that he was able to find places for the bestowal of his household linen, his boxes, and his seldom-used but not-to-be-destroyed accumulation of papers.

It was early spring that Oleron entered on his tenancy, and he was anxious to have *Romilly* ready for publication in the coming autumn. Nevertheless, he did not intend to force its production. Should it demand longer in the doing, so much the worse; he realized its importance, its crucial importance, in his artistic development, and it must have its own length and time. In the workroom he had recently left he had been making excellent progress; *Romilly* had begun, as the saying is, to speak and act of herself; and he did not doubt she would continue to do so the moment the distraction of his removal was over. This distraction was almost over; he told himself it was time he pulled himself together again; and on a March morning he went out and returned again with two great bunches of yellow daffodils, placed one bunch on his mantelpiece between the Sheffield sticks and the other on the table before him, and took out the half-completed manuscript of *Romilly Bishop*.

But before beginning work he went to a small rosewood cabinet and took from a drawer his check-book and pass-book. He totted them up, and his monk-like face grew thoughtful. His installation had cost him more than he had intended it should, and his balance was rather less than fifty pounds, with no immediate prospect of more.

"Hm! I'd forgotten rugs and chintz curtains and so forth mounted up so," said Oleron. "But it would have been a pity to spoil the place for the want of ten pounds or so. . . . Well, *Romilly* simply *must* be out for the autumn, that's all. So here goes———"

He drew his papers toward him.

But he worked badly; or, rather, he did not work at all. The square outside had its own noises, frequent and new, and Oleron could only hope that he would speedily become accustomed to these. First came hawkers, with their carts and cries; at midday the children, returning from school, trooped into the square and swung on Oleron's gate; and when the children had departed again for afternoon school, an itinerant musician with a mandoline posted himself beneath Oleron's window and began to strum. This was a not unpleasant distraction, and Oleron, pushing up his window, threw the man a penny. Then he returned to his table again. . . .

But it was no good. He came to himself, at long intervals, to find that he had been looking about his room and wondering how it had formerly been furnished—whether a settee in buttercup or petunia satin had stood under the farther window, whether from the center molding of the light lofty ceiling had depended a glimmering crystal chandelier, or where the tambour-frame or the piquet-table had stood. . . . No, it was no good; he had far better be frankly doing nothing than getting fruitlessly tired; and he decided that he would take a walk, but, chancing to sit down for a moment, dozed in his chair instead.

"This won't do," he yawned when he awoke at half-past four in the afternoon; "I must do better than this tomorrow——"

And he felt so deliciously lazy that for some minutes he even contemplated the breach of an appointment he had for the evening.

The next morning he sat down to work without even permitting himself to answer one of his three letters—two of them tradesman's accounts, the third a note from Miss Bengough, forwarded from his old address. It was a jolly day of white and blue, with a gay noisy wind and a subtle turn in the color of growing things; and over and over again, once or twice a minute, his room became suddenly light and then subdued again, as the shining white cloud rolled northeastward over the square. The soft fitful illumination was reflected in the polished surface of the table and even in the footworn old floor; and the morning noises had begun again.

Oleron made a pattern of dots on the paper before him, and then broke off to move the jar of daffodils exactly opposite the center of a creamy panel. Then he wrote a sentence that ran continuously for a couple of lines, after which it broke off into notes and jottings. For a time he succeeded in persuading himself that in making these memoranda he was really working; then he rose and began to pace his room. As he did so, he was struck by an idea. It was that the place might possibly be a little better for more positive color. It was, perhaps, a thought *too* pale—mild and sweet as a kind old face, but a little devitalized, even wan. . . . Yes, decidedly it would bear a robuster note—more and richer flowers, and possibly some warm and gay stuff for cushions for the window-seats. . . .

"Of course, I really can't afford it," he muttered, as he went for a two-foot and began to measure the width of the window recesses. . . .

In stooping to measure a recess, his attitude suddenly changed to one of interest and attention. Presently he rose again, rubbing his hands with gentle glee.

"Oho, oho!" he said. "These look to me very much like window-boxes, nailed up. We must look into this! Yes, those are boxes, or I'm . . . oho, this is an adventure!"

On that wall of his sitting room there were two windows (the third was in another corner), and, beyond the open bedroom door, on the same wall, was another. The seats of all had been painted, repainted, and painted again; and Oleron's investigating finger had barely detected the old nailheads beneath the paint. Under the ledge over which he stooped an old keyhole also had been puttied up. Oleron took out his penknife.

He worked carefully for five minutes, and then went into the kitchen for a hammer and chisel. Driving the chisel cautiously under the seat, he started the whole lid slightly. Again using the penknife, he cut along the hinged edge and outward along the ends; and then he fetched a wedge and a wooden mallet.

"Now for our little mystery——" he said.

The sound of the mallet on the wedge seemed, in that sweet and pale apartment, somehow a little brutal—nay, even shocking. The paneling rang and rattled and vibrated to the blows like a sounding-board. The whole house seemed to echo; from the roomy cellarage to the garrets above a flock of echoes seemed to awake; and the sound got a little on Oleron's nerve.

All at once he paused, fetched a duster, and muffled the mallet. . . . When the edge was sufficiently raised he put his fingers under it and lifted. The paint flaked and starred a little; the rusty old nails squeaked and grunted; and the lid came up, laying open the box beneath. Oleron looked into it. Save for a couple of inches of scurf and mold and old cobwebs it was empty.

"No treasure there," said Oleron, a little amused that he should have fancied there might have been. "*Romilly* will still have to be out by the autumn. Let's have a look at the others."

He turned to the second window.

The raising of the two remaining seats occupied him until well into the afternoon. That of the bedroom, like the first, was empty; but from the second seat of his sitting room he drew out something yielding and folded and furred over an inch thick with dust. He carried the object into the kitchen, and having swept it over a bucket, took a duster to it.

It was some sort of a large bag, of an ancient frieze-like material, and when unfolded it occupied the greater part of the small kitchen floor. In shape it was an irregular, a very irregular, triangle, and it had a couple of wide flaps, with the remains of straps and buckles. The patch that had been uppermost in the folding was of a faded yellowish brown; but the rest of it was of shades of crimson that varied according to the exposure of the parts of it.

"Now whatever can that have been?" Oleron mused as he stood surveying it. . . . "I give it up. Whatever it is, it's settled my work for today, I'm afraid——."

He folded the object up carelessly and thrust it into a corner of the kitchen; then, taking pans and brushes and an old knife, he returned to the sitting room and began to scrape and to wash and to line with paper, his newly discovered receptacles. When he had finished, he put his spare boots and books and papers into them; and he closed the lids again, amused with his little adventure, but also a little anxious for the hour to come when he should settle fairly down to his work again.

III

It piqued Oleron a little that his friend, Miss Bengough, should dismiss with a glance the place he himself had found so singularly winning. Indeed she scarcely lifted her eyes to it. But then she had always been more or less like that—a little indifferent to the graces of life, careless of appearances, and perhaps a shade more herself when she ate biscuits from a paper bag than when she dined with greater observance of the convenances. She was an unattached journalist of thirty-four, large, showy, fair as butter, pink as a dogrose, reminding one of a florist's picked specimen bloom, and given to sudden and ample movements and moist and explosive utterances. She "pulled a better living out of the pool" (as she expressed it) than Oleron did; and by cunningly disguised puffs of drapers and haberdashers she "pulled" also the greater part of her very varied wardrobe. She left small whirlwinds of air behind her when she moved, in which her veils and scarves fluttered and spun.

Oleron heard the flurry of her skirts on his staircase and her single loud knock at his door when he had been a month in his new abode. Her garments brought in the outer air, and she flung a bundle of ladies' journals down on a chair.

"Don't knock off for me," she said across a mouthful of large-headed hatpins as she removed her hat and veil. "I didn't know whether you were straight yet, so I've brought some sandwiches for lunch. You've got coffee, I suppose? No, don't get up—I'll find the kitchen——"

"Oh, that's all right, I'll clear these things away. To tell the truth, I'm rather glad to be interrupted," said Oleron.

He gathered his work together and put it way. She was already in the kitchen; he heard the running of water into the kettle. He joined her, and ten minutes later followed her back to the sitting room with the coffee and sandwiches on a tray. They sat down, with the tray on a small table between them.

"Well, what do you think of the new place?" Oleron asked as she poured out coffee.

"Hm! . . . Anybody'd think you were going to get married, Paul."

He laughed.

"Oh no. But it's an improvement on some of them, isn't it?"

"Is it? I suppose it is; I don't know. I liked the last place, in spite of the black ceiling and no watertap. How's *Romilly*?"

Oleron thumbed his chin.

"Hm! I'm rather ashamed to tell you. The fact is, I've not got on very well with it. But it will be all right on the night, as you used to say."

"Stuck?"

"Rather stuck."

"Got any of it you care to read to me? . . ."

Oleron had long been in the habit of reading portions of his work to Miss Bengough occasionally. Her comments were always quick and practical, sometimes directly useful, sometimes indirectly suggestive. She, in return for his confidence, always kept all mention of her own work sedulously from him. His, she said, was "real work"; hers merely filled space, not always even grammatically.

"I'm afraid there isn't," Oleron replied, still meditatively dry-shaving his chin. Then he added, with a little burst of candor, "The fact is, Elsie, I've not written—not actually written—very much more of it—*any* more of it, in fact. But, of course, that doesn't mean I haven't progressed. I've progressed, in one sense, rather alarmingly. I'm now thinking of reconstructing the whole thing."

Miss Bengough gave a gasp. "Reconstructing!"

"Making Romilly herself a different type of woman. Somehow, I've begun to feel that I'm not getting the most out of her. As she stands, I've certainly lost interest in her to some extent."

"But—but——" Miss Bengough protested, "you had her so real, so *living*, Paul!"

Oleron smiled faintly. He had been quite prepared for Miss Bengough's disapproval. He wasn't surprised that she liked Romilly as she at present existed; she would. Whether she realized it or not, there was much of herself in his fictitious creation. Naturally Romilly would seem "real," "living," to her. . . .

"But are you really serious, Paul?" Miss Bengough asked presently, with a round-eyed stare.

"Quite serious."

"You're really going to scrap those fifteen chapters?"

"I didn't exactly say that."

"That fine, rich love-scene?"

"I should only do it reluctantly, and for the sake of something I thought better."

"And that beautiful, *beau*tiful description of Romilly on the shore?"

"It wouldn't necessarily be wasted," he said a little uneasily.

But Miss Bengough made a large and windy gesture, and then let him have it.

"Really, you are *too* trying!" she broke out. "I do wish sometimes you'd remember you're human, and live in a world! You know I'd be the *last* to wish you to lower your standard one inch, but it wouldn't be lowering it to bring it within human comprehension. Oh, you're sometimes altogether too godlike! . . . Why, it would be a wicked, criminal waste of your powers to destroy those fifteen chapters! Look at it reasonably, now. You've been working for nearly twenty years; you've now got what you've been working for almost within your grasp; your affairs are at a most critical stage (oh, don't tell me; I know you're about at the end of your money); and here you are, deliberately proposing to withdraw a thing that will probably make your name, and to substitute for it something that ten to one nobody on earth will ever want to read—and small blame to them! Really, you try my patience!"

Oleron had shaken his head slowly as she had talked. It was an old story between them. The noisy, able practical journalist was an admirable friend—up to a certain point; beyond that . . . well, each of us knows that point beyond which we stand alone. Elsie Bengough sometimes said that had she had one-tenth part of Oleron's genius there were few things she could not have done—thus making that genius a quantitatively divisible thing, a sort of ingredient, to be added to or to be subtracted from in the admixture of his work. That it was a qualitative thing, essential, indivisible, informing, passed her comprehension. Their spirits parted company at that point. Oleron knew it. She did not appear to know it.

"Yes, yes, yes," he said a little wearily, by-and-by, "practically you're quite right, entirely right, and I haven't a word to say. If I could only turn *Romilly* over to you you'd make an enormous success of her. But that can't be, and I, for my part, am seriously doubting whether she's worth my while. You know what that means."

"What does it mean?" she demanded bluntly.

"Well," he said, smiling wanly, "what *does* it mean when you're convinced a thing isn't worth doing? You simply don't do it."

Miss Bengough's eyes swept the ceiling for assistance against this impossible man.

"What utter rubbish!" she broke out at last. "Why, when I saw you last you were simply oozing *Romilly*; you were turning her off at the rate of four chapters a week; if you hadn't moved you'd have had her three parts done by now. What on earth possessed you to move right in the middle of your most important work?"

Oleron tried to put her off with a recital of inconveniences, but she wouldn't have it. Perhaps in her heart she partly suspected the reason. He was simply mortally weary of the narrow circumstances of his life. He had had twenty years of it—twenty years of garrets and roof-chambers and dingy flats and shabby lodgings, and he was tired of dinginess and shabbiness. The reward was as far off as ever—or if it was not, he no longer cared as once he would have cared to put out his hand and take it. It is all very well to tell a man who is at the point of exhaustion that only another effort is required of him; if he cannot make it he is as far off as ever. . . .

"Anyway," Oleron summed up, "I'm happier here than I've been for a long time. That's some sort of a justification."

"And doing no work," said Miss Bengough pointedly.

At that a trifling petulance that had been gathering in Oleron came to a head.

"And why should I do nothing but work?" he demanded. "How much happier am I for it? I don't say I don't love my work—when it's done; but I hate doing it. Sometimes it's an intolerable burden that I simply long to be rid of. Once in many weeks it has a moment, one moment, of glow and thrill for me; I remember the days when it was all glow and thrill; and now I'm forty-four, and it's becoming drudgery. Nobody wants it; I'm ceasing to want it myself; and if any ordinary sensible man were to ask me whether I didn't think I was a fool to go on, I think I should agree that I was."

Miss Bengough's comely pink face was serious.

"But you knew all that, many, many years ago, Paul—and still you chose it," she said in a low voice.

"Well, and how should I have known?" he demanded. "I didn't know. I was told so. My heart, if you like, told me so, and I thought I knew. Youth always thinks it knows; then one day it discovers that it is nearly fifty——"

"Forty-four, Paul——"

"—forty-four, then—and it finds that the glamour isn't in front, but behind. Yes, I knew and chose, if *that's* knowing and choosing . . . but it's a costly choice we're called on to make when we're young!"

Miss Bengough's eyes were on the floor. Without moving them she said: "You're not regretting it, Paul?"

"Am I not?" he took her up. "Upon my word, I've lately thought I am! What *do* I get in return for it all?"

"You know what you get," she replied.

He might have known from her tone what else he could have had for the holding up of a finger—herself. She knew, but could not tell him, that he could have done no better thing for himself. Had he, any time these ten years, asked her to marry him, she would have replied quietly, "Very well; when?" He had never thought of it. . . .

"Yours is the real work," she continued quietly. "Without

you we jackals couldn't exist. You and a few like you hold everything upon your shoulders."

For a minute there was a silence. Then it occurred to Oleron that this was common vulgar grumbling. It was not his habit. Suddenly he rose and began to stack cups and plates on the tray.

"Sorry you catch me like this, Elsie," he said, with a little laugh. . . . "No, I'll take them out; then we'll go for a walk, if you like. . . ."

He carried out the tray, and then began to show Miss Bengough round his flat. She made few comments. In the kitchen she asked what an old faded square of reddish frieze was, that Mrs. Barrett used as a cushion for her wooden chair.

"That? I should be glad if you could tell *me* what it is," Oleron replied as he unfolded the bag and related the story of its finding in the window-seat.

"I think I know what it is," said Miss Bengough. "It's been used to wrap up a harp before putting it into its case."

"By Jove, that's probably just what it was," said Oleron. "I could make neither head nor tail of it. . . ."

They finished the tour of the flat, and returned to the sitting room.

"And who lives in the rest of the house?" Miss Bengough asked.

"I dare say a tramp sleeps in the cellar occasionally. Nobody else."

"Hm! . . . Well, I'll tell you what I think about it, if you like."

"I should like."

"You'll never work here."

"Oh?" said Oleron quickly. "Why not?"

"You'll never finish *Romilly* here. Why, I don't know, but you won't. I know it. You'll have to leave before you get on with that book."

He mused for a moment, and then said:

"Isn't that a little—prejudiced, Elsie?"

"Perfectly ridiculous. As an argument it hasn't a leg to stand on. But there it is," she replied, her mouth once more full of the large-headed hat pins.

Oleron was reaching down his hat and coat. He laughed.

"I can only hope you're entirely wrong," he said, "for I shall be in a serious mess if *Romilly* isn't out in the autumn."

IV

As Oleron sat by his fire that evening, pondering Miss Bengough's prognostication that difficulties awaited him in his work, he came to the conclusion that it would have been far better had she kept her beliefs to herself. No man does a thing better for having his confidence damped at the outset, and to speak of difficulties is in a sense to make them. Speech itself becomes a deterrent act, to which other discouragements accrete until the very event of which warning is given is as likely as not to come to pass. He heartily confounded her. An influence hostile to the completion of *Romilly* had been born.

And in some illogical, dogmatic way women seem to have, she had attached this antagonistic influence to his new abode. Was ever anything so absurd! "You'll never finish *Romilly* here." . . . Why not? Was this her idea of the luxury that saps the spring of action and brings a man down to indolence and dropping out of the race? The place was well enough—it was entirely charming, for that matter—but it was not so demoralizing as all that! No; Elsie had missed the mark that time. . . .

He moved his chair to look round the room that smiled, positively smiled, in the firelight. He too smiled, as if pity was to be entertained for a maligned apartment. Even that slight lack of robust color he had remarked was not noticeable in the soft glow. The drawn chintz curtains—they had a flowered and trellised pattern, with baskets and oaten pipes—fell in long quiet folds to the window-seats; the rows of bindings in old bookcases took the light richly; the last trace of sallowness had gone with the daylight; and, if the truth must be told, it had been Elsie herself who had seemed a little out of the picture.

That reflection struck him a little, and presently he returned to it. Yes, the room had, quite accidentally, done Miss Bengough a disservice that afternoon. It had, in some subtle but unmistakable way, placed her, marked a contrast of qualities. Assuming for the sake of argument the slightly ridiculous proposition that the room in which Oleron sat *was* characterized by a certain sparsity and lack of vigor; so much the worse for Miss Bengough; she certainly erred on the side of redundancy and general muchness. And if one must contrast abstract qualities, Oleron inclined to the austere in taste. . . .

Yes, here Oleron had made a distinct discovery; he wondered he had not made it before. He pictured Miss Bengough again as she had appeared that afternoon—large, showy, mostly pink, with that quality of the prize bloom exuding, as it were, from her; and instantly she suffered in his thought. He even recognized now that he had noticed something odd at the time, and that unconsciously his attitude, even while she had been there, had been one of criticism. The mechanism of her was a little obvious; her melting humidity was the result of analyzable processes; and behind her there had seemed to lurk some dim shape emblematic of mortality. He had never, during the ten years of their intimacy, dreamed for a moment of asking her to marry him; nonetheless, he now felt for the first time a thankfulness that he had not done so. . . .

Then, suddenly and swiftly, his face flamed that he should be thinking thus of his friend. What! Elsie Bengough, with whom he had spent weeks and weeks of afternoons—she, the good chum, on whose help he would have counted had all the rest of the world failed him—she, whose loyalty to him would not, he knew, swerve as long as there was breath in her—Elsie to be even in thought dissected thus! He was an ingrate and a cad. . . .

Had she been there in that moment he would have abased himself before her.

For ten minutes and more he sat, still gazing into the fire, with that humiliating red fading slowly from his cheeks. All was still within and without, save for a tiny musical tinkling that came from his kitchen—the dripping of water from an imperfectly turned-off tap into the vessel beneath it. Mechanically he began to beat with his fingers to the faintly heard falling of the drops; the tiny regular movement seemed to hasten that shameful withdrawal from his face. He grew cool once more; and when he resumed his meditation he was all unconscious that he took it up again at the same point. . . .

It was not only her florid superfluity of build that he had approached in the attitude of criticism; he was conscious also of the wide differences between her mind and his own. He felt no thankfulness that up to a certain point their natures had ever run companionably side by side; he was now full of questions beyond that point. Their intellects diverged; there was no denying it; and, looking back, he was inclined to doubt whether there had been any real coincidence. True, he had read his writings to her and she had appeared to speak comprehendingly and to the point; but what can a man do who, having assumed that another sees as he does, is suddenly brought up sharp by something that falsifies and discredits all that has gone before? He doubted all now. . . . It did for a moment occur to him that the man who demands of a friend more than can be given to him is in danger of losing that friend, but he put the thought aside.

Again he ceased to think, and again moved his finger to the distant dripping of the tap. . . .

And now (he resumed by-and-by), if these things were true of Elsie Bengough, they were also true of the creation of which she was the prototype—Romilly Bishop. And since he could say of Romilly what for very shame he could not say of Elsie, he gave his thoughts rein. He did so in that smiling, fire-lighted room, to the accompaniment of the faintly heard tap.

There was no longer any doubt about it; he hated the central character of his novel. Even as he had described her physically she overpowered the senses; she was coarse-fibered, overcolored, rank. It became true the moment he formulated his thought; Gulliver had described the Brobdingnagian maids-of-honor thus: and mentally and spiritually she corresponded—was unsensitive, limited, common. The model (he closed his eyes for a moment)—the model stuck out through fifteen vulgar and blatant chapters to such a pitch that, without seeing the reason, he had been unable to begin the sixteenth. He marveled that it had only just dawned upon him.

And *this* was to have been his Beatrice, his vision! As Elsie she was to have gone into the furnace of his art, and she was to have come out the Woman all men desire! Her thoughts were to have been culled from his own finest, her form from his dearest dreams, and her setting wherever he could find one fit for her worth. He had brooded long before making the attempt; then one day he had felt her stir within him as a mother feels a quickening, and he had begun to write; and so he had added chapter to chapter. . . .

And those fifteen sodden chapters were what he had produced!

Again he sat, softly moving his finger. . . .

Then he bestirred himself.

She must go, all fifteen chapters of her. That was settled. For what was to take her place his mind was a blank; but one thing at a time; a man is not excused from taking the wrong course because the right one is not immediately revealed to him. Better would come if it was to come; in the meantime——

He rose, fetched the fifteen chapters, and read them over before he should drop them into the fire.

But instead of putting them into the fire he let them fall from his hand. He became conscious of the dripping of the tap again. It had a tinkling gamut of four or five notes, on which it rang irregular changes, and it was foolishly sweet and dulcimer-like. In his mind Oleron could see the gathering of each drop, its little tremble on the lip of the tap, and the tiny percussion of its fall "Plink—plunk," minimized almost to inaudibility. Following the lowest note there seemed to be a brief phrase, irregularly repeated; and presently Oleron found himself waiting for the recurrence of this phrase. It was quite pretty. . . .

But it did not conduce to wakefulness, and Oleron dozed over his fire.

When he awoke again the fire had burned low and the flames of the candles were licking the rims of the Sheffield sticks. Sluggishly he rose, yawned, went his nightly round of door-locks, and window-fastenings, and passed into his bedroom. Soon, he slept soundly.

But a curious little sequel followed on the morrow. Mrs. Barrett usually tapped, not at his door, but at the wooden wall beyond which lay Oleron's bed; and then Oleron rose, put on his dressing-gown, and admitted her. He was not conscious that as he did so that morning he hummed an air; but Mrs. Barrett lingered with her hand on the doorknob and her face a little averted and smiling.

"De-ar me!" her soft falsetto rose. "But that will be a very o-ald tune, Mr. Oleron! I will not have heard it this for-ty years!"

"What tune?" Oleron asked.

"The tune, indeed, that you was humming, sir."

Oleron had his thumb in the flap of a letter. It remained there.

"*I* was humming? . . . Sing it, Mrs. Barrett."

Mrs. Barrett prut-prutted.

"I have no voice for singing, Mr. Oleron; it was Ann Pugh was the singer of our family; but the tune will be very o-ald, and it is called 'The Beckoning Fair One.'"

"Try to sing it," said Oleron, his thumb still in the envelope; and Mrs. Barrett, with much dimpling and confusion, hummed the air.

"They do say it was sung to a harp, Mr. Oleron, and it will be very o-ald," she concluded.

"And *I* was singing that?"

"Indeed you was. I would not be likely to tell you lies."

With a "Very well—let me have breakfast," Oleron opened his letter; but the trifling circumstance struck him as more odd than he would have admitted to himself. The phrase he had hummed had been that which he had associated with the falling from the tap on the evening before.

V

Even more curious than that the commonplace dripping of an ordinary water-tap should have tallied so closely with an actually existing air was another result it had, namely, that it awakened, or seemed to awaken, in Oleron an abnormal sensitiveness to other noises of the old house. It has been remarked that silence obtains its fullest and most impressive quality when it is broken by some minute sound; and, truth to tell, the place was never still. Perhaps the mildness of the spring air operated on its torpid old timbers; perhaps Oleron's fires caused it to stretch its old anatomy; and certainly a whole world of insect life bored and burrowed in its baulks and joists. At any rate Oleron had only to sit quiet in his chair and to wait for a minute or two in order to become aware of such a change in the auditory scale as comes upon a man who, conceiving the midsummer woods to be motionless and still, all at once finds his ear sharpened to the crepitation of a myriad insects.

And he smiled to think of man's arbitrary distinction between that which has life and that which has not. Here, quite apart from such recognizable sounds as the scampering of mice, the falling of plaster behind his paneling, and the popping of purses or coffins from his fire, was a whole house talking to him had he but known its language. Beams settled with a tired sigh into their old mortises; creatures ticked in the walls; joists cracked, boards complained; with no palpable stirring of the air window-sashes changed their positions with a soft knock in their frames. And whether the place had life in this sense or not, it had at all events a winsome personality. It needed but an hour of musing for Oleron to conceive the idea that, as his own body stood in friendly relation to his soul, so, by an extension and an attenuation, his habitation might fantastically be supposed to stand in some relation to himself. He even amused himself with the far-fetched fancy that he might so identify himself with the place that some future tenant, taking possession, might regard it as in a sense haunted. It would be rather a joke if he, a perfectly harmless author, with nothing on his mind worse than a novel he had discovered he must begin again, should turn out to be laying the foundation of a future ghost! . . .

In proportion, however, as he felt this growing attachment to the fabric of his abode, Elsie Bengough, from being merely un attracted, began to show a dislike of the place that was more and more marked. And she did not scruple to speak of her aversion.

"It doesn't belong to today at all, and for you especially it's bad," she said with decision. "You're only too ready to let go your hold on actual things and to slip into apathy; *you* ought to be in a place with concrete floors and a patent gas-meter and a tradesman's lift. And it would do you all the good in the world if you had a job that made you scramble and rub elbows with your fellow-men. Now, if I could get you a job, for, say, two or three days a week, one that would allow you heaps of time for your proper work—would you take it?"

Somehow, Oleron resented a little being diagnosed like this. He thanked Miss Bengough, but without a smile.

"Thank you, but I don't think so. After all each of us has his own life to live," he could not refrain from adding.

"His own life to live! . . . How long is it since you were out, Paul?"

"About two hours."

"I don't mean to buy stamps or to post a letter. How long is it since you had anything like a stretch?"

"Oh, some little time perhaps. I don't know."

"Since I was here last?"

"I haven't been out much."

"And has *Romilly* progressed much better for your being cooped up?"

"I think she has. I'm laying the foundations of her. I shall begin the actual writing presently."

It seemed as if Miss Bengough had forgotten their tussle about the first *Romilly*. She frowned, turned half away, and then quickly turned again.

"Ah! . . . So you've still got that ridiculous idea in your head?"

"If you mean," said Oleron slowly, "that I've discarded the old *Romilly*, and am at work on a new one, you're right. I have still got that idea in my head."

Something uncordial in his tone struck her; but she was a

fighter. His own absurd sensitiveness hardened her. She gave a "Pshaw!" of impatience.

"Where is the old one?" she demanded abruptly.

"Why?" asked Oleron.

"I want to see it. I want to show some of it to you. I want, if you're not wool-gathering entirely, to bring you back to your senses."

This time it was he who turned his back. But when he turned round again he spoke more gently.

"It's no good, Elsie. I'm responsible for the way I go, and you must allow me to go it—even if it should seem wrong to you. Believe me, I am giving thought to it. . . . The manuscript? I was on the point of burning it, but I didn't. It's in that window-seat, if you must see it."

Miss Bengough crossed quickly to the window-seat, and lifted the lid. Suddenly she gave a little exclamation, and put the back of her hand to her mouth. She spoke over her shoulder:

"You ought to knock those nails in, Paul," she said.

He strode to her side.

"What? What is it? What's the matter?" he asked. "I did knock them in—or, rather, pulled them out."

"You left enough to scratch with," she replied, showing her hand. From the upper wrist to the knuckle of the little finger a welling red wound showed.

"Good gracious!" Oleron ejaculated. . . . "Here, come to the bathroom and bathe it quickly——"

He hurried her to the bathroom, turned on warm water, and bathed and cleansed the bad gash. Then, still holding the hand, he turned cold water on it, uttering broken phrases of astonishment and concern.

"Good Lord, how did that happen! As far as I knew I'd . . . is this water too cold? Does that hurt? I can't imagine how on earth . . . there; that'll do——"

"No—one moment longer—I can bear it," she murmured, her eyes closed. . . .

Presently he led her back to the sitting room and bound the hand in one of his handkerchiefs; but his face did not lose its expression of perplexity. He had spent half a day in opening and making serviceable the three window-boxes, and he could not conceive how he had come to leave an inch and a half of rusty nail standing in the wood. He himself had opened the lids of each of them a dozen times and had not noticed any nail; but there it was. . . .

"It shall come out now, at all events," he muttered, as he went for a pair of pincers. And he made no mistake about it that time.

Elsie Bengough had sunk into a chair, and her face was rather white; but in her hand was the manuscript of *Romilly*. She had not finished with *Romilly* yet. Presently she returned to the charge.

"Oh, Paul, it will be the greatest mistake you ever, *ever* made if you do not publish this!" she said.

He hung his head, genuinely distressed. He couldn't get that incident of the nail out of his head, and *Romilly* occupied a second place in his thoughts for the moment. But still she insisted; and when presently he spoke it was almost as if he asked her pardon for something.

"What can I say, Elsie? I can only hope that when you see the new version, you'll see how right I am. And if in spite of all you *don't* like her, well . . ." he made a hopeless gesture. "Don't you see that I *must* be guided by my own lights?"

She was silent.

"Come, Elsie," he said gently. "We've got along well so far; don't let us split on this."

The last words had hardly passed his lips before he regretted them. She had been nursing her injured hand, with her eyes once more closed; but her lips and lids quivered simultaneously. Her voice shook as she spoke.

"I can't help saying it, Paul, but you are so greatly changed."

"Hush, Elsie," he murmured soothingly; "you've had a shock; rest for a while. How could I change?"

"I don't know, but you are. You've not been yourself ever since you came here. I wish you'd never seen the place. It's stopped your work, it's making you into a person I hardly know, and it's made me horribly anxious about you. . . . Oh, how my hand is beginning to throb!"

"Poor child!" he murmured. "Will you let me take you to a doctor and have it properly dressed?"

"No—I shall be all right presently—I'll keep it raised——"

She put her elbow on the back of her chair, and the bandaged hand rested lightly on his shoulder.

At that touch an entirely new anxiety stirred suddenly within him. Hundreds of times previously, on their jaunts and excursions, she had slipped her hand within his arm as she might have slipped it into the arm of a brother, and he had accepted the little affectionate gesture as a brother might have accepted it. But now, for the first time, there rushed into his mind a hundred startling questions. Her eyes were still closed, and her head had fallen pathetically back; and there was a lost and ineffable smile on her parted lips. The truth broke in upon him. Good God! . . . And he had never divined it!

And stranger than all was that, now that he did see that she was lost in love of him, there came to him, not sorrow and humility and abasement, but something else that he struggled in vain against—something entirely strange and new, that, had he analyzed it, he would have found to be petulance and irritation and resentment and ungentleness. The sudden selfish prompting mastered him before he was aware. He all but gave it words. What was she doing there at all? Why was she not getting on with her own work? Why was she here interfering with his? Who had given her this guardianship over him that lately she had put forward so assertively? "Changed?" It was she, not himself, who had changed. . . .

But by the time she had opened her eyes again he had overcome his resentment sufficiently to speak gently, albeit with reserve.

"I wish you would let me take you to a doctor."

She rose.

"No, thank you, Paul," she said. "I'll go now. If I need a dressing I'll get one; take the other hand, please. Good-bye——"

He did not attempt to detain her. He walked with her to the foot of the stairs. Halfway along the narrow alley she turned.

"It would be a long way to come if you happened not to be in," she said. "I'll send you a postcard the next time."

At the gate she turned again.

"Leave here, Paul," she said, with a mournful look. "Everything's wrong with this house."

Then she was gone.

Oleron returned to his room. He crossed straight to the window-box. He opened the lid and stood long looking at it. Then he closed it again and turned away.

"That's rather frightening," he muttered. "It's simply not possible that I should not have removed that nail. . . ."

VI

Oleron knew very well what Elsie had meant when she had said that her next visit would be preceded by a postcard. She, too, had realized that at last, at last he knew—knew, and didn't want her. It gave him a miserable, pitiful pang, therefore, when she came again within a week, knocking at the door unannounced. She spoke from the landing; she did not intend to stay, she said; and he had to press her before she would so much as enter.

Her excuse for calling was that she had heard of an inquiry for short stories that he might be wise to follow up. He thanked her. Then, her business over, she seemed anxious to get away again. Oleron did not seek to detain her; even he saw through the pretext of the stories; and he accompanied her down the stairs.

But Elsie Bengough had no luck whatever in that house. A second accident befell her. Halfway down the staircase there was the sharp sound of splintering wood, and she checked a loud cry. Oleron knew the woodwork to be old, but he himself had ascended and descended frequently enough without mishap. . . .

Elsie had put her foot through one of the stairs.

He sprang to her side in alarm.

"Oh, I say! My poor girl!"

She laughed hysterically.

"It's my weight—I know I'm getting fat——"

"Keep still—let me clear these splinters away," he muttered between his teeth.

She continued to laugh and sob that it was her weight—she was getting fat——

He thrust downward at the broken boards. The extrication was no easy matter, and her torn boot showed him how badly the foot and ankle within it must be abraded.

"Good God—good God!" he muttered over and over again.

"I shall be too heavy for anything soon," she sobbed and laughed.

But she refused to reascend and to examine her hurt.

"No, let me go quickly—let me go quickly," she repeated.

"But it's a frightful gash!"

"No—not so bad—let me get away quickly—I'm—I'm not wanted."

At her words, that she was not wanted, his head dropped as if she had given him a buffet.

"Elsie!" he choked, brokenly and shocked.

But she too made a quick gesture, as if she put something violently aside.

"Oh, Paul, not *that*—not *you*—of course I do mean that too in a sense—oh, you know what I mean! . . . But if the other can't be, spare me this now! I—I wouldn't have come, but—but oh, I did, I *did* try to keep away!"

It was intolerable, heartbreaking; but what could he do—what could he say? He did not love her. . . .

"Let me go—I'm not wanted—let me take away what's left of me——"

"Dear Elsie—you are very dear to me——"

But again she made the gesture, as of putting something violently aside.

"No, not that—not anything less—don't offer me anything less—leave me a little pride——"

"Let me get my hat and coat—let me take you to a doctor," he muttered.

But she refused. She refused even the support of his arm. She gave another unsteady laugh.

"I'm sorry I broke your stairs, Paul. . . . You will go and see about the short stories, won't you?"

He groaned.

"Then if you won't see a doctor, will you go across the square and let Mrs. Barrett look at you? Look, there's Barrett passing now——"

The long-nosed Barrett was looking curiously down the alley, but as Oleron was about to call him he made off without a word. Elsie seemed anxious for nothing so much as to be clear of the place, and finally promised to go straight to a doctor, but insisted on going alone.

"Good-bye," she said.

And Oleron watched her until she was past the hatchet-like "To Let" boards, as if he feared that even they might fall upon her and maim her.

That night Oleron did not dine. He had far too much on his mind. He walked from room to room of his flat, as if he could have walked away from Elsie Bengough's haunting cry that still rang in his ears. "I'm not wanted—don't offer me anything less —let me take away what's left of me——"

Oh, if he could only have persuaded himself that he loved her!

He walked until twilight fell, then, without lighting candles, he stirred up the fire and flung himself into a chair.

Poor, poor Elsie! . . .

But even while his heart ached for her, it was out of the question. If only he had known! If only he had used common observation! But those walks, those sisterly takings of the arm —what a fool he had been! . . . Well, it was too late now. It was she, not he, who must now act—act by keeping away. He would help her all he could. He himself would not sit in her presence. If she came, he would hurry her out again as fast as he could. . . . Poor, poor Elsie!

His room grew dark; the fire burned dead; and he continued

to sit, wincing from time to time as a fresh tortured phrase rang again in his ears.

Then suddenly, he knew not why, he found himself anxious for her in a new sense—uneasy about her personal safety. A horrible fancy that even then she might be looking over an embankment down into dark water, that she might even now be glancing up at the hook on the door, took him. Women had been known to do those things. . . . Then there would be an inquest, and he himself would be called upon to identify her, and would be asked how she had come by an ill-healed wound on the hand and a bad abrasion of the ankle. Barrett would say that he had seen her leaving his house. . . .

Then he recognized that his thoughts were morbid. By an effort of will he put them aside, and sat for a while listening to the faint creakings and tickings and rappings within his paneling. . . .

If only he could have married her! . . . But he couldn't. Her face had risen before him again as he had seen it on the stairs, drawn with pain and ugly and swollen with tears. Ugly—yes, positively blubbered; if tears were women's weapons, as they were said to be, such tears were weapons turning against themselves . . . suicide again. . . .

Then all at once he found himself attentively considering her two accidents.

Extraordinary they had been, both of them. He *could not* have left that old nail standing in the wood; why, he had fetched tools specially from the kitchen; and he was convinced that that step that had broken beneath her weight had been as sound as the others. It was inexplicable. If these things could happen, anything could happen. There was not a beam nor a jamb in the place that might not fall without warning, not a plank that might not crash inward, not a nail that might not become a dagger. The whole place was full of life even now; as he sat there in the dark he heard its crowds of noises as if the house had been one great microphone. . . .

Only half conscious that he did so, he had been sitting for some time identifying these noises, attributing to each crack or creak or knock its material cause; but there was one noise which, again not fully conscious of the omission, he had not sought to account for. It had last come some minutes ago; it came again now—a sort of soft sweeping rustle that seemed to hold an almost inaudible minute crackling. For half a minute or so it had Oleron's attention; then his heavy thoughts were of Elsie Bengough again.

He was nearer to loving her in that moment than he had ever been. He thought how to some men their loved ones were but the dearer for those poor mortal blemishes that tell us we are but sojourners on earth, with a common fate not far distant that makes it hardly worth while to do anything but love for the time remaining. Strangling sobs, blearing tears, bodies buffeted by sickness, hearts and minds callous and hard with the rubs of the world—how little love there would be were these things a barrier to love! In that sense he did love Elsie Bengough. What her happiness had never moved in him her sorrow almost woke. . . .

Suddenly his meditation went. His ear had once more become conscious of that soft and repeated noise—the long sweep with the almost inaudible crackle in it. Again and again it came, with a curious insistence, and urgency. It quickened a little as he became increasingly attentive . . . it seemed to Oleron that it grew louder. . . .

All at once he started bolt upright in his chair, tense and listening. The silky rustle came again; he was trying to attach it to something. . . .

The next moment he had leapt to his feet, unnerved and terrified. His chair hung poised for a moment, and then went over, setting the fire-irons clattering as it fell. There was only one noise in the world like that which had caused him to spring thus to his feet. . . .

The next time it came Oleron felt behind him at the empty air with his hand, and backed slowly until he found himself against the wall.

"God in Heaven!" The ejaculation broke from Oleron's lips. The sound had ceased.

The next moment he had given a high cry.

"What is it? What's there? *Who's* there?"

A sound of scuttling caused his knees to bend under him for a moment; but that, he knew, was a mouse. That was not something that his stomach turned sick and his mind reeled to entertain. That other sound, the like of which was not in the world, had now entirely ceased; and again he called. . . .

He called and continued to call; and then another terror, a terror of the sound of his own voice, seized him. He did not dare to call again. His shaking hand went to his pocket for a match, but found none. He thought there might be matches on the mantelpiece——

He worked his way to the mantelpiece round a little recess, without for a moment leaving the wall. Then his hand encountered the mantelpiece, and groped along it. A box of matches fell to the hearth. He could just see them in the firelight, but his hand could not pick them up until he had cornered them inside the fender.

Then he rose and struck a light.

The room was as usual. He struck a second match. A candle stood on the table. He lighted it, and the flame sank for a moment and then burned up clear. Again he looked round.

There was nothing.

There was nothing; but there had been something, and might still be something. Formerly, Oleron had smiled at the fantastic thought that, by a merging and interplay of identities between himself and his beautiful room, he might be preparing a ghost for the future; it had not occurred to him *that there might have been a similar merging and coalescence in the past*. Yet with this staggering impossibility he was now face to face. Something did persist in the house; it had a tenant other than himself; and that tenant, whatsoever or whosoever, had appalled Oleron's soul by producing the sound of a woman brushing her hair.

VII

Without quite knowing how he came to be there Oleron found himself striding over the loose board he had temporarily placed on the step broken by Miss Bengough. He was hatless and descending the stairs. Not until later did there return to him a hazy memory that he had left the candle burning on the table, had opened the door no wider than was necessary to allow the passage of his body, and had sidled out, closing the door softly behind him. At the foot of the stairs another shock awaited him. Something dashed with a flurry up from the disused cellars and disappeared out of the door. It was only a cat, but Oleron gave a childish sob.

He passed out of the gate, and stood for a moment under the "To Let" boards, plucking foolishly at his lip and looking up at the glimmer of light behind one of his red blinds. Then, still looking over his shoulder, he moved stumblingly up the square. There was a small public-house round the corner; Oleron had never entered it; but he entered it now, and put down a shilling that missed the counter by inches.

"B—b—bran—brandy," he said, and then stooped to look for the shilling.

He had the little sawdusted bar to himself; what company there was—carters and laborers and the small tradesmen of the neighborhood—was gathered in the farther compartment, beyond the space where the white-haired landlady moved among her taps and bottles. Oleron sat down on a hardwood settee with a perforated seat, drank half his brandy, and then, thinking he might as well drink it as spill it, finished it.

Then he fell to wondering which of the men whose voices he heard across the public-house would undertake the removal of his effects on the morrow.

In the meantime he ordered more brandy.

For he did not intend to go back to that room where he had left the candle burning. Oh no! He couldn't have faced even the entry and the staircase with the broken step—certainly not that pith-white, fascinating room. He would go back for the present to his old arrangement, of workroom and separate sleeping-quarters; he would go to his old landlady at once—presently—when he had finished his brandy—and see if she could put him up for the night. His glass was empty now. . . .

He rose, had it refilled, and sat down again.

And if anybody asked his reason for removing again? Oh, he had reason enough—reason enough! Nails that put themselves back into wood again and gashed people's hands, steps that broke when you trod on them, and women who came into a man's place and brushed their hair in the dark, were reasons enough! He was querulous and injured about it all. He had taken the place for himself, not for invisible women to brush their hair in; that lawyer fellow in Lincoln's Inn should be told so, too, before many hours were out; it was outrageous, letting people in for agreements like that!

A cut-glass partition divided the compartment where Oleron sat from the space where the white-haired landlady moved; but it stopped seven or eight inches above the level of the counter. There was no partition at the further bar. Presently Oleron, raising his eyes, saw that faces were watching him through the aperture. The faces disappeared when he looked at them.

He moved to a corner where he could not be seen from the other bar; but this brought him into line with the white-haired landlady.

She knew him by sight—had doubtless seen him passing and repassing; and presently she made a remark on the weather. Oleron did not know what he replied, but it sufficed to call forth the further remark that the winter had been a bad one for influenza, but that the spring weather seemed to be coming at last. . . . Even this slight contact with the commonplace steadied Oleron a little; an idle, nascent wonder whether the landlady brushed her hair every night, and, if so, whether it gave out those little electric cracklings, was shut down with a snap; and Oleron was better. . . .

With his next glass of brandy he was all for going back to his flat. Not go back? Indeed, he would go back! They should very soon see whether he was to be turned out of his place like that! He began to wonder why he was doing the rather unusual thing he was doing at that moment, unusual for him—sitting hatless, drinking brandy, in a public-house. Suppose he were to tell the white-haired landlady all about it—to tell her that a caller had scratched her hand on a nail, had later had the bad luck to put her foot through a rotten stair, and that he himself, in an old house full of squeaks and creaks and whispers, had heard a minute noise and had bolted from it in fright—what would she think of him? That he was mad, of course. . . . Pshaw! The real truth of the matter was that he hadn't been doing enough work to occupy him. He had been dreaming his days away, filling his head with a lot of moonshine about a new *Romilly* (as if the old one was not good enough), and now he was surprised that the devil should enter an empty head!

Yes, he would go back. He would take a walk in the air first—he hadn't walked enough lately—and then he would take himself in hand, settle the hash of that sixteenth chapter of *Romilly* (fancy, he had actually been fool enough to think of destroying fifteen chapters!) and thenceforward he would remember that he had obligations to his fellow men and work to do in the world. There was the matter in a nutshell.

He finished his brandy and went out.

He had walked for some time before any other bearing of the matter than that on himself occurred to him. At first, the fresh air had increased the heady effect of the brandy he had drunk; but afterwards his mind grew clearer than it had been since morning. And the clearer it grew, the less final did his boastful self-assurances become, and the firmer his conviction that, when all explanations had been made, there remained something that could not be explained. His hysteria of an hour before had passed; he grew steadily calmer; but the disquieting conviction remained. A deep fear took possession of him. It was a fear for Elsie.

For something in his place was inimical to her safety. Of themselves, her two accidents might not have persuaded him of this; but she herself had said it. *"I'm not wanted here. . . ."* And she had declared that there was something wrong with the place. She had seen it before he had. Well and good. One thing stood out clearly: namely, that if this was so, she must be kept away for quite another reason than that which had so confounded and humiliated Oleron. Luckily she had expressed her intention of staying away; she must be held to that intention. He must see to it.

And he must see to it all the more that he now saw his first example, never to set foot in the place again, was absurd. People did not do that kind of thing. With Elsie made secure, he could not with any respect to himself suffer himself to be turned out by a shadow, nor even by a danger merely because it was a danger. He had to live somewhere, and he would live there. He must return.

He mastered the faint chill of fear that came with the decision, and turned in his walk abruptly. Should fear grow on him again he would, perhaps, take one more glass of brandy. . . .

But by the time he reached the short street that led to the square he was too late for more brandy. The little public-house was still lighted, but closed, and one or two men were standing talking on the curb. Oleron noticed that a sudden silence fell on them as he passed, and he noticed further that the long-nosed Barrett, whom he passed a little lower down, did not return his good-night. He turned in at the broken gate, hesitated merely an instant in the alley, and then mounted his stairs again.

Only an inch of candle remained in the Sheffield stick, and Oleron did not light another one. Deliberately he forced himself to take it up and to make the tour of his five rooms before retiring. It was as he returned from the kitchen across his little hall that he noticed that a letter lay on the floor. He carried it into his sitting room, and glanced at the envelope before opening it.

It was unstamped, and had been put into the door by hand. Its handwriting was clumsy, and it ran from beginning to end without comma or period. Oleron read the first line, turned to the signature, and then finished the letter.

It was from the man Barrett, and it informed Oleron that he, Barrett, would be obliged if Mr. Oleron would make other arrangements for the preparing of his breakfasts and the cleaning out of his place. The sting lay in the tail, that is to say, the postscript. This consisted of a text of Scripture. It embodied an allusion that could only be to Elsie Bengough. . . .

A seldom-seen frown had cut deeply into Oleron's brow. So! That was it! Very well; they would see about that on the morrow. . . . For the rest, this seemed merely another reason why Elsie should keep away. . . .

Then his suppressed rage broke out. . . .

The foul-minded lot! The devil himself could not have given a leer at anything that had ever passed between Paul Oleron and Elsie Bengough, yet this nosing rascal must be prying and talking! . . .

Oleron crumpled the paper up, held it in the candle flame, and then ground the ashes under his heel.

One useful purpose, however, the letter had served: it had created in Oleron a wrathful blaze that effectually banished pale shadows. Nevertheless, one other puzzling circumstance was to close the day. As he undressed, he chanced to glance at his bed. The coverlets bore an impress as if somebody had lain on them. Oleron could not remember that he himself had lain down during the day—off-handed, he would have said that certainly he had not; but after all he could not be positive. His indignation for Elsie, acting possibly with the residue of the brandy in him, excluded all other considerations; and he put out his candle, lay down, and passed immediately into a deep and dreamless sleep, which, in the absence of Mrs. Barrett's morning call, lasted almost once round the clock.

VIII

To the man who pays heed to that voice within him which warns him that twilight and danger are settling over his soul, terror is apt to appear an absolute thing, against which his heart must be safeguarded in a twink unless there is to take place an alteration in the whole range and scale of his nature. Mercifully, he has never far to look for safeguards. Of the immediate and small and common and momentary things of life, of usages and observances and modes and conventions, he builds up fortifications against the powers of darkness. He is even content that, not terror only, but joy also, should for working purposes be placed in the category of the absolute things; and the last treason he will commit will be that breaking down of terms and limits that strikes, not at one man, but at the welfare of the souls of all.

In his own person, Oleron began to commit this treason. He began to commit it by admitting the inexplicable and horrible to an increasing familiarity. He did it insensibly, unconsciously, by a neglect of the things that he now regarded it as an impertinence in Elsie Bengough to have prescribed. Two months before, the words "a haunted house," applied to his lovely bemusing dwelling, would have chilled his marrow; now his scale of sensation becoming depressed, he could ask "Haunted by what?" and remain unconscious that horror, when it can be proved to be relative, by so much loses its proper quality. He was setting aside the landmarks. Mists and confusion had begun to enwrap him.

And he was conscious of nothing so much as of a voracious inquisitiveness. He wanted *to know*. He was resolved to know. Nothing but the knowledge would satisfy him; and craftily he cast about for means whereby he might attain it.

He might have spared his craft. The matter was the easiest imaginable. As in time past he had known, in his writing, moments when his thoughts had seemed to rise of themselves and to embody themselves in words not to be altered afterwards, so now the questions he put himself seemed to be answered even in the moment of their asking. There was exhilaration in the swift, easy processes. He had known no such joy in his own power since the days when his writing had been a daily freshness and a delight to him. It was almost as if the course he must pursue was being dictated to him.

And the first thing he must do, of course, was to define the problem. He defined it in terms of mathematics. Granted that he had not the place to himself; granted that the old house had inexpressibly caught and engaged his spirit; granted that, by virtue of the common denominator of the place, this unknown co-tenant stood in some relation to himself: what next? Clearly, the nature of the other numerator must be ascertained.

And how? Ordinarily this would not have seemed simple, but

to Oleron it was now pellucidly clear. The key, *of course,* lay in his half-written novel—or rather, in both *Romillys,* the old and the proposed new one.

A little while before Oleron would have thought himself mad to have embraced such an opinion; now he accepted the dizzying hypothesis without a quiver.

He began to examine the first and second *Romillys.*

From the moment of his doing so the thing advanced by leaps and bounds. Swiftly he reviewed the history of the *Romilly* of the fifteen chapters. He remembered clearly now that he had found her insufficient on the very first morning on which he had sat down to work in his new place. Other instances of his aversion leaped up to confirm his obscure investigation. There had come the night when he had hardly forborne to throw the whole thing into the fire; and the next morning he had begun the planning of the new *Romilly.* It had been on that morning that Mrs. Barrett, overhearing him humming a brief phrase that the dripping of a tap the night before had suggested, had informed him that he was singing some air he had never in his life heard before, called "The Beckoning Fair One." . . .

The Beckoning Fair One! . . .

With scarcely a pause in thought he continued:

The first *Romilly* having been definitely thrown over, the second had instantly fastened herself upon him, clamoring for birth in his brain. He even fancied now, looking back, that there had been something like passion, hate almost, in the supplanting, and that more than once a stray thought given to his discarded creation had—(it was astonishing how credible Oleron found the almost unthinkable idea)—had offended the supplanter.

Yet that a malignancy almost homicidal should be extended to his fiction's poor mortal prototype. . . .

In spite of his inuring to a scale in which the horrible was now a thing to be fingered and turned this way and that, a "Good God!" broke from Oleron.

This intrusion of the first *Romilly's* prototype into his thought again was a factor that for the moment brought his inquiry into the nature of his problem to a termination; the mere thought of Elsie was fatal to anything abstract. For another thing, he could not yet think of that letter of Barrett's, nor of a little scene that had followed it, without a mounting of color and a quick contraction of the brow. For, wisely or not, he had had that argument out at once. Striding across the square on the following morning, he had bearded Barrett on his own doorstep. Coming back again a few minutes later, he had been strongly of opinion that he had only made matters worse. The man had been vagueness itself. He had not been able to be either challenged or browbeaten into anything more definite than a muttered farrago in which the words "Certain things . . . Mrs. Barrett . . . respectable house . . . if the cap fits . . . proceedings that shall be nameless," had been constantly repeated.

"Not that I make any charge——" he had concluded.

"Charge!" Oleron had cried.

"I 'ave my idears of things, as I don't doubt you 'ave yours——"

"Ideas—mine!" Oleron had cried wrathfully, immediately dropping his voice as heads had appeared at windows of the square. "Look you here, my man; you've an unwholesome mind, which probably you can't help, but a tongue which you can help, and shall! If there is a breath of this repeated . . ."

"I'll not be talked to on my own doorstep like this by anybody . . ." Barrett had blustered. . . .

"You shall, and I'm doing it . . ."

"Don't you forget there's a Gawd above all, Who 'as said . . ."

"You're a low scandalmonger! . . ."

And so forth, continuing badly what was already badly begun. Oleron had returned wrathfully to his own house and thenceforward, looking out of his windows, had seen Barrett's face at odd times, lifting blinds or peering round curtains, as if he sought to put himself in possession of Heaven knew what evidence, in case it should be required of him.

The unfortunate occurrence made certain minor differences in Oleron's domestic arrangements. Barrett's tongue, he gathered, had already been busy; he was looked at askance by the dwellers of the square; and he judged it better, until he should be able to obtain other help, to make his purchases of provisions a little farther afield rather than at the small shops of the immediate neighborhood. For the rest, housekeeping was no new thing to him, and he would resume his old bachelor habits. . . .

Besides, he was deep in certain rather abstruse investigations, in which it was better that he should not be disturbed. He was looking out of his window one midday rather tired, not very well, and glad that it was not very likely he would have to stir out of doors, when he saw Elsie Bengough crossing the square towards his house. The weather had broken; it was a raw and gusty day; and she had to force her way against the wind that set her ample skirts bellying about her opulent figure and her veil spinning and streaming behind her.

Oleron acted swiftly and instinctively. Seizing his hat, he sprang to the door and descended the stairs at a run. A sort of panic had seized him. She must be prevented from setting foot in the place. As he ran along the alley he was conscious that his eyes went up to the eaves as if something drew them. He did not know that a slate might not accidentally fall. . . .

He met her at the gate, and spoke with curious volubleness.

"This is really too bad, Elsie! Just as I'm urgently called away! I'm afraid it can't be helped though, and that you'll have to think me an inhospitable beast." He poured it out just as it came into his head.

She asked if he was going to town.

"Yes, yes—to town," he replied. "I've got to call on—on Chambers. You know Chambers, don't you? No, I remember you don't; a big man you once saw me with. . . . I ought to have gone yesterday, and"—this he felt to be a brilliant effort—"and he's going out of town this afternoon. To Brighton. I had a letter from him this morning."

He took her arm and led her up the square. She had to remind him that his way to town lay in the other direction.

"Of course—how stupid of me!" he said, with a little loud laugh. "I'm so used to going the other way with you—of course;

it's the other way to the bus. Will you come along with me? I am so awfully sorry it's happened like this. . . ."

They took the street to the bus terminus.

This time Elsie bore no signs of having gone through interior struggles. If she detected anything unusual in his manner she made no comment, and he, seeing her calm, began to talk less recklessly through silences. By the time they reached the bus terminus, nobody, seeing the pallid-faced man without an overcoat and the large ample-skirted girl at his side, would have supposed that one of them was ready to sink on his knees for thankfulness that he had, as he believed, saved the other from a wildly unthinkable danger.

They mounted to the top of the bus, Oleron protesting that he should not miss his overcoat, and that he found the day, if anything, rather oppressively hot. They sat down on a front seat.

Now that this meeting was forced upon him, he had something else to say that would make demands upon his tact. It had been on his mind for some time, and was, indeed, peculiarly difficult to put. He revolved it for some minutes, and then, remembering the success of his story of a sudden call to town, cut the knot of his difficulty with another lie.

"I'm thinking of going away for a little while, Elsie," he said.

She merely said: "Oh?"

"Somewhere for a change. I need a change. I think I shall go tomorrow, or the day after. Yes, tomorrow, I think."

"Yes," she replied.

"I don't quite know how long I shall be," he continued. "I shall have to let you know when I am back."

"Yes, let me know," she replied in an even tone.

The tone was, for her, suspiciously even. He was a little uneasy.

"You don't ask me where I'm going," he said, with a little cumbrous effort to rally her.

She was looking straight before her, past the bus driver.

"I know," she said.

He was startled. "How, you know?"

"You're not going anywhere," she replied.

He found not a word to say. It was a minute or so before she continued, in the same controlled voice she had employed from the start.

"You're not going anywhere. You weren't going out this morning. You only came out because I appeared; don't behave as if we were strangers, Paul."

A flush of pink had mounted to his cheeks. He noticed that the wind had given her the pink of early rhubarb. Still he found nothing to say.

"Of course, you ought to go away," she continued. "I don't know whether you look at yourself often in the glass, but you're rather noticeable. Several people have turned to look at you this morning. So, of course, you ought to go away. But you won't, and I know why."

He shivered, coughed a little, and then broke silence.

"Then if you know, there's no use in continuing this discussion," he said curtly.

"Not for me, perhaps, but there is for you," she replied. "Shall I tell you what I know?"

"No," he said in a voice slightly raised.

"No?" she asked, her round eyes earnestly on him.

"No."

Again he was getting out of patience with her; again he was conscious of the strain. Her devotion and fidelity and love plagued him; she was only humiliating both herself and him. It would have been bad enough had he ever, by word or deed, given her cause for thus fastening herself on him ... but there; that was the worst of that kind of life for a woman. Women such as she, business women, in and out of offices all the time, always, whether they realized it or not, made comradship a cover for something else. They accepted the unconventional status, came and went freely, as men did, were honestly taken by men at their own valuation—and then it turned out to be the other thing after all, and they went and fell in love. No wonder there was gossip in shops and squares and public-houses! In a sense the gossipers were in the right of it. Independent, yet not efficient; with some of womanhood's graces foregone, and yet with all the woman's hunger and need; half sophisticated yet not wise; Oleron was tired of it all. . . .

And it was time he told her so.

"I suppose," he said tremblingly, looking down between his knees, "I suppose the real trouble is in the life women who earn their own living are obliged to lead."

He could not tell in what sense she took the lame generality; she merely replied: "I suppose so."

"It can't be helped," he continued, "but you do sacrifice a good deal."

She agreed: a good deal; and then she added after a moment: "What, for instance?"

"You may or may not be gradually attaining a new status, but you're in a false position today."

It was very likely, she said; she hadn't thought of it much in that light——

"And," he continued desperately, "you're bound to suffer. Your most innocent acts are misunderstood; motives you never dreamed of are attributed to you; and in the end it comes to"— he hesitated a moment and then took the plunge—"to the sidelong look and the leer."

She took his meaning with perfect ease. She merely shivered a little as she pronounced the name.

"Barrett?"

His silence told her the rest.

Anything further that was to be said must come from her. It came as the bus stopped at a stage and fresh passengers mounted the stairs.

"You'd better get down here and go back, Paul," she said. "I understand perfectly—perfectly. It isn't Barrett. You'd be able to deal with Barrett. It's merely convenient for you to say it's Barrett. I know what it is . . . but you said I wasn't to tell you that. Very well. But before you go let me tell you why I came up this morning."

In a dull tone he asked her why. Again she looked straight before her as she replied:

"I came to force your hand. Things couldn't go on as they have been going, you know; and now that's all over."

"All over," he repeated stupidly.

"All over. I want you now to consider yourself, as far as I'm concerned, perfectly free. I make only one reservation."

He hardly had the spirit to ask her what that was.

"If *I* merely need *you*," she said, "please don't give that a thought; that's nothing; I shan't come near for that. But," she dropped her voice, "if *you're* in need of *me*, Paul—I shall know if you are, *and you will be*—then I shall come at no matter what cost. You understand that?"

He could only groan.

"So that's understood," she concluded. "And I think that's all. Now go back. I should advise you to walk back, for you're shivering—good-bye——"

She gave him a cold hand, and he descended. He turned on the edge of the curb as the bus started again. For the first time in all the years he had known her she parted from him with no smile and no wave of her long arm.

IX

He stood on the curb plunged in misery, looking after her as long as she remained in sight; but almost instantly with her disappearance he felt the heaviness lift a little from his spirit. She had given him his liberty; true, there was a sense in which he had never parted with it, but now was no time for splitting hairs; he was free to act, and all was clear ahead. Swiftly the sense of lightness grew on him: it became a positive rejoicing in his liberty; and before he was halfway home he had decided what must be done next.

The vicar of the parish in which his dwelling was situated lived within ten minutes of the square. To his house Oleron turned his steps. It was necessary that he should have all the information he could get about this old house with the insurance marks and the sloping "To Let" boards, and the vicar was the person most likely to be able to furnish it. This last preliminary out of the way, and—aha! Oleron chuckled—things might be expected to happen!

But he gained less information than he had hoped for. The house, the vicar said, was old—but there needed no vicar to tell Oleron that; it was reputed (Oleron pricked up his ears) to be haunted—but there were few old houses about which some such rumor did not circulate among the ignorant; and the deplorable lack of Faith of the modern world, the vicar thought, did not tend to dissipate these superstitions. For the rest, his manner was the soothing manner of one who prefers not to make statements without knowing how they will be taken by his hearer. Oleron smiled as he perceived this.

"You may leave my nerves out of the question," he said. "How long has the place been empty?"

"A dozen years, I should say," the vicar replied.

"And the last tenant—did you know him—or her?" Oleron was conscious of a tingling of his nerves as he offered the vicar the alternative of sex.

"Him," said the vicar. "A man. If I remember rightly, his name was Madley; an artist. He was a great recluse; seldom went out of the place, and"—the vicar hesitated and then broke into a little gush of candor—"and since you appear to have come for this information, and since it is better that the truth should be told than that garbled versions should get about, I don't mind saying that this man Madley died there, under somewhat unusual circumstances. It was ascertained at the post-mortem that there was not a particle of food in his stomach, although he was found to be not without money. And his frame was simply worn out. Suicide was spoken of, but you'll agree with me that deliberate starvation is, to say the least, an uncommon form of suicide. An open verdict was returned."

"Ah!" said Oleron. . . . "Does there happen to be any comprehensive history of this parish?"

"No; partial ones only. I myself am not guiltless of having made a number of notes on its purely ecclesiastical history, its registers and so forth, which I shall be happy to show you if you would care to see them; but it is a large parish, I have only one curate, and my leisure, as you will readily understand . . ."

The extent of the parish and the scantiness of the vicar's leisure occupied the remainder of the interview, and Oleron thanked the vicar, took his leave, and walked slowly home.

He walked slowly for a reason, twice turning away from the house within a stone's throw of the gate and taking another turn of twenty minutes or so. He had a very ticklish piece of work now before him; it required the greatest mental concentration; it was nothing less than to bring his mind, if he might, into such a state of unpreoccupation and receptivity that he should see the place as he had seen it on that morning when, his removal accomplished, he had sat down to begin the sixteenth chapter of the first *Romilly*.

For, could he recapture that first impression, he now hoped for far more from it. Formerly, he had carried no end of mental lumber. Before the influence of the place had been able to find him out at all, it had had the inertia of those dreary chapters to overcome. No results had shown. The process had been one of slow saturation, charging, filling up to a brim. But now he was light, unburdened, rid at last both of that *Romilly* and of her prototype. Now for the new unknown, coy, jealous, bewitching Beckoning Fair! . . .

At half-past two of the afternoon he put his key into the Yale lock, entered, and closed the door behind him. . . .

His fantastic attempt was instantly and astonishingly successful. He could have shouted with triumph as he entered the room; it was as if he had *escaped* into it. Once more, as in the days when his writing had had a daily freshness and wonder and promise for him, he was conscious of that new ease and mastery and exhilaration and release. The air of the place seemed to hold more oxygen; as if his own specific gravity had changed, his very tread seemed less ponderable. The flowers in the bowls, the fair proportions of the meadowsweet-colored panels and moldings, the polished floor, and the lofty and faintly starred ceiling, fairly laughed their welcome. Oleron actually laughed back, and spoke aloud.

"Oh, you're pretty, pretty!" he flattered it.

Then he lay down on his couch.

He spent that afternoon as a convalescent who expected a dear visitor might have spent it—in a delicious vacancy, smiling now and then as if in his sleep, and ever lifting drowsy and contented eyes to his alluring surroundings. He lay thus until darkness came, and, with darkness, the nocturnal noises of the old house. . . .

But if he waited for any specific happening, he waited in vain.

He waited similarly in vain on the morrow, maintaining, though with less ease, that sensitized lake-like condition of his mind. Nothing occurred to give it an impression. Whatever it was which he so patiently wooed, it seemed to be both shy and exacting.

Then on the third day he thought he understood. A look of gentle drollery and cunning came into his eyes, and he chuckled.

"Oho, oho! . . . Well, if the wind sits in *that* quarter we must see what else there is to be done. What is there, now? . . . No, I won't send for Elsie; we don't need a wheel to break the butterfly on; we won't go to those lengths, my butterfly. . . ."

He was standing musing, thumbing his lean jaw, looking aslant; suddenly he crossed to his hall, took down his hat, and went out.

"My lady is coquettish, is she? Well, we'll see what a little neglect will do," he chuckled as he went down the stairs.

He sought a railway station, got into a train, and spent the rest of the day in the country. Oh, yes: Oleron thought *he* was the man to deal with Fair Ones who beckoned, and invited, and then took refuge in shyness and hanging back!

He did not return until after eleven that night.

"*Now*, my Fair Beckoner!" he murmured as he walked along the alley and felt in his pocket for his keys. . . .

Inside his flat, he was perfectly composed, perfectly deliberate, exceedingly careful not to give himself away. As if to intimate that he intended to retire immediately, he lighted only a single candle; and as he set out with it on his nightly round he affected to yawn. He went first into his kitchen. There was a full moon, and a lozenge of moonlight, almost peacock-blue by contrast with his candle-flame, lay on the floor. The window was uncurtained, and he could see the reflection of the candle, and, faintly, that of his own face, as he moved about. The door of the powder-closet stood a little ajar, and he closed it before sitting down to remove his boots on the chair with the cushion made of the folded harp-bag. From the kitchen he passed to the bathroom. There, another slant of blue moonlight cut the window-sill and lay across the pipes on the wall. He visited his seldom-used study, and stood for a moment gazing at the silvered roofs across the square. Then, walking straight through his sitting room, his stockinged feet making no noise, he entered his bedroom and put the candle on the chest of drawers. His face all this time wore no expression save that of tiredness. He had never been wilier nor more alert.

His small bedroom fireplace was opposite the chest of drawers on which the mirror stood, and his bed and the window occupied the remaining sides of the room. Oleron drew down his blind, took off his coat, and then stooped to get his slippers from under the bed.

He could have given no reason for the conviction, but that the manifestation that for two days had been withheld was close at hand he never for an instant doubted. Nor, though he could not form the faintest guess of the shape it might take, did he experience fear. Startling or surprising it might be; he was prepared for that; but that was all; his scale of sensation had become depressed. His hand moved this way and that under the bed in search of his slippers. . . .

But for all his caution and method and preparedness, his heart all at once gave a leap and a pause that was almost horrid. His hand had found the slippers, but he was still on his knees; save for this circumstance he would have fallen. The bed was a low one; the groping for the slippers accounted for the turn of his

THE BECKONING FAIR ONE 239

head to one side; and he was careful to keep the attitude until he had partly recovered his self-possession. When presently he rose there was a drop of blood on his lower lip where he had caught at it with his teeth, and his watch had jerked out of the pocket of his waistcoat and was dangling at the end of its short leather guard. . . .

Then, before the watch had ceased its little oscillation, he was himself again.

In the middle of his mantelpiece there stood a picture, a portrait of his grandmother; he placed himself before this picture, so that he could see in the glass of it the steady flame of the candle that burned behind him on the chest of drawers. He could see also in the picture-glass the little glancings of light from the bevels and facets of the objects about the mirror and candle. But he could see more. These twinklings and reflections and re-reflections did not change their position; but there was one gleam that had motion. It was fainter than the rest, and it moved up and down through the air. It was the reflection of the candle on Oleron's black vulcanite comb, and each of its downward movements was accompanied by a silky and crackling rustle.

Oleron, watching what went on in the glass of his grandmother's portrait, continued to play his part. He felt for his dangling watch and began slowly to wind it up. Then, for a moment ceasing to watch, he began to empty his trousers' pockets and to place methodically in a little row on the mantelpiece the pennies and halfpennies he took from them. The sweeping, minutely electric noise filled the whole bedroom, and had Oleron altered his point of observation he could have brought the dim gleam of the moving comb so into position that it would almost have outlined his grandmother's head.

Any other head of which it might have been following the outline was invisible.

Oleron finished the emptying of his pockets; then, under cover of another simulated yawn, not so much summoning his resolution as overmastered by an exorbitant curiosity, he swung suddenly round. That which was being combed was still not to be seen, but the comb did not stop. It had altered its angle a little, and had moved a little to the left. It was passing, in fairly regular sweeps, from a point rather more than five feet from the ground, in a direction roughly vertical, to another point a few inches below the level of the chest of drawers.

Oleron continued to act to admiration. He walked to his little washstand in the corner, poured out water, and began to wash his hands. He removed his waistcoat, and continued his preparations for bed. The combing did not cease, and he stood for a moment in thought. Again his eyes twinkled. The next was very cunning——

"Hm! . . . *I think I'll read for a quarter of an hour,*" he said aloud. . . .

He passed out of the room.

He was away a couple of minutes; when he returned again the room was suddenly quiet. He glanced at the chest of drawers; the comb lay still, between the collar he had removed and a pair of gloves. Without hesitation Oleron put out his hand and picked it up. It was an ordinary eighteen-penny comb, taken from a card in a chemist's shop, of a substance of a definite specific gravity, and no more capable of rebellion against the Laws by which it existed than are the worlds that keep their orbits through the void. Oleron put it down again; then he glanced at the bundle of papers he held in his hand. What he had gone to fetch had been the fifteen chapters of the original *Romilly*.

"Hm!" he muttered as he threw the manuscript into a chair. . . . "As I thought. . . . She's just blindly, ragingly, murderously jealous."

. . . . .

On the night after that, and on the following night, and for many nights and days, so many that he began to be uncertain about the count of them, Oleron, courting, cajoling, neglecting, threatening, beseeching, eaten out with unappeased curiosity and regardless that his life was becoming one consuming passion and desire, continued his search for the unknown co-numerator of his abode.

X

As time went on, it came to pass that few except the postman mounted Oleron's stairs; and since men who do not write letters receive few, even the postman's tread became so infrequent that it was not heard more than once or twice a week. There came a letter from Oleron's publishers, asking when they might expect to receive the manuscript of his new book; he delayed for some days to answer it, and finally forgot it. A second letter came, which also he failed to answer. He received no third.

The weather grew bright and warm. The privet bushes among the chopper-like notice-boards flowered, and in the streets where Oleron did his shopping the baskets of flower-women lined the curbs. Oleron purchased flowers daily; his room clamored for flowers, fresh and continually renewed; and Oleron did not stint its demands. Nevertheless, the necessity for going out to buy them began to irk him more and more, and it was with a greater and ever greater sense of relief that he returned home again. He began to be conscious that again his scale of sensation had suffered a subtle change—a change that was not restoration to its former capacity, but an extension and enlarging that once more included terror. It admitted it in an entirely new form. *Lux orco, tenebræ Jovi.* The name of this terror was agoraphobia. Oleron had begun to dread air and space and the horror that might pounce upon the unguarded back.

Presently he so contrived it that his food and flowers were delivered daily at his door. He rubbed his hands when he had hit upon this expedient. That was better! Now he could please himself whether he went out or not. . . .

Quickly he was confirmed in his choice. It became his pleasure to remain immured.

But he was not happy—or, if he was, his happiness took an extraordinary turn. He fretted discontentedly, could sometimes have wept for mere weakness and misery; and yet he was dimly conscious that he would not have exchanged his sadness for all the noisy mirth of the world outside. And speaking of noise: noise, much noise, now caused him the acutest discomfort. It was hardly more to be endured than that new-born fear that kept him, on the increasingly rare occasions when he did go out, sidling close to walls and feeling friendly railings with his hand. He moved from room to room softly and in slippers, and sometimes stood for many seconds closing a door so gently that not a sound broke the stillness that was in itself a delight. Sunday now became an intolerable day to him, for, since the coming of the fine weather, there had begun to assemble in the square under his windows each Sunday morning certain members of the sect to which the long-nosed Barrett adhered. These came with a great drum and large brass-bellied instruments; men and women uplifted anguished voices, struggling with their God; and Barrett himself, with upraised face and closed eyes and working brows, prayed that the sound of his voice might penetrate the ears of all unbelievers—as it certainly did Oleron's. One day, in the middle of one of these rhapsodies, Oleron sprang to his blind and pulled it down, and heard, as he did so, his own name made the object of a fresh torrent of outpouring.

And sometimes, but not as expecting a reply, Oleron stood still and called softly. Once or twice he called "Romilly!" and then waited; but more often his whispering did not take the shape of a name.

There was one spot in particular of his abode that he began to haunt with increasing persistency. This was just within the opening of his bedroom door. He had discovered one day that by opening every door in his place (always excepting the outer one, which he only opened unwillingly) and by placing himself on this particular spot, he could actually see to a greater or less extent into each of his five rooms without changing his position. He could see the whole of his sitting room, all of his bedroom except the part hidden by the open door, and glimpses of his kitchen, bathroom, and of his rarely used study. He was often in this place, breathless and with his finger on his lip. One day, as he stood there, he suddenly found himself wondering whether this Madley, of whom the vicar had spoken, had ever discovered the strategic importance of the bedroom entry.

Light, moreover, now caused him greater disquietude than did darkness. Direct sunlight, of which as the sun passed daily round the house, each of his rooms had now its share, was like a flame in his brain; and even diffused light was a dull and numbing ache. He began, at successive hours of the day, one after another, to lower his crimson blinds. He made short and daring excursions in order to do this; but he was ever careful to leave his retreat open, in case he should have sudden need of it. Presently this lowering of the blinds had become a daily methodical exercise, and his rooms, when he had been his round, had the blood-red half-light of a photographer's darkroom.

One day, as he drew down the blind of his little study and backed in good order out of the room again, he broke into a soft laugh.

"*That* bilks Mr. Barrett!" he said; and the baffling of Barrett continued to afford him mirth for an hour.

But on another day, soon after, he had a fright that left him trembling also for an hour. He had seized the cord to darken the window over the seat in which he had found the harp-bag, and was standing with his back well protected in the embrasure, when he thought he saw the tail of a black-and-white check skirt disappear round the corner of the house. He could not be sure—had he run to the window of the other wall, which was blinded, the skirt must have been already past—but he was *almost* sure that it was Elsie. He listened in an agony of suspense for her tread on the stairs. . . .

But no tread came, and after three or four minutes he drew a long breath of relief.

"By Jove, but that would have compromised me horribly!" he muttered. . . .

And he continued to mutter from time to time: "Horribly compromising . . . *no* woman would stand that . . . not *any* kind of woman . . . oh, compromising in the extreme!"

Yet he was not happy. He could not have assigned the cause of the fits of quiet weeping which took him sometimes; they came and went, like the fitful illumination of the clouds that traveled over the square; and perhaps, after all, if he was not happy, he was not unhappy. Before he could be unhappy something must have been withdrawn, and nothing had been granted. He was waiting for that granting, in that flower-laden, frightfully enticing apartment of his, with the pith-white walls tinged and subdued by the crimson blinds to a blood-like gloom.

He paid no heed to it that his stock of money was running perilously low, nor that he had ceased to work. Ceased to work? He had not ceased to work. They knew very little about it who supposed that Oleron had ceased to work! He was in truth only now beginning to work. He was preparing such a work . . . such a work . . . such a Mistress was a-making in the gestation of his Art . . . let him but get this period of probation and poignant waiting over and men should see. . . . How *should* men know her, this Fair One of Oleron's, until Oleron himself knew her? Lovely radiant creations are not thrown off like How-d'ye-do's. The men to whom it is committed to father them must weep wretched tears, as Oleron did, must swell with vain presumptuous hopes, as Oleron did, must pursue, as Oleron pursued, the capricious, fair, mocking, slippery, eager Spirit that, ever eluding, ever sees to it that the chase does not slacken. Let Oleron but hunt this Huntress a little longer . . . he would have her sparkling and panting in his arms yet. . . . Oh, no: they were very far from the truth who supposed that Oleron had ceased to work!

And if all else was falling away from Oleron, gladly he was letting it go. So do we all when our Fair Ones beckon. Quite at the beginning we wink, and promise ourselves that we will put Her Ladyship through her paces, neglect her for a day, turn her own jealous wiles against her, flout and ignore her when she comes wheedling; perhaps there lurks within us all the time a heartless sprite who is never fooled; but in the end all falls away. She beckons, beckons, and all goes. . . .

And so Oleron kept his strategic post within the frame of his bedroom door, and watched, and waited, and smiled, with his finger on his lips. . . . It was his duteous service, his worship, his troth-plighting, all that he had ever known of Love. And when he found himself, as he now and then did, hating the dead man Madley, and wishing that he had never lived, he felt that that, too, was an acceptable service. . . .

But, as he thus prepared himself, as it were, for a Marriage, and moped and chafed more and more that the Bride made no sign, he made a discovery that he ought to have made weeks before.

It was through a thought of the dead Madley that he made it. Since that night when he had thought in his greenness that a little studied neglect would bring the lovely Beckoner to her knees, and had made use of her own jealousy to banish her, he had not set eyes on those fifteen discarded chapters of *Romilly*. He had thrown them back into the window seat, forgotten their very existence. But his own jealousy of Madley put him in mind of hers, of her jilted rival of flesh and blood, and he remembered them. . . . Fool that he had been! Had he, then, expected his Desire to manifest herself while there still existed the evidence of his divided allegiance? What, and she with a passion so fierce and centered that it had not hesitated at the destruction, twice attempted, of her rival? Fool that he had been! . . .

But if *that* was all the pledge and sacrifice she required she should have it—ah, yes, and quickly!

He took the manuscript from the window-seat, and brought it to the fire.

He kept his fire always burning now; the warmth brought out the last vestige of odor of the flowers with which his room was banked. He did not know what time it was; long since he had allowed his clock to run down—it had seemed a foolish measurer of time in regard to the stupendous things that were happening to Oleron; but he knew it was late. He took the *Romilly* manuscript and knelt before the fire.

But he had not finished removing the fastening that held the sheets together before he suddenly gave a start, turned his head over his shoulder, and listened intently. The sound he had heard had not been loud—it had been, indeed, no more than a tap, twice or thrice repeated—but it had filled Oleron with alarm. His face grew dark as it came again.

He heard a voice outside on his landing.

"Paul! . . . Paul! . . ."

It was Elsie's voice.

"Paul! . . . I know you're in . . . I want to see you. . . ."

He cursed her under his breath, but kept perfectly still. He did not intend to admit her.

"Paul! . . . You're in trouble. . . . I believe you're in danger . . . at least come to the door! . . ."

Oleron smothered a low laugh. It somehow amused him that she, in such danger herself, should talk to him of *his* danger! . . . Well, if she was, serve her right; she knew, or said she knew, all about it. . . .

"Paul! . . . Paul! . . ."

"Paul! . . . Paul! . . ." He mimicked her under his breath.

"Oh, Paul, it's *horrible*! . . ."

Horrible was it? thought Oleron. Then let her get away. . . .

"I only want to help you, Paul. . . . I didn't promise not to come if you needed me. . . ."

He was impervious to the pitiful sob that interrupted the low cry. The devil take the woman! Should he shout to her to go away and not come back? No: let her call and knock and sob. She had a gift for sobbing; she mustn't think her sobs would move him. They irritated him, so that he set his teeth and shook his fist at her, but that was all. Let her sob.

"Paul! . . . Paul! . . ."

With his teeth hard set, he dropped the first page of *Romilly* into the fire. Then he began to drop the rest in, sheet by sheet.

For many minutes the calling behind his door continued; then suddenly it ceased. He heard the sound of feet slowly descending the stairs. He listened for the noise of a fall or a cry or the crash of a piece of the handrail of the upper landing; but none of these things came. She was spared. Apparently her rival suffered her to crawl abject and beaten away. Oleron heard the passing of her steps under his window; then she was gone.

He dropped the last page into the fire, and then, with a low laugh, rose. He looked fondly round his room.

"Lucky to get away like that," he remarked. "She wouldn't have got away if I'd given her as much as a word or a look! What devils these women are! . . . But no; I oughtn't to say that; one of 'em showed forbearance. . . ."

Who showed forbearance? And what was forborne? Ah, Oleron knew! . . . Contempt, no doubt, had been at the bottom of it, but that didn't matter: the pestering creature had been allowed to go unharmed. Yes, she was lucky; Oleron hoped she knew it. . . .

And now, now, now for his reward!

Oleron crossed the room. All his doors were open; his eyes shone as he placed himself within that of his bedroom.

Fool that he had been, not to think of destroying the manuscript sooner! . . .

How, in a houseful of shadows, should he know his own Shadow? How, in a houseful of noises, distinguish the summons he felt to be at hand? Ah, trust him! He would know! The place was full of a jugglery of dim lights. The blind at his elbow that allowed the light of a street lamp to struggle vaguely through—the glimpse of greeny blue moonlight seen through the distant kitchen door—the sulky glow of the fire under the black ashes of the burnt manuscript—the glimmering of the tulips and the moon-daisies and narcissi in the bowls and jugs and jars—these did not so trick and bewilder his eyes that he would not know his Own! It was he, not she, who had been delaying the shadowy Bridal; he hung his head for a moment in mute acknowledgment; then he bent his eyes on the deceiving, puzzling gloom again. He would have called her name had he known it—but now he would not ask her to share even a name with the other. . . .

His own face, within the frame of the door, glimmered white as the narcissi in the darkness. . . .

A shadow, light as fleece, seemed to take shape in the kitchen (the time had been when Oleron would have said that a cloud had passed over the unseen moon). The low illumination on the blind at his elbow grew dimmer (the time had been when Oleron would have concluded that the lamplighter going his rounds had turned low the flame of the lamp). The fire settled, letting down the black and charred papers; a flower fell from a bowl, and lay indistinct upon the floor; all was still; and then a stray draught moved through the old house, passing before Oleron's face. . . .

Suddenly, inclining his head, he withdrew a little from the doorjamb. The wandering draught caused the door to move a little on its hinges. Oleron trembled violently, stood for a moment longer, and then, putting his hand out to the knob, softly drew the door to, sat down on the nearest chair, and waited, as a man might await the calling of his name that should summon him to some weighty, high and privy Audience. . . .

XI

One knows not whether there can be human compassion for anæmia of the soul. When the pitch of Life is dropped, and the spirit is so put over and reversed that that only is horrible which before was sweet and worldly and of the day, the human relation disappears. The sane soul turns appalled away, lest not merely itself, but sanity should suffer. We are not gods. We cannot drive out devils. We must see selfishly to it that devils do not enter into ourselves.

And this we must do even though Love so transfuse us that we may well deem our nature to be half divine. We shall but speak of honor and duty in vain. The letter dropped within the dark door will lie unregarded, or, if regarded for a brief instant between two unspeakable lapses, left and forgotten again. The telegram will be undelivered, nor will the whistling messenger (wiselier guided than he knows to whistle) be conscious as he walks away of the drawn blind that is pushed aside an inch by a finger and then fearfully replaced again. No: let the miserable wrestle with his own shadows; let him, if indeed he be so mad, clip and strain and enfold and crouch the succubus; but let him do so in a house into which not an air of Heaven penetrates, nor a bright finger of the sun pierces the filthy twilight. The lost must remain lost. Humanity has other business to attend to.

For the handwriting of the two letters that Oleron, stealing noiselessly one June day into his kitchen to rid his sitting room of an armful of fetid and decaying flowers, had seen on the floor within his door, had had no more meaning for him than if it had belonged to some dim and far-away dream. And at the beating of the telegraph-boy upon the door, within a few feet of the bed where he lay, he had gnashed his teeth and stopped his ears. He had pictured the lad standing there, just beyond his partition, among packets of provisions and bundles of dead and dying flowers. For his outer landing was littered with these. Oleron had feared to open his door to take them in. After a week, the errand lads had reported that there must be some mistake about the order, and had left no more. Inside, in the red twilight, the old flowers turned brown and fell and decayed where they lay.

Gradually his power was draining away. The Abominaton fastened on Oleron's power. The steady sapping sometimes left him for many hours of prostration gazing vacantly up at his red-tinged ceiling, idly suffering such fancies as came of themselves to have their way with him. Even the strongest of his memories had no more than a precarious hold upon his attention. Sometimes a flitting half-memory, of a novel to be written, a novel it was important that he should write, tantalized him for a space before vanishing again; and sometimes whole novels, perfect, splendid, established to endure, rose magically before him. And sometimes the memories were absurdly remote and trivial, of garrets he had inhabited and lodgings that had sheltered him, and so forth. Oleron had known a good deal about such things in his time, but all that was now past. He had at last found a place which he did not intend to leave until they fetched him out—a place that some might have thought a little on the green-sick side, that others might have considered to be a little too redolent of long-dead and morbid things for a living man to be mewed up in, but ah, so irresistible, with such an authority of its own, with such an associate of its own, and a place of such delights when once a man had ceased to struggle against its inexorable will! A novel? Somebody ought to write a novel about a place like that! There must be lots to write about in a place like that if one could but get to the bottom of it! It had probably already been painted, by a man called Madley who had lived there . . . but Oleron had not known this Madley—had a strong feeling that he wouldn't have liked him—would rather he had lived somewhere else—really couldn't stand the fellow—hated him, Madley, in fact. (Aha! That was a joke!) He seriously doubted whether the man had led the life he ought; Oleron was in two minds sometimes whether he wouldn't tell that long-nosed guardian of the public morals across the way about him; but probably he knew, and had made his praying hullabaloos for him also. That was his line. Why, Oleron himself had had a dust-up with him about something or other . . . some girl or other . . . Elsie Bengough her name was, he remembered. . . .

Oleron had moments of deep uneasiness about this Elsie Bengough. Or rather, he was not so much uneasy about her as restless about the things she did. Chief of these was the way in which she persisted in thrusting herself into his thoughts; and, whenever he was quick enough, he sent her packing the moment she made her appearance there. The truth was that she was not merely a bore; she had always been that; it had now come to the pitch when her very presence in his fancy was inimical to the full enjoyment of certain experiences. . . . She had no tact; really ought to have known that people are not at home to the thoughts of everybody all the time; ought in mere politeness to have allowed him certain seasons quite to himself; and was monstrously ignorant of things if she did not know, as she appeared not to know, that there were certain special hours when a man's veins ran with fire and daring and power, in which . . . well, in which he had a reasonable right to treat folk as he had treated that prying Barrett—to shut them out completely. . . . But no, up she popped: the thought of her, and ruined all. Bright towering fabrics, by the side of which even those perfect, magical novels of which he dreamed were dun and gray, vanished utterly at her intrusion. It was as if a fog should suddenly quench some fair-beaming star, as if at the threshold of some golden portal prepared for Oleron a pit should suddenly gape, as if a bat-like shadow should turn the growing dawn to murk and darkness again. . . . Therefore, Oleron strove to stifle even the nascent thought of her.

Nevertheless, there came an occasion on which this woman Bengough absolutely refused to be suppressed. Oleron could not have told exactly when this happened; he only knew by the glimmer of the street lamp on his blind that it was some time during the night, and that for some time she had not presented herself.

He had no warning, none, of her coming; she just came—was there. Strive as he would, he could not shake off the thought of her nor the image of her face. She haunted him.

But for her to come at *that* moment of all moments! . . . Really, it was past belief! How *she* could endure it, Oleron could not conceive! Actually, to look on, as it were, at the triumph of a Rival. . . . Good God! It was monstrous! tact—reticence—he had never credited her with an overwhelming amount of either; but he had never attributed mere—oh, there was no word for it! Monstrous—monstrous! Did she intend thenceforward. . . . Good God! To look on! . . .

Oleron felt the blood rush up to the roots of his hair with anger against her.

"Damnation take her!" he choked. . . .

But the next moment his heat and resentment had changed to a cold sweat of cowering fear. Panic-stricken, he strove to comprehend what he had done. For though he knew not what, he knew he had done something, something fatal, irreparable, blasting. Anger he had felt, but not *this* blaze of ire that suddenly flooded the twilight of his consciousness with a white infernal light. *That* appalling flash was not his—not his *that* open rift of bright and searing Hell—not his, not his! His had been the hand of a child, preparing a puny blow; but what was *this other* horrific hand that was drawn back to strike in the same place? Had *he* set that in motion? Had *he* provided the spark that had touched off the whole accumulated power of that formidable and relentless place? He did not know. He only knew that that poor igniting particle in himself was blown out, that—— Oh, impossible!—a clinging kiss (how else to express it?) had changed on his very lips to a gnashing and a removal, and that for very pity of the awful odds he must cry out to her against whom he had lately ranged to guard herself . . . guard herself. . . .

"*Look out!*" he shieked aloud. . . .

The revulsion was instant. As if a cold slow billow had broken over him, he came to find that he was lying in his bed, that the mist and horror that had for so long enwrapped him had departed, that he was Paul Oleron, and that he was sick, naked, helpless, and unutterably abandoned and alone. His faculties, though weak, answered at last to his calls upon them; and he knew that it must have been a hideous nightmare that had left him sweating and shaking thus.

Yes, he was himself, Paul Oleron, a tired novelist, already past the summit of his best work, and slipping downhill again empty-handed from it all. He had struck short in his life's aim. He had tried too much, had overestimated his strength, and was a failure, a failure. . . .

It all came to him in the single word, enwrapped and complete; it needed no sequential thought; he was a failure. He had missed. . . .

And he had missed not one happiness, but two. He had missed the ease of this world, which men love, and he had missed also that other shining prize for which men forego ease, the snatching and holding and triumphant bearing up aloft of which is the only justification of the mad adventurer who hazards the enterprise. And there was no second attempt. Fate has no morrow. Oleron's morrow must be to sit down to profitless, ill-done, unrequired work again, and so on the morrow after that, and the morrow after that, and as many morrows as there might be. . . .

He lay there, weakly yet sanely considering it. . . .

And since the whole attempt had failed, it was hardly worth while to consider whether a little might not be saved from the general wreck. No good would ever come out of that half-finished novel. He had intended that it should appear in the autumn; was under contract that it should appear; no matter; it was better to pay forfeit to his publishers than to waste what days were left. He was spent; age was not far off; and paths of wisdom and sadness were the properest for the remainder of the journey. . . .

If only he had chosen the wife, the child, the faithful friend at the fireside, and let them follow an *ignis fatuus* that list! . . .

In the meantime it began to puzzle him exceedingly why he should be so weak, that his room should smell so overpoweringly of decaying vegetable matter, and that his hand, chancing to stray to his face in the darkness, should encounter a beard.

"Most extraordinary!" he began to mutter to himself. "Have I been ill? Am I ill now? And if so, why have they left me alone? . . . Extraordinary! . . ."

He thought he heard a sound from the kitchen or bathroom. He rose a little on his pillow, and listened. . . . Ah! He was not alone, then! It certainly would have been extraordinary if they had left him ill and alone—— Alone? Oh, no. He would be looked after. He wouldn't be left, ill, to shift for himself. If everybody else had forsaken him, he could trust Elsie Bengough, the dearest chum he had, for that . . . bless her faithful heart!

But suddenly a short, stifled, spluttering cry rang sharply out:

"*Paul!*"

It came from the kitchen.

And in the same moment it flashed upon Oleron, he knew not how, that two, three, five, he knew not how many minutes before, another sound, unmarked at the time, but suddenly transfixing his attention now, had striven to reach his intelligence. This sound had been the slight touch of metal on metal— just such a sound as Oleron made when he put his key into the lock.

"Hallo! . . . Who's that?" he called sharply from his bed. He had no answer.

He called again. "Hallo! . . . Who's there? . . . Who is it?"

This time he was sure he heard noises, soft and heavy, in the kitchen.

"This is a queer thing altogether," he muttered. "By Jove, I'm as weak as a kitten, too. . . . Hallo, there! Somebody called, didn't they? . . . Elsie! Is that you? . . ."

Then he began to knock with his hand on the wall at the side of his bed.

"Elsie! . . . Elsie! . . . You called, didn't you? . . . Please come here, whoever it is! . . ."

There was a sound as of a closing door, and then silence. Oleron began to get rather alarmed.

"It may be a nurse," he muttered: "Elsie'd have to get me a nurse, of course. She'd sit with me as long as she could spare the time, brave lass, and she'd get a nurse for the rest. . . . But it was awfully like her voice. . . . Elsie, or whoever it is! . . . I can't make this out at all. I must go and see what's the matter. . . ."

He put one leg out of bed. Feeling its feebleness, he reached with his hand for the additional support of the wall. . . .

But before putting out the other leg he stopped and considered, picking at his new-found beard. He was suddenly wondering whether he *dared* go into the kitchen. It was such a frightfully long way; no man knew what horror might not leap and huddle on his shoulders if he went so far; when a man has an overmastering impulse to get back into bed he ought to take heed of the warning and obey it. Besides, why should he go? What was there to go for? If it was that Bengough creature again, let her look after herself; Oleron was not going to have things cramp themselves on his defenseless back for the sake of such a spoil-sport as *she*! . . . If she was in, let her let herself out again, and the sooner the better for her! Oleron simply couldn't be bothered. He had his work to do. On the morrow, he must set about the writing of a novel with a heroine so winsome, capricious, adorable, jealous, wicked, beautiful, inflaming, and altogether evil, that men should stand amazed. She was coming over him now; he knew by the alteration of the very air of the room when she was near him; and that soft thrill of bliss that had begun to stir in him never came unless she was beckoning, beckoning. . . .

He let go the wall and fell back into bed again as—oh, unthinkable!—the other half of that kiss that a gnash had interrupted was placed (how else convey it?) on his lips, robbing him of very breath. . . .

XII

In the bright June sunlight a crowd filled the square, and looked up at the windows of the old house with the antique insurance marks on its walls of red brick and the agents' noticeboards hanging like wooden choppers over the paling. Two constables stood at the broken gate of the narrow entrance alley, keeping folk back. The women kept to the outskirts of the throng, moving now and then as if to see the drawn red blinds of the old house from a new angle, and talking in whispers. The children were in the houses, behind closed doors.

A long-nosed man had a little group about him, and he was telling some story over and over again; and another man, little and fat and wide-eyed, sought to capture the long-nosed man's audience with some relation in which a key figured.

". . . and it was revealed to me that there'd been something that very afternoon," the long-nosed man was saying. "I was standing there, where Constable Saunders is—or rather, I was passing about my business, when they came out. There was no deceiving me, oh, no deceiving *me*! *I* saw her face. . . .

"What was it like, Mr. Barrett?" a man asked.

"It was like hers whom our Lord said to, 'Woman, doth any man accuse thee?'—white as paper, and no mistake! Don't tell *me*! . . . And so I walks straight across to Mrs. Barrett, and 'Jane,' I says, 'this must stop, and stop at once; we are commanded to avoid evil,' I says, 'and it must come to an end now;

let him get help elsewhere.' And she says to me, 'John,' she says, 'it's four-and-sixpence a week'—them was her words. 'Jane,' I says, 'if it was forty-six thousand pounds it should stop' . . . and from that day to this she hasn't set foot inside that gate."

There was a short silence: then:

"Did Mrs. Barrett ever . . . *see* anything, like?" somebody vaguely inquired.

Barrett turned austerely on the speaker.

"What Mrs. Barrett saw and Mrs. Barrett didn't see shall not pass these lips; even as it is written, keep thy tongue from speaking evil," he said.

Another man spoke.

"He was pretty near canned up in the *Wagon and Horses* that night, weren't he, Jim?"

"Yes, 'e 'adn't 'alf copped it. . . ."

"Not standing treat much, neither; he was in the bar, all on his own. . . ."

"So 'e was; we talked about it. . . ."

The fat, scared-eyed man made another attempt.

"She got the key off of me—she 'ad the number of it—she came into my shop of a Tuesday evening. . . ."

Nobody heeded him.

"Shut your heads," a heavy laborer commented gruffly, "she hasn't been found yet. 'Ere's the inspectors; we shall know more in a bit."

Two inspectors had come up and were talking to the constables who guarded the gate. The little fat man ran eagerly forward, saying that she had bought the key of him. "I remember the number, because of its being three ones and three threes—111333!" he exclaimed excitedly.

An inspector put him aside.

"Nobody's been in?" he asked of one of the constables.

"No, sir."

"Then you, Brackley, come with us; you, Smith, keep the gate. There's a squad on its way."

The two inspectors and the constable passed down the alley and entered the house. They mounted the wide carved staircase.

"This don't look as if he'd been out much lately," one of the inspectors muttered as he kicked aside a litter of dead leaves and paper that lay outside Oleron's door. "I don't think we need knock—break a pane, Brackley."

The door had two glazed panels; there was a sound of shattered glass; and Brackley put his hand through the hole his elbow had made and drew back the latch.

"Faugh!" . . . choked one of the inspectors as they entered. "Let some light and air in, quick. It stinks like a hearse——"

The assembly out in the square saw the red blinds go up and the windows of the old house flung open.

"That's better," said one of the inspectors, putting his head out of a window and drawing a deep breath. . . . "That seems to be the bedroom in there; will you go in, Simms, while I go over the rest? . . ."

They had drawn up the bedroom blind also, and the waxy-white, emaciated man on the bed had made a blinker of his hand against the torturing flood of brightness. Nor could he believe that his hearing was not playing tricks with him, for there were two policemen in his room, bending over him and asking where "she" was. He shook his head.

"This woman Bengough . . . goes by the name of Miss Elsie Bengough . . . d'ye hear? Where is she? . . . No good, Brackley; get him up; be careful with him; I'll just shove *my* head out of the window, I think. . . ."

The other inspector had been through Oleron's study and had found nothing, and was now in the kitchen, kicking aside an ankle-deep mass of vegetable refuse that cumbered the floor. The kitchen window had no blind, and was overshadowed by the blank end of the house across the alley. The kitchen appeared to be empty.

But the inspector, kicking aside the dead flowers, noticed that a shuffling track that was not of his making had been swept to a cupboard in the corner. In the upper part of the door of the cupboard was a square panel that looked as if it slid on runners. The door itself was closed.

The inspector advanced, put out his hand to the little knob, and slid the hatch along its groove.

Then he took an involuntary step back again.

Framed in the aperture, and falling forward a little before it jammed again in its frame, was something that resembled a large lumpy pudding, done up in a pudding-bag of faded browny red frieze.

"Ah!" said the inspector.

To close the hatch again he would have had to thrust that pudding back with his hand; and somehow he did not quite like the idea of touching it. Instead, he turned the handle of the cupboard itself. There was weight behind it, so much weight that, after opening the door three or four inches and peering inside, he had to put his shoulder to it in order to close it again. In closing it he left sticking out, a few inches from the floor, a triangle of black and white check skirt.

He went into the small hall.

"All right!" he called.

They had got Oleron into his clothes. He still used his hands as blinkers, and his brain was very confused. A number of things were happening that he couldn't understand. He couldn't understand the extraordinary mess of dead flowers there seemed to be everywhere; he couldn't understand why there should be police officers in his room; he couldn't understand why one of these should be sent for a four-wheeler and a stretcher; and he couldn't understand what heavy article they seemed to be moving about in the kitchen—his kitchen. . . .

"What's the matter?" he muttered sleepily. . . .

Then he heard a murmur in the square, and the stopping of a four-wheeler outside. A police officer was at his elbow again, and Oleron wondered why, when he whispered something to him, he should run off a string of words—something about "used in evidence against you." They had lifted him to his feet, and were assisting him towards the door. . . .

No, Oleron couldn't understand it at all.

They got him down the stairs and along the alley. Oleron was aware of confused angry shoutings; he gathered that a number

THE BECKONING FAIR ONE

of people wanted to lynch somebody or other. Then his attention became fixed on a little fat frightened-eyed man who appeared to be making a statement that an officer was taking down in a notebook.

"I'd seen her with him . . . they was often together . . . she came into my shop and said it was for him . . . I thought it was all right . . . 111333 the number was," the man was saying.

The people seemed to be very angry; many police were keeping them back; but one of the inspectors had a voice that Oleron thought quite kind and friendly. He was telling somebody to get somebody else into the cab before something or other was brought out; and Oleron noticed that a four-wheeler was drawn up at the gate. It appeared that it was himself who was to be put into it; and as they lifted him up he saw that the inspector tried to stand between him and something that stood behind the cab, but was not quick enough to prevent Oleron seeing that this something was a hooded stretcher. The angry voices sounded like a sea, something hard, like a stone, hit the back of the cab; and the inspector followed Oleron in and stood with his back to the window nearer the side where the people were. The door they had put Oleron in at remained open, apparently till the other inspector should come; and through the opening Oleron had a glimpse of the hatchet-like "To Let" boards among the privet-trees. One of them said that the key was at Number Six. . . .

Suddenly the raging of voices was hushed. Along the entrance alley shuffling steps were heard, and the other inspector appeared at the cab door.

"Right away," he said to the driver.

He entered, fastened the door after him, and blocked up the second window with his back. Between the two inspectors Oleron slept peacefully. The cab moved down the square, the other vehicle went up the hill. The mortuary lay that way.

ON THE BRIGHTON ROAD

BY RICHARD MIDDLETON

Slowly the sun had climbed up the hard white downs, till it broke with little of the mysterious ritual of dawn upon a sparkling world of snow. There had been a hard frost during the night, and the birds, who hopped about here and there with scant tolerance of life, left no trace of their passage on the silver pavements. In places the sheltered caverns of the hedges broke the monotony of the whiteness that had fallen upon the colored earth, and overhead the sky melted from orange to deep blue, from deep blue to a blue so pale that it suggested a thin paper screen rather than illimitable space. Across the level fields there came a cold, silent wind which blew fine dust of snow from the trees, but hardly stirred the crested hedges. Once above the sky-line, the sun seemed to climb more quickly, and as it rose higher it began to give out a heat that blended with the keenness of the wind.

It may have been this strange alternation of heat and cold that disturbed the tramp in his dreams, for he struggled for a moment with the snow that covered him, like a man who finds himself twisted uncomfortably in the bedclothes, and then sat up with staring, questioning eyes. "Lord! I thought I was in bed," he said to himself as he took in the vacant landscape, "and all the while I was out here." He stretched his limbs, and, rising carefully to his feet, shook the snow off his body. As he did so the wind set him shivering, and he knew that his bed had been warm.

"Come, I feel pretty fit," he thought. "I suppose I am lucky

ON THE BRIGHTON ROAD

to wake at all in this. Or unlucky—it isn't much of a business to come back to." He looked up and saw the downs shining against the blue like the Alps on a picture-postcard. "That means another forty miles or so, I suppose," he continued grimly. "Lord knows what I did yesterday. Walked till I was done, and now I'm only about twelve miles from Brighton. Damn the snow, damn Brighton, damn everything!" The sun crept up higher and higher, and he started walking patiently along the road with his back turned to the hills.

"Am I glad or sorry that it was only sleep that took me, glad or sorry, glad or sorry?" His thoughts seemed to arrange themselves in a metrical accompaniment to the steady thud of his footsteps, and he hardly sought an answer to his question. It was good enough to walk to.

Presently, when three milestones had loitered past, he overtook a boy who was stooping to light a cigarette. He wore no overcoat, and looked unspeakably fragile against the snow. "Are you on the road, guv'nor?" asked the boy huskily as he passed.

"I think I am," the tramp said.

"Oh, then I'll come a bit of the way with you if you don't walk too fast. It's a bit lonesome walking this time of day." The tramp nodded his head, and the boy started limping along by his side.

"I'm eighteen," he said casually. "I bet you thought I was younger."

"Fifteen, I'd have said."

"You'd have backed a loser. Eighteen last August, and I've been on the road six years. I ran away from home five times when I was a little 'un, and the police took me back each time. Very good to me, the police was. Now I haven't got a home to run away from."

"Nor have I," the tramp said calmly.

"Oh, I can see what you are," the boy panted; "you're a gentleman come down. It's harder for you than for me." The tramp glanced at the limping, feeble figure and lessened his pace.

"I haven't been at it as long as you have," he admitted.

"No, I could tell that by the way you walk. You haven't got tired yet. Perhaps you expect something the other end?"

The tramp reflected for a moment. "I don't know," he said bitterly, "I'm always expecting things."

"You'll grow out of that," the boy commented. "It's warmer in London, but it's harder to come by grub. There isn't much in it really."

"Still, there's the chance of meeting somebody there who will understand——"

"Country people are better," the boy interrupted. "Last night I took a lease of a barn for nothing and slept with the cows, and this morning the farmer routed me out and gave me tea and toke because I was little. Of course, I score there; but in London, soup on the Embankment at night, and all the rest of the time coppers moving you on."

"I dropped by the roadside last night and slept where I fell. It's a wonder I didn't die," the tramp said. The boy looked at him sharply.

"How do you know you didn't?" he said.

"I don't see it," the tramp said, after a pause.

"I tell you," the boy said hoarsely, "people like us can't get away from this sort of thing if we want to. Always hungry and thirsty and dog-tired and walking all the time. And yet if anyone offers me a nice home and work my stomach feels sick. Do I look strong? I know I'm little for my age, but I've been knocking about like this for six years, and do you think I'm not dead? I was drowned bathing at Margate, and I was killed by a gipsy with a spike; he knocked my head right in, and twice I was froze like you last night, and a motor cut me down on this very road, and yet I'm walking along here now, walking to London to walk away from it again, because I can't help it. Dead! I tell you we can't get away if we want to."

The boy broke off in a fit of coughing, and the tramp paused while he recovered.

"You'd better borrow my coat for a bit, Tommy," he said, "your cough's pretty bad."

"You go to hell!" the boy said fiercely, puffing at his cigarette; "I'm all right. I was telling you about the road. You haven't got down to it yet, but you'll find out presently. We're all dead, all of us who're on it, and we're all tired, yet somehow we can't leave it. There's nice smells in the summer, dust and hay and the wind smack in your face on a hot day; and it's nice waking up in the wet grass on a fine morning. I don't know, I don't know——" He lurched forward suddenly, and the tramp caught him in his arms.

"I'm sick," the boy whispered—"sick."

The tramp looked up and down the road, but he could see no houses or any sign of help. Yet even as he supported the boy doubtfully in the middle of the road a motor-car suddenly flashed in the middle distance, and came smoothly through the snow.

"What's the trouble?" said the driver quietly as he pulled up. "I'm a doctor." He looked at the boy keenly and listened to his strained breathing.

"Pneumonia," he commented. "I'll give him a lift to the infirmary, and you, too, if you like."

The tramp thought of the workhouse and shook his head. "I'd rather walk," he said.

The boy winked faintly as they lifted him into the car.

"I'll meet you beyond Reigate," he murmured to the tramp. "You'll see." And the car vanished along the white road.

All the morning the tramp splashed through the thawing snow, but at midday he begged some bread at a cottage door and crept into a lonely barn to eat it. It was warm in there, and after his meal he fell asleep among the hay. It was dark when he woke, and started trudging once more through the slushy roads.

Two miles beyond Reigate a figure, a fragile figure, slipped out of the darkness to meet him.

"On the road, guv'nor?" said a husky voice. "Then I'll come a bit of the way with you if you don't walk too fast. It's a bit lonesome walking this time of day."

"But the pneumonia!" cried the tramp aghast.

"I died at Crawley this morning," said the boy.

THE CONSIDERATE HOSTS

BY THORP McCLUSKY

Midnight.

It was raining, abysmally. Not the kind of rain in which people sometimes fondly say they like to walk, but rain that was heavy and pitiless, like the rain that fell in France during the war. The road, unrolling slowly beneath Marvin's headlights, glistened like the flank of a great backsnake; almost Marvin expected it to writhe out from beneath the wheels of his car. Marvin's small coupé was the only man-made thing that moved through the seething night.

Within the car, however, it was like a snug little cave. Marvin might almost have been in a theater, unconcernedly watching some somber drama in which he could revel without really being touched. His sensation was almost one of creepiness; it was incredible that he could be so close to the rain and still so warm and dry. He hoped devoutly that he would not have a flat tire on a night like this!

Ahead a tiny red pinpoint appeared at the side of the road, grew swiftly, then faded in the car's glare to the bull's-eye of a lantern, swinging in the gloved fist of a big man in a streaming rubber coat. Marvin automatically braked the car and rolled the right-hand window down a little way as he saw the big man come splashing toward him.

"Bridge's washed away," the big man said. "Where you going, Mister?"

"Felders, damn it!"

"You'll have to go around by Little Rock Falls. Take your

THE CONSIDERATE HOSTS

left up that road. It's a county road, but it's passable. Take your right after you cross Little Rock Falls bridge. It'll bring you into Felders."

Marvin swore. The trooper's face, black behind the ribbons of water dripping from his hat, laughed.

"It's a bad night, Mister."

"Gosh, yes! Isn't it!"

Well, if he must detour, he must detour. What a night to crawl for miles along a rutty back road!

Rutty was no word for it. Every few feet Marvin's car plunged into water-filled holes, gouged out from beneath by the settling of the light roadbed. The sharp, cutting sound of loose stone against the tires was audible even above the hiss of the rain.

Four miles, and Marvin's motor began to sputter and cough. Another mile, and it surrendered entirely. The ignition was soaked; the car would not budge.

Marvin peered through the moisture-streaked windows, and, vaguely, like blacker masses beyond the road, he sensed the presence of thickly clustered trees. The car had stopped in the middle of a little patch of woods. "Judas!" Marvin thought disgustedly. "What a swell place to get stalled!" He switched off the lights to save the battery.

He saw the glimmer then, through the intervening trees, indistinct in the depths of rain.

Where there was a light there was certainly a house, and perhaps a telephone. Marvin pulled his hat tightly down upon his head, clasped his coat collar up around his ears, got out of the car, pushed the small coupé over on the shoulder of the road, and ran for the light.

The house stood perhaps twenty feet back from the road, and the light shone from a front-room window. As he plowed through the muddy yard—there was no sidewalk—Marvin noticed a second stalled car—a big sedan—standing black and deserted a little way down the road.

The rain was beating him, soaking him to the skin; he pounded on the house door like an impatient sheriff. Almost instantly the door swung open, and Marvin saw a man and a woman standing just inside, in a little hallway that led directly into a well-lighted living-room.

The hallway itself was quite dark. And the man and woman were standing close together, almost as though they might be endeavoring to hide something behind them. But Marvin, wholly preoccupied with his own plight, failed to observe how unusual it must be for these two rural people to be up and about, fully dressed, long after midnight.

Partly shielded from the rain by the little overhang above the door, Marvin took off his dripping hat and urgently explained his plight.

"My car. Won't go. Wires wet, I guess. I wonder if you'd let me use your phone? I might be able to get somebody to come out from Little Rock Falls. I'm sorry that I had to——"

"That's all right," the man said. "Come inside. When you knocked at the door you startled us. We—we really hadn't—well, you know how it is, in the middle of the night and all. But come in."

"We'll have to think this out differently, John," the woman said suddenly.

Think what out differently? thought Marvin absently.

Marvin muttered something about you never can be too careful about strangers, what with so many hold-ups and all. And, oddly, he sensed that in the half darkness the man and woman smiled briefly at each other, as though they shared some secret that made any conception of physical danger to themselves quietly, mildly amusing.

"We weren't thinking of you in that way," the man reassured Marvin. "Come into the living-room."

The living-room of that house was—just ordinary. Two overstuffed chairs, a davenport, a bookcase. Nothing particularly modern about the room. Not elaborate, but adequate.

In the brighter light Marvin looked at his hosts. The man was around forty years of age, the woman considerably younger, twenty-eight, or perhaps thirty. And there was something definitely attractive about them. It was not their appearance so much, for in appearance they were merely ordinary people; the woman was almost painfully plain. But they moved and talked with a curious singleness of purpose. They reminded Marvin of a pair of gray doves.

Marvin looked around the room until he saw the telephone in a corner, and he noticed with some surprise that it was one of the old-style, coffee-grinder affairs. The man was watching him with peculiar intentness.

"We haven't tried to use the telephone tonight," he told Marvin abruptly, "but I'm afraid it won't work."

"I don't see how it *can* work," the woman added.

Marvin took the receiver off the hook and rotated the little crank. No answer from Central. He tried again, several times, but the line remained dead.

The man nodded his head slowly. "I didn't think it would work," he said, then.

"Wires down or something, I suppose," Marvin hazarded. "Funny thing, I haven't seen one of those old-style phones in years. Didn't think they used 'em any more."

"You're out in the sticks now," the man laughed. He glanced from the window at the almost opaque sheets of rain falling outside.

"You might as well stay here a little while. While you're with us you'll have the illusion, at least, that you're in a comfortable house."

What on earth is he talking about? Marvin asked himself. Is he just a little bit off, maybe? That last sounded like nonsense.

Suddenly the woman spoke.

"He'd better go, John. He can't stay here too long, you know. It would be horrible if someone took his license number and people—jumped to conclusions afterward. No one should know that he stopped here."

The man looked thoughtfully at Marvin.

"Yes, dear, you're right. I hadn't thought that far ahead. I'm afraid, sir, that you'll have to leave," he told Marvin. "Something extremely strange———"

Marvin bristled angrily, and buttoned his coat with an air of affronted dignity.

"I'll go," he said shortly. "I realize perfectly that I'm an intruder. You should not have let me in. After you let me in I began to expect ordinary human courtesy from you. I was mistaken. Good night."

The man stopped him. He seemed very much distressed.

"Just a moment. Don't go until we explain. We have never been considered discourteous before. But tonight—tonight . . .

"I must introduce myself. I am John Reed, and this is my wife, Grace."

He paused significantly, as though that explained everything, but Marvin merely shook his head. "My name's Marvin Phelps, but that's nothing to you. All this talk seems pretty needless."

The man coughed nervously. "Please understand. We're only asking you to go for your own good."

"Oh, sure," Marvin said. "Sure. I understand perfectly. Good night."

The man hesitated. "You see," he said slowly, "things aren't as they seem. We're really ghosts."

"You don't say!"

"My husband is quite right," the woman said loyally. "We've been dead twenty-one years."

"Twenty-two years next October," the man added, after a moment's calculation. "It's a long time."

"Well, I never heard such hooey!" Marvin babbled. "Kindly step away from that door, Mister, and let me out of here before I swing from the heels."

"I know it sounds odd," the man admitted, without moving, "and I hope that you will realize that it's from no choosing of mine that I have to explain. Nevertheless, I was electrocuted, twenty-one years ago, for the murder of the Chairman of the School Board, over in Little Rock Falls. Notice how my head is shaved, and my split trouser-leg? The fact is, that whenever we materialize we have to appear exactly as we were in our last moment of life. It's a restriction on us."

Screwy, certainly screwy. And yet Marvin hazily remembered

THE CONSIDERATE HOSTS

that School Board affair. Yes, the murderer *had* been a fellow named Reed. The wife had committed suicide a few days after burial of her husband's body.

It was such an odd insanity. Why, they *both* believed it. They even dressed the part. That odd dress the woman was wearing. 'Way out of date. And the man's slit trouser-leg. The screwy cluck had even shaved a little patch on his head, too, and his shirt was open at the throat.

They didn't look dangerous, but you never can tell. Better humor them, and get out of here as quick as I can.

Marvin cleared his throat.

"If I were you—why, say, I'd have lots of fun materializing. I'd be at it every night. Build up a reputation for myself."

The man looked disgusted. "I should kick you out of doors," he remarked bitterly. "I'm trying to give you a decent explanation, and you keep making fun of me."

"Don't bother with him, John," the wife exclaimed. "It's getting late."

"Mr. Phelps," the self-styled ghost doggedly persisted, ignoring the woman's interruption, "perhaps you noticed a car stalled on the side of the road as you came into our yard. Well, that car, Mr. Phelps, belongs to Lieutenant-Governor Lyons, of Felders, who prosecuted me for that murder and won a conviction, although he knew that I was innocent. Of course he wasn't Lieutenant-Governor then; he was only County Prosecutor. . . .

"That was a political murder, and Lyons knew it. But at that time he still had his way to make in the world—and circumstances pointed toward me. For example, the body of the slain man was found in the ditch just beyond my house. The body had been robbed. The murderer had thrown the victim's pocketbook and watch under our front steps. Lyons said that I had *hidden* them there—though obviously I'd never have done a suicidal thing like that, had I really been the murderer. Lyons knew that, too—but he had to burn somebody.

"What really convicted me was the fact that my contract to teach had not been renewed that spring. It gave Lyons a ready-made motive to pin on me.

"So he framed me. They tried, sentenced, and electrocuted me, all very neatly and legally. Three days after I was buried, my wife committed suicide."

Though Marvin was a trifle afraid, he was nevertheless beginning to enjoy himself. Boy, what a story to tell the gang! If only they'd believe him!

"I can't understand," he pointed out slyly, "how you can be so free with this house if, as you say, you've been dead twenty-one years or so. Don't the present owners or occupants object? If I lived here I certainly wouldn't turn the place over to a couple of ghosts—especially on a night like this!"

The man answered readily, "I told you that things are not as they seem. This house has not been lived in since Grace died. It's not a very modern house, anyway—and people have natural prejudices. At this very moment you are standing in an empty room. Those windows are broken. The wallpaper has peeled away, and half the plaster has fallen off the walls. There is really no light in the house. If things appeared to you as they really are you could not see your hand in front of your face."

Marvin felt in his pocket for his cigarettes. "Well," he said, "you seem to know all the answers. Have a cigarette. Or don't ghosts smoke?"

The man extended his hand. "Thanks," he replied. "This is an unexpected pleasure. You'll notice that although there are ash-trays about the room there are no cigarettes or tobacco. Grace never smoked, and when they took me to jail she brought all my tobacco there to me. Of course, as I pointed out before, you see this room exactly as it was at the time she killed herself. She's wearing the same dress, for example. There's a certain form about these things, you know."

Marvin lit the cigarettes. "Well!" he exclaimed. "Brother, you certainly seem to think of everything! Though I can't understand, even yet, why you want me to get out of here. I should think that after you've gone to all this trouble, arranging your effects and so on, you'd want somebody to haunt."

The woman laughed dryly.

"Oh, you're not the man we want to haunt, Mr. Phelps. You

THE CONSIDERATE HOSTS 271

came along quite by accident; we hadn't counted on you at all. No, Mr. Lyons is the man we're interested in."

"He's out in the hall now," the man said suddenly. He jerked his head toward the door through which Marvin had come. And all at once all this didn't seem half so funny to Marvin as it had seemed a moment before.

"You see," the woman went on quickly, "this house of ours is on a back road. Nobody ever travels this way. We've been trying for years to—to haunt Mr. Lyons, but we've had very little success. He lives in Felders, and we're pitifully weak when we go to Felders. We're strongest when we're in this house, perhaps because we lived here so long.

"But tonight, when the bridge went out, we knew that our opportunity had arrived. We knew that Mr. Lyons was not in Felders, and we knew that he would have to take this detour in order to get home.

"We felt very strongly that Mr. Lyons would be unable to pass this house tonight.

"It turned out as we had hoped. Mr. Lyons had trouble with his car, exactly as you did, and he came straight to this house to ask if he might use the telephone. Perhaps he had forgotten us, years ago—twenty-one years is a long time. Perhaps he was confused by the rain, and didn't know exactly where he was.

"He fainted, Mr. Phelps, the instant he recognized us. We have known for a long time that his heart is weak, and we had hoped that seeing us would frighten him to death, but he is still alive. Of course while he is unconscious we can do nothing more. Actually, we're almost impalpable. If you weren't so convinced that we are real you could pass your hand right through us.

"We decided to wait until Mr. Lyons regained consciousness and then to frighten him again. We even discussed beating him to death with one of those non-existent chairs you think you see. You understand, his body would be unmarked; he would really die of terror. We were still discussing what to do when you came along.

"We realized at once how embarrassing it might prove for you if Mr. Lyons' body were found in this house tomorrow and the police learned that you were also in the house. That's why we want you to go."

"Well," Marvin said bluntly, "I don't see how I can get my car away from here. It won't run, and if I walk to Little Rock Falls and get somebody to come back here with me the damage'll be done."

"Yes," the man admitted thoughtfully. "It's a problem."

For several minutes they stood like a tableau, without speaking. Marvin was uneasily wondering: Did these people really have old Lyons tied up in the hallway; were they really planning to murder the man? The big car standing out beside the road belonged to *somebody*. . . .

Marvin coughed discreetly.

"Well, it seems to me, my dear shades," he said, "that unless you are perfectly willing to put me into what might turn out to be a very unpleasant position you'll have to let your vengeance ride, for tonight, anyway."

"There'll never be another opportunity like this," the man pointed out. "That bridge won't go again in ten lifetimes."

"We don't want the young man to suffer though, John."

"It seems to me," Marvin suggested, "as though this revenge idea of yours is overdone, anyway. Murdering Lyons won't really do you any good, you know."

"It's the customary thing when a wrong has been done," the man protested.

"Well, maybe," Marvin argued, and all the time he was wondering whether he were really facing a madman who might be dangerous or whether he were at home dreaming in bed; "but I'm not so sure about that. Hauntings are pretty infrequent, you must admit. I'd say that shows that a lot of ghosts really don't care much about the vengeance angle, despite all you say. I think that if you check on it carefully you'll find that a great many ghosts realize that revenge isn't so much. It's really the thinking about revenge, and the planning it, that's all the fun. Now, for the sake of argument, what good would it do you to put old Lyons away? Why, you'd hardly have any incentive to be ghosts any more. But if you let him go, why, say, any time you wanted to, you could start to scheme up a good scare for him, and begin to calculate how it would work, and time would fly like everything. And on top of all that, if anything happened to me on account of tonight, it would be just too bad for you. *You'd* be haunted, really. It's a bad rule that doesn't work two ways."

The woman looked at her husband. "He's right, John," she said tremulously. "We'd better let Lyons go."

The man nodded. He looked worried.

He spoke very stiffly to Marvin. "I don't agree entirely with all you've said," he pointed out, "but I admit that in order to protect you we'll have to let Lyons go. If you'll give me a hand we'll carry him out and put him in his car."

"Actually, I suppose, I'll be doing all the work."

"Yes," the man agreed, "you will."

They went into the little hall, and there, to Marvin's complete astonishment, crumpled on the floor lay old Lyons. Marvin recognized him easily from the newspaper photographs he had seen.

"Hard-looking duffer, isn't he?" Marvin said, trying to stifle a tremor in his voice.

The man nodded without speaking.

Together, Marvin watching the man narrowly, they carried the lax body out through the rain and put it into the big sedan. When the job was done the man stood silently for a moment, looking up into the black invisible clouds.

"It's clearing," he said matter-of-factly. "In an hour it'll be over."

"My wife'll kill me when I get home," Marvin said.

The man made a little clucking sound. "Maybe if you wiped your ignition now your car'd start. It's had a chance to dry a little."

"I'll try it," Marvin said. He opened the hood and wiped the distributor cap and points and around the spark plugs with his handkerchief. He got in the car and stepped on the starter, and the motor caught almost immediately.

The man stepped toward the door, and Marvin doubled his right fist, ready for anything. But then the man stopped.

"Well, I suppose you'd better be going along," he said. "Good night."

"Good night," Marvin said. "And thanks. I'll stop by one of these days and say hello."

"You wouldn't find us in," the man said simply.

By Heaven, he *is* nuts, Marvin thought. "Listen, brother," he said earnestly, "you aren't going to do anything funny to old Lyons after I'm gone?"

The other shook his head. "No. Don't worry."

Marvin let in the clutch and stepped on the gas. He wanted to get out of there as quickly as possible.

In Little Rock Falls he went into an all-night lunch and telephoned the police that there was an unconscious man sitting in a car three or four miles back on the detour. Then he drove home.

Early the next morning, on his way to work, he drove back over the detour.

He kept watching for the little house, and when it came in sight he recognized it easily from the contour of the rooms and the spacing of the windows and the little overhang above the door.

But as he came closer he saw that it was deserted. The windows were out, the steps had fallen in. The clapboards were gray and weather-beaten, and naked rafters showed through holes in the roof.

Marvin stopped his car and sat there beside the road for a little while, his face oddly pale. Finally he got out of the car and walked over to the house and went inside.

There was not one single stick of furniture in the rooms. Jagged scars showed in the ceilings where the electric fixtures had been torn away. The house had been wrecked years before by vandals, by neglect, by the merciless wearing of the sun and the rain.

In shape alone were the hallway and living-room as Marvin

THE CONSIDERATE HOSTS

remembered them. *"There,"* he thought, "is where the bookcases were. The table was *there*—the davenport *there*."

Suddenly he stooped, and stared at the dusty boards underfoot.

On the naked floor lay the butt of a cigarette. And, a half-dozen feet away, lay another cigarette that had not been smoked —that had not even been lighted!

Marvin turned around blindly, and, like an automaton, walked out of that house.

Three days later he read in the newspapers that Lieutenant-Governor Lyons was dead. The Lieutenant-Governor had collapsed, the item continued, while driving his own car home from the state capital the night the Felders bridge was washed out. The death was attributed to heart disease. . . .

After all, Lyons was not a young man.

So Marvin Phelps knew that, even though his considerate ghostly hosts had voluntarily relinquished their vengeance, blind, impartial nature had meted out justice. And, in a strange way, he felt glad that that was so, glad that Grace and John Reed had left to Fate the punishment they had planned to impose with their own ghostly hands. . . .

AUGUST HEAT

BY W. F. HARVEY

Phenistone Road, Clapham,

August 20th, 190—. I have had what I believe to be the most remarkable day in my life, and while the events are still fresh in my mind, I wish to put them down on paper as clearly as possible.

Let me say at the outset that my name is James Clarence Withencroft.

I am forty years old, in perfect health, never having known a day's illness.

By profession I am an artist, not a very successful one, but I earn enough money by my black-and-white work to satisfy my necessary wants.

My only near relative, a sister, died five years ago, so that I am independent.

I breakfasted this morning at nine, and after glancing through the morning paper I lighted my pipe and proceeded to let my mind wander in the hope that I might chance upon some subject for my pencil.

The room, though door and windows were open, was oppressively hot, and I had just made up my mind that the coolest and most comfortable place in the neighborhood would be the deep end of the public swimming bath, when the idea came.

I began to draw. So intent was I on my work that I left my lunch untouched, only stopping work when the clock of St. Jude's struck four.

The final result, for a hurried sketch, was, I felt sure, the best thing I had done.

It showed a criminal in the dock immediately after the judge had pronounced sentence. The man was fat—enormously fat. The flesh hung in rolls about his chin; it creased his huge, stumpy neck. He was clean shaven (perhaps I should say a few days before he must have been clean shaven) and almost bald. He stood in the dock, his short, stumpy fingers clasping the rail, looking straight in front of him. The feeling that his expression conveyed was not so much one of horror as of utter, absolute collapse.

There seemed nothing in the man strong enough to sustain that mountain of flesh.

I rolled up the sketch, and without quite knowing why, placed it in my pocket. Then with the rare sense of happiness which the knowledge of a good thing well done gives, I left the house.

I believe that I set out with the idea of calling upon Trenton, for I remember walking along Lytton Street and turning to the right along Gilchrist Road at the bottom of the hill where the men were at work on the new tram lines.

From there onward I have only the vaguest recollections of where I went. The one thing of which I was fully conscious was the awful heat, that came up from the dusty asphalt pavement as an almost palpable wave. I longed for the thunder promised by the great banks of copper-colored cloud that hung low over the western sky.

I must have walked five or six miles, when a small boy roused me from my reverie by asking the time.

It was twenty minutes to seven.

When he left me I began to take stock of my bearings. I found myself standing before a gate that led into a yard bordered by a strip of thirsty earth, where there were flowers, purple stock and scarlet geranium. Above the entrance was a board with the inscription—

CHAS. ATKINSON
MONUMENTAL MASON
WORKER IN ENGLISH AND ITALIAN MARBLES

From the yard itself came a cheery whistle, the noise of hammer blows, and the cold sound of steel meeting stone.

A sudden impulse made me enter.

A man was sitting with his back toward me, busy at work on a slab of curiously veined marble. He turned round as he heard my steps and stopped short.

It was the man I had been drawing, whose portrait lay in my pocket.

He sat there, huge and elephantine, the sweat pouring from his scalp, which he wiped with a red silk handkerchief. But though the face was the same, the expression was absolutely different.

He greeted me smiling, as if we were old friends, and shook my hand.

I apologized for my intrusion.

"Everything is hot and glary outside," I said. "This seems an oasis in the wilderness."

"I don't know about the oasis," he replied, "but it certainly is hot, as hot as hell. Take a seat, sir!"

He pointed to the end of the gravestone on which he was at work, and I sat down.

"That's a beautiful piece of stone you've got hold of," I said.

He shook his head. "In a way it is," he answered; "the surface here is as fine as anything you could wish, but there's a big flaw at the back, though I don't expect you'd ever notice it. I could never make really a good job of a bit of marble like that. It would be all right in the summer like this; it wouldn't mind the blasted heat. But wait till the winter comes. There's nothing like frost to find out the weak points in stone."

"Then what's it for?" I asked.

The man burst out laughing.

"You'd hardly believe me if I was to tell you it's for an exhibition, but it's the truth. Artists have exhibitions: so do grocers and butchers; we have them too. All the latest little things in headstones, you know."

He went on to talk of marbles, which sort best withstood wind and rain, and which were easiest to work; then of his garden

AUGUST HEAT

and a new sort of carnation he had bought. At the end of every other minute he would drop his tools, wipe his shining head, and curse the heat.

I said little, for I felt uneasy. There was something unnatural, uncanny, in meeting this man.

I tried at first to persuade myself that I had seen him before, that his face, unknown to me, had found a place in some out-of-the-way corner of my memory, but I knew that I was practicing little more than a plausible piece of self-deception.

Mr. Atkinson finished his work, spat on the ground, and got up with a sigh of relief.

"There! what do you think of that?" he said, with an air of evident pride.

The inscription which I read for the first time was this—

SACRED TO THE MEMORY
OF
JAMES CLARENCE WITHENCROFT.
BORN JAN. 18TH, 1860.
HE PASSED AWAY VERY SUDDENLY
ON AUGUST 20TH, 190–

"In the midst of life we are in death."

For some time I sat in silence. Then a cold shudder ran down my spine. I asked him where he had seen the name.

"Oh, I didn't see it anywhere," replied Mr. Atkinson. "I wanted some name, and I put down the first that came into my head. Why do you want to know?"

"It's a strange coincidence, but it happens to be mine."

He gave a long, low whistle.

"And the dates?"

"I can only answer for one of them, and that's correct."

"It's a rum go!" he said.

But he knew less than I did. I told him of my morning's work. I took the sketch from my pocket and showed it to him. As he looked, the expression of his face altered until it became more and more like that of the man I had drawn.

"And it was only the day before yesterday," he said, "that I told Maria there were no such things as ghosts!"

Neither of us had seen a ghost, but I knew what he meant.

"You probably heard my name," I said.

"And you must have seen me somewhere and have forgotten it! Were you at Clacton-on-Sea last July?"

I had never been to Clacton in my life. We were silent for some time. We were both looking at the same thing, the two dates on the gravestone, and one was right.

"Come inside and have some supper," said Mr. Atkinson.

His wife is a cheerful little woman, with the flaky red cheeks of the country-bred. Her husband introduced me as a friend of his who was an artist. The result was unfortunate, for after the sardines and watercress had been removed, she brought me out a Doré Bible, and I had to sit and express my admiration for nearly half an hour.

I went outside, and found Atkinson sitting on the gravestone smoking.

We resumed the conversation at the point we had left off.

"You must excuse my asking," I said, "but do you know of anything you've done for which you could be put on trial?"

He shook his head.

"I'm not a bankrupt, the business is prosperous enough. Three years ago I gave turkeys to some of the guardians at Christmas, but that's all I can think of. And they were small ones, too," he added as an afterthought.

He got up, fetched a can from the porch, and began to water the flowers. "Twice a day regular in the hot weather," he said, "and then the heat sometimes gets the better of the delicate ones. And ferns, good Lord! they could never stand it. Where do you live?"

I told him my address. It would take an hour's quick walk to get back home.

"It's like this," he said. "We'll look at the matter straight. If you go back home to-night, you take your chance of accidents. A cart may run over you, and there's always banana skins and orange peel, to say nothing of fallen ladders."

AUGUST HEAT

He spoke of the improbable with an intense seriousness that would have been laughable six hours before. But I did not laugh.

"The best thing we can do," he continued, "is for you to stay here till twelve o'clock. We'll go upstairs and smoke; it may be cooler inside."

To my surprise I agreed.

We are sitting in a long, low room beneath the eaves. Atkinson has sent his wife to bed. He himself is busy sharpening some tools at a little oilstone, smoking one of my cigars the while.

The air seems charged with thunder. I am writing this at a shaky table before the open window. The leg is cracked, and Atkinson, who seems a handy man with his tools, is going to mend it as soon as he has finished putting an edge on his chisel

It is after eleven now. I shall be gone in less than an hour.

But the heat is stifling.

It is enough to send a man mad.

THE RETURN OF
ANDREW BENTLEY

BY AUGUST W. DERLETH AND
MARK SCHORER

A weird shape with flaffing black cape strove to drag the body of Amos Wilder from the vault in which it had been laid.

It is with considerable hesitation that I here chronicle the strange incidents which marked my short stay at the old Wilder homestead on the banks of the Wisconsin River not far from the rustic village of Sac Prairie. My reluctance is not entirely dispelled by the conviction that some record of these events should emphatically be made, if only to stop the circulation of unfounded rumors which have come into being since my departure from the vicinity.

The singular chain of events began with a peremptory letter from my aging uncle, Amos Wilder, ordering me to appear at the homestead, where he was then living with a housekeeper and a caretaker. Communications from my Uncle Amos were not only exceedingly rare, but usually tinged with biting and withering comments about my profession of letters, which he held in great scorn. Previous to this note, we had not seen each other for over four years. His curt note hinted that there was something of vital importance to both of us which he wished to take up with me, and though I had no inkling of what this might be, I did not hesitate to go.

The old house was not large. It stood well back in the

rambling grounds, its white surface mottled by the shadows of leafy branches in the warm sunlight of the day on which I arrived. Green shutters crowded upon the windows, and the door was tightly closed, despite the day's somnolent warmth. The river was cerulean and silver in the immediate background, and farther beyond, the bluffs on the other side of the river rose from behind the trees and were lost in the blue haze of distance to the north and south.

My uncle had grown incredibly old, and now hobbled about with the aid of a cane. On the morning of my arrival he was dressed in a long, ragged black robe that trailed along the floor; beneath this garment he wore a threadbare black jersey and a pair of shabby trousers. His hair was unkempt, and on his chin was a rough beard, masking his thin, sardonic mouth. His eyes, however, had lost none of their fire, and I felt his disapproval of me as clearly as ever. His expression was that of a man who is faced with an unpleasant but necessary task.

At last, after a rude scrutiny, he began to speak, having first made certain that no one lurked within earshot.

"It's hardly necessary for me to say I'm not too certain I've done a wise thing in choosing you," he began. "I've always considered you somewhat of a milksop, and you've done nothing to change my opinion."

He watched my face closely as he spoke, to detect any resentment that I might feel; but I had heard this kind of speech from him too often before to feel any active anger. He sensed this, apparently, for he went on abruptly.

"I'm going to leave everything I've got to you, but there'll be a condition. You'll have to spend most of your time here, make this your home, of course, and there are one or two other small things you'll have to see to. Mind, I'm not putting anything in my will; I want only your word. Do you think you can give it? Think you can say, 'Yes' to my terms?"

He paused, and I said, "I see no reason why I shouldn't—if you can guarantee that your terms won't interfere with my writing."

My uncle smiled and shook his head as if in exasperation.

"Nothing is easier," he replied curtly. "Your time for writing will be virtually unlimited."

"What do you want me to do?" I asked.

"Spend most of your time here, as I said before. Let no day go by during which you do not examine the vault behind the house. My body will lie there, and the vault will be sealed; I want to know that I can depend upon you to prevent anything from entering that vault. If at any time you discover that some one has been tampering, you will find written instructions for your further procedure in my library desk. Will you promise me to attend to these things without too much curiosity concerning them?"

I promised without the slightest hesitation, though there were perplexing thoughts crowding upon my mind.

Amos Wilder turned away, his eyes glittering. Then he looked through the window directly opposite me and began to chuckle in a curiously guttural tone. At last he said, his eyes fixed upon a patch of blue sky beyond the tree near the window, "Good. I'll block him yet! Amos Wilder is still a match for you—do you hear, Andrew?"

What his words might portend I had no means of knowing, for he turned abruptly to me and said in his clipped, curt way, "You must go now, Ellis. I shall not see you again." With that, he left the room, and as if by magic, old Jacob Kinney, the caretaker, appeared to show me from the grounds, his lugubrious face regarding me with apologetic eyes from the doorway through which his master had so abruptly vanished but a moment before.

My uncle's strange words puzzled me, and it occurred to me that the old man was losing his mind. That I then did him an injustice I subsequently learned, but at the time all evidence pointed to mental derangement. I finally contented myself with this explanation, though it did not account for the old man's obvious rationality during most of the conversation. Two points struck me: my uncle had put particular stress upon the suggestion that something might enter his vault. And secondly, what was the meaning of his last words, and to whom was my uncle referring when he said, "I'll block him yet!" and "Amos Wilder is still a match for you—do you hear, Andrew?" Conjecture, however, was futile; for, since I knew very little of my uncle's personal affairs, any guesses I might have made as to his obscure references, if indeed he was not losing his mind, would be fruitless.

I left the old homestead that day in May only to find myself back there again within forty-eight hours, summoned by Thomas Weatherbee of Sac Prairie, my uncle's solicitor, whose short telegram apprising me of Amos Wilder's death reached me within three hours of my return to the St. Louis apartment which served me as my temporary home. My shock at the news of his sudden death was heightened when I learned that the circumstances surrounding his decease indicated suicide.

Weatherbee told me the circumstances of my uncle's singular death. It appeared that Jacob Kinney had found the old man in the very room in which he and I had discussed his wishes only a day before. He was seated at the table, apparently asleep. One hand still grasped a pen, and before him lay a sheet of note-paper upon which he had written my name and address, nothing more. It was presumed at first that he had had a heart attack, but a medical examination had brought forth the suspicion that the old man had made away with himself by taking an overdose of veronal. There was, however, considerable reluctance to presume suicide, for an overdose of veronal might just as likely be accident as suicide. Eventually a coroner's jury decided that my uncle had met his death by accident, but from the first I was convinced that Amos Wilder had killed himself. In the light of subsequent events and of his own cryptic words to me, "I shall not see you again," my suspicion was, I feel, justified, though no definite and conclusive evidence emerged.

My uncle was buried, as he had wished, in the long-disused family vault behind the house, and the vault was sealed from the outside with due ceremony and in the presence of witnesses. The reading of the will was a short affair, for excepting bequests made to the housekeeper and caretaker, I inherited everything.

My living was thus assured, and as my uncle had said, I found the future holding many hours of leisure in which to pursue letters.

And yet, despite the apparent rosiness of the outlook, there was from the first a peculiar restraint upon my living in the old homestead. It was indefinable and strange, and numerous small incidents occurred to supplement this odd impression. First old Jacob Kinney wanted to leave. With great effort I persuaded him to stay, and dragged from him his reason for wanting to go.

"There've been mighty strange things a-goin' on about this house, Mr. Wilder, all the time your uncle was alive—and I'm afraid things'll be goin' on again after a bit."

More than that cryptic utterance I could not get out of him. I took the liberty shortly after to repeat Kinney's words to the housekeeper, Mrs. Seldon. The startled expression that passed over her countenance did not escape me, and her immediate assurance that Jake Kinney was in his dotage did not entirely reassure me.

Then there was the daily function of examining the seal on the vault. The absurdity of my uncle's request began to grow on me, and my task, trivial as it was, became daily more irritating. Yet, having given my promise, I could do no more than fulfill it.

On the third night following my uncle's interment, my sleep was troubled by a recurrent dream which gave me no little thought when I remembered its persistence on the following day. I dreamed that my Uncle Amos stood before me, clad as I had last seen him on the visit just preceding his strange death. He regarded me with his beady eyes, and then abruptly said in a mournful and yet urgent voice, "You must bring Burkhardt back here. He forgot to protect me against them. You must get him to do so. If he will not, then see those books on the second shelf of the seventh compartment of my library."

This dream was repeated several times, and it had a perfectly logical basis, which was briefly this: My uncle was buried by Father Burkhardt, the Sac Prairie parish priest, who was not

THE RETURN OF ANDREW BENTLEY 287

satisfied with the findings of the coroner's jury, and consequently, in the belief that Amos Wilder had killed himself, had refused to bless the grave of a suicide. Yet, what the dream-shape of the night before had obviously meant when he spoke of what Father Burkhardt had forgotten to do, was the blessing of the grave.

I spent some time mulling over this solution of the dream, and at length went to see the priest. My efforts, however, were futile. The old man explained his attitude with great patience, and I was forced to agree with him.

On the following night the dream recurred, and in consequence, since a visit to Father Burkhardt had already failed to achieve the desired effect, I turned, impelled largely by curiosity, to the books on the second shelf of the seventh compartment indicated by the dream-figure of my uncle. From the moment that I opened the first of those books, the entire complexion of the occurrences at the homestead changed inexplicably, and I found myself involved in a chain of incidents, the singularity of which continues to impress me even as I write at this late date. For the books on the second shelf of the seventh compartment in my dead uncle's library were books on black magic—books long out of print, and apparently centuries old, for in many of them the print had faded almost to illegibility.

The Latin in which most of the books were written was not easily translated, but fortunately it was not necessary for me to search long for the portions indicated by my uncle, for in each book paragraphs were marked for my attention. The subjects of the marked portions were strangely similar. After some difficulty I succeeded in translating the first indicated paragraph to catch my eye. "For Protection from Things That Walk in the Night," it read. "There are many things stalking abroad by darkness, perhaps ghouls, perhaps evil demons lured from outer space by man's own ignorance, perhaps souls isolated in space, havenless and alone, and yet strongly attached to the things of this earth. Let no bodies be exposed to their evil wrath. Let there be all manner of protection for vaults and graves, for the dead as well as the living; for ghouls, incubi, and succubi haunt the near places as well as the far, and seek always to quench the fire of their unholy desire. . . . Take blessed water from a church and mix it with the blood of a young babe, be it ever so small a measure, and with this cross the grave or the door of the vault thrice at the full of the moon."

If this was what my Uncle Amos desired me to do, I knew at once that the task had devolved upon the wrong man; for I could certainly not see myself going about collecting holy water and the blood of a young child and then performing ridiculous rites over the vault with an odious mixture of the two. I put the books aside and returned to my work, which seemed suddenly more inviting than it had ever been before.

Yet what I had read disturbed me, and the suggestion that my uncle had come to believe in the power of black magic—perhaps even more than this, for all I knew—was extremely distasteful to me. In consequence, my writing suffered, and immediately after my supper that evening, I went for a long walk on the river bank.

A half-moon high in the sky made the countryside bright and clear, and since the night was balmy and made doubly inviting by the sweet mystery of night sounds—the gasping and gurgling of the water, the splashing of distant fish, the muted cries of night-birds, particularly the *peet, peet* of the nighthawk and the eery call of the whippoorwill, and the countless mysterious sounds from the underbrush in the river bottoms—I extended my walk much farther than I had originally intended; so that it was shortly after midnight when I approached the house again, and the moon was close upon the western horizon.

As I came quietly along in the now still night, my eye caught a movement in the shadowy distance. The movement had come from the region of the large old elm which pressed close upon the house near the library window, and it was upon this tree that I now fixed my eyes. I had not long to wait, for presently a shadow detached itself from the giant bole and went slowly around the house toward the darkness behind. I could see the figure quite clearly, though I did not once catch sight of its face, despite the fact that the man, for man it was, wore no hat. He walked with a slight limp, and wore a long black cape. He was near medium height, but quite bent, so that his back was unnaturally hunched. His hands were strikingly white in the fading light of the moon, and he walked with a peculiar flaffing motion, despite his obvious limp. He passed beyond the house with me at his heels, for I was determined to ascertain if possible what design had brought him to the old house.

I lost sight of him for a few moments while I gained the shelter of the house, but in a minute I saw him again, and with a gasp of astonishment realized that he was making directly for the vault in which my Uncle Amos lay buried. I stifled an impulse to shout at him, and made my way cautiously in the shadow of a row of lilac bushes toward the vault, before which he was now standing. The darkness here was intense, owing to the fact that the trees from the surrounding copse pressed close upon this corner of the estate; yet I could see from my crouching position that the mysterious intruder was fumbling with the seals of the vault. My purpose in following him so closely was to collar him while he was engaged with the seals, but this design was now for the moment thwarted by his stepping back to survey the surface of the vault door. He remained standing in silence for some while, and I had almost decided that it might be just as easy to capture him in this position, when he moved forward once more. But this time he did not fumble with the seals. Instead, he seemed to flatten himself against the door of the vault. Then, incredible as it may seem, his figure began to grow smaller, to shrink, save for his gaunt and gleaming white fingers and arms!

With a strangled gasp, I sprang forward.

My memory at this point is not quite clear. I remember seizing the outstretched fingers of the man at the vault door, feeling something within my grasp. Then something struck me at the same moment that the intruder whirled and leaped away. I had the fleeting impression that a second person had leaped upon me from behind. I went down like a log.

I came to my senses not quite an hour later, and lay for a moment recalling what had happened. I remembered having made a snatch at the intruder's fingers, and being struck. There was an appreciable soreness of the head, and a sensitive bruise on my forehead when finally I felt for it. But what most drew my attention was the thing that I held tightly in my left hand, the hand which had grasped at the strangely white fingers of the creature pressed against the door of the Wilder vault. I had felt it within my grasp from the first moment of consciousness, but from its roughness, I had taken it for a small twig caught up from the lawn. In consequence, it was not until I reached the security of the house that I looked at it. I threw it upon the table in the dim glow of the table lamp—and almost fell in my utter amazement; for the thing I had held in my hand was a fragment of human bone—the unmistakable first two joints of the little finger!

This discovery loosed a flood of futile conjectures. Was it after all a man I had surprised at the vault, or was it—something else? . . . That my uncle was in some way vitally concerned now became apparent, if it had not been entirely so before. The fact that Amos Wilder had looked for some such interruption of his repose in the old vault led me to believe that whatever he feared derived from some source in the past. Accordingly, I gave up all conjecture for the time, and promised myself that in the morning I would set on foot inquiries designed to make me familiar with my secluded uncle's past life.

I was destined to receive a shock in the morning. Determined to prosecute my curiosity concerning my uncle without loss of time, I summoned Jacob Kinney, whose surliness had noticeably increased during the few days I had been at the old Wilder house. Instead of asking directly about my uncle, I began with a short account of the figure I had seen outside the preceding night.

"I was out quite late last night, Jake," I began, "and when I came home I noticed a stranger on the grounds."

Kinney's eyebrows shot up in undisguised curiosity, but he

said nothing, though he began to exhibit signs of uneasiness which did not escape my notice.

"He was about five feet tall, I should say, and wore no hat," I went on. "He wore a long black cape, and walked with a slight limp."

Abruptly Kinney came to his feet, his eyes wide with fear. "What's that you say?" he demanded hoarsely. "Walked with a limp—wore a cape?"

I nodded, and would have continued my narrative, had not Kinney cut in.

"My God!" he exclaimed. "Andrew Bentley's back!"

"Who's Andrew Bentley?" I asked.

But Kinney did not hear. He had whirled abruptly and run from the room as fast as his feeble legs would allow him to go. My astonishment knew no bounds, nor did subsequent events in any way lessen it; for Jacob Kinney ran not only from the house, but from the grounds, and his flight was climaxed shortly after by the appearance of a begrimed youth representing himself as the old man's nephew, who came for "Uncle Jake's things." From him I learned that Kinney was leaving his position at once, and would forfeit any wages due him, plus any amount I thought fit to recompense me for his precipitate flight.

Kinney's unaccountable action served only to sharpen my already keen interest, and I descended upon Mrs. Seldon posthaste. But the information which she was able to offer me was meager indeed. Andrew Bentley had arrived in the neighborhood only a few years back. He and my uncle had immediately become friends, and the friendship, despite an appearance of strain, had ended only when Bentley mysteriously disappeared about a year ago. She confirmed my description of the figure I had seen as that of Bentley. Mrs. Seldon, too, was inexplicably agitated, and when I sought to probe for the source of this agitation she said only that there were some very strange stories extant about Bentley, and about my uncle as well, and that most of the people in the neighborhood had been relieved of a great fear when Bentley disappeared from the farm adjoining the Wilder estate. This farm, which he had inhabited for the years of his residence, but had not worked, and had yet always managed to exist without trouble, was now uninhabited. This, together with a passing hint that Thomas Weatherbee might be able to add something, was the sum of what Mrs. Seldon knew.

I lost no time in telephoning Weatherbee and making an appointment for that afternoon. On the way to the attorney's office I had ample time to think over the events of the last ten days. That it was Andrew Bentley whom my Uncle Amos had referred to when he spoke so cryptically with me before his death, I had no longer any doubt. Evidently then, he, too, feared his strange neighbor, but how he hoped to thwart any attempt that Bentley might make to get the body—for what reason he might want it I could not guess—with black magic, was beyond my comprehension.

Thomas Weatherbee was a short and rather insignificant man, but his attitude was conducive to business, and he made clear to me that he had only a limited time at my disposal. I came directly to the matter of Andrew Bentley.

"Andrew Bentley," began Weatherbee with some reluctance, "was a man with whom I had no dealings, with whom I cared to have none. I have seldom met any one whose mere presence was so innately evil. Your uncle took up with him, it is true, but I believe he regretted it to the end of his days."

"What exactly was wrong with Bentley?" I cut in.

Weatherbee smiled grimly, regarded me speculatively for a moment or two, and said, "Bentley was an avowed sorcerer."

"Oh, come," I said; "that sort of thing isn't believed in any more." But a horrible suspicion began to grow in my mind.

"Perhaps not generally," replied Weatherbee at once. "But I can assure you that most of us around here believe in the power of black magic after even so short an acquaintance as ours with Andrew Bentley. Consider for a moment that you have spent the greater part of your life in a modern city, away from the countrysides where such beliefs flourish, Wilder."

He stopped with an abrupt gesture, and took a portfolio from

THE RETURN OF ANDREW BENTLEY

a cabinet. From this he took a photograph, looked at it with a slight curl of disgust on his lips, and passed it over to me.

It was a snapshot, apparently made surreptitiously, of Andrew Bentley, and it had been taken evidently at considerable risk after sunset, for the general appearance of the picture led me to assume that its vagueness was caused by the haziness of dusk —a supposition which Weatherbee confirmed. The figure, however, was quite clear, save for blurred arms, which had evidently been moving during the exposure, and for the head. The view had been taken from the side, and showed Andrew Bentley, certainly identified for me by the long cape he wore, standing as if in conversation with some one. Yet it struck me as strange that Bentley could have stood quietly during the exposure with no incentive to do so, and I commented upon it at once.

Weatherbee looked at me queerly. "Wilder," he said, "there was another person there—or should I say *thing*? And this thing was directly in line with the lens, for he was standing very close to Bentley—and yet, there is nothing on the snapshot, nor is there any evidence on the exposed negative itself that any one stood there; for, as you can see, the landscape is unbroken."

It was as he said.

"But this other person," I put in. "He was seen, and yet does not appear. Apparently the camera was out of focus, or the film was defective."

"On the contrary. There are logical explanations for the non-appearance of something on a film. You can't photograph a dream. And you can't photograph something that has no material form—I say *material* advisedly—even though our own eyes give that thing a physical being."

"What do you mean?"

"Father Burkhardt would call it a familiar," he said, clipping his words. "A familiar, in case you don't know, is an evil spirit summoned by a sorcerer to wait upon his desires. That tall, gaunt man was never seen by day—always by night, and never without Bentley. I can give you no more of my time now, but if you can bring yourself to accept what I have to say at face value, I'll be glad to see you again."

My interview with Thomas Weatherbee left me considerably shaken, and I found myself discarding all my previously formed beliefs regarding black magic. I went immediately to my late uncle's store of books, and began to read through them for further information, in the hope that something I might learn would enable me to meet Andrew Bentley on more equal footing, should he choose to call.

I read until far into the night, and what inconceivable knowledge I assimilated lingers clearly in my mind as I write. I read of age-old horror summoned from the abyss by the ignorance of men, of cosmic ghouls that roamed the ether in search of prey, and of countless things that walk by night. There were many legends of familiars, ghastly demons called forth from the depths at the whims of long-dead sorcerers; and it was significant that each legend had been heavily scored along the margins, and in one case the name "Andrew Bentley" was written in my uncle's hand. In another place my uncle had written, "We are fools to play with powers of whose scope even the wisest of us has no knowledge!"

It was at this point that it occurred to me that my uncle had left a letter of sealed instructions for me in case the vault was tampered with. This letter was to be in the library desk, where I found it with little trouble, a long, legal-looking envelope with my name inscribed very formally. The handwriting was undoubtedly my uncle's, and the letter within was the thing that finally dispelled all doubt from my mind as to the reality of the sorcery that had been and was still being practiced near the Wilder homestead; for it made clear what had happened between my uncle and Andrew Bentley—and that other.

"My Dear Ellis:
"If indeed they have come for me, as they must have if you read this, there is but one thing you can do. Bentley's body must be found and utterly destroyed; surely there cannot be much left of it now. Perhaps you have seen him in the night when he walks—as I have. He is not alive. I know, because I killed him a year ago—stabbed him with

your grandfather's hunting-knife—which must yet lie in his black skeleton.

"I think both Burkhardt and Weatherbee suspected that I aided Bentley to his black rites, but that was long before I dreamed of what depths of evil lurked in his soul. And when he began to hound me so, when he brought forward that other, that hellish thing he had conjured up from the nethermost places of evil—could I do otherwise than rid myself of his evil presence? My mind was at stake—and yes, my body. When you read this, only my body is at stake. For they want it—conceive if you can the ghastly irony of my lifeless body given an awful new existence by being inhabited by Bentley's familiar!

"The body—Bentley's body—I put it in the vault, but that other removed it and hid it somewhere on the grounds. I have not been able to find it, and this past year has been a living hell for me—they have hounded me nightly, and though I can protect myself from them, I cannot stop them from appearing to taunt me. And when I am dead, my protection must come from you. But I hope that Burkhardt will have closed his eyes and blessed the vault, for this I think will be strong enough to keep them away—and yet, I cannot tell.

"And perhaps even this is being read too late—for if once they have my body, destroy me, too, with Bentley's remains—by fire.

"AMOS WILDER."

I put down this letter and sat for a moment in silence. But what thoughts crowded upon my mind were interrupted by an odd sound from outside the window, a sound that was unnaturally striking in the still night. I glanced at my watch; it was one o'clock in the morning. Then I turned out the small reading-lamp and moved quietly toward the window, immediately beyond which stood the giant elm beneath which on the previous night I had first seen the ghostly figure of Andrew Bentley—for since he had been killed a year before, what I had seen could have been none other than his specter.

Then a thought struck me that paralyzed me with horror. Suppose I had been struck by *that other*? It seemed to me that the blow which had knocked me out had been struck from behind. At the same instant my eyes caught sight of the faintest movement beyond the window. The moon hung in a hazy sky and threw a faint illumination about the tree, despite the fairly heavy shadow of its overhanging limbs. There was a man pressed close to the bole of the tree, and even as I looked another seemed to rise up out of the ground at his side. And the second man was Andrew Bentley! I looked again at the first, and saw a tall, gaunt figure with malevolent red eyes, *through* whom I could see the line of moonlight and shadow on the lawn beyond the tree. They stood there together for only a moment, and then went quickly around the house— toward the vault!

From that instant events moved rapidly to a climax.

My eyes fixed themselves upon that place in the ground from which the figure of Andrew Bentley had sprung, and saw there an opening in the trunk of the old tree—for the elm was hollow, and its bole held the remains of Andrew Bentley! Small wonder that my uncle had been haunted by the presence of the man he had killed, when his remains were hidden in the tree near the library window!

But I stood there only for a fraction of a minute. Then I went quickly to the telephone, and after an agonizing delay got Weatherbee on the wire and asked him to come out at once, hinting enough of what was happening to gain his assent. I suggested also that he bring Father Burkhardt along, and this he promised to do.

Then I slipped silently from the house into the shadowy garden. I think the sight of those two unholy figures hovering about the door of the vault was too much for me, for I launched myself at them, heedless of my danger. But realization came almost instantly, for Andrew Bentley did not even turn at my appearance. Instead, the other looked abruptly around, fixed me with his red and fiery eyes, smiled wickedly so that his leathery face was weirdly creased, and leisurely watched my approach. Instinct, I believe, whirled me about and sent me flying from the garden.

The thing was somewhat surprised at my abrupt bolt, and this momentary hesitation on its part I continue to believe is responsible for my being alive to write this. For I knew that I was flying for my life, and I ran with the utmost speed of which I was capable. A fleeting glance showed me that the thing loped after me, a weirdly flaffing shape seeming to come with the wind in the moonlight night, and struck shuddery horror into my heart.

I made for the river, because I remembered reading in one of my uncle's old books that certain familiars could not cross water unless accompanied by those whose sorcery had summoned them to earth. I leaped into the cold water, tense with the hope that the thing behind could not follow.

It could not.

I saw it raging up and down along the river bank, impotent and furious at my fortunate escape, while I kept myself afloat in mid-current. The current carried me rapidly downstream, and I kept my eyes fixed upon the thing I had eluded until it turned and sped back toward the vault. Only when I was completely out of its sight did I make for the bank once more.

I ran madly down the road along which Weatherbee and the priest must come, flinging off some of my wet clothes as I went. What was happening at the vault I did not know—at the moment my only thought was temporary safety from the thing whose power I had so thoughtlessly challenged.

I had gone perhaps a half-mile beyond the estate when the headlights of Weatherbee's car swept around a curve and outlined me in the road. The car ground to an emergency stop, and Weatherbee's voice called out. I jumped into the car, and explained as rapidly as I could what had happened.

Father Burkhardt regarded me quizzically, half smiling.

"You've had a narrow escape, my boy," he said, "a very narrow escape. Now if only we can get to the vault before they succeed in their evil design. Such a fate is too harsh a punishment even for the sins of Amos Wilder."

He shuddered as he spoke, and Weatherbee's face was grim.

None of us wasted a moment when the car came to a stop near the house. Father Burkhardt, despite his age, led the way, marshaling us behind him, for he went ahead with a crucifix extended.

But even he faltered at the horrifying sight that met our eyes when we rounded the house and came into the garden. For the vault was open, and from it emerged the skeletal Bentley and his familiar, and between them they dragged the lifeless body of my Uncle Amos! Burkhardt's hesitation, however, was only momentary, for he ran forward immediately; nor were Weatherbee and I far behind.

At the same moment the two at the vault caught sight of us. With a shrill scream, the tall, gaunt thing loosed his hold of the corpse and launched himself forward. But the crucifix served us well, for the thing fell shuddering away from it. Father Burkhardt immediately pressed his advantage, and following his sharp command, Weatherbee and I rushed at Bentley, who had up to this moment remained beside the corpse, still keeping hold of one dead arm.

But at our advance, Bentley wavered a moment, and then turned and took flight, dodging nimbly past us and running for the house. We were at his heels, and saw him when he vanished in the deep shadows of the tree near the library window.

Father Burkhardt presently made his appearance, walking warily, for the thing was still at bay but eager to attack.

"Find the bones," directed the priest. "They're in the tree, I suspect."

I bent obediently, and presently my searching hand encountered a scooped-out hollow in the trunk just above the opening at the base of the tree. In this lay the skeleton of Andrew Bentley, together with the weapon by which he had met his death, and here it had lain ever since the thing Bentley had summoned from the depths had removed the sorcerer's body from the old vault. Small wonder that it had never been discovered!

Father Burkhardt stood protectingly close while Weatherbee and I prepared a pyre to consume the remains of the sorcerer.

"But what can we do about that?" I asked once, pointing to the familiar that now raged in baffled fury just beyond us.

"We need not bother about that," said the priest. "He is held to earth only by the body of the man who summoned him from below. When once that body is destroyed, he must return. That's why they were after your uncle's body. If the

THE RETURN OF ANDREW BENTLEY

familiar could inhabit a body fresh from a new grave, he could walk by day as well as by night, and need have no fear of having to return."

Once or twice the thing did rush at us—but each time its charge was arrested by the power of that crucifix held unfalteringly aloft by Father Burkhardt, and each time the thing shrank away, wailing.

It was over at last, but not without a short period of ghastly doubt. The remains of Andrew Bentley were reduced to ashes, utterly destroyed, and yet the thing Bentley had called from outside lingered beyond us, strangely quiet now, regarding us malevolently.

"I don't understand," admitted Father Burkhardt at last. "Now that Bentley's ashes alone remain, the thing should go back into the depths."

But if the priest did not understand, I did. Abruptly I ran to the library window, raised it as far as it would go, and scrambled into the room. In a moment I emerged, bearing the fragment of Bentley's little finger which I had snatched from the skeletal hand the night before. I threw it into the flames already dying down in the shadow of the tree.

In a moment it had caught fire, and at the same instant the thing hovering near gave a chilling scream of pain and fury, pushed madly toward us, and then abruptly shot into space and vanished like the last fragment of an unholy, ghastly nightmare.

"*Requiescat in pace,*" said Father Burkhardt softly, looking at the ashes at our feet. But the dubious expression in his eyes conveyed his belief that for the now-released spirit of Andrew Bentley a greater and longer torture had just begun.

THE SUPPER AT ELSINORE

BY ISAK DINESEN

Upon the corner of a street of Elsinore, near the harbor, there stands a dignified old gray house, built early in the eighteenth century, and looking down reticently at the new times grown up around it. Through the long years it has been worked into a unity, and when the front door is opened on a day of north-north-west the door of the corridor upstairs will open out of sympathy. Also when you tread upon a certain step of the stair, a board of the floor in the parlor will answer with a faint echo, like a song.

It had been in the possession of the family De Coninck for many years, but after the state bankruptcy of 1813 and simultaneous tragic happenings within the family itself, they gave it up and moved to their house in Copenhagen. An old woman in a white cap looked after the old house for them, with a man to assist her, and, living in the old rooms, would think and talk of old days. The two daughters of the house had never married, and were now too old for it. The son was dead. But in summers of long ago—so Madam Bæk would recount—on Sunday afternoons when the weather was fine, the Papa and Mamma De Coninck, with the three children, used to drive in a landaulet to the country house of the old lady, the grandmother, where they would dine, as the custom was then, at three o'clock, outside on the lawn under a large elm tree which, in June, scattered its little round and flat brown seeds thickly upon the grass. They would partake of duck with green peas and of strawberries with cream, and the little boy would run to and fro, in white nankeens, to feed his grandmother's Bolognese dogs.

The two young sisters used to keep, in cages, the many birds presented to them by their seafaring admirers. When asked if they did not play the harp, old Madam Bæk would shrug her shoulders over the impossibility of giving any account of the many perfections of the young ladies. As to their adorers, and the proposals which had been made them, this was a hopeless theme to enter upon. There was no end to it.

Old Madam Bæk, who had herself been married for a short time to a sailor, and had, when he was drowned, reëntered the service of the De Coninck family as a widow, thought it a great pity that neither of the lovely sisters had married. She could not quite get over it. Toward the world she held the theory that they had not been able to find any man worthy of them, except their brother. But she herself felt that her doctrine would not hold water. If this had been the two sisters' trouble, they ought to have put up with less than the ideal. She herself, on their behalf, would have done so, although it would have cost her much. Also, in her heart she knew better. She was seventeen years older than the elder sister, Fernande, whom they called Fanny, and eighteen years older than the younger, Eliza, who was born on the day of the fall of the Bastille, and she had been with them for the greater part of her life. Even if she was unable to put it into words, she felt keenly enough, as with her own body and soul, the doom which hung over the breed, and which tied these sisters and this brother together and made impossible for them any true relation to other human beings.

While they had been young, no event in the social world of Elsinore had been a success without the lovely De Coninck sisters. They were the heart and soul of all the gayety of the town. When they entered its ballrooms, the ceilings of sedate old merchants' houses seemed to lift a little, and the walls to spring out in luminous Ionian columns, bound with vine. When one of them opened the ball, light as a bird, bold as a thought, she consecrated the gathering to the gods of true joy of life, from whose presence care and envy are banished. They could sing duets like a pair of nightingales in a tree, and imitate without effort and without the slightest malice the voices of all the *beau monde* of Elsinore, so as to make the paunches of their father's friends, the matadors of the town, shake with laughter around their card tables. They could make up a charade or a game of forfeits in no time, and when they had been out for their music lessons, or to the Promenade, they came back brimful of tales of what had happened, or of tales out of their own imaginations, one whim stumbling over the other.

And then, within their own rooms, they would walk up and down the floor and weep, or sit in the window and look out over the harbor and wring their hands in their laps, or lie in bed at night and cry bitterly, for no reason in the world. They would talk, then, of life with the black bitterness of two Timons of Athens, and give Madam Bæk an uncanny feeling, as in an atmosphere of corrodent rust. Their mother, who did not have the curse in her blood, would have been badly frightened had she been present at these moments, and would have suspected some unhappy love affair. Their father would have understood them, and have grieved on their behalf, but he was occupied with his affairs, and did not come into his daughters' rooms. Only this elderly female servant, whose temperament was as different as possible from theirs, would understand them in her way, and would keep it all within her heart, as they did themselves, with mingled despair and pride. Sometimes she would try to comfort them. When they cried out, "Hanne, is it not terrible that there is so much lying, so much falsehood, in the world?" she said, "Well, what of it? It would be worse still if it were actually true, all that they tell."

Then again the girls would get up, dry their tears, try on their new bonnets before the glass, plan their theatricals and sleighing parties, shock and gladden the hearts of their friends, and have the whole thing over again. They seemed as unable to keep from one extremity as from the other. In short, they were born melancholiacs, such as make others happy and are themselves helplessly unhappy, creatures of playfulness, charm and salt tears, of fine fun and everlasting loneliness.

Whether they had ever been in love, old Madam Bæk herself could not tell. They used to drive her to despair by their hard skepticism as to any man being in love with them, when she, indeed, knew better, when she saw the swains of Elsinore grow pale and worn, go into exile or become old bachelors from love of them. She also felt that could they ever have been quite convinced of a man's love of them, that would have meant salvation to these young flying Dutchwomen. But they stood in a strange, distorted relation to the world, as if it had been only their reflection in a mirror which they had been showing it, while in the background and the shadow the real woman remained a looker-on. She would follow with keen attention the movements of the lover courting her image, laughing to herself at the impossibility of the consummation of their love, when the moment should come for it, her own heart hardening all the time. Did she wish that the man would break the glass and the lovely creature within it, and turn around toward herself? Oh, that she knew to be out of the question. Perhaps the lovely sisters derived a queer pleasure out of the adoration paid to their images in the mirror. They could not do without it in the end.

Because of this particular turn of mind they were predestined to be old maids. Now that they were real old maids, of fifty-two and fifty-three, they seemed to have come to better terms with life, as one bears up with a thing that will soon be over. That they were to disappear from the earth without leaving any trace whatever did not trouble them, for they had always known that it would be so. It gave them a certain satisfaction to feel that they were disappearing gracefully. They could not possibly putrefy, as would most of their friends, having already been, like elegant spiritual mummies, laid down with myrrh and aromatic herbs. When they were in their sweet moods, and particularly in their relations with the younger generation, the children of their friends, they even exhaled a spiced odor of sanctity, which the young people remembered all their lives.

The fatal melancholy of the family had come out in a different manner in Morten, the boy, and in him had fascinated

Madam Bæk even to possession. She never lost patience with him, as she sometimes did with the girls, because of the fact that he was male and she female, and also by reason of the true romance which surrounded him as it had never surrounded his sisters. He had been, indeed, in Elsinore, as another highborn young dandy before him, the observed of all observers, the glass of fashion and the mold of form. Many were the girls of the town who had remained unmarried for his sake, or who had married late in life one having a likeness, perhaps not quite *en face* and not quite in profile, to that god-like young head which had, by then, forever disappeared from the horizon. And there was even the girl who had been, in the eyes of all the world, engaged to be married to Morten, herself married now, with children—*aber frage nur nicht wie!* She had lost that radiant fairness which had in his day given her the name, in Elsinore, of "golden lambkin," so that where that fairy creature had once pranced in the streets a pale and quiet lady now trod the pavement. But still this was the girl whom, when he had stepped out of his barge on a shining March day at the pier of Elsinore, with the whole population of the town waving and shouting to him, he had lifted from the ground and held in his arms, while all the world had swung up and down around her, had whirled fans and long streamers in all the hues of the rainbow.

Morten De Coninck had been more reticent of manner than his sisters. He had no need to exert himself. When he came into a room, in his quiet way, he owned and commanded it. He had all the beauty of limb and elegance of hands and feet of the ladies of the family, but not their fineness of feature. His nose and mouth seemed to have been cut by a rougher hand. But he had the most striking, extraordinarily noble and serene forehead. People talking to him lifted their eyes to that broad pure brow as if it had been radiant with the diamond tiara of a young emperor, or the halo of a saint. Morten De Coninck looked as if he could not possibly know either guilt or fear. Very likely he did not. He played the part of a hero to Elsinore for three years.

This was the time of the Napoleonic wars, when the world was trembling on its foundations. Denmark, in the struggle of the Titans, had tried to remain free and to go her own ways, and had had to pay for it. Copenhagen had been bombarded and burned. On that September night, when the sky over the town had flamed red to all Sealand, the great chiming bells of Frue Kirke, set going by the fire, had played, on their own, Luther's hymn, *Ein fester Burg ist unser Gott*, just before the tall tower fell into ruins. To save the capital the government had had to surrender the fleet. The proud British frigates had led the warships of Denmark—the apples of her eye, a string of pearls, a flight of captive swans—up through the Sound. The empty ports cried to heaven, and shame and hatred were in all hearts.

It was in the course of the struggles and great events of the following years of 1807 and 1808 that the flotilla of privateers sprang up, like live sparks from a smoking ruin. Driven forth by patriotism, thirst of revenge, and hope of gain, the privateers came from all the coasts and little islands of Denmark, manned by gentlemen, ferrymen and fishermen, idealists and adventurers—gallant seamen all of them. As you took out your letter of marque you made your own cause one with that of the bleeding country; you had the right to strike a blow at the enemy whenever you had the chance, and you might come out of the rencounter a rich man. The privateer stood in a curious relationship to the state: it was a sort of acknowledged maritime love-affair, a left-handed marriage, carried through with passionate devotion on both sides. If she did not wear the epaulets and sanctifying bright metal of legitimate union, she had at least the burning red kiss of the crown of Denmark on her lips, and the freedom of the concubine to enchant her lord by these wild whims which queens do not dream of. The royal navy itself—such as was left of it in those ships which had been away from Copenhagen that fatal September week—took a friendly view of the privateer flotilla and lived with it on congenial terms; on such terms, probably, as those on which Rachel lived with her maid Bilhah, who accomplished what she could not do herself. It was a great time for grave men. There were cannons singing once more in the Danish fairways, here and there, and where they were least expected, for the privateers very rarely worked together; every one of them was out on its own. Incredible, heroic deeds were performed, great prizes were snatched away under the very guns of the conveying frigates and were brought into port, by the triumphant wild little boats with their rigging hanging down in rags, amid shouts of exultation. Songs were made about it all. There can rarely have been a class of heroes who appealed more highly and deeply to the heart and imagination of the common people, and to all the boys, of a nation.

It was soon found that the larger type of ship did not do well for this traffic. The ferryboat or snow, with a station bill of twelve to twenty men, and with six to ten swivel guns, handy and quick in emergencies, was the right bird for the business. The nautical skill of the captain and his knowledge of the seaways played a great part, and the personal bravery of the crew, their artfulness with the guns, and, in boarding, with hand weapons, carried the point. Here were the honors of war to be won; and not only honor, but gold; and not gold alone, but revenge upon the violator, sweet to the heart. And when they came in, these old and young sea dogs, covered with snow, their whole rigging sometimes coated with ice until the ship looked as if it were drawn with chalk upon a dark sea, they had their hour of glory behind them, but a great excitement in front, for they made a tremendous stir in the little seaport towns. Then came the judgment of the prize, and the sale of the salved goods, which might be of great value. The government took its share, and each man on board came in for his, from the captain, gunner, and mate to the boys, who received one-third of a man's share. A boy might have gone to sea possessing nothing but his shirt, trousers and trouser-strap, and come back with those badly torn and red-stained, and a tale of danger and high seas to tell his friends, and might be jingling five hundred riksdaler in his pocket a fortnight later, when the sale was over. The Jews of Copenhagen and Hamburg, each in three tall hats, one on top of the other, made their appearance upon the spot quickly, to play a great rôle at the sale, or, beforehand, to coax the prize-marks out of the pockets of impatient combatants.

Soon there shot up, like new comets, the names of popular heroes and their boats, around whose fame myths gathered daily. There was Jens Lind, of the *Cort Adeler,* the one they called "Velvet" Lind because he was such a swell, and who played the rôle of a great nabob for some years, and then, when all gain was spent, finished up as a bear-leader. There was Captain Raaber, of *The Revenger,* who was something of a poet; the brothers Wulffsen, of *The Mackerel* and the *Madame Clark,* who were gentlemen of Copenhagen; and Christen Kock, of the *Æolus,* whose entire crew—every single man—was killed or wounded in her fight with a British frigate off Læssø; and there was young Morten De Coninck, of the *Fortuna II.*

When Morten first came to his father and asked him to equip a privateer for him, the heart of old Mr. De Coninck shrank a little from the idea. There were many rich and respectable shipowners of Copenhagen, some of them greater merchants than he, who had in these days launched their privateers, and Mr. De Coninck, who yielded to no one in patriotic feeling, had himself suffered heavy losses at the hands of the British. But the business was painful to him. There was to his mind something revolting in the idea of attacking merchant ships, even if they did carry contraband. It seemed to him like assaulting ladies or shooting albatrosses. Morten had to turn for support to his father's cousin, Fernand De Coninck, a rich old bachelor of Elsinore whose mother was French and who was an enthusiastic partisan of the Emperor Napoleon. Morten's two sisters masterfully assisted him in getting around Uncle Fernand, and in November, 1807, the young man put to sea in his own boat. The uncle never regretted his generosity. The whole business rejuvenated him by twenty years, and he possessed, in the end, a collection of souvenirs from the ships of the enemy that gave him great pleasure.

The *Fortuna II* of Elsinore, with a crew of twelve and four swivel guns, received her letter of marque on the second of November—was not this date, and the dates of exploits following it, written in Madam Bæk's heart, like the name of Calais in Queen Mary's, now, thirty-three years after? Already on the fourth the *Fortuna II* surprised an English brig off Hveen. An English man-of-war, hastening to the spot, shot at the privateer, but her crew managed to cut the cables of the prize and bring her into safety under the guns of Kronborg.

On the twentieth of November the boat had a great day. From a convoy she cut off the British brig, *The William*, and the snow, *Jupiter*, which had a cargo of sail cloth, stoneware, wine, spirits, coffee, sugar and silks. The cargo was unloaded at Elsinore, but both prizes were brought to Copenhagen, where they were condemned. Two hundred Jews came to Elsinore to bid at the auction sale of the *Jupiter's* cargo, on the thirtieth of December. Morten himself bought in a piece of white brocade which was said to have been made in China and sent from England for the wedding dress of the Czar's sister. At this time Morten had just become engaged, and all Elsinore laughed and smiled at him as he walked away with the parcel under his arm.

Many times he was pursued by the enemy's men-of-war. Once, on the twenty-seventh of May, in flight from a British frigate, he ran ashore near Aarhus, but escaped by throwing his ballast of iron overboard, and got in under the guns of the Danish batteries. The burghers of Aarhus provided the illustrious young privateersman with new iron for his ballast, free of charge. It was said that the little seamstresses brought him their pressing-irons, and kissed them in parting with them, to bring him luck.

On the fifteenth of January the *Fortuna* had, together with the privateer *Three Friends*, captured six of the enemy's ships, and with these was bearing in with Drogden, to have them realized in Copenhagen, when one of the prizes ran ashore on the Middelgrund. It was a big British brig loaded with sail cloth, valued at 100,000 riksdaler, which the privateers had, on the morning of the same day, cut off from an English convoy. The British men-of-war were still pursuing them. At the sight of the accident the pursuing ships instantly dispatched a strong detachment of six longboats to recapture their brig. The privateers, on their side, were not disposed to give her up, and beat up against the British, who were driven away by a fire of grape-

THE SUPPER AT ELSINORE 309

shot and had to give up the recapture. But the ship was to be lost all the same. The prizemaster on board her, at the sight of the enemy's boats with their greatly superior forces, had put fire to the brig so that she should not fall again into the hands of the British. The fire spread so violently that the ship could not be saved, and all night the people of Copenhagen watched the tall, terrible beacon to the north. The five remaining prizes were taken to Copenhagen.

It was in the summer of the same year that the *Fortuna II* came in for a life-and-death fight off Elsinore. She had by then become a thorn in the flesh of the British, and on a dark night in August they made ready, from the men-of-war stationed on the Swedish coast, to capture her. Two big launches were sent off, their holes bound with wool. The crew of the privateer had turned in, and only young Morten himself and his balker were on deck when the launches, manned by thirty-five sailors, grated against the *Fortuna's* sides, and the boarding pikes were planted in her boards. From the launches shots were fired, but on board the privateer there was neither time nor room for using the guns. It became a struggle of axes, broadswords and knives. The enemy swarmed on deck from all sides; men were cutting at the chain-cable and hanging in the figurehead. But it did not last long. The *Fortuna's* men put up a desperate fight, and in twenty minutes the deck was cleared. The enemy jumped into its boats and pushed off. The guns were used then, and three canister shots were fired after the retreating British. They left twelve dead and wounded men on the deck of the *Fortuna II*.

At Elsinore the people had heard the musketry fire from the longboats, but no reply from the *Fortuna*. They gathered at the harbor and along the ramparts of Kronborg, but the night was dark, and although the sky was just reddening in the east, no one could see what was happening. Then, just as the first light of morning was filling the dull air, three shots rang out, one after another, and the boys of Elsinore said that they could see the white smoke run along the dark waves. The *Fortuna II* bore in with Elsinore half an hour later. She looked black against the eastern sky. It was apparent that her rigging had been badly crippled, and gradually the people on land were able to distinguish the little dark figures on board, and the red on the deck. It was said that there was not a single broadsword or knife on board that was not red, and all the netting from stern to main chains had been soaked with blood. There was not one man on board, either, who had not been wounded, but only one was badly hurt. This was a West-Indian Negro, from the Danish colonies there—"black in skin but a Dane in heart," the newspapers of Elsinore said the next day. Morten himself, fouled with gunpowder, a bandage down over one eye, white in the morning light and wild still from the fight, lifted both his arms high in the air to the cheering crowd on shore.

In the autumn of that same year the whole privateer trade was suddenly prohibited. It was thought that it drew the enemy's frigates to the Danish seas, and constituted a danger to the country. Also, it was on many sides characterized as a wild and inhuman way of fighting. This broke the hearts of many gallant sailors, who left their decks to wander all over the world, unable to settle down again to their work in the little towns. The country grieved over her birds of prey.

To Morten De Coninck, all people agreed, the new order came conveniently. He had gathered his laurels and could now marry and settle down in Elsinore.

He was then engaged to Adrienne Rosenstand, the falcon to the white dove. She was the bosom friend of his sisters, who treated her much as if they had created her themselves, and took pleasure in dressing up her loveliness to its greatest advantage. They had refined and decided tastes, and spent as much time on the choice of her trousseau as if it had been their own. Between themselves they were not always so lenient to their frail sister-in-law, but would passionately deplore to one another the mating of their brother with a little *bourgeoise*, an ornamental bird out of the poultry yard of Elsinore. Had they thought the matter over a little, they ought to have congratulated themselves. The timidity and conventionality of Adrienne still allowed them to shine unrivaled within their sphere of daring and fantasy; but what figures would the falcon's sisters

THE SUPPER AT ELSINORE

have cut, had he, as might well have happened, brought home a young eagle-bride?

The wedding was to take place in May, when the country around Elsinore is at its loveliest, and all the town was looking forward to the day. But it did not come off in the end. On the morning of the marriage the bridegroom was found to be missing, and he was never seen again in Elsinore. The sisters, dissolved in tears of grief and shame, had to take the news to the bride, who fell down in a swoon, lay ill for a long time, and never quite recovered. The whole town seemed to have been struck dumb by the blow, and to wrap up its head in sorrow. No one made much out of this unique opportunity for gossip. Elsinore felt the loss its own, and the fall.

No direct message from Morten De Coninck ever reached Elsinore. But in the course of the years strange rumors of him drifted in from the West. He was a pirate, it was said first of all, and that was not an unheard-of fate for a homeless privateer. Then it was rumored that he was in the wars in America, and had distinguished himself. Later it was told that he had become a great planter and slave-owner in the Antilles. But even these rumors were lightly handled by the town. His name was hardly ever mentioned, until, after long years, he could be talked about as a figure out of a fairy tale, like Bluebeard or Sindbad the Sailor. In the drawing-rooms of the De Coninck house he ceased to exist after his wedding-day. They took his portrait down from the wall. Madame De Coninck took her death over the loss of her son. She had a great deal of life in her. She was a stringed instrument from which her children had many of their high and clear notes. If it were never again to be used, if no waltz, serenade, or martial march were ever to be played upon it again, it might as well be put away. Death was no more unnatural to her than silence.

To Morten's sisters the infrequent news of their brother was manna on which they kept their hearts alive in a desert. They did not serve it to their friends, nor to their parents; but within the distillery of their own rooms they concocted it according to many recipes. Their brother would come back an admiral in a foreign fleet, his breast covered with unknown stars, to marry the bride waiting for him, or come back wounded, broken in health, but highly honored, to die in Elsinore. He would land at the pier. Had he not done so, and had they not seen it with their own eyes? But even this spare food came in time to be seasoned with much pungent bitterness. They themselves, in the end, would rather have starved than have swallowed it, had they had the choice. Morten, it was told, far from being a distinguished naval officer or a rich planter, had indeed been a pirate in the waters around Cuba and Trinidad—one of the last of the breed. But, pursued by the ships *Albion* and *Triumph*, he had lost his ship near Port of Spain, and himself had a narrow escape. He had tried to make his living in many hard ways and had been seen by somebody in New Orleans, very poor and sick. The last thing that his sisters heard of him was that he had been hanged.

From Morten's wedding day, Madam Bæk had carried her wound in silence for thirty years. The sophistries of his sisters she never chose to make use of; she let them go in at one ear and out at the other. She was very humble and attentive to the deserted bride, when she again visited the family, yet she never showed her much sympathy. Also she knew, as was ever the case in the house, more than any other inhabitant of it. It cannot be said that she had seen the catastrophe approach, but she had had strange warnings in her dreams. The bridegroom had been in the habit, from childhood, of coming and sitting with her in her little room from time to time. He had done that while they were making great preparations for his happiness. Over her needlework and her glasses she had watched his face. And she, who often worked late at night, and who would be up in the linen-room before the early summer sun was above the Sound, was aware of many comings and goings unknown to the rest of the household. Something had happened to the engaged people. Had he begged her to take him and hold him, so that it should no longer be in his power to leave her? Madam Bæk could not believe that any girl could refuse Morten anything. Or had she yielded, and found the magic ineffective?

Or had she been watching him, daily slipping away from her, and still had not the strength to offer the sacrifice which might have held him?

Nobody would ever know, for Adrienne never talked of these things; indeed, she could not have done so if she had wanted to. Ever since her recovery from her long illness she seemed to be a little hard of hearing. She could only hear the things which could be talked about very loudly, and finished her life in an atmosphere of high-shrieked platitudes.

For fifteen years the lovely Adrienne waited for her bridegroom, then she married.

The two sisters De Coninck attended the wedding. They were magnificently attired. This was really the last occasion upon which they appeared as the belles of Elsinore, and although they were then in their thirties, they swept the floor with the young girls of the town. Their wedding present to the bride was no less imposing. They gave her their mother's diamond earrings and brooch, a *parure* unique in Elsinore. They had likewise robbed the windows of their drawing-rooms of all their flowers to adorn the altar, this being a December wedding. All the world thought that the two proud sisters were doing these honors to their friend to make amends for what she had suffered at their brother's hands. Madam Bæk knew better. She knew that they were acting out of deep gratitude, that the diamond *parure* was a thank-offering. For now the fair Adrienne was no longer their brother's virgin widow, and held no more the place next to him in the eyes of all the world. When the gentle intruder now walked out of their house, the least they could do was to follow her to the door with deep courtesies. To her children, later in life, they also for the same reason showed the most excessive kindness, leaving them, in the end, most of their worldly goods; and to all this they were driven by their thankfulness to that pretty brood of ornamental chickens out of the poultry yard of Elsinore, because they were not their brother's children.

Madam Bæk herself had been asked to the wedding, and had a pleasant evening. When the ice was being served, she suddenly thought of the icebergs in the great black ocean, of which she had read, and of a lonely young man gazing at them from the deck of a ship, and at that moment her eyes met those of Miss Fanny, at the other end of the table. These dark eyes were all ablaze, and shone with tears. With all her De Coninck strength the distinguished old maid was suppressing something: a great longing, or shame, or triumph.

But there was another girl of Elsinore whose story may rightly be told, very briefly, in this place. That was an innkeeper's daughter of Sletten, by the name of Katrine, of the blood of the charcoal burners who live near Elsinore and are in many ways like gypsies. She was a big, handsome, dark and red-cheeked girl, and was said to have been, at a time, the sweetheart of Morten De Coninck. This young woman had a sad fate. She was thought to have gone a little out of her head. She took to drink and to worse ways, and died young. To this girl, Eliza, the younger of the sisters, showed great kindness. Twice she started her in a little milliner's shop, for the girl was talented and had an eye for elegance, and advertised it herself by wearing no bonnets but hers, and to the end of her life she gave her money. When, after many scandals in Elsinore, Katrine moved to Copenhagen, and took up her residence in the street of Dybensgade, where, in general, the ladies of the town never set foot, Eliza De Coninck still went to see her, and seemed to come back having gathered strength and a secret joy from her visits. For this was the way in which a girl beloved and deserted by Morten De Coninck ought to behave. This plain ruin, misery and degradation were the only harmonious accompaniment to the happenings, which might resound in and rejoice the heart of the sister while she stopped her ears to the words of comfort of the world. Eliza sat at Katrine's deathbed like a witch attentively observing the working of the deadly potion, holding her breath for the fulfillment of it.

The winter of 1841 was unusually severe. The cold began before Christmas, but in January it turned into a deadly still, continuous frost. A little snow in spare hard grains came down from time to time, but there was no wind, no sun, no movement

THE SUPPER AT ELSINORE

in air or water. The ice was thick upon the Sound, so that people could walk from Elsinore to Sweden to drink coffee with their friends, the fathers of whom had met their own fathers to the roar of cannons on the same waters, when the waves had gone high. They looked like little rows of small black tin soldiers upon the infinite gray plane. But at night, when the lights from the houses and the dull street lamps reached only a little way out on the ice, this flatness and whiteness of the sea was very strange, like the breath of death over the world. The smoke from the chimneys went straight up in the air. The oldest people did not remember another such winter.

Old Madam Bæk, like other people, was very proud of this extraordinarily cold weather, and much excited about it, but during these winter months she changed. She probably was near her end, and was going off quickly. It began by her fainting in the dining-room one morning when she had been out by herself to buy fish, and for some time she could hardly move. She became very silent. She seemed to shrink, and her eyes grew pale. She went about in the house as before, but now it seemed to her that she had to climb an endless steep hill when in the evenings, with her candlestick and her shadow, she walked up the stair; and she seemed to be listening to sounds from far away when, with her knitting, she sat close to the crackling tall porcelain stove. Her friends began to think that they should have to cut out a square hole for her in that iron ground before the thaw of spring would set in. But she still held on, and after a time she seemed to become stronger again, although more rigid, as if she herself had frozen in the hard winter with a frost that would not thaw. She never got back that gay and precise flow of speech which, during seventy years, had cheered so many people, kept servants in order, and promoted or checked the gossip of Elsinore.

One afternoon she confided to the man who assisted her in the house her decision to go to Copenhagen to see her ladies. The next day she went out to arrange for her trip with the hackney man. The news of her project spread, for the journey from Elsinore to Copenhagen is no joke. On a Thursday morning she was up by candlelight and descended the stone steps to the street, her carpetbag in her hand, while the morning light was still dim.

The journey was no joke. It is more than twenty-six miles from Elsinore to Copenhagen, and the road ran along the sea. In many places there was hardly any road; only a track that went along the seashore. Here the wind, blowing onto the land, had swept away the snow, so that no sledges could pass, and the old woman went in a carriage with straw on the floor. She was well wrapped up, still, as the carriage drove on and the winter day came up and showed all the landscape so silent and cold, it was as if nothing at all could keep alive here, least of all an old woman all by herself in a carriage. She sat perfectly quiet, looking around her. The plane of the frozen Sound showed gray in the gray light. Here and there seaweed strewn upon the beach marked it with brown and black. Near the road, upon the sand, the crows were marching martially about, or fighting over a dead fish. The little fishermen's houses along the road had their doors and windows carefully shut. Sometimes she would see the fishermen themselves, in high boots that came above their knees, a long way out on the ice, where they were cutting holes to catch cod with a tin bait. The sky was the color of lead, but low along the horizon ran a broad stripe the color of old lemon peel or very old ivory.

It was many years since she had come along this road. As she drove on, long-forgotten figures came and ran alongside the carriage. It seemed strange to her that the indifferent coachman in a fur cap and the small bay horses should have it in their power to drive her into a world of which they knew nothing.

They came past Rungsted, where, as a little girl, she had served in the old inn, red-tiled, close to the road. From here to town the road was better. Here had lived, for the last years of his life, in sickness and poverty, the great poet Ewald, a genius, the swan of the North. Broken in health, deeply disappointed in his love for the faithless Arendse, badly given to drink, he still radiated a rare vitality, a bright light that had fascinated the little girl. Little Hanne, at the age of ten, had been sensitive to the magnetism of the great mysterious powers of life, which she did not understand. She was happy when she could be with him. Three things, she had learned from the talk of the landlady, he was always begging for: to get married, since to him life without women seemed unbearably cold and waste; alcohol of some sort—although he was a fine connoisseur of wine, he could drink down the crass gin of the country as well; and, lastly, to be taken to Holy Communion. All three were firmly denied him by his mother and stepfather, who were rich people of Copenhagen, and even by his friend, Pastor Schoenheyder, for they did not want him to be happy in either of the first two ways, and they considered that he must alter his ways before he could be made happy in the third. The landlady and Hanne were sorry for him. They would have married him and given him wine and taken him to Holy Communion, had it lain with them. Often, when the other children had been playing, Hanne had left them to pick early spring violets for him in the grass with cold fingers, looking forward to the sight of his face when he smelled the little bunches of flowers. There was something here which she could not understand, and which still held all her being strongly—that violets could mean so much. Generally he was very gay with her, and would take her on his knees and warm his cold hands on her. His breath sometimes smelled of gin, but she never told anybody. Even three years later, when she was confirmed, she imagined the Lord Jesus with his long hair in a queue, and with that rare, wild, broken and arrogant smile of the dying poet.

Madam Bæk came through the East Gate of Copenhagen just as people were about to light their lamps. She was held up and questioned by the toll collectors, but when they found her to be an honest woman in possession of no contraband they let her pass. So she would appear at the gate of heaven, ignorant of what was wanted of her, but confident that if she behaved correctly, according to her lights, others would behave correctly, according to theirs.

She drove through the streets of Copenhagen, looking around —for she had not been there for many years—as she would look around to form an opinion of the new Jerusalem. The streets here were not paved with gold or chrysoprase, and in places there was a little snow; but such as they were she accepted them. She likewise accepted the stables, where she was to get out, and the walk in the icy-cold blue evening of Copenhagen to Gammeltorv, where lay the house of her ladies.

Nevertheless she felt, as she took her way slowly through the streets, that she was an intruder and did not belong. She was not even noticed, except by two young men, deep in a political discussion, who had to separate to let her pass between them, and by a couple of boys, who remarked upon her bonnet. She did not like this sort of thing, it did not take place in Elsinore.

The windows of the first floor of the Misses De Conincks' house were brightly lighted. Remembering it to be Fernande's birthday, Madam Bæk, down in the square, reasoned that the ladies would be having a party.

This was the case, and while Madam Bæk was slowly ascending the stair, dragging her heavy feet and her message from step to step, the sisters were merrily entertaining their guests in their warm and cozy gray parlor with its green carpet and shining mahogany furniture.

The party was characteristic of the two old maids by being mostly composed of gentlemen. They existed, in their pretty house in Gammeltorv, like a pair of prominent spiritual courtesans of Copenhagen, leading their admirers into excesses and seducing them into scattering their spiritual wealth and health upon their charms. As a couple of corresponding young courtesans of the flesh would be out after the great people and princes of this world, so were they ever spreading their snares for the *honoratiori* of the world spiritual, and tonight could lay on the table no meaner acquisition than the Bishop of Sealand, the director of the Royal Theater of Copenhagen, who was himself a distinguished dramatic and philosophical scribe, and a famous old painter of animals, just back from Rome, where he had been shown great honor. An old commodore with a fresh face, who had carried a wound since 1807, and a lady-in-waiting to the Dowager Queen, elegant and a good listener, who looked as if her voluminous skirt was absolutely massive, from her waist down, completed the party, all of whom were old friends, but were there chiefly to hold the candle.

If these sisters could not live without men, it was because they had the firm conviction, which, as an instinct, runs in the blood of seafaring families, that the final word as to what you are really worth lies with the other sex. You may ask the members of your own sex for their opinion and advice as to your compass and crew, your cuisine and garden, but when it comes to the matter of what you yourself are worth, the words of even your best friends are void and good for nothing, and you must address yourself to the opposite sex. Old white skippers, who have been round the Horn and out in a hundred hurricanes, know the law. They may be highly respected on the deck or in the mess, and honored by their staunch gray contemporaries, but it is, finally the girls who have the say as to whether they are worth keeping alive or not. The old sailors' women are aware of this fact, and will take a good deal of trouble to impress even the young boys toward a favorable judgment. This doctrine, and this quick estimating eye is developed in sailors' families because there the two sexes have the chance to see each other at a distance. A sailor, or a sailor's daughter, judges a person of the other sex as quickly and surely as a hunter judges a horse; a farmer, a head of cattle; and a soldier, a rifle. In the families of clergymen and scribes, where the men sit in their houses all their days, people may judge each other extremely well individually, but no man knows what a woman is, and no woman what a man is; they cannot see the wood for trees.

The two sisters, in caps with lace streamers, were doing the honors of the house gracefully. In those days, when gentlemen did not smoke in the presence of ladies, the atmosphere of an evening party remained serene to the end, but a very delicate aromatic and exotic stream of steam rose from the tumblers of rare old rum with hot water, lemon and sugar, upon the table in the soft glow of the lamp. None of the company was quite uninfluenced by this nectar. They had a moment before been conjuring forth their youth by the singing of old songs which they themselves remembered their fathers' friends singing over their wine in the really good old days. The Bishop, who had a very sweet voice, had been holding up his glass while giving the ancient toast to the old generation:

Let the old ones be remembered now; they once were gay and free. And that they knew to love, my dear, the proof thereof are we!

The echo of the song—for she now declared that it was a five-minutes' course from her ear to her mind—was making Miss Fanny De Coninck thoughtful and a little absentminded. What a strange proof, she thought, are these dry old bodies here tonight of the fact that young men and women, half a century ago, sighed and shivered and lost themselves in ecstasies. What a curious proof is this gray hand of the follies of young hands upon a night in May long, long ago.

As she was standing, her chin, in this intensive dreaming, pressed down a little upon the black velvet ribbon around her throat, it would have been difficult for anyone who had not known her in her youth to find any trace of beauty in Fanny's face. Time had played a little cruelly with her. A slight wryness of feature, which had been an adorable piquantry once, was now turned into an uncanny little disfigurement. Her birdlike lightness was caricatured into abrupt little movements in fits and starts. But she had her brilliant dark eyes still, and was, all in all, a distinguished, and slightly touching, figure.

After a moment she took up again the conversation with the Bishop as animatedly as before. Even the little handkerchief in her fingers and the small crystal buttons down her narrow silk bosom seemed to take part in the argument. No pythoness on her tripod, her body filled with inspiring fumes, could look more prophetic. The theme under discussion was the question whether, if offered a pair of angel's wings which could not be removed, one would accept or refuse the gift.

"Ah, Your Right Worshipfulness," said Miss Fanny, "in walking up the aisle you would convert the entire congregation with your back. There would not be a sinner left in Copenhagen. But remember that even you descend from the pulpit at twelve o'clock every Sunday. It must be difficult enough for you as it is, but how would you, in a pair of white angel's wings, get out of——" What she really wanted to say was, "get out of using a chamber-pot?" Had she been forty years younger she would have said it. The De Coninck sisters had not been acquainted with sailors all of their lives for nothing. Very vigorous expressions, and oaths even, such as were never found in the mouths of the other young ladies of Elsinore, came naturally to their rosy lips, and used to charm their admirers into idolatry. They knew a good many names for the devil, and in moments of agitation would say, "Hell—to hell!" Now the long practice of being a lady and a hostess prevented Fanny, and she said instead very sweetly, "of eating a roast white turkey?" For that was what the Bishop had been doing at dinner with obvious delight. Still, her imagination was so vividly at work that it was curious that the prelate, gazing, at close quarters, with a fatherly smile into her clear eyes, did not see there the picture of himself, in his canonicals, making use of a chamber-pot in a pair of angel's wings.

The old man was so enlivened by the debate that he spilled a few drops from his glass onto the carpet. "My dear charming Miss Fanny," he said, "I am a good Protestant and flatter myself that I have not quite failed in making things celestial and terrestrial go well together. In that situation I should look down and see, in truth, my celestial individuality reflected in miniature, as you see yours every day in the little bit of glass in your fair hand."

The old professor of painting said: "When I was in Italy I was shown a small, curiously shaped bone, which is found only in the shoulder of the lion, and is the remains of a wing bone, from the time when lions had wings, such as we still see in the lion of St. Mark. It was very interesting."

"Ah, indeed, a fine monumental figure on that column," said the Bishop, who had also been in Italy, and who knew that he had a leonine head.

"Oh, if I had a chance of those wings," said Miss Fanny, "I

should not care a hang about my fine or monumental figure. But, by St. Anne, I should fly."

"Allow me," said the Bishop, "to hope, Miss Fanny, that you would not. We may have our reasons to mistrust a flying lady. You have, perhaps, heard of Adam's first wife, Lilith? She was, in contradistinction to Eve, made all out of earth, like himself. What was the first thing that she did? She seduced two angels and made them betray to her the secret word which opens heaven, and so she flew away from Adam. That goes to teach us that where there is too much of the earthly element in a woman, neither husband nor angels can master her.

"Indeed," he went on, warming to his subject, his glass still in his hand, "in woman, the particularly heavenly and angelic attributes, and those which we most look up to and worship, all go to weigh her down and keep her on the ground. The long tresses, the veils of pudicity, the trailing garments, even the adorable womanly forms in themselves, the swelling bosom and hip, are as little as possible in conformity with the idea of flying. We, all of us, willingly grant her the title of angel, and the white wings, and lift her up on our highest pedestal, on the one inevitable condition that she must not dream of, must even have been brought up in absolute ignorance of, the possibility of flight."

"Ah, la la," said Fanny, "we are aware of that, Bishop, and so it is ever the woman whom you gentlemen do not love or worship, who possesses neither the long lock nor the swelling bosom, and who has had to truss up her skirts to sweep the floor, who chuckles at the sight of the emblem of her very thralldom, and anoints her broomstick upon the eve of Walpurgis."

The director of the Royal Theater rubbed his delicate hands gently against each other. "When I hear the ladies complain of their hard task and restrictions in life," he said, "it sometimes reminds me of a dream that I once had. I was at the time writing a tragedy in verse. It seemed to me in my dream that the words and syllables of my poem made a rebellion and protested, 'Why must we take infinite trouble to stand, walk and behave according to difficult and painful laws which the words of your prose do not dream of obeying?' I answered, 'Mesdames, because you are meant to be poetry. Of prose we think, and demand, but little. It must exist, if only for the police regulations and the calendar. But a poem which is not lovely has no *raison d'être.*' God forgive me if I have ever made poems which had in them no loveliness, and treated ladies in a manner which prevented them from being perfectly lovely—my remaining sins I can shoulder easily then."

"How," said the old commodore, "could I entertain any doubts as to the reality of wings, who have grown up amongst sailing ships and amongst the ladies of the beginning of our century? The beastly steamships which go about these days may well be a species of witches of the sea—they are like self-supporting women. But if you ladies are contemplating giving up being white-sailed ships and poems—well, we must be perfectly lovely poems ourselves, then, and leave you to make up the police regulations. Without poetry no ship can be sailed. When I was a cadet, on the way to Greenland, and in the Indian Ocean, I used to console myself, on the middle watch, by thinking, in consecutive order, of all the women I knew, and by quoting poetry that I had learned by heart."

"But you have always been a poem, Julian," said Eliza, "a roundel." She felt tempted to put her arms round her cousin, they had always been great friends.

"Ah, in talking about Eve and Paradise," said Fanny, "you all still remain a little jealous of the snake."

"When I was in Italy," said the professor, "I often thought what a curious thing it is that the serpent, which, if I understand the Scripture, opened the eyes of man to the arts, should be, in itself, an object impossible to get into a picture. A snake is a lovely creature. At Naples they had a large reptile house, and I used to study the snakes there for many hours. They have skins like jewels, and their movements are wonderful performances of art. But I have never seen a snake done successfully in a picture. I could not paint it myself."

"Do you remember," said the commodore, who had been following his own thoughts, "the swing that I put up for you, at

Øregaard, on your seventeenth birthday, Eliza? I made a poem about it."

"Yes, I do, Julian," said Eliza, her face brightening, "it was made like a ship."

It was a curious thing about the two sisters, who had been so unhappy as young women, that they should take so much pleasure in dwelling upon the past. They could talk for hours of the most insignificant trifles of their young days, and these made them laugh and cry more heartily than any event of the present day. Perhaps to them the first condition for anything having real charm was this: that it must not really exist.

It was another curious phenomenon about them that they, to whom so very little had happened, should talk of their married friends who had husbands, children and grandchildren with pity and slight contempt, as of poor timid creatures whose lives had been dull and uneventful. That they themselves had had no husbands, children or lovers did not restrain them from feeling that they had chosen the more romantic and adventurous part. The explanation was that to them only possibilities had any interest; realities carried no weight. They had themselves had all possibilities in hand, and had never given them away in order to make a definite choice and come down to a limited reality. They might still take part in elopements by rope-ladder, and in secret marriages, if it came to that. No one could stop them. Thus their only intimate friends were old maids like themselves, or unhappily married women, dames of the round table of possibilities. For their happily married friends, fattened on realities, they had, with much kindness, a different language, as if these had been of a slightly lower caste, with whom intercourse had to be carried on with the assistance of interpreters.

Eliza's face had brightened, like a fine, pure jar of alabaster behind which a lamp is lighted, at mention of the swing, made like a boat, which had been given her for her seventeenth birthday. She had always been by far the loveliest of the De Coninck children. When they were young their old French aunt had named them *la Bonté, la Beauté* and *l'Esprit,* Morten being *la Bonté.*

THE SUPPER AT ELSINORE

She was as fair as her sister was dark, and in Elsinore, where at the time a fashion for surnames had prevailed, they had called her "Ariel," or "The Swan of Elsinore." There had been that particular quality about her beauty that it seemed to hold promise, to be only the first step of the ladder of some extraordinary career. Here was this exceptional young female creature who had had the inspiration to be, from head to foot, strikingly lovely. But that was only the beginning of it. The next step was perhaps her clothes, for Eliza had always been a great swell, and had run up heavy debts—for which at times her brother had taken the responsibility before their father—on brocades, cashmeres, and plumes ordered from Copenhagen and Hamburg, and even from Paris. But that was also only the beginning of something. Then came the way in which she moved, and danced. There was about it an atmosphere of suspense which caused onlookers to hold their breaths. What was this extraordinary girl to do next? If at this time she had indeed unfolded a pair of large white wings, and had soared from the pier of Elsinore up into the summer air, it would have surprised no one. It was clear that she must do something extraordinary with such an abundance of gifts. "There is more strength in that girl," said the old boatswain of *La Fortuna*, when upon a spring day she came running down to the harbor, bareheaded, "than in all *Fortuna's* crew." Then in the end she had done nothing at all.

At Grammeltorv she was quietly, as if intentionally, fading day by day, into an even more marble-like loveliness. She could still span her waist with her two long slim hands, and moved with much pride and lightness, like an old Arab mare a little stiff, but unmistakably noble, at ease in the sphere of war and fantasias. And there was still that about her which kept open a perspective, the feeling that somewhere there were reserves and it was not out of the question that extraordinary things might happen.

"God, that swing, Eliza!" said the commodore. "You had been so hard on me in the evening that I actually went out into the garden of Øregaard, on that early July morning, resolved to hang myself. And as I was looking up into the crown of the great elm, I heard you saying behind me: 'That would be a good branch.' That, I thought, was cruelly said. But as I turned around, there you were, your hair still done up in curling papers, and I remembered that I had promised you a swing. I could not die, in any case, till you had had it. When I got it up, and saw you in it, I thought: If it shall be my lot in life to be forever only ballast to the white sails of fair girls, I still bless my lot."

"That is what we have loved you for all your life," said Eliza.

An extremely pretty young maid, with pale blue ribbons on her cap—kept by the pair of old spiritual courtesans to produce an equilibrium in the establishment, in the way in which two worldly young courtesans might have kept, to the same end, an ugly and misshapen servant, a dwarf with wit and imagination—brought in a tray filled with all sorts of delicacies: Chinese ginger, tangerines, and crystallized fruit. In passing Miss Fanny's chair she said softly, "Madam Bæk has come from Elsinore, and waits in the kitchen."

Fanny's color changed, she could never receive calmly the news that anybody had arrived, or had gone away. Her soul left her and flew straight to the kitchen, from where she had to drag it back again.

"In that summer of 1806," she said, "the *Odyssey* had been translated into Danish for the first time, I believe. Papa used to read it to us in the evenings. Ha, how we played the hero and his gallant crew, braved the Cyclops and cruised between the island of the Læstrygones and the Phæacian shores! I shall never be made to believe that we did not spend that summer in our ships, under brown sails."

Shortly after this the party broke up, and the sisters drew up the blinds of their window to wave to the four gentlemen who helped Miss Bardenfleth into her court carriage and proceeded in a gayly talking group across the little iron-gray desert of nocturnal Gammeltorv, remarking, in the midst of philosophical and poetic discussions, upon the extraordinary cold.

This moment at the end of their parties always went strangely to the sisters' hearts. They were happy to get rid of their guests; but a little silent, bitter minute accompanied the pleasure. For they could still make people fall in love with them. They had the radiance in them which could refract little rainbow effects in the atmosphere of Copenhagen existence. But who could make them feel in love? That glass of mental and sentimental alcohol which made for warmth and movement within the old phlebolitic veins of their guests—from where were they themselves to get it? From each other, they knew, and in general they were content with the fact. Still, at this moment, the *tristesse* of the eternal hostess stiffened them a little.

Not so tonight, for no sooner had they lowered the blind again than they were off to the kitchen, making haste to send their pretty maid to bed, as if they knew the real joy of life to be found solely amongst elderly women. They made Madam Bæk and themselves a fresh cup of coffee, lifting down the old copper kettle from the wall. Coffee, according to the women of Denmark, is to the body what the word of the Lord is to the soul.

Had it been in the old days that the sisters and their servant met again after a long separation, the girls would have started at once to entertain the widow with accounts of their admirers. The theme was ever fascinating to Madam Bæk, and dear to the sisters by reason of the opportunity it gave them of shocking her. But these days were past. They gave her the news of the town—an old widower had married again, and another had gone mad—also a little gossip of the Court, such as she would understand, which they had heard from Miss Bardenfleth. But there was something in Madam Bæk's face which caught their attention. It was heavy with fate; she brought news herself. Very soon they paused to let her speak.

Madam Bæk allowed the pause to wax long.

"Master Morten," she said at last, and at the sound of her own thoughts of these last long days and nights she herself grew very pale, "is at Elsinore. He walks in the house."

At this news a deadly silence filled the kitchen. The two sisters felt their hair stand on end. The terror of the moment lay, for them, in this: that it was Madam Bæk who had recounted such news to them. They might have announced it to her, out of perversity and fancies, and it would not have meant much. But that

Hanne, who was to them the principle of solidity and equilibrium for the whole world, should open her mouth to throw at them the end of all things—that made these seconds in their kitchen feel to the two younger women like the first seconds of a great earthquake.

Madam Bæk herself felt the unnatural in the situation, and all which was passing through the heads of her ladies. It would have terrified her as well, had she still had it in her to be terrified. Now she felt only a great triumph.

"I have seen him," she said, "seven times."

Here the sisters took to trembling so violently that they had to put down their coffee cups.

"The first time," said Madam Bæk, "he stood in the red dining-room, looking at the big clock. But the clock had stopped. I had forgotten to wind it up."

Suddenly a rain of tears sprang out of Fanny's eyes, and bathed her pale face. "Oh, Hanne, Hanne," she said.

"Then I met him once on the stair," said Madam Bæk. "Three times he has come and sat with me. Once he picked up a ball of wool for me, which had rolled onto the floor, and threw it back in my lap."

"How did he look to you?" asked Fanny, in a broken, cracked voice, evading the glance of her sister, who sat immovable.

"He looks older than when he went away," said Madam Bæk. "He wears his hair longer than people do here; that will be the American fashion. His clothes are very old, too. But he smiled at me just as he always did. The third time that I saw him, before he went—for he goes in his own way, and just as you think he is there, he is gone—he blew me a kiss exactly as he used to do when he was a young man and I had scolded him a little."

Eliza lifted her eyes, very slowly, and the eyes of the two sisters met. Never in all their lives had Madam Bæk said anything to them which they had for a moment doubted.

"But," said Madam Bæk, "this last time I found him standing before your two pictures for a long time. And I thought that he wanted to see you, so I have come to fetch you to Elsinore."

At these words the sisters rose up like two grenadiers at

parade. Madam Bæk herself, although terribly agitated, sat where she had sat, as ever the central figure of their gatherings.

"When was it that you saw him?" asked Fanny.

"The first time," said Madam Bæk, "was three weeks ago today. The last time was on Saturday. Then I thought: 'Now I must go and fetch the ladies.'"

Fanny's face was suddenly all ablaze. She looked at Madam Bæk with a great tenderness, the tenderness of their young days. She felt that this was a great sacrifice, which the old woman was bringing out of her devotion to them and her sense of duty. For these three weeks, during which she had been living with the ghost of the outcast son of the De Coninck house, all alone, must have been the great time of Madam Bæk's life, and would remain so for her forever. Now it was over.

It would have been difficult to say if, when she spoke, she came nearest to laughter or tears. "Oh, we will go, Hanne," she said, "we will go to Elsinore."

"Fanny, Fanny," said Eliza, "he is not there; it is not he."

Fanny made a step forward toward the fire, so violently that the streamers of her cap fluttered. "Why not, Lizzie?" she said. "God means to do something for you and me after all. And do you not remember, when Morten was to go back to school after the holiday, and did not want to go, that he made us tell Papa that he was dead? We made a grave under the apple tree, and laid him down in it. Do you remember?" The two sisters at this moment saw, with the eyes of their minds, exactly the same picture of the little ruddy boy, with earth in his curls, who had been lifted out of his grave by their angry young father, and of themselves, with their small spades and soiled muslin frocks, following the procession home like disappointed mourners. Their brother might play a trick on them this time.

As they turned to each other their two faces had the same expression of youthful waggishness. Madam Bæk, in her chair, felt at the sight like a happily delivered lady-in-the-straw. A weight and a fullness had been taken from her, and her importance had gone with it. That was ever the way of the gentry. They would lay their hands on everything you had, even to the ghosts.

Madam Bæk would not let the sisters come back with her to Elsinore. She made them stay behind for a day. She wanted to see for herself that the rooms were warm to receive them, and that there would be hot water bottles in those maiden beds in which they had not slept for so long. She went the next day, leaving them in Copenhagen till the morrow.

It was good for them that they had been given these hours in which to make up their minds and prepare themselves to meet the ghost of their brother. A storm had broken loose upon them, and their boats, which had been becalmed in back waters, were whirled in a blizzard, amongst waves as high as houses. Still they were, in their lappets of lace, no landlubbers in the tempests of life. They were still able to maneuver, and they held their sheets. They did not melt into tears either. Tears were never a solution for them. They came first and were a weakness only; now they were past them, out in the great dilemma. They were themselves acquainted with the old sailors' rule:

> *Comes wind before rain—Topsail down and up again.*
> *Comes rain before wind—Topsail down and all sails in.*

They did not speak together much while waiting for admission to their Elsinore house. Had the day been Sunday they would have gone to church, for they were keen churchgoers, and critics of the prominent preachers of the town, so that they generally came back holding that they could have done it better themselves. In the church they might have joined company; the house of the Lord alone of all houses might have held them both. Now they had to wander in opposite parts of the town, in snowy streets and parks, their small hands in muffs, gazing at cold naked statues and frozen birds in the trees.

How were two highly respected, wealthy, popular and petted ladies to welcome again the hanged boy of their own blood? Fanny walked up and down the linden avenue of the Royal Rose Gardens of Rosenborg. She could never revisit it later, not even in summer time, when it was a green and golden bower, filled like an aviary with children's voices. She carried with her, from one end of it to the other, the picture of her brother, looking at

THE SUPPER AT ELSINORE 331

the clock, and the clock stopped and dead. The picture grew upon her. It was upon his mother's death from grief of him that he was gazing, and upon the broken heart of his bride. The picture still grew. It was upon all the betrayed and broken hearts of the world, all the sufferings of weak and dumb creatures, all injustice and despair on earth, that he was gazing. And she felt that it was all laid upon her shoulders. The responsibility was hers. That the world suffered and died was the fault of the De Conincks. Her misery drove her up and down the avenue like a dry leaf before the wind—a distinguished lady in furred boots, in her own heart a great, mad, wing-clipped bird, fluttering in the winter sunset. Looking askance she could see her own large nose, pink under her veil, like a terrible, cruel beak. From time to time a question came into her mind: What is Eliza thinking now? It was strange that the elder sister should feel thus, with bitterness and fear, that her younger sister had deserted her in her hour of need. She had herself fled her company, and yet she repeated to herself: "What, could she not watch with me one hour?" It had been so even in the old De Coninck home. If things began to grow really difficult, Morten and the Papa and Mamma De Coninck would turn to the quiet younger girl, so much less brilliant than herself: "What does Eliza think?"

Toward evening, as it grew dark, and as she reflected that Madam Bæk must by now be at home in Elsinore, Fanny suddenly stopped and thought, Am I to pray to God? Several of her friends, she knew, had found comfort in prayer. She herself had not prayed since she had been a child. Upon the occasions of her Sundays in church, which were visits of courtesy to the Lord, her little silences of bent head had been gestures of civility. Her prayer now, as she began to form it, did not please her either. She used, as a girl, to read out his correspondence to her papa, so she was well acquainted with the jargon of mendicant letters —". . . Feeling deeply impressed with the magnificence of your noble and well-known loving-kindness . . ." She herself had had many mendicant letters in her days; also many young men had begged her, on their knees, for something. She had been highly generous to the poor, and hard on the lovers. She had not begged herself, nor would she begin it now on behalf of her proud young brother. As her prayer took on a certain likeness to a mendicant letter or to a proposal, she stopped it. "He shall not be ashamed," she thought, "for he has called upon me. He shall not be afraid of ten thousands of people that have set themselves against him round about." Upon this she walked home.

When upon Saturday afternoon the sisters arrived at the house in Elsinore, they went through much deep agitation of the heart. Even the air—even the smell in the hall, that atmosphere of salt and seaweed which ever braces up old seaside houses—went straight through them. They say, thought Miss Fanny, sniffing, that your body is changed completely within the course of seven years. How I have changed, and how I have forgotten! But my nose must be the same. My nose I have still kept and it remembers all. The house was as warm as a box, and this struck them as a sweet compliment, as if an old admirer had put on his gala uniform for them. Many people, in revisiting old places, sigh at the sight of change and age. The De Coninck sisters, on the contrary, felt that the old house might well have deplored the signs of age and decay at this meeting again of theirs, and have cried: Heavens, heavens! Are these the damask-cheeked, silver-voiced girls in dancing sandals who used to slide down the banisters of my stairs?—sighing down its long chimneys, Oh, God! Fare away, fare away! When, then, it chose to pass over its feelings and pretend that they were the same, it was a fine piece of courtesy on its part.

Old Madam Bæk's great and ceremonious delight in their visit was also bound to touch them. She stood out on the steps to receive them; she changed their shoes and stockings for them, and had warm drinks ready. If we can make her happy so easily, they thought, how is it that we never came till now? Was it that the house of their childhood and young days had seemed to them a little empty and cold, a little grave-like, until it had a ghost in it?

Madam Bæk took them around to show them the spots where Morten had stood, and she repeated his gestures many times. The sisters did not care a pin what gestures he would make to anybody but themselves, but they valued the old woman's love of their brother, and listened patiently. In the end Madam Bæk felt very proud, as if she had been given a sacred relic out of the boy's beloved skeleton, a little bone that was hers to keep.

The room in which supper was made ready was a corner room. It turned two windows to the east, from which there was a view of the old gray castle of Kronborg, copper-spired, like a clenched fist out in the Sound. Above the ramparts departed commandants of the fortress had made a garden, in which, in their winter bareness, lindens now showed the world what loosely built trees they are when not drilled to walk, militarily, two by two. Two windows looked south out upon the harbor. It was strange to find the harbor of Elsinore motionless, with sailors walking back from their boats on the ice.

The walls of the room had once been painted crimson, but with time the color had faded into a richness of hues, like a glassful of dying red roses. In the candlelight these flat walls blushed and shone deeply, in places glowing like little pools of dry, burning, red lacquer. On one wall hung the portraits of the two young De Coninck sisters, the beauties of Elsinore. The third portrait, of their brother, had been taken down so long ago that only a faint shadow on the wall showed where it had once been. Some potpourri was being burned on the tall stove, on the sides of which Neptune, with a trident, steered his team of horses through high waves. But the dried rose-petals dated from summers of long ago. Only a very faint fragrance now spread from their funeral pile, a little rank, like the bouquet of fine claret kept too long. In front of the stove the table was laid with a white tablecloth and delicate Chinese cups and plates.

In this room the sisters and the brother De Coninck had in the old days celebrated many secret supper-parties, when preparing some theatrical or fancy-dress show, or when Morten had returned very late at night from an expedition in his sailing boat, of which their parents must know nothing. The eating and drinking at such times had to be carried on in a subdued manner, so as not to wake up the sleeping house. Thirty-five years ago the red room had seen much merriment caused by this precaution.

Faithful to tradition, the Misses De Coninck now came in and took their seats at table, opposite each other, on either side of the stove, and in silence. To these indefatigable old belles of a hundred balls, age and agitation all the same began to assert themselves. Their eyelids were heavy, and they could not have held out much longer if something had not happened.

They did not have to wait long. Just as they had poured out their tea, and were lifting the thin cups to their lips, there was a slight rustle in the quiet room. When they turned their heads a little, they saw their brother standing at the end of the table.

He stood there for a moment and nodded to them, smiling at them. Then he took the third chair and sat down, between them. He placed his hands upon the edge of the table, gently moving them sideward and back again, exactly as he always used to do.

Morten was poorly dressed in a dark gray coat that looked faded and much worn. Still it was clear that he had taken pains about his appearance for the meeting, he had on a white collar and a carefully tied high black stock, and his hair was neatly brushed back. Perhaps he had been afraid, Fanny for a moment thought, that after having lived so long in rough company he should impress his sisters as less refined and well mannered than before. He need not have worried; he would have looked a gentleman on the gallows. He was older than when they had seen him last, but not as old as they. He looked a man of forty.

His face was somehow coarser than before, weather-beaten and very pale. It had, with the dark, always somewhat sunken eyes, that same divine play of light and darkness which had long ago made maidens mad. His large mouth also had its old frankness and sweetness. But to his pure forehead a change had come. It was not that it was now crossed by a multitude of little horizontal lines, for the marble of it was too fine to be marred by such superficial wear. But time had revealed its true character. It was not the imperial tiara, that once had caught all eyes, above his dark brows. It was the grave and noble likeness to a skull. The radiance of it belonged to the possessor, not of the world, but of the grave and of eternity. Now, as his hair had withdrawn from it, it gave out the truth frankly and simply. Also, as you got, from the face of the brother, the key of understanding to this particular type of family beauty, you would recognize it at once in the appearance of the sisters, even in the two youthful portraits on the wall. The most striking characteristic in the three heads was the generic resemblance to the skull.

All in all, Morten's countenance was quiet, considerate, and dignified, as it had always been.

"Good evening, little sisters; well met, well met," he said, "it was very sweet and sisterly of you to come and see me here. You had a—" he stopped a moment, as if searching for his word, as if not in the habit of speaking much with other people —"a nice fresh drive to Elsinore, I should say," he concluded.

His sisters sat with their faces toward him, as pale as he. Morten had always been wont to speak very lowly, in contrast to themselves. Thus a discussion between the sisters might be carried on with the two speaking at the same time, on the chance of the one shrill voice drowning the other. But if you wanted to hear what Morten said, you had to listen. He spoke in just the same way now, and they had been prepared for his appearance, more or less, but not for his voice.

They listened then as they had done before. But they were longing to do more. As they had set eyes on him they had turned their slim torsos all around in their chairs. Could they not touch him? No, they knew that to be out of the question. They had not been reading ghost stories all their lives for nothing. And this very thing recalled to them the old days, when, for these private supper-parties of theirs, Morten had come in at times, his large cloak soaked with rain and sea water, shining, black and rough like a shark's skin, or glazed over with snow, or freshly tarred, so that they had, laughing, held him at arm's length off their frocks. Oh, how thoroughly had the tunes of thirty years ago been transposed from a major to a minor key! From what blizzards had he come in tonight? With what sort of tar was he tarred?

"How are you, my dears?" he asked. "Do you have as merry a time in Copenhagen as in the old days at Elsinore?"

"And how are you yourself, Morten?" asked Fanny, her voice a full octave higher than his. "You are looking a real, fine privateer captain. You are bringing all the full, spiced, trade winds into our nunnery of Elsinore."

"Yes, those are fine winds," said Morten.

"How far away you have been, Morten!" said Eliza, her voice trembling a little. "What a multitude of lovely places you have visited, that we have never seen! How I have wished, how I have wished that I were you."

Fanny gave her sister a quick strong glance. Had their thoughts gone up in a parallel motion from the snowy parks and streets of Copenhagen? Or did this quiet sister, younger than she, far less brilliant, speak the simple truth of her heart?

"Yes, Lizzie, my duck," said Morten. "I remember that. I have thought of that—how you used to cry and stamp your little feet and wring your hands shouting, 'Oh, I wish I were dead.'"

"Where do you come from, Morten?" Fanny asked him.

"I come from hell," said Morten. "I beg your pardon," he added, as he saw his sister wince. "I have come now, as you see, because the Sound is frozen over. I can come then. That is a rule."

Oh, how the heart of Fanny flew upward at his words. She felt it herself, as if she had screamed out, in a shout of deliverance, like a woman in the final moment of childbirth. When the Emperor, from Elba, set foot on the soil of France he brought back the old time with him. Forgotten was red-hot Moscow, and the deadly white and black winter marches. The tricolor was up in the air, unfolded, and the old grenadiers threw up their arms and cried once more: *Vive l'empereur!* Her soul, like they, donned the old uniform. It was for the benefit of onlookers only, and for the fun of the thing, from now, that she was dressed up in the body of an old woman.

"Are we not looking a pair of old scarecrows, Morten?" she asked, her eyes shining at him. "Were not our old aunts right

THE SUPPER AT ELSINORE 337

when they preached to us about our vanity, and the vanity of all things? Indeed, the people who impress on the young that they should purchase, in time, crutches and an ear-trumpet, do carry their point in the end."

"No, you are looking charming, Fanny," he said, his eyes shining gently back. "Like a bumblebee-hawkmoth." For they used to collect butterflies together in their childhood. "And if you were really looking like a pair of old ladies I should like it very much. There have been few of them where I have been, for many years. Now when grandmamma had her birthday parties at Øregaard, that was where you would see a houseful of fine old ladies. Like a grand aviary, and grandmamma amongst them like a proud cockatoo."

"Yet, you once said," said Fanny, "that you would give a year of your existence to be free from spending the afternoon with the old devils."

"Yes, I did that," said Morten, "but my ideas about a year of my existence have changed since then. But tell me, seriously, do they still tie weights to *billets-doux*, and throw them into your carriage when you drive home from the balls?"

"Oh!" said Eliza, drawing in her breath.

> *Was klaget aus dem dunkeln Thal*
> *Die Nachtigall?*
> *Was seufzt darein der Erlenbach*
> *Mit manchem Ach?*

She was quoting a long-forgotten poem by a long-forgotten lover.

"You are not married, my dears, are you?" said Morten, suddenly frightened at the absurd possibility of a stranger belonging to his sisters.

"Why should we not be married?" asked Fanny. "We both of us have husbands and lovers at each finger-tip. I, I married the Bishop of Sealand—he lost his balance a little in our bridal bed because of his wings." She could not prevent a delicate thin little laughter coming out of her in small puffs, like steam from a kettle-spout. The Bishop looked, at the distance of forty-eight hours, ridiculously small, like a little doll seen from a tower. "Lizzie married—" she went on, and then stopped herself. When they were children the young De Conincks had lived under a special superstition, which they had from a marionette comedy. It came to this: that the lies which you tell are likely to become truth. On this account they had always been careful in their choice of what lies they would tell. Thus they would never say that they could not pay a Sunday visit to their old aunts because they had a toothache, for they would be afraid that Nemesis might be at their heels, and that they would indeed have a toothache. But they might safely say that their music master had told them not to practice their gavottes any longer, as they already played them with masterly art. The habit was still in their blood.

"No, to speak the truth, Morten," Fanny said, "we are old maids, all on your account. Nobody would have us. The De Conincks have had a bad name as consorts since you went off and took away the heart and soul and innocence of Adrienne."

She looked at him to see what he would say to this. She had followed his thoughts. They had been faithful, but he—what had he done? He had encumbered them with a lovely and gentle sister-in-law.

Their uncle, Fernand De Coninck, he who had helped Morten to get his ship, had in the old days lived in France during the Revolution. That was the place and the time for a De Coninck to live in. Also he had never got quite out of them again, not even when he had been an old bachelor in Elsinore, and he never felt quite at home in a peaceful life. He had been full of anecdotes and songs of the period, and when they had been children the brother and the sisters had known them by heart from him. After a moment Morten slowly and in a low voice began to quote one of Uncle Fernand's ditties. This had been made on a special occasion, when the old aunts of the King of France had been leaving the country, and the revolutionary police had ordered all their boxes to be opened and examined at the frontier, for fear of treachery.

them? That was the case with me, then, my dears: a bouquet I should say that I may still have had, but no body. I could not sink into friendship, or fear, or any real delight any longer. And still I could not sleep."

The sisters had no need to pretend sympathy with this misfortune. It was their own. All the De Conincks suffered from sleeplessness. When they had been children they had laughed at their father and his sisters when they greeted one another in the morning first of all with minute inquiries and accounts of how they had slept at night. Now they did not laugh; the matter meant much to them also now.

"But when you cannot sleep at night," said Fanny, sighing, "is it that you wake up very early, or is it that you cannot fall asleep at all?"

"Nay, I cannot fall asleep at all," said Morten.

"Is it not, then," asked Fanny, "because you are——" She would have said "cold," but remembering where he had said he came from, she stopped herself.

"And I have known all the time," said Morten, who did not seem to have heard what she said to him, "that I shall never lay me down to rest until I can sleep once more on her, in her, *La Belle Eliza*."

"But you lived ashore, too," said Fanny, her mind running after his, for she felt as if he were about to escape her.

"Yes, I did," said Morten. "I had for some time a tobacco plantation in Cuba. And that was a delightful place. I had a white house with pillars which you would have liked very much. The air of those islands is fine, delicate, like a glass of true rum. It was there that I had the lovely wife, the planter's widow, and two children. There were women to dance with there, at our balls, light like the trade winds—like you two. I had a very pretty pony to ride there, named Pegasus; a little like Papa's Zampa. Do you remember him?"

"And you were happy there?" Fanny asked.

"Yes, but it did not last," said Morten. "I spent too much money. I lived beyond my means, something which Papa had always warned me against. I had to clear out of it." He sat silent for a little while.

"I had to sell my slaves," he said.

At these words he grew so deadly pale, so ashen gray, that had they not known him to be dead for long they would have been afraid that he might be going to die. His eyes, all his features, seemed to sink into his face. It became the face of a man upon the stake, when the flames take hold.

The two women sat pale and rigid with him, in deep silence. It was as if the breath of the hoarfrost had dimmed three windows. They had no word of comfort for their brother in this situation. For no De Coninck had ever parted with a servant. It was a code to them that whoever entered their service must remain there and be looked after by them forever. They might make an exception with regard to marriage or death, but unwillingly. In fact it was the opinion of their circle of friends that in their old age the sisters had come to have only one real object in life, which was to amuse their servants.

Also they felt that secret contempt for all men, as beings unable to raise money at any fatal moment, which belongs to fair women with their consciousness of infinite resources. The sisters De Coninck, in Cuba, would never have allowed things to come to such a tragic point. Could they not easily have sold themselves three hundred times, and made three hundred Cubans happy, and so saved the welfare of their three hundred slaves? There was, therefore, a long pause.

"But the end," said Fanny finally, drawing in her breath deeply, "that was not yet, then?"

"No, no," said Morten, "not till quite a long time after that. When I had no more money I started an old brig in the carrying trade, from Havana to New Orleans first, and then from Havana to New York. Those are difficult seas." His sister had succeeded in turning his mind away from his distress, and as he began to explain to her the various routes of his trade he warmed to his subject. Altogether he had, during the meeting, become more and more sociable and had got back all his old manner of a man who is at ease in company and is in really good understanding with the minds of his convives. "But nothing would go right for me," he went on. "I had one run of bad luck after another. No, in the end, you see, my ship foundered near the Cay Sal bank, where she ran full of water and sank in a dead calm; and with one thing and another, in the end, if you do not mind my saying so, in Havana I was hanged. Did you know that?"

"Yes," said Fanny.

"Did you mind that, I wondered, you two?" he asked

"No!" said his sisters with energy.

They might have answered him with their eyes turned away, but they both looked back at him. And they thought that this might perhaps be the reason why he was wearing his collar and stock so unusually high; there might be a mark on that strong and delicate neck around which they had tied the cambric with great pains when they had been going to balls together.

There was a moment's silence in the red room, after which Fanny and Morten began to speak at the same time.

"I beg your pardon," said Morten.

"No," said Fanny, "no. What were you going to say?"

"I was asking about Uncle Fernand," said Morten. "Is he still alive?"

"Oh, no, Morten, my dear," said Fanny, "he died in 'thirty. He was an old man then. He was at Adrienne's wedding, and made a speech, but he was very tired. In the evening he took me aside and said to me: 'My dear, it is a *gênante fête*.' And he died only three weeks later. He left Eliza his money and furniture. In a drawer we found a little silver locket, set with rose diamonds, with a curl of fair hair, and on it was written, 'The hair of Charlotte Corday.'"

"I see," said Morten. "He had a fine figure, Uncle Fernand. And Aunt Adelaide, is she dead too?"

"Yes, she died even before he did," said Fanny. She meant to tell him something of the death of Madame Adelaide De Coninck, but did not go on. She felt depressed. These people were dead; he ought to have known of them. The loneliness of her dead brother made her a little sick at heart.

"How she used to preach to us, Aunt Adelaide," he said. "How many times did she say to me: 'This melancholy of yours, Morten, this dissatisfaction with life which you and the girls allow yourselves, makes me furious. What is good enough for me is good enough for you. You all ought to be married and have large families to look after; that would cure you.' And you, Fanny, said to her: 'Yes, little Aunt, that was the advice, from an auntie of his, which our Papa did follow.'"

"Toward the end," Eliza broke in, "she would not hear or think of anything that had happened since the time when she was thirty years old and her husband died. Of her grandchildren she said: 'These are some of the new-fangled devices of my young children. They will soon find out how little there is to them.' But she could remember all the religious scruples of Uncle Theodore, her husband, and how he had kept her awake at night with meditations upon the fall of man and original sin. Of those she was still proud."

"You must think me very ignorant," Morten said. "You know so many things of which I know nothing."

"Oh, dear Morten," said Fanny, "you surely know of a lot of things of which we know nothing at all."

"Not many, Fanny," said Morten. "One or two, perhaps."

"Tell us one or two," said Eliza.

Morten thought over her demand for a little while.

"I have come to know of one thing," he said, "of which I myself had no idea once. *C'est une invention très fine, très spirituelle, de la part de Dieu,* as Uncle Fernand said of love. It is this: that you cannot eat your cake and have it. I should never have hit upon that on my own. It is indeed an original idea. But then, you see, he is really *très fin, très spirituel,* the Lord."

The two sisters drew themselves up slightly, as if they had received a compliment. They were, as already said, keen churchgoers, and their brother's words had ever carried great weight with them.

"But do you know," said Morten suddenly, "that little snappy pug of Aunt Adelaide's, Fingal—him I have seen."

"How was that?" Fanny asked. "Tell us about that."

"That was when I was all alone," said Morten, "when my ship had foundered at the Cay Sal bank. We were three who got away in a boat, but we had no water. The others died, and in the end I was alone."

"What did you think of then?" Fanny asked.

"Do you know, I thought of you," said Morten.

"What did you think of us?" Fanny asked again in a low voice.

Morten said, "I thought: we have been amateurs in saying no, little sisters. But God can say no. Good God, how he can say no. We think that he can go on no longer, not even he. But he goes on, and says no once more.

"I had thought of that before, quite a good deal," Morten said, "at Elsinore, during the time before my wedding. And now I kept on thinking upon it. I thought of those great, pure, and beautiful things which say no to us. For why should they say yes to us, and tolerate our insipid caresses? Those who say yes, we get them under us, and we ruin them and leave them, and find when we have left them that they have made us sick. The earth says yes to our schemes and our work, but the sea says no; and we, we love the sea ever. And to hear God say no, in the stillness, in his own voice, that to us is very good. The starry sky came up, there, and said no to me as well. Like a noble, proud woman."

"And did you see Fingal then?" Eliza asked.

"Yes," said Morten. "Just then. As I turned my head a little, Fingal was sitting with me in the boat. You know, he was an ill-tempered little dog always, and he never liked me because I teased him. He used to bite me every time he saw me. I dared not touch him there in the boat. I was afraid that he would snap at me again. Still, there he sat, and stayed with me all night."

"And did he go away then?" Fanny asked.

"I do not know, my dear," Morten said. "An American schooner, bound for Jamaica, picked me up in the early morning. There on board was a man who had bid against me at the sale in Philippsburg. In this way it came to pass that I was hanged—in the end, as you say—at Havana."

"Was that bad?" asked Fanny in a whisper.

"No, my poor Fanny," said Morten.

"Was there anyone with you there?" Fanny whispered.

"Yes, there was a fat young priest there," said Morten. "He was afraid of me. They probably told him some bad things about me. But still he did his best. I asked him: 'Can you obtain for me, now, one minute more to live in?' He said, 'What will you do with one minute of life, my poor son?' I said, 'I will think, with the halter around my neck, for one minute of *La Belle Eliza*.'"

While they now sat in silence for a little while, they heard some people pass in the street below the window, and talk together. Through the shutters they could follow the passing flash of their lanterns.

Morten leaned back in his chair, and he looked now to his sisters older and more worn than before. He was indeed much like their father, when the Papa De Coninck had come in from his office tired, and had taken pleasure in sitting down quietly in the company of his daughters.

"It is very pleasant in here, in this room," he said, "it is just like old days—do you not think so? With Papa and Mamma below. We three are not very old yet. We are good-looking people still."

"The circle is complete again," said Eliza gently, using one of their old expressions.

"Is completed, Lizzie," said Morten, smiling back at her.

"The vicious circle," said Fanny automatically, quoting another of their old familiar terms.

"You were always," said Morten, "such a clever lass."

At these kind direct words Fanny impetuously caught at her breath.

"And, oh, my girls," Morten exclaimed, "how we did long then, with the very entrails of us, to get away from Elsinore!"

His elder sister suddenly turned her old body all around in the chair, and faced him straight. Her face was changed and

THE SUPPER AT ELSINORE

drawn with pain. The long wake and the strain began to tell on her, and she spoke to him in a hoarse and cracked voice, as if she were heaving it up from the innermost part of her chest.

"Yes," she cried, "yes, you may talk. But you mean to go away again and leave me. You! You have been to these great warm seas of which you talk, to a hundred countries. You have been married to five people. Oh, I do not know of it all! It is easy for you to speak quietly, to sit still. You have never needed to beat your arms to keep warm. You do not need to now!"

Her voice failed her. She stuttered in her speech and clasped the edge of the table. "And here," she groaned out, "I am— cold. The world is bitterly cold around me. I am so cold at night, in my bed, that my warming-pans are no good to me!"

At this moment the tall grandfather's clock started to strike, for Fanny had herself wound it up in the afternoon. It struck midnight in a grave and slow measure, and Morten looked quickly up at it.

Fanny meant to go on speaking, and to lift at last all the deadly weight of her whole life off her, but she felt her chest pressed together. She could not out-talk the clock, and her mouth opened and shut twice without a sound.

"Oh, hell," she cried out, "to hell!"

Since she could not speak she stretched out her arms to him, trembling. With the strokes of the clock his face became gray and blurred to her eyes, and a terrible panic came upon her. Was it for this that she had wound up the clock! She threw herself toward him, across the table.

"Morten!" she cried in a long wail. "Brother! Stay! Listen! Take me with you!"

As the last stroke fell, and the clock took up its ticking again, as if it meant to go on doing something, in any case, through all eternity, the chair between the sisters was empty, and at the sight Fanny's head fell down on the table.

She lay like that for a long time, without stirring. From the winter night outside, from far away to the north, came a resounding tone, like the echo of a cannon shot. The children of

Elsinore knew well what it meant: it was the ice breaking up somewhere, in a long crack.

Fanny thought, dully, after a long while, What is Eliza thinking? and laboriously lifted her head, looked up, and dried her mouth with her little hankerchief. Eliza sat very still opposite her, where she had been all the time. She dragged the streamers of her cap downward and together, as if she were pulling a rope, and Fanny remembered seeing her, long, long ago, when angry or in great pain or joy, pulling in the same way at her long golden tresses. Eliza lifted her pale eyes and stared straight at her sister's face.

"To think," said she, "'to think, with the halter around my neck, for one minute of *La Belle Eliza*.'"

THE CURRENT CROP OF GHOST STORIES

BY BENNETT CERF

Do you suffer from dinner parties that sag after the soup course? Do spells of lethargy seize you at literary salons? Are you allergic to moonlight picnics? Try introducing a couple of neatly contrived ghost stories the next time the going is slow, and watch the electrifying results! Guests perk up, goose pimples do likewise, and soon everybody is remembering a story *he* heard about a haunted house, or an ill-mannered ghost, or a thing that behaved in no fashion that was human!

In the following pages I have set down a few of the memorable ghost anecdotes that have been told me in the past few years. Several of them I heard more than once. The minor details varied, but the essentials were always the same. I have tried to keep the stories brief. It seems to me that they are more effective that way.

An intelligent, comely New York girl of twenty-odd summers was invited for the first time to the Carolina estate of some distant relatives. She looked forward to the visit, and bought quite an extensive wardrobe with which to impress her Southern cousins.

The plantation fulfilled her fondest expectations. The grounds, the manor house, the relatives themselves were perfect. She was assigned to a room in the western wing, and prepared to retire for the night in a glow of satisfaction. Her room was drenched with the light of a full moon. Outside was a gravel roadway which curved up to the main entrance of the building.

Just as she was climbing into her bed, she was startled by the sound of horses' hooves on the gravel roadway. She walked to the window, and saw, to her astonishment, a magnificent old coach, drawn by four coal-black horses, pull up sharply directly in front of her window. The coachman jumped from his perch, looked up, and pointed a long, bony finger at her. He was hideous. His face was chalk white. A deep scar ran the length of his left cheek. His nose was beaked. As he pointed at her, he droned in sepulchral tones: "There is room for one more!" Then, as she recoiled in terror, the coach, the horses and the ominous coachman disappeared completely. The roadway stretched empty before her in the moonlight.

The girl slept little that night, but in the reassuring sunlight of the following morning, she was able to convince herself that the sight she had seen had been nothing more than a nightmare, or an obsession caused by a disordered stomach. She said nothing about it to her hosts.

The next night, however, provided an exact repetition of the first night's procedure. The same coach drove up the roadway. The same coachman pointed to her and croaked: "There is room for one more!" Then the entire equipage disappeared again.

The girl, in complete panic, could scarcely wait for morning. She trumped up some excuse to her hosts, and rushed back to New York. Her doctor had an office on the eighteenth floor of a modern medical center. She taxied there from the station, and told him her story in tremulous tones.

The doctor's matter-of-fact acceptance of her tale did much to quiet her nerves. He persuaded her that she had been the victim of a peculiar hallucination, laughed at her terror, kissed her paternally on the brow, and dismissed her in a state of infinite relief. She rang the bell for the elevator, and a door swung open before her.

The elevator was very crowded. She was about to squeeze her way inside when a familiar voice rang in her ear. "There is room for one more!" it said. The operator was the coachman who had pointed at her! She saw his chalk-white face, the livid scar, the beaked nose! She drew back and screamed, and the elevator door banged shut in her face.

A moment later the building shook with a terrific crash. The elevator that had gone on without her broke loose from its cables and plunged eighteen stories to the ground. Everybody in it, of course, was crushed to a pulp.

Ellison was a person who generally minded his own business, but it was impossible to concentrate on his evening paper after the young man had entered the car and slumped into the seat beside him. In all his years of commuting between New York and Stamford, Ellison had never seen anybody so obviously demoralized and on the verge of collapse. His hands trembled violently, his body twitched, he gave the air of seeing nothing around him and neither knowing nor caring exactly where he was. He mumbled to himself occasionally too, but when Ellison pointedly sighed and folded up his newspaper, he pulled himself together sufficiently to apologize for fidgeting and making a nuisance of himself. Ellison did not encourage him in any way, and was rather surprised to find himself suddenly plunged into the middle of the young man's story. He had to tell it to *somebody*, he explained.

Nine years ago, he said, I was elected head of the most exclusive fraternity at ——— College. We had a strict rule that only three members of every new Freshman class be admitted to membership. That kept our active list to an even dozen. Nobody ever refused our bids. Everybody recognized that we were the kingpins of the campus. In what was probably a subconscious effort to prove to ourselves what superior beings we were, our initiations became more and more elaborate and fantastic as the years went by.

I guess it was my idea to take the three neophytes that we selected at the start of my senior year, and bundle them out to a deserted house about fifteen miles from the campus. It had been unoccupied for as long as anybody could remember; it was windowless, sagging, and ugly as it possibly could be. The village legend had it that the house was haunted by the spirit of the man who had lived in it last—a blackguard who murdered his wife and two children, and was probably hanged for his crime. We picked a black, starless night for the initiation, and all the way out to the place poured tales of horror and the supernatural into the ears of our three apprehensive Freshmen.

I picked the frailest of the kids to go into the house first. He was the son of a famous novelist who had won the Pulitzer Prize the year before, and was by way of being a boy prodigy himself. His eyes betrayed his fear when we shipped him off, but he compressed his lips and set out bravely enough. The rest of us built a bonfire and relaxed around it. Ted Williams had brought his guitar. Everybody joined in the songs except the other two Freshmen, who sat off to one side silently, their hands clasped about their knees.

I watched the kid enter the deserted house myself. It was about two hundred yards from where we were gathered. His instructions were to stay inside for a half hour, and then come back to us. When forty-five minutes went by without signs of hide or hair of him, I experienced my first uneasiness.

"We'll pay him back for these smart-aleck shenanigans," I said, and despatched the second Freshman to go fetch him. The boy set out across the field without a word, and entered the house. Ten minutes more went by. Nothing happened. There wasn't a sound anywhere. The fire was burning low. Williams had put aside his guitar. We just sat there watching.

"Damn these kids," I said at last. "They're a little too smart for their own good. Davis, get in there and bring them back fast, or by cracky, we'll skin you alive!" Davis was our prize conquest—a handsome, two-hundred-pound boy whose scholastic records foreshadowed an almost certain place on the next year's All-American squad. He had already been elected President of the Freshman class.

"I'll get 'em," grinned Davis, and loped toward the house.

"Come out of there, you lugs," we heard him call before he disappeared from view.

And then we just sat there. I guess it was only ten minutes, but it seemed like hours. "It looks like my move, fellows," I said finally. "We'll have to teach these brats that they can't play tricks on their elders this way." Nobody said anything at all, and I got up and walked slowly over to the deserted house.

The first thing that struck me when I entered was a musty smell—like the smell of an attic full of old books and newspapers. I yelled for the boys, and poked my flashlight into every corner, but there wasn't a sign of them. Only a faint, steady tap that seemed to come from the roof. Filled with a dread I can't describe to you, I climbed the creaking stairway to the second floor, and the ladder leading to the roof. I stuck my head through the open skylight. There was Davis, stretched out on his stomach! His hair had turned snow white. His eyes rolled in his head. He was mad as a hatter. In his hand he had a hammer covered with blood. He was rapping weakly with it on the tin parapet, in a senseless rhythm. I screamed to him, but he paid no attention to me at all. He just went on tapping with that bloody hammer. I got back to the fellows waiting for me somehow or other, and we managed to carry Davis down from the roof. He died in the college hospital the next morning without uttering a single syllable. We never found the slightest trace of the other two boys. . . .

Ellison fidgeted in his seat, not quite certain whether or not he was being gulled. The young man certainly was in a desperate condition. A drunkard, perhaps, or dope fiend? All this had happened nine years ago according to the young man's own story, he pointed out carefully; surely he had not been in such a state all that time! The young man turned burning eyes upon him.

On the anniversary of that night every year, he explained, one of the nine men who had been on that hazing party had gone stark, raving mad. They were found gibbering nonsense, and tapping the floor with a blood-soaked hammer. They all died within twenty-four hours' time.

Tomorrow, said the young man in low and precise tones, is the ninth anniversary of that night. And I'm the only one left. . . .

A young lady dreamed one night that she was walking along a strange country lane. It led her up a wooded hill whose summit was crowned with the loveliest little white frame house and garden she ever had seen. Unable to conceal her delight, she knocked loudly on the door of the house, and finally it was opened by an old, old man with a long white beard. Just as she started to talk to him, she woke up. Every detail of this dream was so vivid in her memory that she carried it about in her head for days. Then, on three successive nights, she had precisely the same dream again. Always she awakened at the point where her conversation with the old man was about to begin.

A few weeks later, the young lady was motoring to Litchfield for a week-end party, when she suddenly tugged at the driver's sleeve, and begged him to stop. There, at the right of the concrete highway, was the country lane of her dreams! "Wait for me a few moments," she pleaded, and, her heart beating wildly, set out on the lane. She was no longer surprised when it wound to the top of the wooded hill and the house whose every feature was now so familiar to her. The old man responded to her impatient summons. "Tell me," she began, "is this little house for sale?" "That it is," said the man, "but I would scarcely advise you to buy it. You see, young lady, this house is haunted!" "Haunted," echoed the girl. "For heaven's sake, by whom?" "By you," said the old man, and softly closed the door. . . .

John Sullivan was the only son of a doting mother, widowed during the First World War. He was handsome, richly endowed with Irish charm, and a particular favorite of the ladies. They could not resist his fetching smile. In fact, they never tried.

John couldn't explain how he suddenly came to be walking up Euclid Avenue. He had no memory of how he got there, nor of what he had been doing previously that morning. "I must be walking in my sleep," he said to himself in some perplexity. Two lovely young girls were approaching him. John stopped them with the confidence born of years of easy conquest. "Could you be telling me the time?" he asked with his easy smile. To his surprise, one of the girls screamed, and both of them careened past him. Several other people, he noticed, seemed terrified by the sight of him. One man flattened himself against a show window of the Halle Store to get out of his way.

Greatly puzzled, John Sullivan started to climb into a taxi. Just as he was giving the address of his home, however, the driver looked at him for the first time, smothered an exclamation, pushed him out of the cab, and drove off with a grinding of gears.

John's head was spinning. He entered a drugstore, and phoned to his mother. A strange voice answered.

"Mrs. Sullivan?" it echoed. "Now who would be expecting to find her in now? Don't you know that her poor son John was caught in a machine at the bindery yesterday and mangled to death? She's out at the cemetery where they're burying him now!"

Two ladies from the faculty of a famous New England college for women decided to spend one of their vacations in an automobile tour to California and back. They traveled westward by way of the Petrified Forest and the Grand Canyon, and headed for home on the Salt Lake City route. They were two normal, unimaginative women, enjoying to the full a tour of their native country.

Late one evening, they were driving through the flat and monotonous fields of Kansas, intent upon reaching a hostel some thirty miles distant, when their car broke down. They were the kind of drivers who knew nothing whatever about motors. They had no choice but to wait for some good Samaritan to come driving along and help them—and it soon became obvious that no other car was likely to come that way until the next morning.

It was then that one of the ladies noticed a two-story, unpainted farmhouse, set back some distance from the road. They approached it gingerly, wary of watchdogs, and knocked timidly on the front door. Nobody answered. The impression grew on them that the house was uninhabited. When they discovered that the door was unlocked, they entered, calling loudly, and flashing their pocket searchlight in every corner. They found the living room and kitchen in good order, but an undisturbed layer of dust indicated that no human had been in them for days.

The ladies blessed their luck, and decided to spend the night in the living room. The couch was fairly comfortable, and they bundled themselves up in robes which they fetched from the stalled automobile. There were dry logs in the fireplace; the ladies soon had a roaring fire going, and, in the light of the flickering embers, went peacefully to sleep.

Some hours later, one of the ladies awoke with the distinct feeling that somebody had entered the house. Her friend jumped up at precisely the same moment. A chill seemed to run through the room, followed by the unmistakable scent of the salt sea, although the nearest ocean front was over a thousand miles away. Then a young man walked into the room! Rather he *floated* in, because they heard no footsteps. He was dressed in boots and oilskins; seaspray glistened on his rough stubble of reddish beard. He moved to the dying fire, shivering violently, and knelt down before it.

One of the women screamed. The figure turned slowly, gave a sort of mournful sigh, and slowly dissolved into nothingness. The terrified women clutched each other desperately, and lay there until the morning sun poured through the dusty window panes. "I saw it; I know I did!" said one of them. "Of course you did; I saw it too," the other reassured her, and then pointed dramatically to the fireplace. Before it was a small puddle of brackish water, and a piece of slimy green weed!

The ladies made for the open air, but the bolder of the two snatched up the piece of weed before they bolted, and held it gingerly at arm's length. When it dried, she placed it carefully in her bag.

Eventually a car rattled along the highway, and the driver cheerfully consented to tow the ladies to the nearest garage. While the mechanic tinkered with the engine, the ladies asked him about the deserted house some miles back on the road. "That must have been the Newton place," he said with no special show of interest. "Been empty nigh on to two years now. When Old Man Newton died, he left it lock, stock and barrel to his son Tom, who said he didn't like farming, and lit out one day for the East. Spoke of taking to the sea, like his great-grandfather did. Ain't none of us seen hide nor hair of him since that day!"

When the ladies returned to their college, they took the green weed, which still seemed clammy and damp, to the head of the botany department. He readily confirmed their suspicions. "It's seaweed, all right," he told them. "Furthermore, it's a kind that's only found on dead bodies!" The ship news reporter of the *Evening Sun* reported that a Thomas Newton had sailed as first-class seaman on a freighter called the *Robert B. Anthony* on April 14, 1937. It had gone down with all hands aboard in a storm off the Greenland coast six weeks thereafter.

A favorite story of New York literary circles a few years ago concerned the beautiful young girl in the white satin dress. It was one of those anecdotes that everybody swore had actually happened to his first cousin or next-door neighbor, and several narrators got very testy when they were informed that several other people's cousins had evidently undergone the same experience a few weeks before.

At any rate, the legend maintained that a very lovely but poverty-stricken damsel was invited to a formal dance. It was her chance to enter a brand-new world. Who knew but what some rich young man would fall in love with her and lift her out of her life in a box factory? The catch in the matter was that she had no suitable dress to wear for such a great occasion.

"Why don't you rent a costume for the evening?" suggested a friend. She did. She went to a pawnshop near her little flat and for a surprisingly reasonable sum rented a beautiful white satin evening gown with all the accessories to match. Miraculously, it fit her like a glove, and she looked so radiant when she arrived at the party that she created a minor sensation. She was cut in on again and again, and as she whirled happily around the floor she felt that her luck indeed had changed for good.

Then she began to feel faint and nauseated. She fought against a growing discomfort as long as she could, but finally she stole out of the house and had just sufficient strength to stagger into a cab and creep up the stairs to her room. She threw herself onto her bed, broken-hearted, and it was then, possibly in her delirium, that she heard a woman's voice whispering into her ear. It was harsh and bitter. "Give me back my dress," it said. "Give me back my dress! It belongs to the dead. . . ."

The next morning the lifeless body of the young girl was found stretched out on her bed. The unusual circumstances led the coroner to order an autopsy. The girl had been poisoned by embalming fluid, which had entered her pores when she grew overheated from dancing. The pawnbroker was reluctant to admit that he knew where the dress came from, but spoke out when he heard that the District Attorney's office was involved. It had been sold him by an undertaker's assistant, who had taken it from the body of a dead girl just before the casket was nailed down for the last time.

A dozen miles outside of Baltimore, the main road from New York (Route Number One) is crossed by another important highway. It is a dangerous intersection, and there is talk of building an underpass for the east-west road. To date, however, the plans exist only on paper.

Dr. Eckersall was driving home from a country-club dance late one Saturday night. He slowed up for the intersection, and was surprised to see a lovely young girl, dressed in the sheerest

THE CURRENT CROP OF GHOST STORIES 361

of evening gowns, beckoning to him for a lift. He jammed on his brakes, and motioned her to climb into the back seat of his roadster. "All cluttered up with golf clubs and bags up here in front," he explained. "But what on earth is a youngster like you doing out here all alone at this time of night?"

"It's too long a story to tell you now," said the girl. Her voice was sweet and somewhat shrill—like the tinkling of sleigh bells. "Please, please take me home. I'll explain everything there. The address is —— North Charles Street. I do hope it's not too far out of your way!"

The doctor grunted, and set the car in motion. He drove rapidly to the address she had given him, and as he pulled up before the shuttered house, he said, "Here we are." Then he turned around. The back seat was empty!

"What the devil?" the doctor muttered to himself. The girl couldn't possibly have fallen from the car. Nor could she simply have vanished. He rang insistently on the house bell, confused as he had never been in his life before. At long last the door opened. A gray-haired, very tired-looking man peered out at him.

"I can't tell you what an amazing thing has happened," began the doctor. "A young girl gave me this address a while back. I drove her here and——"

"Yes, yes, I know," said the man wearily. "This has happened several other Saturday evenings in the past month. That young girl, sir, was my daughter. She was killed in an automobile accident at that intersection where you saw her almost two years ago. . . ."

The Best of the World's Best Books
COMPLETE LIST OF TITLES IN
THE MODERN LIBRARY

For convenience in ordering use number at right of title

ADAMS, HENRY	The Education of Henry Adams 76
AIKEN, CONRAD (Editor)	A Comprehensive Anthology of American Poetry 101
AIKEN, CONRAD (Editor)	20th-Century American Poetry 127
ALEICHEM, SHOLOM	Selected Stories of 145
ANDERSON, SHERWOOD	Winesburg, Ohio 104
AQUINAS, ST. THOMAS	Introduction to St. Thomas Aquinas 259
ARISTOTLE	Introduction to Aristotle 248
ARISTOTLE	Politics 228
ARISTOTLE	Rhetoric and Poetics 246
AUGUSTINE, ST.	The Confessions of 263
AUSTEN, JANE	Pride and Prejudice and Sense and Sensibility 264
BACON, FRANCIS	Selected Writings of 256
BALZAC	Droll Stories 193
BALZAC	Père Goriot and Eugénie Grandet 245
BEERBOHM, MAX	Zuleika Dobson 116
BELLAMY, EDWARD	Looking Backward 22
BENNETT, ARNOLD	The Old Wives' Tale 184
BERGSON, HENRI	Creative Evolution 231
BIERCE, AMBROSE	In the Midst of Life 133
BLAKE, WILLIAM	Selected Poetry & Prose of 285
BOCCACCIO	The Decameron 71
BOSWELL, JAMES	The Life of Samuel Johnson 282
BRONTË, CHARLOTTE	Jane Eyre 64
BRONTË, EMILY	Wuthering Heights 106
BROWNING, ROBERT	Selected Poetry of 198
BUCK, PEARL	The Good Earth 15
BURCKHARDT, JACOB	The Civilization of the Renaissance in Italy 32
BURK, JOHN N.	The Life and Works of Beethoven 241
BUTLER, SAMUEL	Erewhon and Erewhon Revisited 136
BUTLER, SAMUEL	The Way of All Flesh 13
BYRNE, DONN	Messer Marco Polo 43
BYRON, LORD	The Selected Poetry of 195
BYRON, LORD	Don Juan 24
CALDWELL, ERSKINE	God's Little Acre 51
CALDWELL, ERSKINE	Tobacco Road 249
CANFIELD, DOROTHY	The Deepening Stream 200
CARROLL, LEWIS	Alice in Wonderland, etc. 79
CASANOVA, JACQUES	Memoirs of Casanova 165
CELLINI, BENVENUTO	Autobiography of Cellini 150
CERVANTES	Don Quixote 174
CHAUCER	The Canterbury Tales 161
CHEKHOV, ANTON	Best Plays by 171
CHEKHOV, ANTON	The Short Stories of 50
CICERO	The Basic Works of 272
COLERIDGE	Selected Poetry and Prose of 279
COMMAGER, HENRY STEELE & NEVINS, ALLAN	A Short History of the United States 235

CONFUCIUS	The Wisdom of Confucius 7
CONRAD, JOSEPH	Lord Jim 186
CONRAD, JOSEPH	Nostromo 275
CONRAD, JOSEPH	Victory 34
COOPER, JAMES FENIMORE	The Pathfinder 105
CORNEILLE & RACINE	Six Plays of Corneille and Racine 194
CORVO, FREDERICK BARON	A History of the Borgias 192
CRANE, STEPHEN	The Red Badge of Courage 130
CUMMINGS, E. E.	The Enormous Room 214
DANA, RICHARD HENRY	Two Years Before the Mast 236
DANTE	The Divine Comedy 208
DEFOE, DANIEL	Moll Flanders 122
DEFOE, DANIEL	Robinson Crusoe and A Journal of the Plague Year 92
DEWEY, JOHN	Human Nature and Conduct 173
DICKENS, CHARLES	David Copperfield 110
DICKENS, CHARLES	Pickwick Papers 204
DICKENS, CHARLES	A Tale of Two Cities 189
DICKINSON, EMILY	Selected Poems of 25
DINESEN, ISAK	Out of Africa 23
DINESEN, ISAK	Seven Gothic Tales 54
DONNE, JOHN	Complete Poetry and Selected Prose of 12
DOS PASSOS, JOHN	Three Soldiers 205
DOSTOYEVSKY, FYODOR	The Best Short Stories of 293
DOSTOYEVSKY, FYODOR	The Brothers Karamazov 151
DOSTOYEVSKY, FYODOR	Crime and Punishment 199
DOSTOYEVSKY, FYODOR	The Possessed 55
DOUGLAS, NORMAN	South Wind 5
DOYLE, SIR ARTHUR CONAN	The Adventures and Memoirs of Sherlock Holmes 206
DREISER, THEODORE	Sister Carrie 8
DUMAS, ALEXANDRE	Camille 69
DUMAS, ALEXANDRE	The Three Musketeers 143
DU MAURIER, DAPHNE	Rebecca 227
ELLIS, HAVELOCK	The Dance of Life 160
EMERSON, RALPH WALDO	Essays and Other Writings 91
FAULKNER, WILLIAM	Absalom, Absalom! 271
FAULKNER, WILLIAM	Go Down, Moses 175
FAULKNER, WILLIAM	Light in August 88
FAULKNER, WILLIAM	Sanctuary 61
FAULKNER, WILLIAM	The Sound and the Fury and As I Lay Dying 187
FIELDING, HENRY	Joseph Andrews 117
FIELDING, HENRY	Tom Jones 185
FLAUBERT, GUSTAVE	Madame Bovary 28
FORESTER, C. S.	The African Queen 102
FRANCE, ANATOLE	Penguin Island 210
FRANKLIN, BENJAMIN	Autobiography, etc. 39
FREUD, SIGMUND	The Interpretation of Dreams 96
FROST, ROBERT	The Poems of 242
GALSWORTHY, JOHN	The Apple Tree (in Great Modern Short Stories 168)
GAUTIER, THEOPHILE	Mlle. De Maupin and One of Cleopatra's Nights 53
GEORGE, HENRY	Progress and Poverty 36
GOETHE	Faust 177
GOGOL, NIKOLAI	Dead Souls 40

GOLDSMITH, OLIVER	The Vicar of Wakefield and other Writings 291
GRAVES, ROBERT	I, Claudius 20
GUNTHER, JOHN	Death Be Not Proud 286
HACKETT, FRANCIS	The Personal History of Henry the Eighth 265
HARDY, THOMAS	Jude the Obscure 135
HARDY, THOMAS	The Mayor of Casterbridge 17
HARDY, THOMAS	The Return of the Native 121
HARDY, THOMAS	Tess of the D'Urbervilles 72
HART & KAUFMAN	Six Plays by 233
HARTE, BRET	The Best Stories of 250
HAWTHORNE, NATHANIEL	The Scarlet Letter 93
HEGEL	The Philosophy of 239
HELLMAN, LILLIAN	Four Plays by 223
HENRY, O.	Best Short Stories of 4
HERODOTUS	The Persian Wars 255
HOFFENSTEIN, SAMUEL	The Complete Poetry of 225
HOMER	The Iliad 166
HOMER	The Odyssey 167
HORACE	The Complete Works of 141
HOWELLS, WILLIAM DEAN	The Rise of Silas Lapham 277
HUDSON, W. H.	Green Mansions 89
HUGHES, RICHARD	A High Wind in Jamaica 112
HUGO, VICTOR	The Hunchback of Notre Dame 35
HUXLEY, ALDOUS	Antic Hay 209
HUXLEY, ALDOUS	Brave New World 48
HUXLEY, ALDOUS	Point Counter Point 180
IBSEN, HENRIK	A Doll's House, Ghosts, etc. 6
IRVING, WASHINGTON	Selected Writings of 240
JAMES, HENRY	The Bostonians 16
JAMES, HENRY	The Portrait of a Lady 107
JAMES, HENRY	The Turn of the Screw 169
JAMES, HENRY	Washington Square 269
JAMES, HENRY	The Wings of the Dove 244
JAMES, WILLIAM	The Philosophy of William James 114
JAMES, WILLIAM	The Varieties of Religious Experience 70
JEFFERS, ROBINSON	Roan Stallion; Tamar and Other Poems 118
JEFFERSON, THOMAS	The Life and Selected Writings of 234
JOYCE, JAMES	Dubliners 124
KAFKA, FRANZ	Selected Stories of 283
KANT	The Philosophy of 266
KAUFMAN & HART	Six Plays by 233
KEATS	The Complete Poetry and Selected Prose of 273
KIPLING, RUDYARD	Kim 99
KOESTLER, ARTHUR	Darkness at Noon 74
LAOTSE	The Wisdom of 262
LAWRENCE, D. H.	The Rainbow 128
LAWRENCE, D. H.	Sons and Lovers 109
LAWRENCE, D. H.	Women in Love 68
LEWIS, SINCLAIR	Dodsworth 252
LONGFELLOW, HENRY W.	Poems 56
LOUYS, PIERRE	Aphrodite 77
LUDWIG, EMIL	Napoleon 95
MACHIAVELLI	The Prince and The Discourses 65
MALRAUX, ANDRÉ	Man's Fate 33

MANN, THOMAS	Death in Venice (in Great German Short Novels and Stories 108)
MARQUAND, JOHN P.	The Late George Apley 182
MARX, KARL	Capital and Other Writings 202
MAUGHAM, W. SOMERSET	Cakes and Ale 270
MAUGHAM, W. SOMERSET	The Moon and Sixpence 27
MAUGHAM, W. SOMERSET	Of Human Bondage 176
MAUPASSANT, GUY DE	Best Short Stories 98
MAUROIS, ANDRÉ	Disraeli 46
McCORD, DAVID (Editor)	What Cheer: An Anthology of Humorous and Witty Verse 190
MEAD, MARGARET	Coming of Age in Samoa 126
MELVILLE, HERMAN	Moby Dick 119
MEREDITH, GEORGE	Diana of the Crossways 14
MEREDITH, GEORGE	The Egoist 253
MEREDITH, GEORGE	The Ordeal of Richard Feverel 134
MEREJKOWSKI, DMITRI	The Romance of Leonardo da Vinci 138
MILTON, JOHN	The Complete Poetry and Selected Prose of John Milton 132
MOLIÈRE	Plays 78
MONTAIGNE	Selected Essays of 218
MORIER, JAMES	The Adventures of Hajji Baba of Ispahan 289
NASH, OGDEN	The Selected Verse of Ogden Nash 191
NEVINS, ALLAN & COMMAGER, HENRY STEELE	A Short History of the United States 235
NEWMAN, CARDINAL JOHN H.	Apologia Pro Vita Sua 113
NIETZSCHE, FRIEDRICH	Thus Spake Zarathustra 9
NOSTRADAMUS	Oracles of 81
ODETS, CLIFFORD	Six Plays of 67
O'HARA, JOHN	Appointment in Samarra 42
O'HARA, JOHN	Selected Short Stories of 211
O'NEILL, EUGENE	The Emperor Jones, Anna Christie and The Hairy Ape 146
O'NEILL, EUGENE	The Long Voyage Home: Seven Plays of the Sea 111
PALGRAVE, FRANCIS (Editor)	The Golden Treasury 232
PARKER, DOROTHY	The Collected Short Stories of 123
PARKER, DOROTHY	The Collected Poetry of 237
PARKMAN, FRANCIS	The Oregon Trail 267
PASCAL, BLAISE	Pensées and The Provincial Letters 164
PATER, WALTER	Marius the Epicurean 90
PATER, WALTER	The Renaissance 86
PEPYS, SAMUEL	Passages from the Diary of 103
PERELMAN, S. J.	The Best of 247
PETRONIUS ARBITER	The Satyricon 156
PLATO	The Republic 153
PLATO	The Works of Plato 181
POE, EDGAR ALLAN	Selected Poetry and Prose 82
POLO, MARCO	The Travels of Marco Polo 196
POPE, ALEXANDER	Selected Works of 257
PORTER, KATHERINE ANNE	Flowering Judas 284
PORTER, KATHERINE ANNE	Pale Horse, Pale Rider 45
PROUST, MARCEL	The Captive 120
PROUST, MARCEL	Cities of the Plain 220
PROUST, MARCEL	The Guermantes Way 213
PROUST, MARCEL	The Past Recaptured 278
PROUST, MARCEL	Swann's Way 59

PROUST, MARCEL	The Sweet Cheat Gone 260
PROUST, MARCEL	Within a Budding Grove 172
RACINE & CORNEILLE	Six Plays by 194
READE, CHARLES	The Cloister and the Hearth 62
REED, JOHN	Ten Days that Shook the World 215
RENAN, ERNEST	The Life of Jesus 140
RICHARDSON, SAMUEL	Clarissa 10
ROSTAND, EDMOND	Cyrano de Bergerac 154
ROUSSEAU, JEAN JACQUES	The Confessions of 243
RUSSELL, BERTRAND	Selected Papers of Bertrand Russell 137
SAKI	The Short Stories of 280
SANTAYANA, GEORGE	The Sense of Beauty 292
SCHOPENHAUER	The Philosophy of Schopenhauer 52
SCHULBERG, BUDD	What Makes Sammy Run? 281
SHAKESPEARE, WILLIAM	Tragedies, 1, 1A—complete, 2 vols.
SHAKESPEARE, WILLIAM	Comedies, 2, 2A—complete, 2 vols.
SHAKESPEARE, WILLIAM	Histories, 3 } complete, 2 vols. Histories, Poems, 3A
SHAW, BERNARD	Four Plays by 19
SHAW, BERNARD	Saint Joan, Major Barbara, and Androcles and the Lion 294
SHELLEY	The Selected Poetry & Prose of 274
SMOLLETT, TOBIAS	Humphry Clinker 159
SPINOZA	The Philosophy of Spinoza 60
STEINBECK, JOHN	In Dubious Battle 115
STEINBECK, JOHN	The Grapes of Wrath 148
STEINBECK, JOHN	Of Mice and Men 29
STEINBECK, JOHN	Tortilla Flat 216
STENDHAL	The Red and the Black 157
STERNE, LAURENCE	Tristram Shandy 147
STEWART, GEORGE R.	Storm 254
STOKER, BRAM	Dracula 31
STONE, IRVING	Lust for Life 11
STOWE, HARRIET BEECHER	Uncle Tom's Cabin 261
STRACHEY, LYTTON	Eminent Victorians 212
SUETONIUS	Lives of the Twelve Caesars 188
SWIFT, JONATHAN	Gulliver's Travels, A Tale of a Tub, The Battle of the Books 100
SYMONDS, JOHN A.	The Life of Michelangelo 49
TACITUS	The Complete Works of 222
TENNYSON	Selected Poetry of 230
THACKERAY, WILLIAM	Henry Esmond 80
THACKERAY, WILLIAM	Vanity Fair 131
THOMPSON, FRANCIS	Complete Poems 38
THOREAU, HENRY DAVID	Walden and Other Writings 155
THUCYDIDES	The Complete Writings of 58
TOLSTOY, LEO	Anna Karenina 37
TROLLOPE, ANTHONY	Barchester Towers and The Warden 41
TROLLOPE, ANTHONY	The Eustace Diamonds 251
TURGENEV, IVAN	Fathers and Sons 21
TWAIN, MARK	A Connecticut Yankee in King Arthur's Court 162
VEBLEN, THORSTEIN	The Theory of the Leisure Class 63
VIRGIL	The Aeneid, Eclogues & Georgics 75
VOLTAIRE	Candide and Other Writings 47
WALPOLE, HUGH	Fortitude 178
WALTON, IZAAK	The Compleat Angler 26
WARREN, ROBERT PENN	All The King's Men 170

WEBB, MARY	Precious Bane 219
WELLS, H. G.	Tono Bungay 197
WELTY, EUDORA	Selected Stories of 290
WHARTON, EDITH	The Age of Innocence 229
WHITMAN, WALT	Leaves of Grass 97
WILDE, OSCAR	Dorian Gray, De Profundis 125
WILDE, OSCAR	The Plays of Oscar Wilde 83
WILDE, OSCAR	Poems and Fairy Tales 84
WORDSWORTH	Selected Poetry of 268
WRIGHT, RICHARD	Native Son 221
YEATS, W. B. (Editor)	Irish Fairy and Folk Tales 44
YOUNG, G. F.	The Medici 179
ZIMMERN, ALFRED	The Greek Commonwealth 207
ZOLA, EMILE	Nana 142
MISCELLANEOUS	An Anthology of American Negro Literature 163
	An Anthology of Irish Literature 288
	The Arabian Nights' Entertainments 201
	Best Amer. Humorous Short Stories 87
	Best Russian Short Stories 18
	Best Spanish Stories 129
	A Comprehensive Anthology of American Poetry 101
	The Consolation of Philosophy 226
	Eight Famous Elizabethan Plays 94
	Eighteenth-Century Plays 224
	Famous Ghost Stories 73
	The Federalist 139
	Five Great Modern Irish Plays 30
	Fourteen Great Detective Stories 144
	Great German Short Novels and Stories 108
	Great Modern Short Stories 168
	Great Tales of the American West 238
	The Greek Poets 203
	The Latin Poets 217
	The Making of Man: An Outline of Anthropology 149
	The Making of Society: An Outline of Sociology 183
	New Voices in the American Theatre 258
	Outline of Abnormal Psychology 152
	Outline of Psychoanalysis 66
	Restoration Plays 287
	Seven Famous Greek Plays 158
	The Short Bible 57
	Six Modern American Plays 276
	Three Famous French Romances 85 Sapho, by Alphonse Daudet Manon Lescaut, by Antoine Prevost Carmen, by Prosper Merimee
	Twentieth-Century Amer. Poetry 127

MODERN LIBRARY GIANTS

A series of full-sized library editions of books that formerly were available only in cumbersome and expensive sets.
THE MODERN LIBRARY GIANTS REPRESENT A SELECTION OF THE WORLD'S GREATEST BOOKS

These volumes contain from 600 to 1,400 pages each

G1. TOLSTOY, LEO. War and Peace.
G2. BOSWELL, JAMES. Life of Samuel Johnson.
G3. HUGO, VICTOR. Les Miserables.
G4. THE COMPLETE POEMS OF KEATS AND SHELLEY.
G5. PLUTARCH'S LIVES (The Dryden Translation).
G6.
G7. GIBBON, EDWARD. The Decline and Fall of the Roman
G8. Empire (Complete in three volumes).
G9. GREAT VOICES OF THE REFORMATION.
G10. TWELVE FAMOUS RESTORATION PLAYS (1660-1820) (Congreve, Wycherley, Gay, Goldsmith, Sheridan, etc.)
G11. JAMES, HENRY. The Short Stories of
G12. THE MOST POPULAR NOVELS OF SIR WALTER SCOTT (Quentin Durward, Ivanhoe and Kenilworth).
G13. CARLYLE, THOMAS. The French Revolution.
G14. BULFINCH'S MYTHOLOGY (Illustrated).
G15. CERVANTES. Don Quixote (Illustrated).
G16. WOLFE, THOMAS. Look Homeward, Angel.
G17. THE POEMS AND PLAYS OF ROBERT BROWNING.
G18. ELEVEN PLAYS OF HENRIK IBSEN.
G19. THE COMPLETE WORKS OF HOMER.
G20. THE LIFE AND WRITINGS OF ABRAHAM LINCOLN.
G21. SIXTEEN FAMOUS AMERICAN PLAYS.
G22. THIRTY FAMOUS ONE-ACT PLAYS.
G23. TOLSTOY, LEO. Anna Karenina.
G24. LAMB, CHARLES. The Complete Works and Letters of
G25. THE COMPLETE PLAYS OF GILBERT AND SULLIVAN.
G26. MARX, KARL. Capital.
G27. DARWIN, CHARLES. Origin of Species & The Descent of Man.
G28. THE COMPLETE WORKS OF LEWIS CARROLL.
G29. PRESCOTT, WILLIAM H. The Conquest of Mexico and The Conquest of Peru.
G30. MYERS, GUSTAVUS. History of the Great American Fortunes.
G31. WERFEL, FRANZ. The Forty Days of Musa Dagh.
G32. SMITH, ADAM. The Wealth of Nations.
G33. COLLINS, WILKIE. The Moonstone and The Woman in White.
G34. NIETZSCHE, FRIEDRICH. The Philosophy of Nietzsche.
G35. BURY, J. B. A History of Greece.
G36. DOSTOYEVSKY, FYODOR. The Brothers Karamazov.
G37. THE COMPLETE NOVELS AND SELECTED TALES OF NATHANIEL HAWTHORNE.
G38. ROLLAND, ROMAIN. Jean-Christophe.
G39. THE BASIC WRITINGS OF SIGMUND FREUD.

G40. THE COMPLETE TALES AND POEMS OF EDGAR ALLAN POE.
G41. FARRELL, JAMES T. Studs Lonigan.
G42. THE POEMS AND PLAYS OF TENNYSON.
G43. DEWEY, JOHN. Intelligence in the Modern World: John Dewey's Philosophy.
G44. DOS PASSOS, JOHN. U. S. A.
G45. LEWISOHN, LUDWIG. The Story of American Literature.
G46. A NEW ANTHOLOGY OF MODERN POETRY.
G47. THE ENGLISH PHILOSOPHERS FROM BACON TO MILL.
G48. THE METROPOLITAN OPERA GUIDE.
G49. TWAIN, MARK. Tom Sawyer and Huckleberry Finn.
G50. WHITMAN, WALT. Leaves of Grass.
G51. THE BEST-KNOWN NOVELS OF GEORGE ELIOT.
G52. JOYCE, JAMES. Ulysses.
G53. SUE, EUGENE. The Wandering Jew.
G54. AN ANTHOLOGY OF FAMOUS BRITISH STORIES.
G55. O'NEILL, EUGENE. Nine Plays by
G56. THE WISDOM OF CATHOLICISM.
G57. MELVILLE. Selected Writings of Herman Melville.
G58. THE COMPLETE NOVELS OF JANE AUSTEN.
G59. THE WISDOM OF CHINA AND INDIA.
G60 DOSTOYEVSKY, FYODOR. The Idiot.
G61. SPAETH, SIGMUND. A Guide to Great Orchestral Music.
G62. THE POEMS, PROSE AND PLAYS OF PUSHKIN.
G63. SIXTEEN FAMOUS BRITISH PLAYS.
G64. MELVILLE, HERMAN. Moby Dick.
G65. THE COMPLETE WORKS OF RABELAIS.
G66. THREE FAMOUS MURDER NOVELS
   Before the Fact, Francis Iles.
   Trent's Last Case, E. C. Bentley.
   The House of the Arrow, A. E. W. Mason.
G67. ANTHOLOGY OF FAMOUS ENGLISH AND AMERICAN POETRY.
G68. THE SELECTED WORK OF TOM PAINE.
G69. ONE HUNDRED AND ONE YEARS' ENTERTAINMENT.
G70. THE COMPLETE POETRY OF JOHN DONNE AND WILLIAM BLAKE.
G71. SIXTEEN FAMOUS EUROPEAN PLAYS.
G72. GREAT TALES OF TERROR AND THE SUPERNATURAL.
G73. A SUB-TREASURY OF AMERICAN HUMOR.
G74. ST. AUGUSTINE. The City of God.
G75. SELECTED WRITINGS OF ROBERT LOUIS STEVENSON.
G76. GRIMM AND ANDERSEN, TALES OF
G77. AN ANTHOLOGY OF FAMOUS AMERICAN STORIES.
G78. HOLMES, OLIVER WENDELL. The Mind and Faith of Justice Holmes.
G79. THE WISDOM OF ISRAEL.
G80. DREISER, THEODORE. An American Tragedy.